ARTIST, SOLDIER, LOVER, MUSE

A Novel

ARTHUR D. HITTNER

D1472532

Apple Ridge Press
Oro Valley, AZ

ISBN 978-0-9989810-1-7

Cover Design by Pure Fusion Media
Formatting by Polgarus Studio

CHAPTER ONE

Eventide

Perspiration flowed from his brow like the paint from his brush as he placed the finishing touches on the canvas. He'd been up all night, hadn't eaten since yesterday morning. Something wasn't right. First it was the ringlets of hair on the head of the infant in the upper center of the picture. He *had* to capture the freshness of a just-bathed child, needed to *feel* and *smell* that dewy moistness. Then it was the confluence of shadow and light on the mother's face. He'd labored for hours to achieve the proper contrast.

His brother, Ben, would arrive at the studio with his pickup truck at eleven that morning. It was ten forty-five. Fortunately, the heavy, gold-leaf frame was already in place. Transporting the mammoth canvas to the Springfield Museum was a two-man job.

It was January 20, 1936, the last day on which entries would be accepted for the competition that drew artists to Massachusetts from throughout the northeast. Drifts of large, wet snowflakes from an early morning squall formed miniature mountain ranges along the ledge outside his studio window. Inside, the logs in the wood stove burned as intensely as the young artist's passion and determination.

He put down his brush and stared at the painting. It was the most ambitious work he'd ever attempted. He'd begun the preliminary studies late last summer, just months after his graduation from Yale; transferred his sketches onto the sixty-by-forty-inch canvas in October; and commenced the long, painstaking process of painting the following month. He'd always worked slowly, meticulously—it was the only way he knew. Now, finally, it was done. It was too late for further revisions. Just as well, or he'd never declare it complete.

He still harbored doubts as he stood before the painting, which he'd titled *Eventide*. The heart of the canvas was dominated by the crouching figure of a young mother in a rose-colored dress, her gaze fixed intently on the naked, curly-haired infant borne protectively in her muscular arms and finely articulated hands. The child is seen from behind; his attention, in turn, is focused down the steps and out the open doorway. There, in the upper right of the composition, the child's father approaches, clad in faded blue overalls, carrying a lunch pail in his right hand, a jacket draped over his left shoulder. It's dusk, the end of a long day of work, the time the poets refer to as eventide. The father's face is drained, his gait deliberate along the packed-dirt path that leads to their modest home. Behind him lies a vista of gentle mountains, a river, and a furrowed field. The sky, however, is ominous, cloudy and gray, darkening as the evening engulfs the horizon. In the foreground and along the left side of the canvas are the trappings of a young family's meager existence: bare wood floors, an old oil lamp, a simple garment hanging on a hook by the doorway. An unadorned window rises to the left. The mood is one of bleak and troubled times, a theme familiar to the rural working poor in the depths of the Depression. Though the parents' expressions betray desperation, their bearing reveals perseverance. While the child clutches his mother and looks to his father for the sustenance he is barely able to provide, a young, hearty plant imbues a ray of hope as it rises from the flowerpot perched upon a stool in the right foreground.

The tall, lanky artist picked up a thin brush, dipped it delicately into a dollop of dark brown paint along the edge of his palette, and signed his name in the bottom right corner of the canvas: "Henry J. Kapler."

The streetlights cast a yellowish pall over the snowy blanket swaddling the Kaplers' Springfield home. Inside the living room window, Dr. Morris Kapler lit the *shamash*, the candle on the elevated perch at the center of the menorah. The family gathered around him: his wife, Ruth, and their three children, twelve-year-old Edith; seven-year-old Henry, and the toddler, Ben. After recitation of the three blessings, Morris handed the *shamash* to Henry. With his father's guiding hand, he lit the first candle and placed it in the receptacle at the end of the menorah.

In accordance with family custom, two neatly wrapped gifts awaited each of the Kapler children after the ceremony. Henry's eyes twinkled like the Hanukkah candle as he sprinted to the dining room table where the gifts were arrayed. He tore through the wrapping of the larger gift first, revealing a worn black bag bearing his father's initials. His face puckered in bewilderment.

"Open it," his father urged.

Henry unclasped the bag. Reaching inside, he withdrew a long, tubular instrument.

"My first medical bag and stethoscope," Morris said proudly. "I wanted you to have them."

Henry glanced at his father, cast the stethoscope aside, and lunged for the second package. His mother watched with anticipation as Henry clawed at the wrapping paper. Inside, he found a set of watercolors and a pad of paper. The youngster beamed.

By week's end, exuberant paintings inundated the Kapler household while the medical kit lay dormant, gathering dust beneath Henry's bed. Ruth marveled at her son's innate talent and enthusiasm, encouraging the boy at every opportunity. Morris, heartbroken, suffered in silence—until that fateful Thanksgiving dinner nearly a decade later when the proverbial feces hit the metaphorical fan.

Thanksgiving offered Henry a well-deserved respite from the rigors of life as a freshman at Yale. He was home, at his familiar place at the dining room table, sharing the holiday feast with his parents, his brother and sister, and his sister's new husband. He should have been happy, partaking liberally in the animated family banter. Instead, he was as apprehensive as he'd been on the day of his bar mitzvah.

Serving himself another helping of Ruth's signature mashed potatoes, Morris inquired about the courses his son had chosen for the upcoming semester. It was the moment that Henry had dreaded. He swallowed hard before reciting the list: Studio Art II, Still Life Painting, Italian Renaissance Art, Eighteenth Century European History, Russian Literature.

Morris rubbed his chin with the thumb and index finger of his left hand. "Thoroughly inappropriate for a young man bound for medical school," he said, his tone leaving scant room for debate. His eyes fixed on those of his eldest son.

Henry squirmed. "Father," he said, "I'm not going to medical school."

Morris sighed heavily, his eyes narrowing. "And what, pray tell, will you do instead?"

"I've decided to become an artist," Henry said.

The clicking of knives and forks ceased. Henry's heart raced. All eyes turned to him, and then to his father.

"You've decided," Morris said, thrusting his left fist into his right palm, "to become a *what?*" It was as if Henry had revealed he was marrying a Catholic.

"An artist," Henry reiterated, evading his father's icy stare. He glanced at his mother for reassurance, but none was forthcoming. Ruth looked downward, her lips pursed.

Morris lowered his head, gathering himself. A tall, gaunt man with a receding hairline and a rabbinical bearing, he lifted the napkin from his lap and placed it upon the table, folding it deliberately. He then removed his delicate, wire-rimmed glasses, setting them down neatly upon the folded napkin.

And then it began: the monologue that would become as much a staple of family meals over the next several years as his wife's mashed potatoes. "I left my homeland," he said in a booming, Russian-accented baritone, "a quarter century ago." His arms rose, his eyes turned toward the ceiling—symbolic, presumably, of the heavens—in righteous indignation. "Three weeks on a stormy ocean, seasick every day and night! In my suitcase, two pairs of trousers, a couple of shirts," he recalled, though the contents of that suitcase would vary with each rendition. He'd "worked like a slave at a drugstore," he reminded his family, "to pay my way through medical school."

Morris reprised the speech at each family gathering, his captive audience listening respectfully though it knew his words by heart. The finale was always the same. "I became a physician to heal the sick," he'd proclaim, "honoring my God and my country."

Invariably, he'd turn to his son. "What will you do, Henry, as an *artist?*" he asked. "Paint pretty pictures to adorn the walls of the haughty?"

Henry endured each recital impassively. *Adorn the walls of the haughty?* What rejoinder could there be for such biblical condemnation?

As the middle child but oldest male, Henry was the natural target of his father's lofty expectations. His sister, Edith, was five years older. She'd married a bright, successful physician who practiced with their father. By that marriage alone, Edith had fulfilled her father's aspirations. All that remained was the manifest destiny of baby production.

Ben, three years Henry's junior, had been eclipsed by Henry's accomplishments, leaving him hopelessly behind and floundering. In his parents' eyes he was, and would always be, the 'baby' of the family, an engaging personality whose charm deflected parental criticism like a shield. Morris had come to view his youngest child as a lost cause, increasing the pressure on Henry.

Henry did little to insulate himself from his parents' expectations. His academic achievements had gratified them, but with each success the bar rose higher. His renunciation of his father's plans for him—a medical career, perhaps a practice together—was the ultimate affront.

On the morning following Henry's pronouncement, after Morris had left for the office, Ruth motioned Henry to join her at the kitchen table. She poured them each a cup of tea.

"He loves you," she said, waiting for the liquid to cool. "He wants what's best for you." Her husband's harsh formality and austere manner stood in contrast to Ruth's nurturing warmth. An ample woman with graying hair and a soft, round face, she'd left Russia for Boston a decade before her husband. They'd met in 1906 and married two years later, relocating to Springfield in 1915, just weeks before Henry's birth.

"But Mother—"

"I know, Henry. I know how much you love your art." Funnels of steam rosé from their teacups. At first blush, Ruth's sympathy for the plight of her son seemed no match for the will of her domineering husband. But she was clever; she knew how to play the hand she'd been dealt.

"I can't abandon—"

"I know, Henry. I know," Ruth said. "But you can meet him halfway."

Henry gave her a quizzical look.

"Take the pre-med courses . . . *along with* the art courses," she counseled. "You'll work twice as hard, but you've always worked hard, Henry. He'll feel better . . . and you'll have the option to attend medical school if you change your mind," she said, "or if life as an artist proves more difficult than you anticipate."

Henry pondered his mother's advice. "Won't I be deceiving him?"

"No, Henry. You'll be serving your needs as well as his. He knows where your heart is, and perhaps, given time, he'll come around. But you can't shatter his dreams all at once any more than he can shatter yours."

Henry slogged through the challenging double major, graduating with honors in June of 1935. His devotion to art never wavered.

Nor did his father's resolve. "You're on your own," Morris informed his son on the day of his graduation, confident that without financial support, Henry would soon recognize the folly of "peddling pictures" in the teeth of a Depression and apply to medical school.

Ruth bristled at her husband's obstinacy. She assured her

son that he could live at home as long as he wanted. It was an offer he couldn't refuse, the conflict with his father notwithstanding. "This is his home too!" she'd barked at Morris when he sought to charge rent.

The fledgling artist secured makeshift studio space on the second floor of a vacant downtown warehouse in exchange for a series of portraits of the landlord's family. It was there that he'd painted *Eventide*.

Now, seven months out of Yale, Henry Kapler needed a triumph, something to announce his presence in the art world, proof that he had the talent required to succeed in a challenging profession. Would *Eventide* be his watershed moment, or was it time to retrieve that old medical bag from beneath his bed?

CHAPTER TWO

Ham Sandwich and a Couple of Doughnuts

Paintings hugged the perimeter of every gallery in the museum, like wallflowers at a high school dance. Four days before the opening, three men in suits plowed through acres of art, pausing briefly here and there to separate the wheat from the chaff. And to this distinguished jury, almost everything was chaff. Of the 350 artworks submitted to the Springfield Art League exhibition, only eighty would survive the withering scrutiny of the jurors. It was the smallest percentage anyone could recall.

Franklin Watkins, a wiry, forty-one-year old Philadelphian with a prominent nose and a receding hairline, led the trio to a canvas comprised of brightly painted geometric shapes arranged in a seemingly random manner. "The colors are vibrant," he said. "They bleed pure emotion!"

"Pure bullshit!" snapped the better dressed of his two companions. About a decade older than Watkins, Eugene Speicher had the slicked-back hair and self-confidence one might expect of an artist that *Esquire* would soon anoint as "America's most important living artist." He puffed at his trademark cigar while he peered dubiously at the non-objective painting through round, wire-rimmed glasses.

The third member of the jury sighed, clearly bored with the

proceedings. He sealed the fate of the painting with a sneer. Tall, bald, and gangly, Edward Hopper was the oldest and most successful of the group, though you'd hardly guess it by his rumpled suit and misshapen fedora. His judgments were swift, callous, and economical, rarely exceeding a sentence in length. "Reminds me of the crap pumped out by Roosevelt's army of WPA dilettantes," he said, expressing disdain for both the President and the artist relief programs he'd established under the Works Progress Administration.

Abstract art, in fact, had little chance with this jury. New Yorkers Speicher and Hopper were staunch traditionalists at the height of their careers. They worked in the predominant style of the day, painting recognizably American subject matter in a realistic fashion. Though Watkins was more daring, he, too, remained firmly tethered to realism.

Leaving the maligned abstraction in its wake, the jury made its way into the fifth and final gallery. The exhibition chairman stomped into the room behind them. He was a rotund man with a barking cough and a disagreeable mien. None of the jurors remembered his name.

"You people are ruthless!" the chairman groused. "There'll be nothing left to exhibit!"

Speicher gave him a scornful stare. "Look, pal," he said with an air of indignation, "you want quantity or quality?"

"From the look of him," Watkins said under his breath, "I suspect he'd be happy with a ham sandwich and a couple of doughnuts."

While Speicher strained to muffle his laughter, Hopper remained stone-faced. "I'd be happy with a check for lodging and carfare," the notoriously tight-fisted artist muttered.

As the four of them marched through the gallery, Hopper and Speicher stopped abruptly before the room's largest work, a majestic family trio in mostly earth tones with the curious title *Eventide.*

Speicher bent down to inspect the signature in the lower right corner of the canvas. "Who's this fellow Kapler?" he asked the dough-faced chairman.

"Local boy. Son of a prominent Jewish doctor. Recent graduate of Yale."

"Hmm," murmured Watkins and Hopper in unison, their eyes lighting up.

"He's pretty good," Speicher said, "and he knows his art history." With his right hand, he extracted the cigar from his mouth, dangling it loosely between his index and middle fingers. "Thing's rife with nods to the Renaissance masters."

"Sort of a Regionalist version of the Holy Family," said Watkins.

"Mary, Joseph and the baby Jesus . . . painted by a Jew! Probably explains the missing halo," Hopper quipped.

Speicher tilted his head and stroked his chin. "I like how the mother looks at the baby, the baby at his father, and the father back at his wife and son. This," he said, turning to his colleagues, "is the best damn painting I've seen today." He returned the smoldering cigar to his lips, launching a cloud of smoke to emphasize his verdict.

"Enough pontification!" Hopper said, his limited patience wearing thin. "How old you say this kid is?" he asked the chairman.

"Twenty-one on opening night."

"Twenty-one-year-old kid hauls in this massive canvas to a top-shelf jury like us? Takes balls," Hopper said. "Deserves a medal for that alone."

"So we've got our winner?" Speicher said.

"Suits me," Watkins said. "Eddie?"

"Yeah, yeah, me too," Hopper confirmed. "Now let's haul our asses out of this mausoleum."

The opening night festivities at the museum had gone on longer than expected. Henry's parents had already retired to bed, his mother bursting with delight over her son's unexpected triumph while his father thrashed in the murky waters between pride and pique. "The dark horse who romped in ahead of the field" is how the newspaper had described Henry, and the characterization was apt. Only in his wildest dreams could he have anticipated first-place honors, or the $500 prize that anointed him a professional artist.

"Quite a night," Ben said to his brother as they invaded the kitchen for a late night snack.

"Couldn't have been any better," Henry replied, reheating a pot of leftover coffee on the stove.

Ben grabbed a large, foil-covered plate from the counter. The brothers took their customary positions opposite one another at the kitchen table. "Guess this means you'll be leaving soon," Ben said. "After all, Springfield's not exactly the art capital of America." The crinkling of the tin foil muffled his words like static as Ben unwrapped the plate of day-old rugelach. The sweet scents of chocolate and cinnamon mingled with the aroma of warm coffee. "Figured you'd be itching to move to New York long before now."

"It's a big step," Henry said as he rose to pour them each a cup, handing one to Ben as he returned to the table. He plunged a teaspoon of sugar into the muddy brown liquid.

"You took that big step tonight. You punched your ticket to New York," Ben said. "And the prize'll cover your rent for a year." He took a bite of the crescent-shaped pastry. "So what're you waiting for?"

Henry remained silent, stirring his coffee long after the sugar had dissolved. Complacency had crept up on him imperceptibly, like the onset of dusk on a balmy summer evening. He'd been content living at home after graduation, spending almost nothing, painting like a dervish in his drafty warehouse studio. He harbored few worries, and his mother's home-cooked meals capped a comfortable, carefree existence.

"Doesn't make it any easier to leave," Henry said, nibbling at his pastry while peppering the tabletop with a dusting of crumbs. "It was the same at Yale."

"What was?"

"That feeling of contentment," he said, "and the reluctance to leave." Henry drained what little remained of his coffee. "I idolized my professors," he sighed wistfully. "They called me the Jewish Thomas Hart Benton—did I ever tell you that?"

"No," Ben laughed, though he'd likely never heard of Benton, the leading proponent of Regionalism, the muscular, hard-edged realism that characterized *Eventide*.

"It's not that I haven't thought about New York," Henry shrugged. "Just need a kick in the pants, I guess."

"Bend over," Ben said. "I can supply that."

Henry chuckled. "The studio lease is up in six months—the end of August . . . maybe then."

It was curious, Henry often thought, how his younger brother had the perspicacity of someone twice his age. Ben understood Henry better than Henry understood himself. If Ben had a failing, it was closer to home.

"Funny how you can give me the same advice that you ignore from everyone else," Henry said. "Instead of college, you work construction gigs with your high school buddies. Where's the future in that?"

Ben smirked. "You sound like Dad. I'm happy, Henry. I don't

have your talent—or your brains. And I don't have your driving ambition to excel." He bit off a mammoth chunk of rugelach. "Hmm . . . good." He dipped the rest into his coffee before devouring it. "When the spirit moves me or the need arises, I'll move on." Satisfied he'd slaked his need for sustenance, Ben rose from the table. "Tonight's not about me, Henry. It's about you and your pursuit of your destiny. Time to get on with it."

Henry basked in the aura of his artistic coup for barely a week before returning to the studio with a vengeance, beginning work on *Dustbowl*, a sort of sequel to *Eventide*. Where *Eventide* examined the plight of the rural poor, *Dustbowl* would take the theme a step further. He'd revisit the family trio of his prize-winning work (the son a little bit older this time), but place them squarely in the American heartland, where persistent drought, devastating erosion, and relentless winds had unleashed the plague of the Dust Bowl. He'd use the same earthy palette, but now the colors would be even more subdued—darker hues to match the even gloomier subject matter.

Henry plotted the composition with his characteristic punctiliousness and tenacity. He persuaded Ben and Edith to pose for him. A neighbor's eight-year-old son modeled in exchange for a couple of Henry's old baseball cards. The kid negotiated like a hardened capitalist, insisting on nothing less than a Babe Ruth and a Lou Gehrig. Seemed like a good deal for everyone—it was just worthless cardboard and the squirt was as happy as if he'd actually met the Bambino.

Henry painted the figure of a barefoot young boy, flanked by his parents, as they trudge dejectedly across the barren, unforgiving landscape, their abandoned home behind them, its porch nearly buried in waves of sand. Their faces are etched with sadness and resignation. The father bears the heavy weight of a sack of belongings over his left shoulder. Henry had struggled with that figure, forcing poor Ben to stand for hours, hunched forward, an overstuffed pillowcase slung over his shoulder. He used a low horizon-line, breaking at his figures' ankles or shins, to silhouette the fleeing family against a vast but sinister morning sky. He chose a murky yellow to depict the rising light of dawn, above which he rendered choking clouds of dust in broad strokes of gray and brown.

Henry had painted a bleak picture, but life in the Dust Bowl *was* bleak—and seemingly hopeless. Where he'd chosen to symbolize hope with a blooming potted plant in *Eventide*, *Dustbowl* offered only a broken tree stump.

He finished *Dustbowl* in May of 1936, in time for inclusion in an exhibition of local artists at the Springfield Museum. Again, he earned plaudits. "They're back," wrote W. D. Danforth, art critic for the *Springfield Union*, referring to the family group that had first appeared in *Eventide*, "and even better this time." While citing the work for "its remarkable handling of atmosphere and light," Danforth tempered his praise with a caveat. "Methinks this talented young artist doth dwell too much with this forlorn family of unfortunate farmers," he alliterated. "As commendable as the artist's sentiment may be, it's time for young Mr. Kapler to cast a wider net for subject matter."

It was perceptive criticism. Henry felt deeply about the plight of the poor and took pride in the social consciousness that pervaded his work. But he was painting what he imagined, not what he knew. His quest for fresh ideas would soon bear fruit—in a most unlikely place.

CHAPTER THREE

A Game for the Aces

The crowd pulsed with anticipation. The grandstands were overflowing, a fanny in every seat. Late arrivals clung like lint to the chain-link fences along the foul lines. Few could recall a crowd of this magnitude at any athletic event in Springfield—much less for a high school baseball game at Forest Park. But this was no ordinary game.

Springfield Classical High School, known as Springfield Central when Henry had graduated five years earlier, was playing host to archrival Springfield Tech. Both were juggernauts. The winner would be the undisputed city and regional champion. But it wasn't just the stakes that had generated this unprecedented level of excitement. It was the pitching match-up: a classic, first-ever duel between the best two young pitchers in the region, perhaps the best of their generation.

On the hill for Classical was seventeen-year-old Victor John Angelo Raschi, a burly six-foot Italian with a scorching fastball and a colorful nickname, the "Springfield Rifle." As a mere freshman, Raschi had piqued the interest of a Yankees scout, later signing an agreement under which the club would foot the bill for his college education for the right to sign him after graduation. The big righthander had been untouchable at

Classical. He came into the contest with a streak of four consecutive shutouts and was primed for another. But though he'd played in the same city, he'd never faced Ernest Taliaferro.

Ernest "Bunny" Taliaferro was every bit the pitcher Raschi was . . . and more. The eighteen-year-old junior was undefeated over his entire high school pitching career—and batted .400 to boot. Ben, a recent Classical grad and an enviable athlete in his own right, had played a year with Raschi on the Classical varsity and with Taliaferro on a summer league team. He swore that Bunny threw harder. But something other than talent set Taliaferro apart from Raschi and every other player on the diamond that day. It was why no Yankee scout would lie in wait. *Bunny Taliaferro was black.*

Though Taliaferro's exploits on the diamonds of Springfield—as well as on its gridirons and basketball courts—were the stuff of legend, his local fame was more the product of an incident that had occurred when Bunny pitched for the otherwise all-white Brightwood American Legion ballclub from Springfield's Post 21. It happened two years earlier, in 1934, after the Post 21 team had won the American Legion baseball championship of Massachusetts and the Northeast sectional championship, qualifying to participate in the Regional tournament at Gastonia, North Carolina. The presence of a black ballplayer on the roster precipitated a maelstrom of hostility in Gastonia, culminating in an ultimatum: the Springfield team would compete without Bunny or it wouldn't compete at all. Bunny urged his teammates to play. Instead, they unanimously elected to withdraw, returning home to a wildly cheering crowd at Springfield's Union Station with their dignity in lieu of a trophy.

The Kapler brothers had arrived at the park early on that balmy late May afternoon, securing prime seats behind home plate. A cadre of fans gathered around the hurlers as they loosened up. The hard *thwack* of fastballs rocketing into the catchers' mitts reverberated through the park like gunshots as the young gladiators readied themselves for combat.

Raschi strolled deliberately to the mound as Classical took the field in the top of the first inning. The umpire barked the obligatory "Play ball!" as the Tech leadoff hitter stepped into the batter's box. Raschi lifted his cap, ran his pitching hand through his thick black hair, carefully replaced the cap on his head, and peered in to the catcher for the sign. Satisfied, he brought his long arms forward, clutching the ball in his right hand as he pressed it into his glove, then rocked back before reuniting hand and glove above his head, pivoting, and propelling the ball toward the plate in a powerful overhand arc. "*Stee-rike one!*" the umpire bellowed as the hitter sneered. The batter fouled off Raschi's second pitch to the right side, unable to measure up to its blazing speed. The third offering, a nifty curveball, twisted him into a pretzel as he unceremoniously struck out. The next two batters suffered similar fates, the Classical partisans gleefully howling with each swing and miss.

Henry poked his brother in the ribs. "Taliaferro throws harder than that?"

"Just wait," Ben said with a knowing grin.

A generous round of applause greeted Bunny Taliaferro as he made his way to the mound for Tech in the bottom of the inning. The tall, slim righthander had a more unorthodox motion, his spindly arms and legs dancing wildly like a stork in heat before uniting in a three-quarter overhand delivery. Whether it was the distraction of his flailing arms and legs, or the prodigious velocity of his fastball, Henry and Ben were convinced that Bunny was even less hittable than the formidable Raschi.

"Jesus!" Henry yelped. "Barely even *saw* that sucker cross the plate!"

"Wait 'til you see his curve ball."

Unlike Raschi, Bunny worked quickly, decoding the catcher's sign and launching into his deceiving motion as soon as he retrieved the ball from his batterymate. Even the *thwack* of ball against glove seemed louder with Bunny on the slab. Like Raschi before him, Bunny struck out the side, embarrassing the third hitter with a curve that broke down and away from the plate by at least two feet. Henry couldn't help but smile.

The smell of popcorn permeated the park as Bunny led off the top of the second for Tech. Raschi gave him a searing look, registered the catcher's sign, reared back, and fired a missile . . . *directly at Bunny's head.* The crowd gasped as Bunny plunged to the ground.

"Kid knows how to throw a purpose pitch," Henry said, chuckling.

Bunny bounced up, brushed himself off, and returned to the batter's box as if nothing had happened. On the next pitch, he lowered the barrel of his bat and laid a perfect bunt halfway down the third base line, beating it out easily for a single.

Bunny danced off first as Raschi scowled. The hurler spun and flung a bullet to his first baseman, but Bunny slid back safely. The lanky baserunner popped up like a jack-in-the-box, dusted himself off, and reclaimed his lead. As Raschi fired to the plate, Bunny pivoted and sprinted to second base, swiping it with the pluck of a cat burglar.

"Even money he steals third," Ben said.

"That's a sucker's bet," Henry replied.

After Raschi fanned the next two hitters, Bunny scampered

to third, well ahead of the catcher's futile throw. Raschi stomped around the mound muttering to himself, but evaded trouble by inducing a weak ground ball that ended the threat.

Two youngsters were stationed behind the right-field fence alongside the manual scoreboard. Henry and Ben watched as they hung up zero after zero. The game remained scoreless through six innings . . . then seven . . . and then eight. Bunny's bunt single had been the game's only hit. He'd struck out seventeen Classical batters (including Raschi, twice) to Raschi's thirteen (including Bunny, once), and both had allowed but two walks.

No one had dared leave the ballpark. The dominance of the young hurlers kept the crowd in their seats as the curtain rose on the ninth inning. In the top of the frame, Raschi would be obliged to face the first three hitters of Tech's lineup.

"Bunny's up fourth this inning," Henry said. "Someone's got to break the ice for him to bat."

"Tall order," said Ben. He sipped absent-mindedly from a bottle of Coca-Cola. "So far, not much evidence of either horse sloughing off."

Sweating profusely, Raschi wiped his brow after every pitch, but continued to throw with the same force and pinpoint control that had characterized his performance all afternoon. He managed to retire Tech's leadoff hitter on a harmless infield pop-up, then fanned the next batter for the fourth time that afternoon. Jim Daly, Tech's stolid third baseman, was next up. Behind in the count two-and-two, Daly smashed a hard comebacker to the mound. But instead of fielding it cleanly for the third out, the big righthander muffed it. The ball bounced off his glove and dropped to his feet, dribbling slowly down the front of the mound. Raschi lurched forward and in a single motion grasped the ball and slung it to first—a split-second too late. Now he'd have to face Bunny Taliaferro.

Bunny grabbed his slab of hickory and sauntered slowly toward the plate. The crowd rose as one. The right-handed hitter dug his cleats into the batter's box and peered out at Raschi. He took a couple of deliberate practice swings before lifting the bat up over his right shoulder. Raschi stared him down, deciphered the sign, leaned back, and flung a rocket that Bunny took for a called strike. Raschi's next pitch, a big, slow curve, was in the dirt for a ball.

The powerful hurler beckoned his catcher to the mound for a conference. Bunny stepped out of the box, his face betraying his impatience. After a few words, pitcher and catcher nodded to each other and reclaimed their positions. The catcher set up on the outside corner. But Raschi's fastball missed the catcher's target, swerving into the inner half of the strike zone. Bunny swung hard, slamming a high drive *deep* down the left field line. The crowd held its collective breath as the ball soared into the late afternoon haze and flew past the left field foul pole—then exhaled in unison as the umpire declared it foul. The throng remained on its feet, buzzing.

Rattled by the near miss, Raschi circled the mound, collecting himself. Hesitant to put anything anywhere near Bunny's wheelhouse, he tried instead to tempt him with a pair of slow, big-breaking curve balls low and away. But Bunny wouldn't bite. He calmly took each pitch for a ball.

With the count now full, Springfield's coach whistled to Raschi, holding up four fingers, the sign for an intentional pass.

"Do you walk Bunny, moving the lead runner into scoring position at second base?" Henry asked rhetorically.

"I would have walked him every time he came up," Ben said.

Raschi glared at his coach and shook his head. The skipper, a portly old-timer with the face of a serial killer, turned bright red, stepped to the top of the dugout, and thrust out the same four fingers more forcefully this time while expelling a colossal stream of tobacco juice from the corner of his mouth.

Raschi stepped back on the rubber, but when the catcher stood up and reached to his right, calling for the soft outside toss required to complete the intentional walk, Raschi waved him back behind the plate. Before his furious skipper could work his way back up the dugout steps to object, Raschi fired what was probably his best fastball of the day right down the heart of the plate.

The only thing louder than the coach's plaintive *"Aw, SHIT!"* was the crack of Bunny's bat colliding with Raschi's fastball. This time, however, there was no uncertainty. Bunny hit that baseball farther than any man had ever hit a baseball in—or in this case, *out*—of Forest Park. The spectators' gasps created a veritable vacuum, fans of both teams inhaling at once in utter amazement as they watched the ball clear the centerfield fence by a good hundred feet. Raschi flung his glove to the ground in disgust while his coach stomped up and down like a spoiled six-year-old before storming out to yank his insubordinate hurler from the contest. While half of the astonished fans were dancing in merriment, the rest slumped to their seats, their heads shaking in disbelief. The crowd generated a continual hum even as a reliever took the mound and quickly erased the last Tech batter on a harmless grounder to third.

Everyone remained glued to their seats for the bottom of the ninth. Henry bit his nails while Ben crossed his fingers. With Taliaferro now three outs from a no-hitter, a hush descended over the ballpark.

Classical brought up its ninth, first, and second hitters to face Bunny. He struck out the first batter on three straight overpowering fastballs. He dealt the same hand to the second batter with the same result, recording his nineteenth strikeout of the afternoon.

"Those were the hardest pitches he's thrown all day!" Henry said.

As the third batter strode reluctantly to the plate, the silence gave way. Two thousand fans were on their feet, stomping, whistling, and screaming encouragement. A communal groan rang out when Bunny started off with a ball. But Bunny hit pay dirt with the next two fastballs and finished off the overmatched hitter handily with a curve ball as crooked as a thief. With an economical ten-pitch inning, Bunny had completed his gem, a twenty-strikeout, 2-0, no-hit victory for the ages—and triggered in the fertile mind of a young artist a notion that could transform his budding career.

CHAPTER FOUR

Gastonia Renaissance

H enry barely slept that night. Bunny's performance and curious history had spawned an idea.

"How well do you know Bunny?" he asked his brother the following morning.

"Well enough, I guess, why?"

"Think I could persuade him to pose for me?"

"For a portrait?"

"Hardly," said Henry cryptically. He then explained what he had in mind.

Ben was skeptical. "That's rather ambitious," he said, "and maybe just a little ambiguous, don't you think?"

"Well, it's a far cry from my forlorn family of unfortunate farmers," Henry said with a smirk.

Henry tracked down Bunny the next morning at his family's home on Montrose Street. It was a small, unassuming ranch house in a part of the city where white visitors were a rarity. After Henry introduced himself as Ben Kapler's artist/brother, the lanky athlete invited him in.

"Is it okay to call you Bunny?"

"Everyone else does."

"Well, then, Bunny," Henry said, "I'd like to paint your picture."

Bunny laughed. "I'm sorry," he said, "I can't hardly pay for an artist to paint my picture."

"No, Bunny, I'm not here to sell you a portrait," Henry said, realizing how foolish his statement must have sounded. He folded himself into the armchair Bunny had offered in his sparsely furnished living room. "I'd like to do a painting of two ballplayers. You, in your American Legion uniform, stepping out of a dugout to shake the hand of another ballplayer . . . a *white* ballplayer with the town name "Gastonia" spelled out across his chest."

Bunny looked puzzled. "I'm afraid that would be a lie, Mr. Kapler."

"Please, call me Henry. And yes, I know that's not what happened. It's what *should* have happened. It's what will happen some day, when people stand up for what's right." Henry feared he'd begun to sound patronizing.

Bunny bit his lip. "I'm not one for instigatin'," he said.

"This painting might ruffle a few feathers, sure," Henry said, doubling down with determination. "But that's my intent. Gastonia shouldn't be swept under the rug. Together we'd be making a statement . . . with subtlety rather than spite."

Bunny stroked his chin. "I'm not sure what to say."

"I'd like you to pose for me in my studio downtown. You can come by nights, weekends, whenever is convenient. I'll pay you for your time. And if you prefer, I'll keep your cooperation under wraps. I'll say I worked from photos. You needn't be implicated."

Bunny fidgeted. "I'm guessing your heart's in the right place. I just don't—"

"Think it over a few days. Then let me know what you decide." As he got up to leave, Henry pressed a card inscribed with his name and address into Bunny's palm. "And . . . by the way," he added, "Ben and I were there for your no-hitter on Saturday. It was a thrill and an honor to watch you play—something I hope to be able to tell my grandchildren about."

Bunny indulged himself a well-earned smile. Henry shook his large right hand and departed.

Three days later, Bunny dropped by Henry's studio. Despite his misgivings, he accepted Henry's offer. He agreed to pose for an hour each weekday evening beginning the following week. After all, he could use the money.

Henry prepared a corner of his studio for his sessions with Bunny. He scrounged an old set of library steps to simulate the steps of a dugout and a well-worn mannequin from a women's clothing store owned by a neighbor. The irony that the mannequin was a naked white female, whose arm would be positioned to reach out to shake the hand of a large black male, was not lost on Henry. It was a redneck's worst nightmare.

Bunny was understandably unsettled by the specter of posing with a white female mannequin and nearly abandoned the project on the very first evening. It took all of Henry's powers of persuasion to assure him that the mannequin was merely a placeholder for the second figure in the painting, and that Henry had described his proposed composition honestly. Henry installed a set of blackout curtains over his studio window lest anyone get the wrong impression. At Henry's request, Bunny posed in his old American Legion uniform, his right hand gripping the mannequin's right hand and his battered old glove on his left.

As the young men became better acquainted, the barriers between them slowly dissolved. When Bunny inquired about the menorah resting on a shelf in Henry's studio, the artist explained the tradition of Hanukkah. He talked of his family's roots in

Russia. Bunny, in turn, recounted the oral tradition of his ancestors' migration from a Virginia plantation by way of the Underground Railroad. Despite their divergent backgrounds, Henry and Bunny had more in common than they might have imagined. Each had spent his entire life in Springfield, loved baseball, and was part of a heritage that had endured—and would continue to endure—intense persecution.

"What happened when your ballclub reached Gastonia in '34?" Henry asked him.

"Well," Bunny said, "somehow word got out before we arrived ... that our club included a Negro. It was even in the papers. We were turned away by restaurants ... by all of the local hotels ... we had to bus a half-hour to Charlotte for lodgings."

"Was this unexpected?"

"The coaches, maybe, had a notion there'd be trouble. But the rest of us were too naïve to realize what we were up against." Bunny shifted uncomfortably as he endeavored to maintain his pose.

"Did you even get to practice?"

"We tried. When we got to the ballpark the next morning, there were hundreds of angry white folks waiting for us. Whole families—even little kids—screaming 'Go home, nigga!' and calling my teammates and Coach Steere 'nigga lovers' ... and worse ... *much* worse. I remember—" Bunny choked up. "I remember a little boy ... couldn't have been more than seven or eight ... comes up to me and spits at me. He looks up at his father and smiles. The father looks down at his son like he'd come home with straight A's."

As Bunny spoke, Henry sketched, stepping forward every so often to make a subtle adjustment to Bunny's position.

"We began infield practice," Bunny continued, "but then

this rowdy bunch of teenagers starts peltin' us with rocks. That's when Coach Steere yelled for us to each pick up a bat and head for the bus. 'Don't you dare swing those bats at anyone 'less you're attacked,' he said. So we rushed to the bus and drove back to our hotel in Charlotte."

Henry was moved by Bunny's account. While he'd read of more lethal incidents in the press, he'd never visited the South nor heard a first-person account of racial abuse. He urged Bunny to continue with his story.

"When we got back to the hotel, Coach called a team meeting. Sid Harris . . . he's the Legion guy who came down with us . . . told us what the Gastonia people had told him. Said that none of our opponents—teams from Maryland, Florida, and North Carolina—would play 'gainst a Negro . . . and that even if they changed their minds, the Gastonia town officials couldn't . . . or *wouldn't* . . . guarantee our safety. We had a choice, Mr. Harris said: play without me, or just go on home."

"What did you say?"

"I told 'em to play without me! We'd traveled so far and played so well. I didn't want to be the one who spoilt it all."

"And then?"

"Well, 'Kingie'—that's Tony King, our second baseman—says that if I don't play, he don't play. Then Moonie Jevanelli says 'I'm with Kingie.' Bits Bazzoni says 'We're a team . . . we play together or not at all.' Coach Steere says we're gonna take a vote."

"And?"

"And everyone voted not to play."

"How'd that make you feel?" Henry asked.

"It *hurt*," Bunny said, "ya know, 'cause of all that hate. And I felt awful that my teammates couldn't play, but I was proud of every last one of them. And none of 'em was mopin' or nothin'.

They said I shouldn't feel bad, that it wasn't my fault. That we'd go home with our heads held high."

"I remember the news reports when you got back," Henry said. "A thousand people at Union Station cheering when your train arrived."

"Yeah, that was really something."

"Seems to me that in the end, you won," Henry said, "maybe not on the field, but you stood up for your principles."

"Yeah," Bunny said. "I guess so. And I guess that's what makes this picture of yours important." Bunny relaxed, backing down the library steps and releasing his hand from the grasp of the mannequin. "I'm glad we're doing this," he said, "and I guess I really don't mind people knowing I cooperated— as long as no one ever finds out I've been shakin' hands with a bony-legged, naked white girl all week!"

Henry coaxed his brother into modeling for the second figure in his composition, the ballplayer from Gastonia. Their mother also pitched in, taking an old pinstriped uniform that Ben had worn when he'd played varsity ball, carefully removing the applied lettering, and replacing it with eight black felt capital letters she'd cut out to spell 'GASTONIA.' At six-foot-two and 190 pounds, Ben was the perfect counterpart to Bunny and just the right size and build for the player that Henry envisioned reaching down from the left side of the canvas to shake Bunny's hand. Henry didn't want the Gastonia player to actually *be* Ben, so he altered the working sketches to eliminate any resemblance.

After he'd completed his drawings of Ben, Henry made a foray to Forest Park to prepare studies of the dugout, from the top step that would appear in the foreground of the painting to the bench that would stretch across the background. He wanted more than just the right shape for that top step—he sought to capture the coarse texture of the concrete, its pockmarks, dirt and tobacco stains, chips, and peeling paint. As he glanced into the dugout, he observed the long, horizontal slats of the bench. Studying the light, he noted how it receded into darkness as he moved his eyes from the floor to the roof of the dugout. It gave him an idea.

Henry stopped at Bunny's after leaving his studio that evening. From their conversations, he knew that Bunny was playing summer ball in an industrial league for a team in neighboring Chicopee.

"When and where's your next game?" Henry asked.

"Saturday afternoon at Gaylord Park in Chicopee," Bunny replied. "Three o'clock."

"Perfect," Henry said, realizing that the shadows at that time might be exactly what he was hoping for. "Do they have traditional dugouts there? Like at Forest Park?"

"Yeah, sure, though the grandstand's much smaller."

"That's not a problem. Do you think you can arrange for me to spend a few minutes on the field, outside the dugout, just before the game starts . . . to take some photos of the guys on the bench?"

"Uh, yeah, I guess so."

"Great. See you then."

Henry borrowed his parent's car and Leica camera, bought some film, and drove to Chicopee that Saturday afternoon. Bunny had made all the necessary arrangements. The light and timing were perfect. Henry waited until close to game time, when every seat on the bench was occupied. It was what Henry had hoped for: players gesturing to one another, one bending forward with his head in his hands, another pondering his glove. The ballplayers' heads were obliterated by the shadows. He shot a dozen photographs.

A week later, Henry had his photos... and his ideal background. Using elements from each of the snapshots, he made rough composite drawings of the players on the dugout bench. He settled on a frieze consisting of three ballplayers: one with his head in his hands, another leaning over to converse with the player beside him, and the third with his arms folded neatly across his chest. Facial details were obliterated by the shadows cast by the dugout roof. He would place the background frieze just below the center of the canvas, between the two key figures in the foreground that would dominate the painting.

After weeks of preparation, Henry had his final sketch. He blocked out a grid on both the sketch and the canvas to facilitate transfer of the image. Only then could he begin to paint.

Henry worked day and night through the first few weeks of July, hoping to finish the painting in time for the Springfield Museum's late summer showcase of regional art. He paused only occasionally for meals, sleeping on a cot in the corner of his studio. No one, not even his family, was permitted to disturb him or to view his work in progress.

He applied his last brushstroke on July 28th. He'd labored to get everything right: the texture and folds of the uniforms, the expression on Bunny's face (mild surprise mixed with welcome satisfaction) and the face of the fictional Gastonia ballplayer (generosity without condescension). Henry titled the work *Gastonia Renaissance.*

The first person he contacted was Bunny, who wasted little time in coming to see the work. The look on his face was *exactly* the same as Henry had captured on canvas.

"It's amazing!" Bunny gushed. "Absolutely amazing!"

CHAPTER FIVE

Kudos and Brickbats

PAINTING BY LOCAL ARTIST STIRS CONTROVERSY
Special to the Springfield Union
by W. D. Danforth, Art Critic for the Springfield Union

SPRINGFIELD, August 10, 1936. There was a new twist when the
Springfield Museum of Fine Arts opened its annual late summer
exhibition of the work of area artists last night. Setting itself apart
from the usual staid selection of tasteful, if *de rigueur*, landscapes,
portraits, and still lifes, was the latest work by local painter Henry
J. Kapler, which he graces with the curious title *Gastonia
Renaissance*. Kapler, you'll recall, is the twenty-one-year-old
prodigy, lately graduated from Yale, who shocked the local art
world in February when he waltzed off with first prize in the oil
painting category for his ambitious family triumvirate, *Eventide.*

Gastonia Renaissance conveys a message, placing itself
squarely within the territory of the provocative band of Social
Realists now gaining traction in New York. The subject of the
painting is the well-known, local Negro athlete Ernest "Bunny"
Taliaferro, the young man whose presence on his American
Legion baseball team gave rise to an unfortunate racial incident
two years ago in Gastonia, North Carolina, the putative site of
Kapler's painting. Subject to racial taunts and threats of violence,
the team chose to abandon the competition with integrity rather
than playing without its dark-skinned star. But instead of painting
history as it was, Kapler has chosen to paint a world in which Mr.
Taliaferro is graciously welcomed by the host city of Gastonia, as
personified by a second figure clad in a pinstriped uniform with

Gastonia emblazoned across his chest. This imaginary character reaches down from field level to shake our local hero's hand, as the latter makes his way up the dugout steps. The conceit here is, one must presume, that the white man has endorsed, even encouraged, the Negro to be lifted from the depths and hoisted onto an equal playing field, if you'll forgive the pun.

While I, and all others who viewed the work, found it technically satisfying, a division of opinion arose as to the efficacy of its message. For some, it was a none-too-subtle effort to excoriate the South by illustrating the chasm between what is and what should be; for others, it let the evil Jim Crow off the hook far too easily by failing to accurately depict the shameful reception accorded a legendary local athlete who, by dint of fortune, just happens to be of the Negro race. Yet no matter what side of the debate you claim, there can be no doubt that *Gastonia Renaissance* made its presence felt in no small way, garnering virtually all of the kudos and brickbats in an otherwise pedestrian exhibition.

CHAPTER SIX

Grand Central

Thunderstorms pelted New Haven Railroad's Train 53 as it splashed its way from Springfield to New York's Grand Central Terminal. Henry sat by a window in the thinly populated railcar, his view obscured by the incessant rain. The first half of the ride was familiar: he'd taken it to Yale for the past four years.

The showers let up briefly as the train pulled into New Haven's Union Station, the spare, brick building that had served as Henry's portal to and from college. He'd thrived on Yale's stately campus, pursuing what he loved, honing his skills, supported by prosperous parents who'd financed his world-class education while shielding him from the anxiety and despair of the Depression. Henry resisted the impulse to get off, to return, if he could, to the nurturing sanctuary of the ivory tower. But Yale, he knew, had been prologue; his future lay in New York. The stop in New Haven was brief. Passengers trudged off, umbrellas in tow, their places quickly taken by grim-faced, Gotham-bound travelers in dripping raincoats and soaked fedoras.

Henry remained pensive as Train 53 clattered slowly from the bowels of the station on the final leg of its journey. Undercurrents of insecurity tempered his optimism. Was he talented enough to make an impression in the chaotic world of art, a world that swallowed many more aspiring entrants than it rewarded? Could he make the connections necessary to enhance his career? And, even more vexing, could he support himself in a country wracked by economic depression? His Yale degree would count for little in the pursuit of his craft, and his meager savings left little margin for error.

As if on cue, the skies cleared and the sun emerged as the train rolled into Grand Central. Buoyed by the meteorological transformation, Henry alighted the railcar, lugging his battered suitcase along the platform, up a stairway, and through the cavernous main concourse of the lavish Beaux Arts edifice. Shafts of sunlight poured through semi-circular windows high above the west side of the concourse, bathing bustling commuters and a hopeful young artist in an almost ethereal light.

New York City beckoned like a swanky suit in a department store window. Activity was everywhere. Traffic rumbled, horns blared, pedestrians hustled down crowded sidewalks. For a buck and a half, Henry secured a clean bed with a shared bath in a nondescript hotel a few blocks from the terminal, mustered a generous helping of lamb stew and a cup of coffee at a nearby cafeteria for a quarter more, and retired early in preparation for the next day's assault on the city.

Henry was no stranger to New York—he'd spent a summer in Union Square before the Crash, while his father served a stint at a nearby hospital. The area was home to some of the painters he most admired, including Reginald Marsh, Kenneth Hayes Miller, Edward Laning, and Raphael Soyer. Hoping perhaps that their talent might rub off on him, or that he might more easily make their acquaintance, Henry canvassed the neighborhood for a modest apartment that could double as a studio.

Henry needed a place with light enough to paint and room enough to live—a tall order with a slim budget of thirty-five bucks a month. After rejecting a dozen possibilities, he stumbled upon an old office space recently converted into a studio apartment on the fourth floor of a five-story commercial building at 12 E. Seventeenth Street, near the corner of Fifth Avenue and the north end of Union Square. The room featured two large windows, a small kitchenette, and an alcove where he could sleep. An exposed bank of iron piping along the back wall delivered adequate heat during business hours, while a small, pot-bellied coal stove provided auxiliary heating for weeknights and weekends. Coal was available in the basement, although Henry was obliged to shovel it himself and haul it up four flights of stairs. While it wasn't fancy, it was equipped, at least, with hot running water, a private toilet, and a small icebox—not bad for $35 a month. But its most impressive aspect was one he hadn't noticed until he'd signed a lease and added his name to the ground floor directory: his apartment was immediately beneath the residence and studio of Edward Laning, one of the city's leading painters and muralists.

The task of relocating his studio to New York was daunting. Since the new space was so much smaller than his Springfield studio, Henry entrusted his parents with most of his paintings, electing to bring with him but one large canvas, *Gastonia Renaissance*, fresh from its controversial Springfield debut, and a smattering of smaller works with sentimental value. He'd need his two easels, together with his stock of paints, brushes, and assorted artists' materials. Ben had volunteered to pack and load it all into his pick-up and drive down that weekend, but he couldn't do it alone. Henry suggested that he enlist Bunny to assist him in exchange for a spirited weekend in The City that Never Sleeps.

Ben and Bunny made the five-hour drive from Springfield on the first weekend in September. Never having been to New York, Bunny was easily recruited. He'd imposed just one condition: a visit to the Cotton Club, the legendary nightclub and jazz venue that had recently relocated to the Broadway Theater District from Harlem. Henry was more than happy to oblige.

"You failed to mention the three flights of stairs," Ben grumbled as he carried the larger of Henry's easels past the third-floor landing, huffing and puffing along with his older brother who bore the weight at the lower end.

"You didn't ask," Henry said between gasps. Meanwhile, Bunny alone carried twice as much at twice the pace with half the strain.

"You're embarrassing us!" Ben complained.

"Not hardly working," Bunny said with a grin. "Saving my energy for the Cotton Club."

It took all three of them to maneuver *Gastonia Renaissance* up the compact staircase, navigating the painting gingerly around each turn. At the fourth floor landing, they encountered a man in shirtsleeves descending from the floor above. Thirtyish, with wavy, sandy-colored hair and a friendly demeanor, he was blocked by the heavily swaddled canvas that clogged the stairwell.

"Don't tell me we have another artist in the building," he said.

"Guilty as charged," Henry replied. The young men shifted the canvas into the hallway and put it down, allowing Henry to introduce himself and his crew.

"Nice to meet you, fellas," the man said. "I'm Edward Laning."

"I surmised," Henry said. "I've looked forward to meeting you."

Laning motioned toward the bundled artwork. "Mind if I take a look?"

"I'd be honored." Henry tried valiantly to banish the pangs of self-doubt that gathered like storm clouds in the presence of the older artist.

Laning waited while the young men steered the painting through the apartment door. Once inside, they propped it against a wall where Henry unwrapped it.

Laning beamed when *Gastonia Renaissance* emerged from its cocoon. "Very impressive," he said, smiling broadly. Henry maintained his outward composure while turning emotional cartwheels inside.

Laning stepped back, taking it all in. He glanced at Bunny and then back at the painting. "That's you, isn't it?" he said to Bunny, who nodded in acknowledgment, prompting Henry to relate a much-abbreviated version of Bunny's Gastonia ordeal.

"A shame you had to endure that kind of treatment," Laning said to Bunny. "Henry, I trust we'll have the pleasure of getting to know one another better," Laning said as he turned to leave.

"I hope so, Mr. Laning."

"Edward," Laning insisted, closing the door behind him.

CHAPTER SEVEN

Night at the Savoy

The cabbie gave Henry a fierce, cross-eyed look when he asked him to take them to the Cotton Club.

"Ain't no coloreds allowed there, pal, don't ya know?" he said, without rancor, tilting his head in Bunny's direction. "Be better off uptown . . . at the Savoy."

"Sorry, Bunny," Henry said. He turned to the cabbie. "The Savoy, then." Bunny was dismayed—and angered—to think that a nightclub where blacks filled the stage would bar them from the audience. After all, this was New York City, not Gastonia!

Rain had begun to fall by the time the cab pulled up to the corner of Lenox Avenue and 141st Street, the heart of the Harlem nightclub district. From the cab, they made a dash for the shelter of the glittering Savoy Ballroom marquee.

None of them had ever been to Harlem. Their preconceptions were molded by assumptions and biases over which they had little control. Each was surprised, in his own way, by the spectacle that greeted them: hordes of mostly young revelers, both black and white, men and women, some in sharp suits and fashionable dresses, others clad in the everyday garb of factory workers or laborers. Wealth and skin color mattered little—everyone had come to dance.

Scores milled about at the entrance, awaiting admission. A pair of bouncers, enormous black men in tuxedos, scrutinized the trio closely before waving them through. Inside, the rhythms of jazz tugged at them as they paid their fifty-cent covers, passed under the enormous cut-glass chandelier, and ascended the grand marble stairway and through the double doors that opened into the massive second-floor ballroom.

Henry had never seen anything quite like it: several *thousand* patrons gyrating like tops, spinning to the beat of the music. Banks of multicolored lights illuminated the elegant ballroom, reflecting off the mirrored walls like shooting stars. The sheer energy of the place could have powered the city for a month.

The wonder on the faces of the three young men betrayed them as first-time visitors. A young, black woman approached them, her attire as glamorous as it was revealing. She identified herself as one of the Savoy hostesses.

"Hey," she said, loudly enough to be heard over the music. "Welcome to the Savoy. Guessin' its your first visit . . . right?"

"Yes, Ma'm," Bunny confessed, transfixed by her statuesque beauty.

"No matter. Name's Thelma. Lemme show you around."

Though more intrigued with Bunny than the Kapler boys, Thelma gladly shepherded the trio along the perimeter of the ballroom. They passed two separate bandstands. "That's so that when one band needs a breather, another's primed and ready to go!" Thelma explained. She pointed to the principal bandstand where a short, hunched musician presided over a gaggle of performers and an array of drums. "That there's Chick Webb and his band. Best in the biz!"

Bunny motioned toward a tall, spindly young woman scat-singing at the front of the orchestra. "Who's the lady singing with the band?"

"Oh, that's Ella . . . Ella Fitzgerald. Just nineteen and what a voice, don't you agree?"

"And how!" Bunny said.

The activity on the dance floor was feverish and unrelenting.

"They call the dance floor 'The Track' . . . on account of its shape," Thelma said. The Track was as wide as the city block on which the ballroom stood, and a good fifty feet deep. Every square inch was occupied.

Thelma led them toward the north corner of the ballroom. "This here's 'Cat's Corner,'" she told them. It was where the real entertainment took place, she said, where the flashiest and most inventive dancers strutted their stuff before a ring of captivated spectators. This was where the cream rose to the top, where the best of the best honed their skills and debuted their latest moves. "They're dancin' the Lindy Hop," she said. "If you like, I can teach you."

"Hell, yeah!" Bunny said, jumping at her offer.

"Uh, no thanks," groaned the Kapler boys.

As Bunny went off with Thelma to master the Lindy Hop, Henry and Ben remained in Cat's Corner, mesmerized by the activity unfolding before them.

From the left side of Cat's Corner, a wiry kid in a loose-fitting suit sauntered out onto the dance floor with his partner, a lean, athletic girl with her hair tied back in a bun. The other dancers quickly backed away, yielding the couple a broad swath of The Track. Their routine was daring, acrobatic and wildly energetic, with rapid circular movements, flips, twists, and bounces, always in step with the rollicking beat.

"Do you know who they are?" Henry asked a spectator.

"That's Frankie Manning, king of the Lindy Hop. His partner's Frieda Washington. Cat's meow, don'tcha think?"

This was what Henry wanted to paint next: Frankie and

Frieda performing the Lindy Hop in Cat's Corner at the Savoy Ballroom. He'd capture them at the height of activity, with an audience of dazzled onlookers, just as he witnessed them now. He revealed his plan to his brother, then waited for the couple to take a break so that he could broach the idea with them.

Henry followed Frankie Manning off the floor, catching him as he headed toward the lounge. He introduced himself and asked if he could sketch, and then paint, the pair in action.

"Don't see why not," Frankie said. "Why don't you come by on Monday, 'bout six o'clock. We'll be practicin' then."

"Great!" Henry said, thanking him profusely, barely able to contain his excitement.

Henry bounded down the stairs from his apartment just after five o'clock on Monday evening. He joined the tide of rush hour commuters descending into the Fourteenth Street station at Union Square. Teeming crowds converged upon the turnstiles from every direction, pressing forward relentlessly, jostling each other without apology as they jockeyed for position on the narrow subway platform. He rubbed elbows with men in suits reading newspapers; men in workclothes carrying lunch pails; well-dressed women clutching shopping bags stuffed with the latest bargains from Klein's, Hearn's, and Ohrbach's; office girls with rouged cheeks and brightly painted lips; beggars in ragged clothes with vacant expressions, outstretched hands, and empty tin cups. The cloying aroma of ladies' perfume mingled uneasily with the odors of grime and sweat while the rumble and shriek of the braking trains assaulted his eardrums.

Henry emerged from the choking underground at 145th Street in Harlem. In the span of thirty minutes, a sea of white faces had transformed completely into shades of black.

The Savoy, too, seemed different. No one lingered under the

big marquee. At the six o'clock hour, the ballroom was virtually empty but for a cluster of dancers in Cat's Corner perfecting their routines in collaboration with a handful of musicians.

Frankie Manning was easy to spot, with his energy and effervescent smile. He broke away from his partner when he saw Henry approach.

"Hey, man, how ya' doin'?"

"Good, Frankie, how 'bout you?"

"I'm dancin', ain't I?"

Henry smiled. Frankie put an arm around Henry's shoulder and led him toward Cat's Corner. He pulled out a stool and placed it at the edge of The Track.

"You can jus' sit here and doodle away to your heart's content," he told Henry before reclaiming his place on the dance floor. He whispered something into Frieda Washington's ear. She glanced at Henry briefly, offering a smile and a wave. She then took Frankie's hand and they plunged back into the music like sun-drenched seals returning to sea.

Henry sketched for close to an hour. Capturing his subjects in constant motion was challenging, but it was that very movement that he sought to portray. Each time the dancers took a break, the young artist coaxed one of them to pose for a close-up study. He drew as fast as he could, knowing he lacked the luxury of time that Bunny and Ben had afforded him as he worked on *Gastonia Renaissance.*

Henry made the long trip uptown daily for two weeks. Frankie and Frieda did their best to accommodate him, making him feel at ease. They wandered over from time to time for a glimpse at his sketches. Savoy employees were equally hospitable, plying him with complimentary refreshments while ogling his growing accumulation of pencil, charcoal, and watercolor studies. On several occasions he stayed on well past midnight, when the Ballroom filled, to capture the postures and expressions of the spectators who surrounded the dancers as they refined their routines into the early morning.

Henry treasured his time at the Savoy. It was an oasis, an antidote to Gastonia and the Cotton Club, a place where races mixed easily, where skin color conferred no burdens or advantages, and where all that mattered was music and dance.

CHAPTER EIGHT

The Abstract Carpenter

It was in mid-October when Henry next encountered Edward Laning. Ascending the stairwell late one morning, Henry happened upon the artist dragging a large roll of canvas up the stairs above him. An attractive dark-haired woman, slightly taller than Laning, was assisting him when the bundle slipped from her grasp and began to unfurl. Henry rushed to their aid. Once they'd maneuvered the recalcitrant roll into the Lanings' top-floor loft, Edward thanked his new neighbor and introduced his wife, Mary.

"This is Henry, the young painter from Springfield I told you about... in the apartment below us," he told Mary. She was gracious and friendly despite a stern, Midwestern countenance.

"Can I offer you a Coke... or maybe a Ballantine?" she asked.

"A Coke would be swell," Henry said with a warm smile as he surveyed the studio. Two skylights flooded the loft with light. A large, movable wooden partition rested against a back wall.

"I use that contraption to stretch canvas for my mural work," Edward explained. He described his current commission, a 190-foot mural for the dining hall at Ellis Island on the role of the immigrant in the industrialization of

America. "This monstrosity lets me work on the murals right here in the studio . . . so I don't have to commute to the island each day—"

"Truth be told," Mary interrupted, "so you don't have to deal with the constant meddling of that idiot Immigration Commissioner . . ."

". . . who's a royal pain in the ass," Edward agreed. "A young, abstract artist built it for me."

"Not much call for abstraction on the WPA mural circuit," Mary said, laughing, "so they found him a gig as a carpenter."

"An abstract carpenter?" Henry teased. "I'd hate to climb one of his scaffolds."

Edward chuckled. "Turns out he's a talented craftsman."

"At least they found him some work they could pay him for," Mary said. "Like most artists, he needs the dough." Henry could certainly relate to that.

A large, unfinished canvas rested on an easel in a corner of the room. A pen-and-ink sketch was tacked to the wall beside it.

"Your latest work?" Henry asked Edward.

"When I'm not slaving over murals, I chip away at that," he acknowledged. "I don't have much time for easel paintings these days," he said with a hint of resignation. Edward grabbed a cigarette from a pack lying on the edge of a small worktable near the easel. "Cigarette?"

Henry politely declined as Edward lit up. "Can I take a look at your sketch?" Edward nodded. It was an elaborate composition with a range of figures, many with upraised arms caught up in what appeared to be a religious frenzy.

"A Bar Mitzvah?" Henry deadpanned.

Edward laughed. "The complete opposite," he said. "A revival meeting. One of these crazy spectacles I remember from my childhood in rural Illinois. The preacher would stand up at the podium and declare everyone sinners ... and the sinners would wail and moan and beg for penance and forgiveness like a pack of coyotes in heat. It'll be called *Camp Meeting* ... if I ever find the time to finish it."

"It'll be wonderful," Henry said. "And how about that one?" He gestured toward a painting hanging above the sofa.

"That's mine," Mary said. Four office girls, strong, confident, and sensual, basked in the hot summer sun on a city rooftop during their lunch break. "I call it *Place in the Sun*."

Mary Fife Laning might have been as talented as her better-known husband, but like so many artist-wives, her primary allegiance was to her husband's career. *Place in the Sun*, an ironic title evocative of the recognition that eluded so many female artists, was the only evidence of Mary's art in the loft.

Edward snuffed out his cigarette. "By the way, Henry ... ran into Eddie Hopper last week. Said he was in Springfield last winter judging a show won by ... and I'm quoting him now ... 'some goddang Jewish kid from Yale.' I mentioned your name. 'Yeah, that's the one!' he said. I described your baseball painting but he said that wasn't it."

Henry was tickled by the recognition. "No, it was a painting of a poor rural family. I'm surprised he remembered."

"Me too," Edward said. "He usually only remembers imagined slights by friends and critics." Mary laughed at her husband's astute characterization.

"And what are you working on now?" Mary asked. Henry described his infatuation with the Savoy Ballroom and the Lindy Hop.

"Swell idea," Edward said.

Henry took a last swig of Coke, thanked the Lanings for their hospitality, and turned to leave.

"Oh . . . I almost forgot," Edward said as he walked Henry to the door. "I've got a meeting here tomorrow with Walter Garrison . . . he's the director of the Corcoran Gallery in Washington. Also the administrator on a mural project I'm doing for some podunk post office in North Carolina. Regs require that he check up on me now and again. While he's here, thought I might take him downstairs for a gander at your baseball painting . . . if you wouldn't mind."

"Really?" Henry was thrilled by the prospect.

"Why not?" Edward said as he opened the door. "Maybe he'll make your day."

Henry was poring over perspective drawings for his Savoy Ballroom piece the next afternoon when he heard the rapping on his door. A spasm of anxiety surged through his body. He'd been unable to concentrate all day. A studio visit by Walter Garrison could jumpstart his career.

Garrison looked as if he'd been cast by Hollywood for the part of the distinguished museum director. Tall, bespectacled, gray-haired, and gray-bearded, he was at least seventy-five. He was bent and walked with the aid of a cane. How he managed to scale the four flights required to reach the Lanings' studio was a mystery, but no matter—he was now entering Henry's own modest studio with Edward Laning at his side.

"This, Walter, is Henry Kapler, the young painter I told you about."

"Honored to meet you, sir," Henry said with a nervous smile. "Please come in. Can I offer you something to drink?"

"No, no. I'm fine," Garrison muttered. He cleared his throat and got right to the point. "Now let me see your work, young man."

Except for his baseball painting, propped up against a wall

at the rear of the studio, Henry had little to show the museum director. His Savoy piece was still in the planning stages. Hanging on a wall near the entryway was a small, endearing portrait of his father that Henry had painted from memory that spring. He'd planned to bring it with him on his next trip home, as a kind of peace offering. With his downward gaze, wire-rimmed glasses, and slightly pursed lips, Dr. Kapler looked both pensive and formidable. Garrison studied the portrait.

"Hmm," he growled.

Adjacent to his father's portrait hung a small still life that Henry had begun in Springfield but finished shortly after his arrival in New York. A vase, a pitcher of flowers, and a couple of pears on a tabletop had been rendered with plasticity, color, and life.

"Hmm," Garrison groaned.

"Uh ... let me show you something a bit more substantial," Henry said, leading them to the rear of his studio.

"Aaaahhh!" the director purred with evident satisfaction upon encountering *Gastonia Renaissance*.

Henry's heart thumped. He glanced at Edward, who smiled back encouragingly.

"I thought you might like it, Walter," Edward said.

"Well ... I do," Garrison replied. "It's technically sound, well-composed, and, I daresay, edgy. I like that."

Not more than five minutes into his visit, the director abruptly turned to leave. "Must be off!" he said as he shuffled toward the door. The young artist escorted them both from his studio.

Henry sat down on a tattered old wing chair, one of only two pieces of upholstered furniture in his apartment. He exhaled deeply. His thoughts were muddled. Though his reaction to *Gastonia Renaissance* was encouraging, Garrison's visit was as brief as it was anticlimactic. What had Henry expected? The director hadn't asked for the story behind the work, nor had Henry the presence of mind to relate it.

An envelope arrived in the mail a week later. Henry shivered at the return address—the Corcoran Gallery of Art in Washington.

The letter was neatly typed. It was as succinct as the director's visit. "If you would be amenable," Garrison wrote, "I would like to include *Gastonia Renaissance* in the Fifteenth Biennial Exhibition of Contemporary American Oil Paintings at the Corcoran Gallery of Art in the spring of 1937."

Henry emitted a yelp audible throughout Union Square.

CHAPTER NINE

Girls! Girls! Girls!

Henry took the train to Springfield for the Thanksgiving holiday. It felt good to be home. Lacking the luxury of a telephone, he hadn't spoken with his family since his move to New York. He should have written, but he was always too busy with something else.

"Henry brought you something from New York," Ruth told her husband when he returned from the office shortly after Henry's arrival.

"Hmm," Morris sniffed. He acknowledged Henry's presence with a nod.

"This is for you," Henry said, handing his father an object about the size of a box of Corn Flakes, swaddled in a maroon velvet cloth. Morris accepted the gift with a raised eyebrow, peeling away the cloth to reveal his own painted image, mounted in a gold-leaf frame.

Henry and his mother watched closely, their expressions wavering between anticipation and anxiety. At first, Morris stared at the portrait blankly. But within moments, Henry witnessed something he'd never seen: tears welling up in his father's eyes. "It's a fine likeness," Morris said, as impassively as possible, before excusing himself to change for dinner.

As the family devoured its Thanksgiving turkey, Henry shared his news about the Corcoran. He talked glowingly of New York, its energy, commerce, and culture, while glossing over its noise, filth, and tawdriness. But even as he extolled the virtues of the city, he realized how little of it he'd actually experienced. Henry was like the business traveler who rarely emerges from his hotel room. He worked constantly, and though he enjoyed his work, he never played. He was alone—and lonely. Besides the Lanings, he'd met virtually no one. He was anonymous in a city of seven million.

Henry didn't share these misgivings with his parents. But later, when they'd gone to bed, he expressed them to Ben.

"You need to go out, have fun," Ben counseled. It was a prescription that would have come more easily to Ben than to Henry. Though his prospects were uncertain, Ben had a wide circle of friends and a penchant for fun, much more so than his nose-to-the-grindstone brother.

"It's not in my nature to go out carousing," Henry said, "especially by myself."

"Take *yourself* out of the equation! Go out and *see* what the city has to offer. Go to a dance hall . . . heck, maybe even a burlesque show. After all, how can you paint what you barely know? And . . . who knows? Maybe you'll meet someone in the process."

"Ha! Can you see me in a burlesque theater, falling for a burlesque queen?"

"No, Henry, I can't. And that's just my point."

Henry couldn't fault Ben's logic. He resolved that when he returned to New York, he'd redouble his efforts to assimilate into the fabric of the city—whether he liked it or not.

Henry found a note wedged under his door when he returned from Springfield—an invitation to a New Year's Eve party from

Mary Laning. "There will be artists, and maybe a former student or two from Edward's classes at the Art Students League," she wrote. "You'll have fun," Mary assured him. "Absolutely nobody goes home sober—except for the Hoppers!" Of course he'd go. It was just what the son of the doctor had ordered.

Meanwhile, Henry resumed work on his Savoy Ballroom piece. He'd finished his preliminary studies and completed a detailed sketch. Instead of oils, he'd decided to paint in tempera, for which he'd need powdered pigments.

The art supply shop was ten blocks away. Bundled against the cold, Henry crossed Union Square. He walked down Fourteenth Street, past the movie houses, penny emporiums, pool halls, dance halls, and burlesque theaters that choked the southern side of the street between Third and Fourth Avenues. It was late afternoon. The sidewalks were clogged with bands of young women provocatively dressed for a night on the town, packs of young men on the prowl for young women, older men looking to sate their sexual appetites, beggars seeking what they could extract from passersby. Touts worked the crowds like grizzled cowboys roping in strays. The tackiness and titillation both repelled and beguiled him.

Henry purchased his pigments and headed home. As he circled back across the raunchiest stretch of Fourteenth Street, he paused beneath the marquee of a popular burlesque hall. "Girls! Girls! Girls!" beckoned a flashing neon sign in bright red letters. His brother's challenge fairly rang in his ears. He was torn. Was it fear, embarrassment, or guilt that restrained him? It felt as if he'd borne a devil on one shoulder and a saint on the other.

"Dammit!" he muttered, "I'm going in!" He stepped up to the kiosk, bought a ticket, and entered the seamy world of burlesque.

The theater was larger than he'd imagined, its decor

incongruously neo-Baroque. Several hundred people—all of them men—packed the venue. Henry had a curious compulsion to paint the look of depravity etched on their faces.

When the crowd settled in, an emcee in a double-breasted plaid suit and a straw boater emerged from the left wing. After a few introductory remarks, he welcomed a pair of comedians onstage to a smattering of applause.

"I'm ready for a vacation," said the chubby foil to his straight man. "Only this year's gonna be different."

"How so?" asked his tall, handsome partner.

"Well, the last few years, I took your advice on where to go. Couple o' years ago, you said to go to Atlantic City, so I went to Atlantic City, and Ruthie got pregnant."

"Uh huh," muttered the straight man.

"Last year, you told me to go to the Poconos, I went to the Poconos, and *again* Ruthie got pregnant."

"So what's gonna be different about this year?"

"This year," the rotund comic said, winking at the audience, "Ruth's coming with me!"

It was the first of an endless stream of sexually suggestive jokes, mining the lewd imaginations of the patrons with the subtlety of a sledgehammer. Hecklers abounded, their barbs predictable enough to have been scripted.

The rabble salivated for more, and the house delivered. To the accompaniment of a bawdy march, a line of chorus girls spilled from the wings, merged mid-stage, and proceeded along the runway that bisected the theater. Henry had taken a seat toward the rear of the room—to facilitate his escape if he lost his nerve. But the chorus line readily commanded his attention. The women were young and pretty. Some wore canned smiles; others made no effort to mask their boredom. All were clad in glittering costumes leaving little to the imagination.

From start to finish, the performance was an exercise in titillation, progressing from the sexual innuendo of the comic sequences to the wholesale exhibitionism of the striptease acts.

Precisely choreographed, the stripteases were fittingly climactic. To the suggestive flourishes of trumpets and trombones, the coquette removed a glove here, a sleeve there, until, to the ascendant beat of the orchestra, she ultimately shed ... *in excruciatingly deliberate fashion* ... her blouse, skirt, brassiere, and panties, the crowd goading her on relentlessly with its hooting and hollering. As the lights dimmed, her pasties flew off, one by one. Then, with the music at a crescendo, she deftly released her g-string and the house went suddenly dark.

When the lights were restored, Henry rose to leave. Though loath to admit it, he found himself breathless. He'd attended solely for the experience, he told himself, like a wide-eyed freshman on a high school field trip. What dismayed his saintly psyche had been nectar to its satanic counterpart, and his ambivalence had yielded to a sense of achievement. Ben would have heartily approved.

Filing toward the exit, he passed a stocky, balding man, in his late thirties, still seated on the aisle, placing finishing touches on a sketch of the final performer. Henry considered addressing the artist but hesitated, reluctant to interrupt his intense concentration, and—his own sense of achievement notwithstanding—conflicted about announcing his presence at the sleazy spectacle. He continued up the aisle, through the lobby, and into the street.

Henry arose early the next morning. The prior day's escapades lingered in his consciousness like a cloying melody. He inhaled a bowl of cereal, prepared a cup of coffee, and repaired to the worktable beside his easel to begin the final stage of his work on *Night at the Savoy*.

Banishing all distraction, he prepared his tempera colors meticulously, mixing each of the powdered pigments with an emulsion of egg yolk and oil, adhering carefully to the recipe he'd learned from a professor at Yale. When the colors were ready, Henry began filling in the outlines he'd transferred to the canvas from his final sketch. Because the medium dried faster, he worked more quickly in tempera than he could in oil.

Henry labored over the painting through the December cold, slaking the thirst of the pot-bellied stove with coal to keep warm. Mary Laning dropped by periodically to check on his progress and offer encouragement. Finally, on New Year's Eve, *Night at the Savoy* was finished.

Henry was pleased with how he'd captured the intensity of the dancers, the way their bodies unraveled, pulling in opposite directions, while their outstretched arms and conjoined hands were poised to reunite them, like the imminent recoil of a stretched rubber band. Their feet hovered above the ground, poised to land and pivot. The elation on their faces shone through, as did the awe in the expressions of the spectators behind them. The tempera had intensified the naturally rich colors of the dancers' ebony skin, rendering it luminous in a way that would have been hard to achieve using oils.

It was eight o'clock in the evening. In a few hours, Henry would pop upstairs for the Lanings' New Year's Eve celebration, a long overdue diversion. Little did he know he'd be launching more than a new year.

CHAPTER TEN

Constipation and Diarrhea

The raspy contralto of Billie Holiday drifted like incense from the phonograph as Henry entered the Lanings' smoke-filled loft. Guests gathered in animated clusters, oblivious to the beefy immigrant railroad workers nearly leaping out from the Ellis Island mural panels looming behind them.

Mary greeted Henry, introducing the star-struck young artist to a veritable who's who in American art. He met the towering Edward Hopper and his petite artist wife, Jo; the Social Realist painter Philip Evergood and his wife, Julia; Stuart Davis and his girlfriend, Roselle.

Off in a corner, a broad-shouldered gentleman sat alone, drawing. Henry recognized him at once as the man he'd seen sketching at the burlesque show.

"Who's that with the sketchpad?" he asked Mary.

"Oh, that's Reggie Marsh," she said. "When he's not the center of attention, he retreats to a corner and sketches . . . and before you know it," she added with a chuckle, "everyone comes by to peek and he's the center of attention again. Go ahead, say hello."

Henry was well acquainted with Marsh's work, much of which focused on the denizens and amusements of Coney

Island, Fourteenth Street, and the Bowery. He also knew that Marsh had attended Yale.

Henry approached the stocky, round-faced artist with the freckled, balding pate. "Sorry to disturb you, Mr. Marsh," he said, "but I very much wanted to meet you." Marsh was so thoroughly engrossed with his drawing that he didn't immediately respond. When he finally did glance up with his piercing blue eyes, Henry introduced himself as "Henry Kapler, Yale '35."

"Well, well, another Yalie," Marsh mumbled, the words dribbling from his tiny mouth. "Mary mentioned you . . . the artist downstairs, right? Said that you'd been working on a Savoy Ballroom picture."

"Negro dancers doing the Lindy Hop," Henry acknowledged.

"Did a couple of Savoy paintings myself," Marsh said, "back in '31 or '32. Love to see yours sometime."

"I'd be honored, Mr. Marsh."

"Reggie."

Henry noticed Reggie's eyes drift back to his sketchpad. "I should leave you to your sketching . . ."

"Nah. Time to put the pad away. I have a bad habit . . . my wife calls it 'with*drawing*,'" he said, placing a decided emphasis on the latter two syllables. "Guess I'd just rather observe than partake in some asinine discussion about Communists or the WPA. Here," he said, depositing pad and pencil on the table beside him, "let's go see what the fuss is about." Henry followed Marsh across the room where the Lanings, Hoppers, and several others were engaged in an animated discussion.

"You can't really tell me the public understands any of this shit you pump out, can you Stuart?" Edward Laning roared at the modernist painter Stuart Davis.

"Who gives a rat's ass what the so-called public

understands?" said Davis, a small, intense man in his early forties. "Would a brilliant, highly articulate writer write like a third-grader just so everyone could *understand* him?" He puffed vigorously from his pipe. "You, Eddie, and Reggie over there . . . you guys are all static, your art never changes. Some day, modernism and abstraction will relegate you fossils to the dustbins of art history!"

"Fat chance!" Hopper blurted out.

"I paint what I *see*," Reggie said, "not what I conjure up in my screwball imagination."

"That's because you're a fuckin' *voyeur*, Reggie . . . and you *have* no imagination!" Stuart shot back. "You paint strippers and bums. Only a pervert wants that stuff on his walls!"

"*All* artists are voyeurs," Laning said. "Reggie's a voyeur of crowds . . . Hopper trains his brush on the lonely."

"At least I'm not some misogynist bent on objectifying women," Davis said, directing his accusation at Marsh, known for his frequent depictions of chorus girls and burlesque queens.

Felicia Marsh rose up quickly in her husband's defense. She was much younger than Reggie—about Henry's age—with short, dark hair and plain features. "That's not fair, Stuart," she protested. "Reggie just paints it like it is."

"Reggie's burlesque girls are simply women trying to make ends meet like the rest of us," Mary said. "These are hard times . . . and young women do what they've gotta do, just like everyone else, Stuart."

Philip Evergood, a small man with a moustache clinging to his upper lip like a misplaced eyebrow, joined the conversation. His proper English upbringing lent a tinge of accent to his halting but booming voice. "As I see it, art is power . . . a means to an end . . . and in the right hands, a weapon for the promotion of justice and social welfare."

"Dammit, Philip. What good does it do to paint gas masks and dive bombers?" Laning said, a lighted cigarette swaying precipitously from his lips.

"—or to paint J.P. Morgan with a pig's nose?" Marsh snickered. Hopper puffed on a cigarette, a look of annoyance gathering upon his face.

"I'm not afraid to inject sentiment into my art . . . or *politics*, for that matter," Evergood said. "You paint what you see, Reggie . . . but I paint what I *feel* and *think*."

"Don't even listen to him, Reggie," Hopper chimed in, his patience spent. "Phil's a damn Commie!"

"Jeez, Hopper, you're such a cantankerous old relic!" Evergood snapped, provoking laughter. "If it were up to you, that milquetoast Hoover would still be president."

"In which case we'd've probably had the revolution by now," Davis said smugly to a chorus of groans.

While Henry was enjoying the repartee, he was too intimidated to join in the conversation. He spotted an attractive young woman pouring herself a glass of wine from a makeshift bar across the room. Henry walked over and introduced himself.

"Hello, Henry," she said. "Fiona Harlsweger . . . sorry, I know it's a mouthful."

"Not at all . . . but I think I'll stick with Fiona."

She laughed. "That'll work just fine."

Fiona was tall and lean with adorable brown eyes, a narrow but well-proportioned nose, and curly brown hair that she'd combed away from her face and clipped in the back. Her skin was flawless and her thin-lipped smile easy and engaging. She'd been Edward's student at the Art Students League in 1933, she said, when he'd temporarily taken over the teaching duties of his mentor, Kenneth Hayes Miller. "Edward was a great instructor . . . taught me a lot," she recalled. "Of course I was just nineteen . . . with a lot to learn. I wish he'd stayed at the League, but he's got his hands full now with his mural commissions." Fiona took a sip from her glass of burgundy. "You're an artist, too?"

"Afraid so," Henry said. "I live in a little studio apartment one floor down." At Fiona's urging, Henry offered a brief sketch of his background and even briefer career, mentioning that he'd just finished his latest work.

"Can I see it?"

Henry wondered if Fiona was truly interested or simply being polite. Either way, he figured, was okay with him, so the two young artists slipped away for the first unofficial unveiling of *Night at the Savoy*. He admired her grace as she led the way out of the Lanings' loft and down the stairway to the fourth floor. Henry unlocked the door, flipped on the lights, and followed her inside.

"Gee, Henry," she said when she came upon the large painting propped upon Henry's easel. "It's marvelous! You learned to paint like that at Yale?"

"Well, I suppose some of it came naturally, but Yale *was* pretty rigorous," he said. "I'm hoping to scrape up enough to take a course or two at the League in the spring."

They sat on a pair of raised stools and spent the next hour in rapt conversation. Henry felt oddly at ease, captivated by Fiona's intelligence, class, and stylish good looks. She told Henry that she'd grown up in Maryland, near Washington. Eager to pursue a career in art, she'd left Georgetown University after her sophomore year and moved to New York, working as a receptionist by day and taking League courses at night. Like most of her peers, she couldn't make ends meet as an artist alone. "A year ago, my company went under and I lost my job. Edward, God bless him, was kind enough to find me a spot as his assistant on the Ellis Island mural project."

"Do you work there . . . or in Edward's studio?"

"A little of both, but mostly here."

"You've been upstairs all this time . . . and I didn't even know it?"

"Gosh, Henry, I guess so," she said with a smile.

Henry had lost track of time. Suddenly, the couple heard a rhythmic stomping from the loft above, accompanied by a familiar countdown. "Five . . . four . . . three . . . two . . . one . . . Happy New Year!" Firecrackers exploded in the street below while car horns blared. They both laughed. Then Fiona got up, leaned forward, and planted a kiss on Henry's lips.

"Happy New Year, Henry," she purred.

Henry dropped by the Lanings' loft a few days later, ostensibly to thank them for the party. He'd hoped to find Fiona there.

"Edward's out at Ellis Island," Mary said.

"Well, please tell him I stopped by to thank both of you. I had a great time." He quickly surveyed the loft. "Um . . . is—"

"Looking for Fiona?" Henry's sheepish grin answered Mary's question. She chuckled. "Sorry, she's with Edward . . . but I figured you'd come looking for her. You two appeared to be getting on pretty well the other night." Mary seemed to be enjoying herself as she gently toyed with Henry. "She's a real peach . . . and smart . . . and, so far as I can tell, Henry . . . she's unattached."

Henry's smile broadened.

"Know what you should do? You should take her to see Reggie's new show at Rehn's gallery on Fifth. I know she admires his work. Come back tomorrow. She'll be here then."

"Thanks for the advice, *Mom*," Henry said, still grinning. "Anyone ever tell you you've got a little bit of the Jewish mother in you?"

"Hah! See you tomorrow."

Henry returned the next morning. Fiona was pleased to see him and eagerly accepted his invitation to join him for the Marsh exhibit. They agreed to meet that Saturday for a quick lunch at the automat before heading off to the gallery.

Henry was the first to arrive at Horn & Hardart's. He'd never been to an automat (it was Fiona's idea), but it was another in a long list of New York institutions that Henry was keen to investigate. He entered through the glass revolving door and sat at the first open table he found, one among a sea of marble-topped tables in the enormous, Art Deco-styled room. Sleek, futuristic grids of steel and glass lined the marble walls, forming four horizontal rows of individual compartments, each housing a serving of hot or cold food. Signs announced the contents of each bank of compartments—sandwiches, hot meals, soups, pies. Adjacent to each compartment was a slot into which one deposited a specified number of nickels before turning a knob. This opened the glass door, allowing the patron to remove its contents. Henry was thoroughly seduced by the novelty of it all.

Women in kiosks dispensed nickels in exchange for bills and larger coins. Henry walked over to change a dollar. While he awaited Fiona's arrival, he decided to put the system to the test by purchasing a cup of coffee. Seemed simple enough. He put a nickel in the slot, turned the knob, and *presto*: a perfectly measured burst of steaming hot coffee poured from a spigot . . . all over the counter. Works better when you remember to place your cup beneath the spigot, he concluded. He slunk back to his table in defeat.

The clock on the wall read 12:15. She was already fifteen minutes late.

Moments later, Fiona emerged from the revolving doors. She wore a long, gray coat and a harried expression.

"So sorry, Henry. Subway broke down again." She gave him a peck on the cheek, then unbuttoned her coat, revealing the deliciously snug red frock beneath it. She wore black shoes with a double strap and chunky heels. Henry was relieved that he'd had the presence of mind to at least don a sport coat.

He proffered a handful of nickels but she declined. "I'm good," she said. Henry followed her as she extracted a couple of quarters from her purse and exchanged them at the kiosk. "I'm having a salad, but I heartily recommend the mac-and-cheese. Best in town," she assured him. "And the pies are out of this world!"

Henry felt like a kid in a candy store with a fistful of coins. They filled their trays and returned to the table. He was fascinated by how the entire operation ran so seamlessly: each time he inserted nickels and removed the contents behind a glass door, someone behind the wall instantly replaced it. And Fiona was right: the mac-and-cheese was outstanding.

"Mary told me you're a fan of Marsh," Henry said.

"Took his course at the League last summer," Fiona said. "He teaches a morning class each summer ... gives him an excuse to avoid joining Felicia and her family in Vermont." She laughed. "And of course he gets to hang out at Coney Island every afternoon."

"Seems like a strange bird."

"Not really," Fiona said. "He'd just rather paint people than rocks and trees."

"And what about you, Fiona?" Henry took a sip from the cup of coffee he'd purchased without incident after his initial calamity. "You never told me what you paint ... when you're not playing muralist."

"Very little, I'm afraid. Edward's murals take up most of my time," she said. "But I've begun to experiment a little bit with non-objective painting."

"Really?" Henry tried to hide his disapproval.

"Yeah. I like the freedom . . . there are no rules."

"What's wrong with rules? They instill discipline."

"And stifle creativity." She slipped a forkful of apple pie elegantly into her mouth. "Look, Henry. It doesn't mean I don't appreciate representation . . . or understand how much more demanding it can be. And those blessed with the talent and discipline to paint the way you paint are worthy of admiration. That's why Marsh's work appeals so much to me."

"Fair enough," Henry said, preferring to end the debate without sounding dismissive.

"So," Fiona asked, "what do *you* paint . . . when you're not painting jitterbugging couples?"

Henry told her about his baseball painting, *Gastonia Renaissance.*

"Why didn't you show it to me the other night?"

"It was packed in a crate in the back of my studio. It's going to the Corcoran for their biennial in March."

"That's fantastic!" She scooped up one last forkful of pie. "And by the way, since you're apparently a baseball fan . . ." Henry's ears perked up. "You'll be interested to know that my cousin, Jake Powell, plays outfield for the New York Yankees—"

"You're kidding!"

"Nope. He can get me top drawer tickets to Yankee Stadium whenever I want . . . that is, if you're interested."

"*Interested?* More like bowled over!" Henry said. "Marry me, Fiona!"

"I'll think about it. Now let's go see some Reginald Marsh."

The Rehn Gallery stretched across the entire fifth floor on Fifth Avenue between 53rd and 54th Streets. The cramped elevator opened into a long room bisected by a row of bins containing prints and works on paper. The surrounding walls were lined with Reggie's paintings. Pride of place was accorded to *Coney Island Beach*, a great big canvas overflowing with frolicking figures, as animated as anything conceived by Hieronymus Bosch. Shapely blonds and musclemen primped and swaggered in the foreground, rising like phoenixes from a jungle of writhing humanity.

Marsh's vision and ingenuity left Henry in awe. "How in the world does he do it?"

"He goes out to the beach with his little sketchbook... tiptoes through the crowds like The Invisible Man ... and just draws," Fiona explained. "It's astounding. He's out there wearing a suit—not a *bathing* suit but a *suit* suit—and he looks ridiculous, but he doesn't care. He just sketches figures and groups, then choreographs it all into a harmonious whole back in his studio."

"How do you know all this?"

"He took a few of his students out with him to Coney Island one afternoon. It was a riot! He's incredibly talented!"

After circumnavigating the main gallery, Fiona and Henry passed through a warren of connecting rooms, each entered through a low archway. Featured in the first of these galleries was *George C. Tilyou's Steeplechase Park*, a large work depicting a clutch of dazed young women swept off their feet by the "Barrel of Fun," a popular Coney Island amusement. The ride challenged participants to maintain their balance while standing on top of a huge, rotating cylinder, while spectators reveled in their inevitable spills.

Hauptmann Must Die anchored the last gallery. It was a

welcome counterpoint to the raucous scenes of beaches, amusement parks, movie houses, and burlesque shows that filled the previous rooms. The painting featured two women seated on a bench in a station, bundled in winter coats and surrounded by valises, a hatbox, purses, and an umbrella. As she waits, one woman reads the *Daily Mirror*. Its headline proclaims "GUILTY: HAUPTMANN MUST DIE," a reference to the verdict rendered in the sensational 1935 trial of German-born carpenter Richard Hauptmann for the abduction and murder of the twenty-month-old son of aviator Charles Lindbergh. Professing his innocence to his death, Hauptmann was executed in 1936.

"Reggie's social realism is subtle," Fiona said. "Evergood would have painted Hauptmann frying in the electric chair."

When they'd retraced their steps to the main gallery, Fiona grabbed Henry's arm. "Mary says that Rehn is also Hopper's dealer," she said. "I'd love to see one of his paintings while we're here."

Fiona approached the desk where Frank Rehn sat dwarfed by a tower of paperwork. She asked if they might see something by Hopper. Rehn smiled, then shook his head apologetically. He was slightly built, with graying hair, a narrow face, and a pencil-thin moustache.

"Can't keep the old boy in stock," he said, gazing up from his papers. "Unlike Mr. Marsh here, Hopper paints like a tortoise." He laughed, arose from his desk and gestured at another of Reggie's pieces on the wall behind him. "You know, Marsh himself said it best. Someone once asked him why he was so prolific and Hopper so slow. 'The trouble with Hopper,' Marsh answered, 'is that Hopper is constipated and I have diarrhea.'"

CHAPTER ELEVEN

The Capital Canvas-Cutting Caper

KAPLER PAINTING INCITES WILD RUCKUS IN CAPITAL
Crazed Culprit Carves Canvas

Special to the Springfield Union
by W. D. Danforth, Art Critic for the Springfield Union

WASHINGTON, D.C., April 1, 1937. It happened again, this time in the nation's capital, where artist Henry J. Kapler, late of Springfield but now of New York City, premiered his recent painting *Gastonia Renaissance* on the national stage at the prestigious Fifteenth Biennial Exhibition of Contemporary American Oil Paintings at the Corcoran Gallery of Art. The painting, you'll recall, depicts local athletic hero Ernest "Bunny" Taliaferro, who just happens to be a Negro, shaking hands atop a baseball dugout with a white ballplayer from Gastonia, North Carolina, the unenlightened backwater where he and his championship American Legion ballclub were sent packing rather than risk life and limb in pursuit of honor on the baseball diamond. Suffice it to say that the event portrayed never happened—it was Mr. Kapler's conception of what *should* have occurred—a veritable slap at the dunderheads who drove our heroes out of town for the alleged crime of color-blindness.

Well, those dunderheads apparently took offense, or at least one of them did. Evidently a fan of neither art nor racial integration, the museum-going moron (who just happens to be a Caucasian Carolinian, we're advised) registered his disapproval with his trusty penknife, plunging the dastardly instrument strategically into the image of our local hero so skillfully rendered by Mr. Kapler. Museum guards came to the rescue of the wounded painting, bravely wrestling the maniac to the floor and averting further damage.

The ruckus, which occurred on the third day of the exhibition, has had the unanticipated but salubrious effect of dramatically boosting interest in the painting and drawing larger than expected crowds to the exhibition. Walter Garrison, the venerable director of the Corcoran, made the courageous decision to keep the damaged work on view, declining to repair it until it completes its exhibition run in early May. "It would be a disservice to the artist and the public to deprive museum-goers of the opportunity to view this accomplished, albeit controversial, artistic expression, even in its slightly altered condition," Mr. Garrison stated in a press release. "The Corcoran is loath," he added, "to render itself complicit in this brazen act of vandalism and censorship by removing the artwork prematurely from public view."

Gastonia Renaissance, you'll remember, provoked mixed reaction the first time it was shown publicly last August at the Springfield Museum of Fine Arts. The question then, it seemed, was whether its criticism of Jim Crow was too subtle. This time, it appears, it was viewed as not subtle enough in its strongly implied criticism of a most pernicious form of Southern bigotry.

While issues of critical judgment have been obscured by the criminal attack on Mr. Kapler's work, suffice it to say that it was well-received by local and national critics who viewed the biennial exhibition. "Mr. Kapler's work is commendable and courageous," *The New York Times* weighed in. "While the unfortunate criminal act has focused considerable attention on Mr. Kapler's work, such attention would have been merited on the strength of the art alone. We look forward," the *Times* critic wrote, "to more of this talented young artist's production."

And so do we.

CHAPTER TWELVE

The Good, the Bad, and the Ugly

"Dear Nigger Lover," it began . . . and went swiftly downhill from there. It was just one of several threatening letters included among the boxful of correspondence addressed to Henry in care of the Corcoran. The gallery's registrar forwarded the envelopes unopened, cautioning him that some might be unwelcome, but considering it inappropriate to screen his mail. "Come to Washingtin, you kike, and you'll go home decapedated," warned another. There was, Henry couldn't help but notice, an inverse relationship between bigotry and spelling prowess.

But there were also letters of admiration and support, praising Henry as much for his painting skills as his courage to challenge the status quo in race relations. These heartened him as much as the others unnerved him. It was also the first time in his young life that he was happy to lack a telephone.

Also among the correspondence was a letter, appearing legitimate, from a self-described entrepreneur in Charlotte who offered Henry the princely sum of $2,000 to purchase *Gastonia Renaissance.* Unlike many others, the letter was literate, and the money it promised would replenish his rapidly dwindling savings. Yet its Southern origin gave Henry pause.

Henry put away the box of letters, showered, and dressed

for his evening date with Fiona. He climbed the flight to the Lanings' studio where she'd been working late on the Ellis Island murals, which had fallen well behind schedule.

Fiona looked chic in a smart blue flower-print dress with puffed sleeves and a high collar. Its slim silhouette, crimped waist, and mid-calf length highlighted her narrow hips and slender frame. A coordinating blue hat with a white faux flower completed the outfit.

"You're all dolled up!" he said. "And here I thought you'd be wearing just a paint-smattered smock."

"And look at you!" she said. "You clean up pretty well yourself." Henry looked uncharacteristically dapper in a light gray double-breasted suit, white shirt, and red-and-white polka-dotted tie.

Mary rather enjoyed watching the evolution of the romantic relationship between the two young artists, ribbing them both at every opportunity. "And where are you lovebirds off to tonight?"

"Actually, Fiona's taking *me* out tonight," Henry said, straightening his tie.

"I'm introducing Henry to the Swing Street jazz scene," Fiona said, referring to the block of West 52nd Street between Fifth and Seventh Avenues in Midtown, where jazz clubs had proliferated in the years following Prohibition.

"What's the occasion?" Edward asked, stepping out from behind the large wooden contraption that held a segment of the nearly completed mural.

"Celebrating Henry's Corcoran Gallery triumph," Fiona said.

"Having your painting slashed by a racist would hardly seem to qualify as a triumph," Henry said.

"Publicity *is* a triumph," Edward said. "Anything you can do to get your work noticed these days is cause for celebration. In fact," he added, "I'm thinking of hiring someone to slash some of *my* paintings to stimulate sales."

"I gotta tell you," Henry said soberly, "it's a double-edged sword."

"Or penknife," quipped Mary.

"Right," Henry said, grinning. He told them about the letters he'd received from the Corcoran. "Some of them were revolting." He also described the offer from the putative buyer in Charlotte. "I could sure use the money," he sighed, "but something just doesn't seem kosher to me."

"I suppose it's at least conceivable that the guy's some rich bigot who'd buy it to finish off what the penknife started," Edward said, "or at least to keep it out of circulation."

"That occurred to me," Henry said.

"Does it matter that much?" Fiona asked. "When you sell a painting, don't you surrender control of its fate?"

"Sure, but you want to protect the integrity of your work, and know it's still alive and kicking if a museum comes around some day looking to exhibit it," Edward said.

"I should be so lucky," Henry said, "but I just put too much of myself into that painting to chance its destruction. So, at least for now, I think I'll hang onto it—at least until my money runs out."

"Well, on that note . . ." Fiona said, taking Henry's arm and heading for the door.

"Don't keep her out too late," Mary said with a smile.

"Behave, kids," Edward added with a paternal grin as he watched them exit the loft.

Fiona directed the cabbie to the Onyx Club at Fifty-Second and Sixth. Beyond the threshold of that nondescript brownstone was an enclave of smoke, liquor, and world-class jazz.

Fiona flashed a smile at the tuxedo-clad gentleman at the door, whispered something into his ear, and coolly slipped a couple of bills into his palm. He looked down briefly, grinned, and escorted the couple through a maze of small, circular tables covered in white tablecloths until he reached an empty table opposite the piano. Henry was impressed: there couldn't have been a better seat in the house. The man pulled out a chair for Fiona while Henry sat down beside her, facing the unoccupied piano.

A waiter accosted them immediately, distributing menus and soliciting drink orders. Fiona ordered a gin fizz; Henry, a Jameson's. Henry perused the pricey menu, feeling uneasy about saddling Fiona with the tab. Drinks were sixty to seventy-five cents each and the less expensive entrees, like the chopped sirloin steak each of them ultimately ordered, began at a buck. A ten- to fifteen-dollar bill would constitute fully half of Fiona's weekly WPA paycheck.

"Relax, Henry," she said, sensing Henry's discomfort. "I've got plenty of cat food in the apartment for the rest of the week. It's a special night . . . let's enjoy it!"

Shortly after they'd placed their order, a member of the Club's staff escorted a young, heavy-set black man with a globe-like face and gargantuan hands to the piano. From his movements and countenance, it was clear he was sightless, or at least nearly so. He smiled, rolled his head several times, and took a swig from the cocktail glass the staffer had placed on the edge of the piano.

"Ladies and gentlemen, clap your hands together for the one and only Art Tatum!"

From Toledo, Ohio, Tatum had swiftly become a jazz world legend. It took only moments to see why. He opened with one of his signature pieces, an upbeat and richly improvisational version of the old standard, *Tea for Two*. As the rhythm intensified, he reached for his drink with his right hand, effortlessly maintaining the melody with his left. His thirst quenched, his right hand fingered *Hallelujah* while his left continued to pound out *Tea for Two*. For several minutes, the two melodies blended harmoniously, drawing enthusiastic applause. Next came *Tiger Rag*, played at the breakneck tempo of a tommy gun barrage.

Tatum's showmanship and virtuosity entranced the young couple. To the accompaniment of improvisational riffs, they savored dinner and another round of drinks. They maintained a respectful silence as Tatum's fingers danced across the keyboard, but their mutually admiring glances spoke volumes.

It was well after one o'clock when Henry and Fiona departed the Onyx. Henry hailed a cab, intending to drop off Fiona at her apartment before continuing on to his own.

"Where to, bud?" the cabbie asked as they slid into the back seat.

"Uh—," Henry began, blanking on Fiona's address.

"12 E. Seventeenth Street," Fiona interrupted. It was Henry's address, and it would be the cabbie's only stop. It was hard to imagine that this night could get any better, but it did.

CHAPTER THIRTEEN

Getting Plastered

H e was intense and passionate, with sparkling eyes, a patrician's nose, bold lips, closely cropped hair—features seemingly chiseled by a sculptor in Caesar's Rome.

Rico Lebrun was a product of Italy, a student of the Italian Renaissance, and an expert on the techniques that Michelangelo used on his great Vatican frescoes. Henry was one of a handful of students eager to unlock the mysteries of fresco painting in Lebrun's course on *Mural Composition and Fresco* at the Art Students League in the spring of 1937.

Like so many artists during the Thirties, Henry was intrigued by the mural revolution. Artistically inspired the great triumvirate of Mexican muralists, Diego Rivera, Jose Clemente Orozco, and David Alfaro Siqueiros, the American movement was fueled by the allocation of public funds for mural production in public buildings under the WPA and other artist relief programs. Few artists made a living selling their paintings in the Thirties. But for many, like Fiona, it was possible to survive on a weekly WPA paycheck while assigned to an undertaking like the Ellis Island project.

Henry needed to develop a skill that might earn him some money. Between rent and his Art Students League fees, his fixed expenses had risen to more than $50 a month. That was *before* food and incidentals. The luxury of a girlfriend had stretched his modest budget even further, virtually wiping out what remained of his art prize and meager savings.

Henry had watched Edward and Fiona fill large swaths of canvas with scenes celebrating the contributions of immigrants to America's industrial development. These would be mounted later on the walls for which they were designed using adhesives. LeBrun, however, taught the more time consuming classical technique of *fresco* in which artists executed murals on site, painting directly upon a layer of wet plaster. This was the technique used by Rivera in his monumental *Detroit Industry* mural cycle at the Detroit Art Institute starting in 1932 and in his ill-fated Rockefeller Center murals shortly thereafter. Henry, like many of his peers, had been appalled by the decision of the Rockefeller family to destroy the latter works rather than allow Rivera the indulgence of pro-leftist imagery.

Lebrun's six-week course began with an appreciation of the murals of the Italian masters. Then came the nitty-gritty— literally—as his students experimented with recipes for the increasingly fine layers of plaster that supported the final painted surface.

"Go home, eat a heaping plate of spaghetti for dinner, and come in tomorrow prepared for a trip to Renaissance Rome," Lebrun directed his charges on the second day of class. "And while you're at it, look up the Roman myth of Romulus and Remus." Henry and his classmates complied, and soon found themselves collaborating on a mural of the outcast mythological twins being suckled by the she-wolf that rescued them after their abandonment on the Tiber River.

As the class sketched out its composition, one of the students, a brash young man with a misogynist streak, directed a question to the lone female in the class.

"Jane, how many teats does a she-wolf have?"

"How the hell should I know!" Jane responded, indignant at his temerity in assuming that the possession of the room's only breasts would qualify her as an expert on wolf teats. To head off the impending kerfuffle, Henry offered a diplomatic solution.

"Listen, let's each submit a guess and use the average."

And so it came to pass that the class fresco featured a wolf with seven-and-a-half teats.

Henry learned the principles of foreshortening, adjusting perspective to correct for the distortion perceived when artworks are viewed from a distance or an angle, and how to enlarge the mural design into a full-sized "cartoon," an outline on thin paper used to transfer the image onto the plaster surface.

Lebrun chose Henry to help him demonstrate how to pin the cartoon to the wall; punch guide holes through it using a small, spiked wheel; and then, using a pouch of red ochre, pounce through the holes in the paper to outline the mural. The next step was to grind pigments and mix them with the proper amounts of water.

Fresco was a revelation to Henry. But for the messy and complicated preparatory steps and his landlord's likely displeasure, he'd have gladly graced his apartment walls with an original mural cycle. He resolved instead to seek an opportunity to apply his newest skills to a more conventional mural project—preferably one that came with a paycheck. And, if all else failed, he could collect his brush and trowel and join the painters and plasterers union.

CHAPTER FOURTEEN

The Brawl in the Ballyard

Though an avid baseball fan for most of his life, Henry had never set foot in a major league ballpark. Springfield was hardly a major league city. He was twenty-two years old, but felt the excitement of a child half that age as he passed through the turnstiles and into the wide concourse that snaked beneath the grandstand. He followed Fiona up the narrow passageway that opened, like the light at the end of a long, dark tunnel, into the blinding sunshine. There, amidst the buzz of the gathering Friday afternoon crowd, the radiance of the lush green grass of Yankee Stadium appeared below him like a glittering emerald on a Bronx sidewalk.

Fiona had planned to fulfill her promise to Henry earlier, but her cousin, Yankee left fielder Jake Powell, had been felled by an attack of appendicitis that spring. Now, on July 9th, back in the lineup after recovering from surgery, he was happy to accommodate Fiona and her now steady beau, securing them seats in the first row of boxes behind the Yankee dugout.

Henry's mornings began with the sports page, so he knew that the Yankees were well on their way to a second consecutive American League pennant. He also knew about Jake Powell. A week shy of his twenty-ninth birthday, Powell was hitting a modest .268, still trying to work himself back into shape. A competent hitter, accomplished defender, and daring baserunner, Powell's signature attribute—if you could call it that—was his bruising style of play.

Six days earlier, playing in Washington's Griffith Stadium against the same club he'd face today, Powell brazenly bulldozed Senators first baseman Joe Kuhel on a routine groundout in the ninth inning, knocking the ball from his grasp, and sparking a rally that ended with Powell scoring the eventual winning run. When he took his position in left field in the bottom of the ninth, angry fans showered him with bottles and bric-a-brac. So the likelihood that the Senators would seek retribution on this steamy afternoon was probably greater than their chance of actually defeating the mighty Bronx Bombers.

Minutes after they'd taken their seats, a young woman made her way across the aisle and sat down in the seat beside Henry. She offered a polite smile and a perfunctory "hello," both of which Henry returned in kind. He casually inquired if she was attending the game alone, an unlikely and rather courageous undertaking for such an attractive young woman.

"My boyfriend's Jake Powell," she said, her inflection revealing her Midwestern roots. "He plays for the Yankees."

"Your *boyfriend*?" Fiona repeated.

"That's right . . . he plays left," she said, giggling.

"Interesting," Fiona said, uttering the word with a decided edge.

Henry wasn't sure what to make of Fiona's chilly reaction. He filled the void with a brief introduction and noted the apparent coincidence of Fiona's connection to Powell.

"Nice to meet you," the young woman said, reaching her hand out first to Henry and then to Fiona. "I'm Alice Woodley."

Henry was struck by an overwhelming sense that he'd seen

Alice before, a feeling that gnawed at him for the remainder of the afternoon. Hers was not a face easily forgotten: she was stunningly beautiful; her perfect, porcelain face framed by cascading curls of blond hair; her lips painted and full; her eyes piercingly blue. She wore a white cotton blouse, a broad-brimmed hat, and gaudy scarlet slacks matching the color of her lipstick.

The contest was never in doubt: the home team went on a rampage, blasting seventeen hits in a 16-2 drubbing of the lowly Senators. Henry witnessed the finest performance yet from the Yankees' extraordinary twenty-two-year-old centerfielder, Joe DiMaggio. The gazelle-like phenom recorded a perfect five-for-five afternoon, driving in seven runs and hitting for the cycle (single, double, triple and two long home runs). Lou Gehrig, dubbed the "Iron Horse" in recognition of a remarkable consecutive game streak now in its eleventh year, knocked in four more runs with three hits, including a homer.

But the real excitement came in the sixth inning. Henry had just returned to his seat with a tub of popcorn and an armful of Cokes when the fireworks began. Cousin Jake grounded to Senator third baseman Buddy Lewis, who fired across the diamond to first baseman Joe Kuhel, the same man that Powell had run down six days earlier in Washington. The throw pulled Kuhel off the bag, forcing him to swat Powell with a hard tag an instant before Jake crossed first base. The tag, to Jake's sensibility, was a tad too aggressive, causing the pugnacious Yankee outfielder to bristle at what he apparently perceived as a breach of decorum. "Jake retraced his steps belligerently," reported *The New York Times* the next morning, "and, after a few words and a slight push, let fly with a hasty right."

Alice jumped from her seat, Fiona let loose with a rare expletive, and Henry lost control of the popcorn, dumping it all over the roof of the Yankee dugout as the melee unfolded. Jake's right hook missed badly, and before he could reload, Washington catcher Walter Millies, clad like a gladiator in mask, chest protector, and shin guards, subdued Powell in a headlock, allowing Kuhel to pound him with impunity. Within seconds, both benches emptied. Players streamed into the fray and fans screamed for blood. It was a scene worthy of a painting by Reginald Marsh—Henry imagined him in suit and tie, weaving through the twisted pile of writhing bodies on the infield grass, sketchbook in hand. While Henry indulged his artistic fantasy, Powell was yanked from the scrum with the help of two umpires. When order was finally restored, Kuhel and Powell were banished from the ballpark.

The rest of the game was anticlimactic. Fiona was ready to leave after the brawl, but Henry resisted, belatedly yielding to Fiona's wishes after the Yankees scored for the sixteenth time in the bottom of the eighth. "Well," Henry said jauntily as they made their way up the ramp toward the exits, "sixteen Yankee runs, long balls by DiMag and Gehrig, and a middleweight fight in which your cousin was beaten to a pulp. Pretty entertaining afternoon, wouldn't you say?"

"Sure . . . if you think I enjoy being embarrassed by the bullshit, juvenile, macho antics of my mother's black-sheep brother's Neanderthal offspring," Fiona said.

"Now there's an impressive mouthful!"

"Jake's an incorrigible hothead," she said, venting her anger. "And today he got what he deserved."

"Well, at least his girlfriend's nice, don't you think?"

"Personification of a pimple-faced teenage boy's wet dream."

"Jeez, Fiona . . ."

"Look, Henry, Jake's *married*. Her name's Beth and she lives in Dayton. And the fact that he's got the nerve . . . you'd call it *chutzpah*, right? . . . to parade this floozy right there in our faces is reprehensible."

"Do you think she knows? Maybe he's deceiving her too," Henry suggested.

"Look, Henry, I doubt she even cares. If you ask me, that sweet, Midwestern façade is too good to be true. After all, this is Jake we're talking about. Not sure 'nice girls' are his thing, particularly when it comes to choosing mistresses."

"I liked her," Henry said.

"I noticed."

"Come on, Fiona. Innocent until proven guilty."

"You or her?"

Henry and Fiona slithered through the throng of departing fans, descended into the subway station at 161st Street, and caught the downtown train. All the way home, and despite his best efforts to the contrary, Henry obsessed over Alice Woodley, enthralled both by her beauty and his conviction that he'd seen her somewhere before. Fiona, on the other hand, suffered in silence.

CHAPTER FIFTEEN

Just What the Doktor Ordered

Since their evening at the Onyx Club in early April (and the transformative night that followed), Fiona had become accustomed to spending nights with Henry whenever she worked late on the Ellis Island murals in the Lanings' studio one flight up. Sure, they'd become lovers, but staying with Henry was also convenient—Fiona wouldn't have to navigate her way to her tiny Greenwich Village apartment late at night. But their time together became more sporadic once she completed the bulk of her work on the murals by mid-July. All that remained was the installation, and for that Fiona spent her days with Edward on Ellis Island and her evenings alone at home, too exhausted for anything (or anyone) else. And although she'd never brought it up again, Henry was convinced that he'd peeved her with his ill-timed and inadvisable defense of—and barely concealed admiration for—Alice Woodley that afternoon at Yankee Stadium. The last night they spent together was in early July, a few days before the ballgame. Was it lack of opportunity or interest? Henry wasn't sure. So he took it as a positive sign a few weeks later when each of them independently accepted Mary's invitation to join the Lanings and Marshes for dinner in the upstairs loft.

Henry and Fiona were the first to arrive. Unaware of any

possible cooling of their relationship, Mary continued to delight in needling the alleged young lovers. "I hope you brought along your pajamas," Mary whispered to Fiona with a sly grin.

"Who needs pajamas?" Fiona responded. The comment, which Henry overheard, was susceptible of contradictory interpretations.

As Mary fixed drinks for Henry and Fiona, Reggie Marsh burst in, his wife Felicia in tow, and a roll of newspapers clenched in his fist.

"Edward! What's all this crap I'm reading about Ellis Island? The press is lambasting you . . . and the entire WPA program!"

"Calm down, Reggie. It's not as bad as it sounds."

"Not bad? Listen to these headlines . . ." Reggie unfurled his *Herald Tribune.* "THAT BIG MURAL WON'T STAY PUT EVEN IF PASTED . . . and here, the *Post* is even better: IMMIGRANTS LOSE APPETITES AS MURAL DOES BUBBLE DANCE!"

"Got to admit, that one's clever," Mary said. "A more appropriate headline would've been something like . . . JUST WHAT THE DOKTOR ORDERED."

"Temporary setback," Edward said. "And Mary's right. It was Raphael Doktor . . . the technical director for the Project . . . who convinced me to use this new-fangled adhesive to paste the canvas to the dining room walls . . . said white lead was old-fashioned. So we used his synthetic crap when we began hanging the murals last Friday."

"Got about a quarter of it hung and trimmed," Fiona said.

"So we come back on Monday morning and it's a disaster . . . all buckled and blistered," Edward said. "Tried rolling out the bumps, but no dice. Finally, we had to cut into the mural in the worst spots, scrape out the hardened globs of glue, re-paste with white lead, and repair and retouch along the incisions."

"Never saw Edward so angry!" Fiona said.

"When we took the ferry back that night, I wanted to jump off . . . end the agony. But I look down from the railing and what do I see floating in the water?" Edward looked at Fiona. "Tell them, Fi."

"Condoms. Everywhere!"

"Enough to—"

"Okay, Edward, they get the idea," Mary said.

"Well, anyway, who'd want to drown himself in that?"

"So you owe your continued existence to a harbor full of condoms?" Felicia asked, gazing at Fiona.

"Don't look at me," Fiona said. "I'm only his assistant. Suicide's not in my job description."

When the laughter and innuendo subsided, Reggie asked how things had ended up.

"The repairs did the trick for the first sections," Edward said. "The rest we're hanging with old-fashioned white lead . . . so far, so good."

"Just goes to show," Reggie said. "You'd have been better off with the fresco technique I'm using on the Custom House project."

"You know that's not true, Reg," Edward said. "Fresco costs more and takes much longer with all that plastering. Plus, we'd have had to do the whole project on site with that cantankerous Immigration Commissioner looking over our shoulders. It was way more pleasant working right here."

"He's right about the cost, Reg," Felicia said. "My financial genius of a husband here took a voluntary cut in pay—from lousy to pathetic—to keep the project afloat with Treasury. Tell them what they're paying you, Reggie."

"Ninety cents an hour," Reggie muttered almost inaudibly.

"Right!" Felicia said. "Treasury Department scale for an assistant clerk . . . isn't that right, Reg? . . . *Ninety cents an hour* for planning, organizing, and executing one of the biggest and most difficult mural projects ever done in New York City! And Mary, tell them what you're making as Reggie's *assistant* on the job."

"Ha! A buck sixty an hour!"

"I rest my case."

"Okay, so maybe it's not cheaper," Reggie conceded, "but I bet I'll get it done quicker and it'll last longer than your murals."

"You're on, Reg—at least on the first part of the bet—we'll make it a bottle of scotch and a box of Cuban cigars!" Edward said, laughing. "Not sure either of us will be around long enough to collect the bet on longevity."

"I sure as hell won't be!" Reggie laughed, expressing confidence more in his mural's lifespan than doubt about his own.

While Henry was generally aware of Mary's involvement with Marsh on a large new mural undertaking, he knew little of the details. Was there a chance to become involved, Henry wondered, in exchange for a government paycheck? Reggie and Mary filled him in during dinner.

"United States Custom House in Lower Manhattan," Reggie said. He took a long sip from his glass of Sauterne. "Built at the turn of the century. Gorgeous building . . . seven stories . . . big rotunda with massive spaces just begging for murals."

"They could've painted the spaces when they built the place, but it was too expensive and too damn hard," Mary said as she passed a bowl of vegetables. "But nothing's too much of a challenge for our hero, Reginald Marsh!"

"Well, yeah, uh . . . thanks, Mary," Reg sputtered, looking up from his plate. "Damn straight I wanted to do it. Who wouldn't?"

"Reggie spent his . . .make that *our* . . . own money to hire some Swede to advise him on the nuances of fresco," Felicia complained.

"If I'm gonna do it, I'm gonna do it right!" Reggie punctuated his proclamation with another long gulp of wine. "I'm using the *dry* fresco method . . . *fresco al secco* . . . same one I used on my Post Office mural in D.C. last year."

"We've spent most of the summer scraping down the walls so they'll hold the plaster," Mary said. "Talk about tedious . . ."

"Put up the first two layers of plaster this month. Two more to go."

"Is this a Treasury project?" Henry asked, looking for an opening.

"Treasury Relief Art Project . . . TRAP for short." Reggie sawed at his brisket like a carpenter.

"Henry took Lebrun's *fresco* course at the League," Edward said. "This spring, wasn't it, Henry?"

"Right," Henry said, "though he taught the wet plaster method, not the dry one you're using."

"Speaking of dry, Mary, isn't this brisket—"

"Hush, Edward," Mary snapped back, irritated.

Reggie diplomatically ignored the interruption. "Not a lot of difference, Henry. Much easier, really, since you don't have to worry about your wet plaster drying up before you can paint it. And instead of full-sized cartoons, I'm using a Balopticon."

"A what?" Fiona asked.

"Balopticon . . . it's a fancy projector. You use it to project the outlines from your drawing right onto the wall so you can trace it directly without having to poke holes through a cartoon."

"What's the theme?" Henry asked as he speared another piece of brisket from the platter at the center of the table. Dry or not, brisket was a treat for an artist with no income.

"The main panels will depict the sequence from an ocean liner's arrival in New York Harbor to the unloading of its cargo onto the docks," Reggie said, pausing for a bite of cauliflower. "The smaller panels will contain portraits of eight great explorers whose names were inscribed on the building when it was finished in '07. You know, Columbus, Vespucci, Henry Hudson . . . the usual suspects."

"That is, unless Kennedy makes us eliminate all the *foreign* explorers," Mary said, chuckling.

"What do you mean?" Fiona asked, patting her lips with her napkin.

"Mary's referring to Joe Kennedy, Chairman of the Maritime Commission," Reggie said. "Bastard wrote to Treasury Secretary Morgenthau to protest our use of foreign vessels in the shipping sequences."

"We submitted sketches of the *Normandie* and the *Queen Mary*, both of which are European liners. Kennedy wanted us to use an American ship name that doesn't even exist yet—and fly American flags on all the vessels!" Mary said.

"I told Morgenthau I'd *consider* doing something about it," Reggie said. "But after considering it for a couple of seconds, I decided he can go to hell. If Kennedy doesn't like it, he can go up there himself and paint over it!"

Henry was virtually salivating. "Is there room for another assistant?"

"Lucarno's leaving next month," Mary reminded Reggie. "Were you planning to replace him?"

"Hadn't even thought about it yet," Reggie said. "We've got eight assistants now . . . but we're getting ready for the busiest phase . . . can't afford to be one short. So why not?" He finished off his glass of wine and then turned to Henry. "Would you be free the third week of September when we're ready to paint?"

"Would I!" Henry was ecstatic. What could be more exciting than earning a paycheck while working on the most spectacular of mural projects with arguably the city's foremost painter?

"Be happy to have you aboard," Reggie said.

"Aye, aye, Captain!" Henry replied.

Reggie smirked. "By the way, Henry ... hope you're not afraid of heights."

"Will you stay the night?" Henry asked Fiona as they departed the Lanings' loft together shortly after midnight. "I miss you."

"I miss you too, Henry." She hadn't answered his question, and both of them knew it.

"Come on in ... at least for a nightcap." Fiona nodded and followed Henry into his apartment. "You're not still sore at me for defending Jake's girlfriend ... are you?"

"Not sure *defending* is the word I'd use ... but no, not really."

Henry walked over to a table in the corner of his studio where he kept the three bottles that comprised his poor man's liquor cabinet. "Bourbon?"

"Sure."

He poured an inch into each of two glasses and handed her one. "Why do I feel we've been growing apart these last few weeks?"

Fiona sat down with her drink on the well-worn wing chair. Her expression turned plaintive. "When I was working late upstairs each night, it was easy to come down here and spend the night with you." She paused for a sip of bourbon. "And when the work upstairs was done and we had to make up for lost time at Ellis Island, it was just as easy—in fact, easier—to go home."

"What are you saying?" Henry asked. But he knew. He'd felt it coming, but it stung nonetheless.

"We miss the easy comfort . . . and maybe the sex. But we're not in love, Henry . . . we're only pretending to be."

Henry took a swig from his glass. Fiona gave him a look of sympathy tinged with sadness. He glanced at the ceiling, then at his drink, swirling the bourbon unconsciously. While he was reluctant to abandon it, he couldn't deny the cooling of their relationship. But Fiona's expression of ambivalence was enough to seal its fate. "I suppose you're right," he conceded with a mix of uncertainty and resignation.

Fiona broke the awkward silence that followed. "So," she said, the hint of a smile emerging from her lips, "how are we going to break the news to poor Mary?"

Henry managed a laugh. "She'll be devastated, won't she?"

"Yep. But she'll get over it . . . in time."

Fiona emptied her glass, got up, and planted a warm kiss on Henry's cheek.

"Can I walk you home?"

"No, Henry. I'll be fine. You take care now, okay?"

"Sure," he said, a sense of emptiness creeping into the pit of his stomach. "You too."

Henry masked his regret with a fragile smile as he watched her walk out the door.

CHAPTER SIXTEEN

The Tower of Terror

Having plowed through the predictable mountain of red tape, Henry reported to work at the Custom House in mid-September. Mary accompanied him that first day as they rode the Broadway bus to Battery Park. She'd taken the news of Henry and Fiona's breakup hard—harder, it seemed, than the former lovers themselves.

As the bus carved its way through the pulsating traffic, Mary shared with Henry a sampling of her experiences on the Custom House project with the obsessive, demanding, and indefatigable Reginald Marsh.

"Reggie wanted sketches of everything: the tugboats, Statue of Liberty, the skyline from Governor's Island. I'd get up at three in the morning to meet him at Battery Park before dawn. He had a wallet full of harbor passes granting access to boats, docks, and buildings." Mary smiled as she recalled her first trip into the harbor on a tug. "Reggie didn't give me any details, so I was hardly dressed for a day on a tugboat. He'd heard that the *Normandie* was coming in and he wanted to see it—from the tug pulling it to port. So I'm standing on the crowded deck of this filthy tug in a dress and heels, struggling to keep from falling on my face . . . and Reggie's laughing."

"What did you do out there?" Henry asked.

"Sketch. What else? He wanted details of lifeboats, davits, hawsers, ventilators, stacks, masts and rigging, sirens, bells, deck-chairs."

"Davits? Hawsers? I haven't a clue what—"

"I didn't either, but I do now," Mary said before she was interrupted by the blare of nearby sirens. "So we both did dozens of drawings, and he was like this little kid watching the big boats. Those huge liners—we sketched both the *Normandie* and the *Queen Mary* on different occasions—fascinated him as much as the bathers on Coney Island."

It was a short walk from Battery Park to the Custom House. Henry was impressed by the building's Beaux Arts grandeur. A carved decorative frieze supported by Corinthian columns lined the granite exterior. Monumental limestone statues by Daniel Chester French, conceived as anthropomorphic representations of the world's four most populous continents, graced the front of the edifice. Inside, an enormous rotunda with massive skylights enclosed a cavernous elliptical space.

Except for portions obscured by two elaborately constructed wooden scaffolds, Henry could see the empty wall panels and niches below the skylights and above the dome's entablature onto which the murals would be painted. He couldn't help but recall Reggie's admonition about heights: the scaffolds were a mind-numbing fifty feet high! A look of concern gripped him as he glanced at Mary.

"I'm working up *there*?"

"Yup."

"Is it safe?"

"Well, Reggie thinks so, but you might get a different answer from that poor plasterer who fell a few weeks back . . . assuming he can still speak."

"Kidding, right?"

"Well . . ."

"Okay. So, are *you* going up there to paint?" Henry asked.

"They don't make brushes long enough to paint from down here," Mary said.

"Okay. I get it. If you can do it, so can I," Henry said in a lame effort to convince himself.

Reggie wasted no time putting Henry to work. He unveiled the famous Balopticon, explaining to Henry that he'd be working at night, tracing the outlines of the sketches onto the wall. It would be impossible to accomplish that task in the daytime, when the daylight streaming through the skylights would dilute the light from the projector.

Reggie was there when Henry arrived for work the following evening. In fact, he'd been there all day. The Balopticon, enclosed in a custom-made wooden platform fitted with wheels, was plugged in and ready to go. Marsh focused its light on the trapezoidal panel for which he'd designed an image of the cruise ship *Normandie* steaming into port, tugboats astride. The lights in the building were shut off and a lantern slide containing Marsh's finished pencil sketch was projected onto the wall. He adjusted the projector until the image fit the empty panel. Satisfied, he restored the lights.

"Okay, Henry, I think we're ready to go. I want you to climb up there on the scaffold and trace the outlines of the image onto the panel."

Henry stared at Reggie and then at the scaffold. It looked like a tower of toothpicks: a tall, vertical cage enclosing a zigzagging staircase with a partially enclosed platform at the summit. To make matters worse, the platform cantilevered inward (to account for the inward slope of the walls), giving the impression that the entire contraption could topple at the least provocation. Henry's heart pounded like a pile driver as he reluctantly began his ascent.

"Can you unfasten that guard rail in the front there?" Reggie asked. "The lower one . . . that's right . . . *that* one. It's blocking the beam from the projector."

"Uh . . . okay," Henry said. He'd never been this uncomfortable in his life. He forced himself not to look down. It was not only harrowing, but the light from the projector was blinding.

"Just relax, Henry," Reggie said. "Remember, you're earning almost twice what I'm making!" You couldn't pay me enough to do this much longer, Henry thought as he assumed a crouching position and began to trace the image with his right hand, clinging for dear life to the scaffold with his left.

In about a half an hour, he was finished. Dripping with sweat, he descended the scaffold. Reggie removed the slide from the projector. A stream of light now illuminated the outlines that Henry had traced. "Nice job, Henry," he said. "Now that wasn't bad at all, was it?"

Breakneck. It was the best word to describe the speed with which Reggie and his eight assistants transformed sixteen empty panels into a *tour de force* of the muralist's craft. And it was also what Henry worried about six days a week, fourteen hours a day, as he stood, kneeled, or prostrated himself, paintbrush in hand, atop a creaky scaffold fifty death-defying feet above the hard marble floor of the Custom House.

Once he'd managed to suppress the fear of imminent annihilation, Henry became Reggie's most proficient assistant, executing some of the larger marine panels in as little as three days and the explorer panels in two. His favorite was the panel depicting Greta Garbo holding court with a flock of reporters and cameramen on the deck of the *Queen Mary*, with the New

York skyline in the background. With the detailed sketch pinned to the railing of the scaffold for reference, Henry spent hours meticulously delineating the dozens of individual figures that Marsh had incorporated into his composition.

Duplicating Marsh's paintings was an education in itself, like copying the work of the Old Masters to unravel the mysteries of their genius. Henry unraveled another mystery one morning in October, when Reggie dispatched him to his studio to retrieve some studies that he'd forgotten to bring to work that day.

Marsh's studio at 1 Union Square West consisted of two rooms on the ninth floor of the old Lincoln Arcade Building on the corner of East Fourteenth Street, overlooking Union Square. If the space had a theme, it was *organized clutter*. Each of the rooms was crammed with paintings in various states of completion. In one of the rooms, two windows opened up on Union Square below. A pair of high-powered binoculars rested on the windowsill, affording the artist a bird's-eye view of the characters populating Union Square and the adjacent rooftops. Unable to resist the temptation, Henry trained the binoculars on a pair of lovers locked in a passionate embrace on a park bench on the edge of the square. Beside them slouched a homeless man, as impervious to their affections as they to his misfortune. The sensation of voyeurism momentarily embarrassed him, but it was part of what made Reggie the master that he was.

At the other end of the studio was a narrow stairway leading to a cramped loft lit by a skylight. It was there that Henry located the studies he'd been sent to retrieve.

As he descended the stairs and retraced his steps through the studio, Henry paused before a stack of framed paintings propped against a wall. Unable to curb his curiosity, he combed through them. He recognized many of the works from the show he'd attended with Fiona that spring. And then he saw it: the alluring figure on the left side of a painting of burlesque chorus girls. *Alice Woodley, Jake Powell's girlfriend! That's* where he'd seen her! At Rehn's! Alice's flowing blond hair and painted lips were unmistakable. She wore a headband with three red ostrich feathers, a black-and-white brassiere with matching panties, one black stocking (on her left leg, with a red bow tied around the top), and nothing else. He slid the canvas out of the stack, flipping it over to decipher the inscription on the stretcher: *Minsky's Chorus/Reginald Marsh/1935.*

His elation surprised and bewildered him. It wasn't sexual obsession that froze him before her image. It was the overwhelming desire to paint her—the inexplicable *compulsion* to paint her. Whatever the reason, Henry desperately wanted Alice to be his muse.

CHAPTER SEVENTEEN

Truth, Actuality, and a Bottle of Scotch

P*eyton Small is ridiculously tall.* That was Henry's first impression of the freakishly elongated young man who sat down in the empty seat beside him on the first day of Yasuo Kuniyoshi's *Life Drawing, Painting, and Composition* class at the Art Students League in early December of 1937. About the same age, the two young painters were among the fifteen students who had managed to scrape together the $17 a month required for enrollment in the popular painting seminar that ran from 9:00 to 12:30 each weekday morning at the League's West 57th Street headquarters.

By early December, the Custom House mural was almost complete. With just a few weeks of work remaining, Reggie had allowed Henry to cut back his hours—from about fourteen a day to eight—to allow him to begin classes at the League. "Take Kuniyoshi's class," Marsh had urged, "you won't regret it."

Kuniyoshi was the most progressive of the dozen instructors offering comparable classes at the League. His background was unusual. He'd emigrated in 1906 as a sixteen-year-old from his native Japan, arriving alone in Seattle. He'd hoped to learn English, perhaps to gain sufficient proficiency to become a translator before returning to his homeland.

Instead, he took courses and worked at menial jobs in Seattle and California. When the unexpected encouragement of an art teacher nudged him into the art field, he relocated to New York where, like Marsh and the Lanings, he studied at the Art Students League. Now a highly regarded modernist painter, he was in his fifth year as an instructor at the institution that gave him his start.

Henry had spent little time in his studio since beginning work at the Custom House. While grateful for the opportunity with Marsh—and the much-needed paycheck—he was desperate to return to his own art. So it was with eager anticipation that he sat in Kuniyoshi's cramped classroom, beside the outlandishly tall Peyton Small, awaiting the arrival of his instructor.

A hush gripped the room when Kuniyoshi entered. Small and slight, he wore round, dark-rimmed glasses, gray trousers, and a black, button-down shirt. A thin black moustache clung to his upper lip. He introduced himself, and then the young lady who would pose for the class that morning. The model undressed, sat on a stool in the corner of the classroom, and the class began. Kuniyoshi encouraged his students to approach the assignment in any manner they pleased, using whatever medium they preferred, on whatever support they chose. This simplicity of approach, low-key tenor, and lack of pretension was what differentiated the League from other art schools and academies. As the students worked, their instructor moved quietly about, offering an occasional suggestion, and otherwise simply registering the disparate visions, skills, and deficiencies of his individual students for later reference or discussion. The only audible sounds were the swooshes of brushes on canvas and the scratches of pencil and charcoal on paper.

Henry drew in charcoal on a large sketchpad while Peyton sketched in oil. Henry couldn't help but be amused at the way his neighbor naturally elongated the limbs and principal features of the model, as if everyone were six-foot-eight like he was.

"You're Henry, I presume," Kuniyoshi said when he gazed over Henry's shoulder for the first time.

"How'd you know?"

"Reggie told me you'd be joining us, and that you'd trained at Yale. The Yale influence is evident in your work." Like many native Japanese, Kuniyoshi often mispronounced or transposed his L and R sounds in English, but his mastery of English vocabulary was extraordinary.

Henry momentarily put down his charcoal. "Is that good or bad?"

"I don't think that's the proper question," the instructor said. "I can see how well you've been trained . . . and how your training has drawn out your natural talent." He paused. "But what I hope you'll discover here is the need to keep moving, to avoid becoming entrenched in a static point of view, however skilled it may be." Henry was intrigued by Kuniyoshi's brief assessment, even if the full scope of its meaning was not yet apparent to him.

After the first day's class, Henry joined Peyton for lunch in the League cafeteria. The atmosphere of the cafeteria was like that of the League: casual and friendly. Students mixed freely with instructors at long tables that encouraged conversation.

Peyton's Southern origins were as obvious as his size. His accent was thick, his manner languid, his language curious and colorful.

"So where, exactly, are you from," Henry asked the big man, "and what brings you to New York?"

"The Great State of South Carolina!" Peyton said. "Eighth generation of the Small family in Charleston. Last three generations of males—that'd be Peyton, Peyton, Jr. and Peyton the Third—were all lawyers and judges, but Peyton the Fourth is breakin' the mold." Peyton the Fourth took a huge bite from his roast beef sandwich. "Took pre-law at the University of South Carolina ... and hated every damn minute. Rather be drawin' than citin' precedent, know what I mean?" Henry nodded. "My Daddy looks at me like I'd dishonored the family and married a damn Yankee," he said, chuckling, "so I thought it wise to skedaddle, cross the old Mason-Dixon and try my luck in the Big City ... where I can chase my dream in peace." He'd arrived in April, he said, settling in a Midtown apartment just blocks from the League. The fact that he was taking afternoon courses as well (William Zorach's sculpture class) and could afford to live alone in Midtown suggested that, unlike Henry's father, Peyton's parents hadn't entirely disowned him.

Henry told Peyton about himself, his supportive mother and headstrong father, and his activities in New York since his arrival in late '36. They might have gone on talking indefinitely, but for Henry there was a half-finished panel at the Custom House in need of attention.

Kuniyoshi huddled his students together by a window at the beginning of the second week of class. He placed his fist on the desk directly in front of the window. "Here's my fist against the sunlight, casting a shadow upon the desk," he said. "The fist represents the Western tradition of painting, and the shadow the Eastern tradition. The fist, you see, is *actuality* ... it has form and substance ... it exists in space. The shadow has shape and depth ... but it's also diffused in mystery." The students looked at each other, not immediately comprehending.

"I've watched you all draw and paint for a week now," Kuniyoshi said. "Each of you is steeped in the Western tradition of art. You paint straight from the model. You strive for *actuality*, but not for *truth*." He let his comments sink in for a few moments before continuing. "The Western eye uses intellect to see what it sees in an object; the Eastern eye seeks the *spirit* of the object and finds the truth from within."

A young woman raised her hand. "Are you saying that we're wrong to paint literally?"

"No, no, no," Kuniyoshi replied. "There *is* no right and wrong in this class—I want to be very clear on that! I'm merely trying to open your eyes and minds to a different way of looking at your art." Kuniyoshi walked around to the center of the group, where Henry and Peyton were seated in front of their respective sketches. "Let me give you an example." He placed his hand on Henry's sketchpad. "May I?" he asked. Henry nodded. Kuniyoshi lifted the pad above his head and pirouetted slowly around in a circle. "Look at how Henry has rendered the model. His sense of anatomy and musculature is superb. He's captured the model's *actuality* as well as anyone in this room." He then moved over to Peyton. "May I, Peyton?" Peyton nodded uneasily as Kuniyoshi lifted and rotated his canvas for all to see. "Now look at how Peyton has rendered the model. It's not as anatomically perfect as Henry's rendering, but it has a lyrical quality that Henry's drawing lacks."

Kuniyoshi wound his way back to the front of the group. "What I'm suggesting to you is that you start with the physical model . . . the *actuality* of that model. And then you abandon the model and paint what you *feel* about what you've observed. The painting itself should be the important thing, not the model. Use your emotional response to the object—instead of your intellect—as your guide. In fact, ladies and gentlemen, I'd prefer that you reserve your intellectual analysis for when you're *not* painting." Kuniyoshi picked up a paintbrush and waved it in the air for emphasis. "And when you *are* painting," he said, "allow yourself to escape into an hypnotic state, painting from your feelings and experiences rather than from your intellect."

Henry had always been among the most technically proficient of his peers. He took pride in that. But now he was being told that proficiency was secondary. He was understandably resistant, but forced himself to consider what his instructor was suggesting. After all, that was why he was here.

When the class concluded, Kuniyoshi approached Henry, drawing him aside as the other students filed out of the room.

"Henry, I want you to understand that I in no way meant to ridicule your work," he said. "In fact, you have more talent than anyone in this class. And if you paint as you've been painting, I think you'll be successful. But change is coming in the art world . . . it always does. And being open to change is, I think, a very good thing, whether you elect to submit to it or not." Henry listened intently but silently. He wasn't really sure what to say.

"I'd like to invite you to visit me in my studio some evening after the holidays," Kuniyoshi said. "I'd like you to see what I'm talking about in reference to my own work. Would you care to come by?"

"Absolutely, Mr. Kuniyoshi. It would be a privilege."

"And my pleasure," Kuniyoshi said.

A few days before Christmas, a bottle of scotch and a box of Cuban cigars arrived at Reginald Marsh's studio. Edward

Laning had lost his bet. The Custom House murals had been completed by the third week in December. Under Reggie's indefatigable direction, the massive undertaking had required just fourteen months, almost a year less time than it had taken for Edward to complete his Ellis Island project. And it was a hell of a bargain for the Treasury Department. At his miniscule ninety-cent-per-hour wage, Marsh received a mere $1,560 for about 1,700 hours of work. At least he had the scotch and the Cubans.

For Henry, there was no such consolation. The completion of the project meant the end of a modest but reliable weekly paycheck. It couldn't have come at a worse time. His prize winnings were long gone, as were most of his savings.

Henry hadn't sold a single work since he'd arrived in New York more than a year earlier. And he had little prospect of doing so. He had no dealer representation and the market for art remained moribund as the Depression lingered. He'd passed on a lucrative offer to sell *Gastonia Renaissance* to a dubious North Carolina purchaser for reasons of artistic integrity that seemed foolhardy now.

The Custom House gig had prompted him to extend his lease for a second year, but he hadn't planned on Reggie's efficiency. Within a few short months, there would be nothing left for rent, let alone anything else.

Henry dismissed—at least for the moment—the possibility of approaching his parents for money. In addition to conceding defeat, there was no assurance that his father would favorably respond. Morris's game plan, after all, had been to starve the young artist into submission, compelling him to take the subsidized detour to medical school. And even if his father relented, he'd gain leverage over Henry's future, something Henry was unwilling to yield.

The Corcoran had returned *Gastonia Renaissance* late that summer following its eventful exhibition and subsequent repair. Deciding he'd sooner sacrifice his painting than his pride, Henry wrote the alleged Charlotte entrepreneur who'd offered to buy the painting eight months earlier. The proceeds of a sale could keep him solvent for another year. It was his last palatable option.

CHAPTER EIGHTEEN

7th Avenue Express
and the Pastrami Local

If there was a silver lining to the rapid completion of the Custom House project—apart from Henry's survival—it was the freedom to paint for the first time in months. So beginning on Christmas Day, Henry plunged into an orgy of creativity. His objective was to submit two works to the annual exhibition at the National Academy of Design in the spring of 1938.

Night at the Savoy, which he'd completed a year ago but never exhibited, seemed a worthy candidate. But he needed another. For that, he'd find his inspiration in the seamy, subterranean netherworld of New York.

The Seventh Avenue Express was the subway Henry knew best. It stopped at Fourteenth Street, running north to Harlem and southeast to Brooklyn. With his sketchbook and a pocket full of tokens, Henry descended into the bowels of the city. He remained submerged for the better part of two weeks, riding from one end of the line to the other, observing and sketching. Surfacing only to eat, sleep, and attend his morning classes at the League, Henry became as much a part of the screeching, grimy, often creepy world of the underground as the foot-long rats that scampered through the stations like frantic commuters.

The stark interior of a subway car was the setting for Henry's opus. Marsh had tackled a similar subject earlier in *Why Not Use the "L"*, portraying the indifference of passengers in documentary fashion. Henry would go further, injecting social commentary by staging a morality play within the confines of his canvas.

Henry sifted through scores of sketches for the characters to inhabit his composition. He roughed out a scene depicting two seated men on the near side of the car to the left, one with his head buried in a newspaper and the other looking blankly ahead; a third man barely awake across the aisle, his elbow resting against the seat back, his right hand propping up his weary head; and a young mother sitting beside him, straining to rein in her fidgety son. One last figure would complete the composition and supply the narrative: a sightless young man in shirtsleeves and dark glasses proceeding down the aisle toward the viewer, his left hand limply grasping a walking cane, his right palm turned upward in supplication. It was an all-too-familiar scene, variations of which he'd witnessed repeatedly during his self-banishment underground: a group of passengers, distracted by their own burdens, studiously ignoring the entreaties of a man less fortunate as he passes by seeking charity.

Henry spent four days on the final sketches for *7th Avenue Express*, leaving him barely two weeks to complete the work before the January 31st deadline.

Henry thrived under pressure. He got up early, worked a couple of hours in the morning, attended Kuniyoshi's class, caught lunch with Peyton at the League cafeteria, and returned home to check the mail (thus far, there'd been no response to his Charlotte letter) and paint until midnight. Afraid that he was skipping meals, Mary dropped by from time to time with generous helpings of food and encouragement. Edward arranged for a friend to transport the paintings to the Academy.

Henry applied his last brushstrokes on the eve of the deadline. He thanked his upstairs neighbors for their kindness and support. Then, physically and mentally exhausted, he slept for twenty-four hours.

Henry finally made his promised visit to Yas Kuniyoshi's studio on a bitterly cold Sunday in early February. The master was astride a stool in front of his easel, clad in a painting smock, brush in hand, when Sara Mazo welcomed Henry into her husband's third floor atelier.

"Sorry it took me so long to come by," Henry said, citing his preoccupation with *7th Avenue Express*.

Yas conveyed a smile of absolution. "Unbroken concentration is the rich soil required for the creation of art," he said.

Henry surveyed his instructor's studio. Floor-to-ceiling windows looked out on Fourteenth Street, providing copious light for Kuniyoshi's easel. Towers of books and art supplies teetered precariously from the shelves of a large bookcase pressed against a rear wall. Vases and antique weathervanes sprouted from tabletops, reappearing in painted form on canvases scattered about the room. Amidst the confusion, a table in the center of the studio was neatly set for lunch.

Sara motioned Henry to the table while Yas removed his smock to join them. "I thought we'd sit and chat over sandwiches before you immerse yourselves in art," Sara said.

She was an attractive woman with short dark hair and warm brown eyes, much younger than her husband and only a few years older than Henry.

"Are you an artist?" Henry asked her.

Sara laughed. "Hardly," she said. "Took lessons a few years back, but to no apparent benefit."

"Sara was a dancer and actress," Yas said. "She was performing in Woodstock when we met."

Henry's eyes sparkled when he glimpsed the sandwiches that Sara had set out on the table. Piled high with pastrami or corned beef, garnished with onions and pickles, and cuddled by dense, springy Jewish rye, they reminded Henry of his favorite deli in Springfield. "This is amazing!" he said as he dug into a pastrami sandwich.

"I was in Midtown this morning and couldn't decide between two wonderful new Jewish delis on Seventh Avenue ... the Stage and the Carnegie," Sara said. "So the pastrami came from the Carnegie and the corned beef from the Stage."

"You're Jewish?" Henry asked.

"Isn't everyone?" Sara laughed.

"Not everyone," Yas grinned. "I've got enough identity confusion as it is."

Henry moaned with delight as he inhaled a tangy dill pickle. "Do you ever miss Japan?" Henry asked.

"I've lived in America twice as long as I lived in Japan," Yas said. He paused, taking a generous bite from his corned beef sandwich. "I went back once ... in '31," he recalled, "but I felt more American than Japanese."

Henry made reference to the growing anti-Japanese sentiment in the United States. "How are you handling it?" he asked his former teacher.

"About as well as can be expected," Sara interjected,

glancing sympathetically at her husband. "I know it hurts him more than he admits."

"Most galling is the law precluding Japanese aliens from attaining American citizenship," Yas said. "Katherine Schmidt, my first wife, was stripped of her citizenship," he lamented, "just for marrying me!"

"Pretty ridiculous . . . this irrational fear of immigrants . . . in a country *built* by immigrants," Sara said as she nibbled at her sandwich. With her napkin, she wiped a fleck of mustard from her lips. "And it just gets worse with the accounts of Japanese soldiers tearing through China committing unspeakable atrocities."

"Despicable acts of barbarity," Yas acknowledged. "I speak out whenever I can," he said, "but it's never enough. People don't dissociate you from your heritage. They blindly assume that your sympathies lie with your homeland."

When they'd finished their lunch, Sara excused herself, returning to the couple's apartment a few blocks away. Yas then took Henry on a tour of his studio, guiding him chronologically through his artistic career. He began with a cache of works from the Twenties—paintings rife with symbolism and childlike imagery, unusual perspectives, and anatomical exaggerations. "These were very personal paintings," he told Henry. "You might call them emotional biography." Henry gave him a quizzical look.

"Take that still life over there." Yas pointed to a drawing of grapes in a bowl. "I painted grapes because they meant something to me. When I first came to America, I worked in a vineyard in California. I'd pick these big, black, dewy clusters of grapes . . . but as I did, I couldn't resist stuffing my mouth with as many as I could. I remember their sweetness, their velvety texture." He sighed deeply, as if to savor the juicy fruits.

"And so, when I paint grapes, they have that special meaning to me."

Yas showed Henry a small picture he'd recently completed. A sophisticated young woman peered out from the canvas. Entitled *Café*, it was painted in a palette of muted earth tones, with thinly applied paint. Kuniyoshi's brushstrokes were light and feathery, producing an ethereal quality and a sense that something more—something non-literal—lay beyond the image itself. *Café* was one of several works featuring sultry, yet cerebral, young women.

"Why do you include the newspaper?" Henry asked, noting a common element in many of these paintings.

"It's my way of tying the inner soul of the painting to the world beyond."

"And why focus now almost exclusively on women?"

"For the same reason I painted grapes. You met Sara, so you can certainly understand my admiration for young women." Yas extracted a wad of tobacco from a pouch and packed it into his pipe. "Women are decorative, Henry . . . and a very effective conduit for emotion."

"Do you use models?" Henry asked.

"Only to begin with, but then . . . as I've mentioned in class . . . I abandon the model and let the painting itself dictate how it develops and what it conveys." He lit the bowl of his pipe and inhaled, drawing the flame into the bowl. "I don't paint *particular* women . . . it's the *universal* woman that I strive for."

Yas described his methodology. "I spend a long time drawing directly on the canvas with charcoal. The drawing maintains its place even as I paint . . . sometimes I scrape back down to it and sometimes it shows through the thin layers of paint . . . as in *Café*. I never use heavy impasto. That robs a work of much of its subtlety, I think." He took a long draw from his pipe, releasing a spiral of fragrant smoke.

Yas looked intently at the younger painter. "Remember, Henry, there's no right way. I show you my work and discuss my methods so you'll understand that there are many avenues to achieve what you want in your painting. You've got enormous talent. I urge you to let it evolve in whatever manner suits you best."

Henry considered it a privilege to view the work of a talented painter through that painter's own eyes. Kuniyoshi wanted him to see the evolution of his work—to understand that a painter could—and should—mature and evolve. The personal interest and attention that the older man bestowed upon the young artist was gratifying. Henry sensed it was Kuniyoshi's way of elevating their relationship from teacher and student to mentor and friend.

CHAPTER NINETEEN

The Quest for Dulcinea

"I need a muse," Henry said to Peyton over lunch at the League cafeteria.

"A what?"

"A muse, Peyton. An inspiring presence."

"Young, female, breathtakingly beautiful . . . right?"

"Of course."

"And where do you plan to find her . . . an art supply shop?"

"Minsky's Burlesque Theater."

"I don't think so, Henry."

"Why not?"

"LaGuardia shut it down about the time I arrived here last spring. Don't you read the papers?"

"Damn." Henry vaguely recalled the well-publicized effort of the popular and perpetually energetic Italian-American mayor to rid Broadway and 42nd Street of "filth." So where was Alice Woodley now?

"Peyton . . . I'm serious. I've already met this girl," he said between spoonfuls of tomato soup. "She was a chorus girl at Minsky's." Henry described his introduction to Alice Woodley at the ballpark eight months earlier and his discovery of her likeness in Reginald Marsh's studio during the fall. "She's *exquisite*."

"Of course she is."

"I *have* to paint her."

"Of course you do."

"Come on, Peyton, I'm serious here."

"Okay, Henry. So she's no longer with Minsky's because there *is* no Minsky's. So do you know where she lives or works?" Peyton took a herculean bite out of his hamburger, leaving streams of ketchup trickling down his chin.

"No. When I met her she was dating Jake Powell, the Yankees' left fielder."

"You mean the hothead that gets into fisticuffs all the time . . . *that* Jake Powell?"

"Yeah. My ex-girlfriend's cousin."

"Let me get this straight. You're obsessed with an ex-chorus girl you met once who was datin' your ex-girlfriend's cousin who is a ragin' lunatic and who would probably beat your skull in with a baseball bat if he knew his girlfriend was modelin' for you—which she isn't anyway because there's not a snowball's chance in hell you'd be able to convince her to do it—that is . . . if you could ever find her. Do I have that right?"

"More or less."

"You're fuckin' nuts!"

Henry was ill-equipped to debate Peyton's logic, but the matter of muses was somewhat beyond the realm of logic to begin with. "So Peyton," he said, "who are *you* painting most often these days in your studio?"

"Uh . . . I guess that would be myself."

"No offense, but who's going to buy a self-portrait of Peyton Small?"

"My mother."

"I rest my case."

A broad smile descended upon Peyton's ketchup-stained

face, a smile of surrender both to the earnestness and the absurdity of Henry's quest. "So how do you plan to find your Dulcinea?"

"I'll reach her through my ex-girlfriend."

"I'm sure she'll be delighted to pimp for you, Henry."

In her eternal crusade to reunite Henry and Fiona, Mary took pains to keep Henry informed as to his ex-girlfriend's status and whereabouts. She revealed to him that Fiona was back at work with Edward on his latest WPA project, a series of murals for the New York Public Library celebrating the history of printing. "They're just beginning to lay out the designs in an old abandoned church on Tenth Avenue," Mary said.

Henry sprinted to Tenth Avenue. While a WPA theater troupe loudly rehearsed on the floor below, Fiona stood in the drafty, echo-infested nave of the old church transferring one of Edward's mural sketches onto a huge canvas. She'd borrowed Reggie Marsh's Balopticon to project the design onto the canvas using a lantern slide made from Edward's drawing.

Fiona looked wonderful. Her hair was a little longer, and it suited her. A pang of regret swept over him as he approached her.

"Well, look what the cat dragged in," she said, smiling at Henry. "To what do I owe this honor?"

"Great to see you, Fiona." It was the first time they'd seen each other since their breakup more than six months earlier. They spent a few moments exchanging compliments and catching up on each other's lives before Henry got to the point of his visit. "I've got a favor to ask, and I hope you won't be angry with me for asking."

"That sounds rather ominous."

"Yeah ... right ... well," Henry stammered. "I suspect you remember Alice Woodley, your cousin's—"

"Yes, Henry," she interrupted with a look registering something between disappointment and disgust.

"I'd like to see if she would consent to modeling for me."

Fiona affected a pained expression. "Jesus, Henry. You're serious?"

"Afraid so." He noted that Reggie Marsh had already painted her and swore that his interest in Alice was purely artistic. "Minsky's is no longer operating and I wondered if ... maybe ... you might be able to help me contact her ... uh ... either directly or through Jake ..."

Fiona had clearly found the inquiry off-putting. She stared at him impassively. Embarrassed, Henry tried to fill the void without making matters worse. He succeeded only in filling the void.

"Is Jake still—"

"Screwing her? Yeah, probably. She was with him the last time I saw him, but we're not exactly bosom buddies, Alice and I." She cringed at her own choice of words.

"Come on, Fiona. Please don't take this personally. Subjects like Alice help to sell paintings. I'm not exactly flush with income now that the Custom House project is over." He leaned back on the edge of a worktable. "I need to get serious about painting salable pictures ... and I thought a model like Alice would help. I intend to pay her, of course."

"Okay, Henry. Look ... I'm sorry. I guess it's just a touchy subject for me ... on several levels." She reached out and grasped Henry's hand. Her touch fairly pulsed through his body. "I think I know how to reach her," she said. "But listen ... I can't predict how Jake might react to something like this ... no matter how innocent your motives. You know as well as I do that he's got an explosive temper. I won't make trouble by telling *him* about it, but I can't be responsible if something goes wrong." She gave him a disparaging look. "You're on your own on this . . . understood?"

"Sure . . . of course." Henry knew he wasn't being entirely rational, and he knew there could be consequences. But for some reason that he couldn't entirely explain, he had to do this—logic be damned.

CHAPTER TWENTY

Academy Rewards

KAPLER PAINTINGS SOAR AT
NATIONAL ACADEMY ANNUAL
Critical Praise for "Night at the Savoy"

Special to the Springfield Union
by W. D. Danforth, Art Critic for the Springfield Union

NEW YORK, N.Y., March 18, 1938. Penknives were nowhere in evidence as the august National Academy of Design lifted the curtain on its 113th Annual Exhibition in New York City on March 16th, an ambitious exhibit that included two remarkable new paintings by the rising young artist Henry J. Kapler, late of Springfield. These were among the 349 works of art shown, just over half of which (including Kapler's pair) were obliged to survive the arduous gauntlet of jury review cruelly inflicted upon non-member submissions. Unlike the sharp-pointed reception accorded *Gastonia Renaissance*, Kapler's provocative interracial treatment of the National Pastime in oil at the Corcoran Gallery last spring, there was no controversy to spoil the debut of our young hero's entries and no knife-wielding attacker to subdue.

7th Avenue Express is Kapler's paean to the subterranean world of the New York City subway. Set within a subway car, Kapler has cast the viewer as a player in a recurring drama unfolding daily in New York as in every other city and town in America. A young blind man with cane and upturned palm approaches us seeking alms while a bevy of riders willfully ignores him. Will the viewer be equally callous? That's the question Kapler seems to ask us.

The work is, as always with this artist, first-rate, and the sentiment is genuine and not the least bit maudlin.

But the better of the two works—and, in the opinion of this reviewer and several others, one of the very best works in the entire show—is a large canvas that Kapler entitled *Night at the Savoy*. This glistening work, expertly painted in tempera, depicts an energetic young Negro couple as they perform the Lindy Hop before a circle of awed admirers inside Harlem's renowned Savoy Ballroom. The dancers are captured at the instant of maximum physical extension, their outstretched arms and clasped hands embodying the tension of a protracted spring about to recoil. William Avery Whyte, critic for *The New York Times*, made special mention of this work, noting that it "manifests the raw energy and unbridled spirit of the Negro race," and excoriating the jury for its "unaccountable failure to accord Kapler's work the honor of a ribbon it so richly deserved." High praise indeed!

Our sources tell us that Mr. Kapler spent the fall assisting Reginald Marsh, acclaimed limner of the denizens of New York, on the installation, in the United States Custom House at the lower tip of Manhattan, of a series of fresco murals celebrating the shipping industry. He is currently taking classes at the Art Students League, the sources report. It is hoped that this latest exposure of Kapler's prodigious talent will only serve to hasten his already rapid ascent in the New York art world.

CHAPTER TWENTY-ONE

A Nice Jewish Girl

By late March of 1938, Henry had completed his fourth month at the Art Students League. Yas took him aside one day after class.

"I don't think there's much point in your continuing here, Henry," Kuniyoshi said. "You've been exposed to all my theories and you've absorbed what you found useful. Your skills were well established when you arrived. I think you'd benefit more by using this time in your studio continuing to hone your art."

Henry was surprised, but not shocked. He'd learned much in these four months, but sketching models in the classroom day after day was yielding diminishing returns. And he would surely benefit from the seventeen dollars a month of tuition he'd save by dropping the course. "Are you breaking up with me, Yas?"

The bespectacled artist laughed heartily. "No, Henry, I'm not. I want you to stop by my studio to talk whenever you feel the urge . . . and I'd like to be able to drop by yours on occasion to see what you're up to."

"I'd like that very much," Henry said.

Henry was at work on his latest painting when Fiona stepped downstairs from Edward's loft and rapped on his door.

"Hi, Henry. Just happened to be passing by," she said, chuckling. Her eyes were drawn to the work-in-progress.

"I call it *Tenements*," he said.

"Clever title," she deadpanned. "Saw your paintings at the National Academy last week... pretty impressive. But this... is *different*," she said, scratching her head, "and rather gloomy."

Fiona was right. The work depicted crumbling tenement buildings glimpsed through a vacant, debris-strewn lot. It was dreary and devoid of figures. Kuniyoshi's influence was readily apparent in the passages of pure texture that defined the building facades, ramshackle fencing, and drying clothes hanging from makeshift clotheslines.

"Experimenting with a lighter, more lyrical touch," Henry said. "Letting the brushwork convey the mood."

"Not sure if I like it," Fiona said with the brutal honesty of an ex-girlfriend.

"Maybe I need a muse, Fiona," Henry replied with mock sarcasm. "A pretty Midwestern girl with a baseball fetish, perhaps?"

"Speaking of which..." Henry perked up. "I talked with Jake's little tart on the telephone yesterday. She's willing, at least, to talk to you about modeling. I figured you'd go all gaga about it so I took the liberty of arranging a meeting for the two of you tomorrow. Noon... lunch at the midtown Horn & Hardart. You're buying."

Henry broke out in an enormous smile and kissed Fiona on the lips. "You're the best ex-girlfriend a guy could ever want!"

She barely flinched. "Imagine what you'd've done if I told you she'd actually said yes."

Henry rushed to the Horn & Hardart late the next morning, hoping to be the first to arrive. It felt strange, sitting at the same table he'd occupied a little more than a year ago, waiting for Fiona to stroll in for their first date. He was wistful recalling his excitement when Fiona had entered the automat, and embarrassed remembering how he flubbed his first attempt to buy a simple cup of coffee.

Alice Woodley entered the room at 12:02. She was stunning. She wore a long, ruffled skirt under a fashionable gray coat and sported a red beret that strained to contain the cascading ringlets of her luxuriant blond hair. Henry stood up so she wouldn't walk right by him and went numb when she acknowledged him.

"Hello, Henry." Her tone was unenthusiastic and her smile contrived.

"Hi, Alice," he sputtered. "Thanks so much for coming."

They grabbed trays and made their choices from the sea of options arranged behind the shiny glass and metal compartment doors. Henry supplied the nickels. When they reconvened at the table, he related the story of his discovery of her image in Reginald Marsh's painting of the chorus line at Minsky's.

"So you've been painted before," Henry told her. She was underwhelmed.

"Creepy, bald guy, freckles . . . big chest, no neck . . . always in the theater drawing."

"That's him," Henry said.

"Hmm." Alice poked indifferently at her Waldorf salad. Her wariness daunted him. This was not the sweet naïf that Henry had imagined. She was aloof and cold. Had he thoroughly misjudged her that day at the ballpark? After all, sweet and innocent weren't the qualities most likely associated with a girl who would date a married ballplayer and dance half-naked in a burlesque show. Was Fiona right about her all along? Was he making a huge mistake in believing this woman could somehow inspire him?

After a few moments of awkward silence, Alice gave Henry a piercing look. "Why do you want to paint me?" she asked him bluntly.

Henry sifted through possible rejoinders. He could have admitted he was obsessed with her, but only an idiot would have done that. He decided instead to appropriate and expand upon the reasoning that Yas had offered him when explaining his own penchant for painting attractive young women.

"Artists paint women because they're beautiful," he prattled, "and because they allow an artist to convey feeling and emotion." He pressed on, improvising liberally. "Throughout art history, beautiful women have always—."

"Henry . . . *please!*" She gave him a look of disdain. "I may have come to New York as a naïve Midwestern hayseed, but those days are long gone. So level with me: are you coming on to me . . . or do you *really* want to paint me?"

Henry had seriously underestimated Alice. He decided to drop the pretensions.

"You're beautiful, Alice," he said, "but you know that. As a suitor, I'm not in your league. But I'm an aspiring artist with prospects. Paintings of you will attract attention . . . and, if I'm lucky, sales. I'll pay you the going rate. Sit for one painting. See if it suits you. I promise you'll be pleased with the results."

"Why didn't you say that in the first place?"

"Well, I—"

"One thing, though," Alice interrupted. "There was this painter back in Cedar Rapids . . . guy named Wood. Painted this picture of his sister and some other poor sap with a pitchfork. Called it *American Catholic*, something like that. Made his sister look stupid. I don't want to look stupid, you understand?"

Henry smiled. "You won't look stupid, Alice, I promise. I'll paint you however you want to be painted, okay?"

"Okay." She looked enviously at his largely untouched plate. "Mind if I finish off your mac-and-cheese?"

Henry took the train to Springfield for Passover. Like the balky rail coach, he was running on fumes. It was mid-April of 1938. By this time next month, he'd be down to his last dollar. He'd given up on the Charlotte businessman, if indeed he ever really existed. Receiving no response from his initial letter, he'd written again, ascribing the failure of correspondence to the vagaries of the United States postal system. But after three months, it was clear there'd be no miraculous rescue from his financial doldrums.

Henry pondered his options as the train rattled on. Should he approach his *mother* for a loan? His father would surely perceive that as an act of cowardice. Should he plunge into the abyss at the beginning of his visit or withhold the request until the end? His alternatives were unappealing.

Henry's resolve dissipated as the engine clattered northward. By the time he reached Springfield's Union Station, he had no idea what to do. If nothing else, he would make amends for his failures as a correspondent. His mother would welcome him with open arms; his father would dish out copious helpings of guilt. It came with the territory.

"The prodigal son has returned!" his father growled as Henry slipped through the front door minutes before sundown on the first night of Passover. His Old Testament father had employed the New Testament reference to deliver the first salvo of guilt. Henry's brother, sister, mother, and brother-in-law had already taken their places around the dining room table where the Seder was about to begin. It was no time to ask for money.

Morris Kapler wore the white robe, or *kittel*, traditionally donned by the family patriarch conducting the ceremonial Passover dinner. Henry seated himself at the table and the six of them proceeded with the traditional rituals as their forebears had observed them for generations in Russia. In between the formalities, Henry caught them up on his life in New York.

"How's your *shiksa* girlfriend?" his father snorted. Ben knew Henry had been dating a gentile and had apparently spilled the beans during a routine parental interrogation.

"You'll be pleased to hear that we broke up," Henry said.

"You'll find a nice Jewish girl," his mother predicted.

"Nice article in the *Union* about the show at the Academy last month," Edith said. "No pictures, though . . . you *never* send us pictures." Another failing, duly noted.

"Speaking of pictures, I got a letter and some photos from my cousin Yuri," Morris said. Yuri Davidov had settled in Amsterdam in 1907 after a pogrom had decimated his Russian village. Now a professor at the University of Amsterdam, he lived there with his wife and their daughter, Lotte, a law student.

"What's the situation in Europe?" Edith asked her father.

"Lotte converses with the young German émigrés who've recently arrived in Amsterdam," he said as he flipped the pages of his prayer book. "Anti-Semitic activity in Germany is accelerating. They say that some Jews have been sent to camps for political prisoners."

"That's discouraging," Ben said. Henry's brother had finally gotten himself on track—and his parents off his back—by enrolling for the spring term at nearby Springfield College.

"Read in today's paper about a pact between Britain and Italy," Edith said. "That certainly sounds hopeful, don't you—"

"War is inevitable," Morris declared with the dolefulness of an undertaker. "It happened quickly in 1914 . . . and it will happen again."

"You really think we'll be involved?" Ben asked.

"Lots of resistance in Washington," Henry said, weighing in. "The isolationists seem intent on keeping us out of European politics."

"Don't fool yourselves," Morris said. "We'll be drawn in . . . eventually."

"God forbid," Henry's mother said. "I don't want my boys in uniform!"

"They'll do what they have to do, Ruth," Morris said sternly, with the conviction of a World War I veteran. Henry said nothing. The last time he'd spoken with his father about such matters was in 1935, after he'd painted an award-winning student piece at Yale called *Soldiers*. It was a haunting indictment of war. He'd first declared himself a pacifist then, a stance that didn't sit well with his father. For an immigrant who'd found a welcoming home in America, Morris Kapler would have done anything to defend his adopted country. He'd served in the Army Medical Corps in the First World War and had always taken a hawkish tone in political discussions. The disagreements between Henry and his father had been theoretical then. But with the growing militarism of both Germany and Japan, Henry knew it would become increasingly difficult to avoid such discussions in the future. Yet for now, he preferred to do just that. Henry didn't need to open yet another battle line in his beleaguered relationship with his father.

Ben knew his brother's views and sought to steer the conversation off its potential collision course. "What're you painting now, Henry?"

"I've found a model to pose for me," Henry said, "so I hope

to do some paintings of her."

"Nice Jewish girl, I presume," Ben said, needling both his brother and his parents.

"Well, frankly, I didn't ask," Henry said. "But I doubt there are many blond-haired Jews from Cedar Rapids."

"Dress her in a shawl and a long skirt . . . no one will know the difference," Edith laughed.

"Just painting her. Not marrying her."

"You never know," Ruth said. "Couldn't she convert?"

"You're all crazy," Henry declared, at which point his father concluded the Seder—as well as the inquisition—with a closing prayer.

Henry never did raise the question of money that weekend. But on the train ride back to the city, Henry noticed a bulge in his coat pocket. Reaching in, he withdrew a folded envelope. Inside were five crisp twenty-dollar bills and a note from his mother. "Don't tell Father," she wrote.

CHAPTER TWENTY-TWO

Waiting

"Like this?" Alice asked as Henry positioned her for his first attempt at painting his new model. He'd suggested that she wear the same clothes she'd worn at the automat, assuming she'd be more comfortable. He resolved to paint her as she was, not as he might have wanted her to be. She was, after all, a chorus girl—or at least that's what she *had* been—and not a debutante.

He posed Alice seated on a chair as if awaiting someone, her torso turned slightly to the viewer's left, her chin up, her gaze off in the distance. She wore her red beret, infusing a strong element of color and furnishing an appealing contrast with her flaxen hair. "Just hold that position as best you can," Henry instructed. "When you get tired, we'll take a break."

"Am I allowed to talk?"

"Sure, please do. Tell me about yourself."

And, much to his surprise, she did. Alice Woodley was twenty-two, a year younger than Henry. Born into a large farming family in central Iowa, she was the eighth of nine siblings. "I didn't want to be a farmer's wife like my mother and grandmothers," she said.

"What did you want to be?"

"An actress," she said without hesitation. She'd dropped out of high school after her junior year, in 1932, moving to Cedar Rapids ("the capital of Nowheresville," she called it), taking a job as a waitress in a diner. "I worked there for two years, dishing out pancakes and omelets, until I saved enough to move to New York."

Henry stepped away from his easel. He reached out and placed his hand gently under Alice's chin and tilted it up and to her right. He returned to his easel and she to her story.

"With the money I saved in Iowa, I rented a room in a boardinghouse in Brooklyn. Took a job waitressing at a greasy spoon." She brushed an errant strand of hair from her face. "One of the other girls in the house knew someone in the chorus line at Minsky's. She arranged for me to meet Morty Minsky." The impresario liked what he saw and offered her a job. Alice was only eighteen when she joined the chorus line in late 1934. "I was still there when they shut us down last spring."

"What are you doing now?"

"Modeling?"

"I know, but—"

"Considering my options," she said without conviction.

"What've you been doing since the show shut down?" Henry asked her.

"This and that," Alice said ambiguously. "Jake has been helping me out a little." She sighed deeply. "How about we take a break?" Henry put down his brush.

"Can I get you a beer?"

"Sure . . . that'd be nice." Now that she no longer had to focus in one direction, she scanned Henry's studio. Just as Bunny Taliaferro had in Springfield, Alice noticed the menorah that Henry displayed prominently on a bookshelf.

"You Jewish?" The question was direct but inoffensive.

"Why do you ask?"

"That candelabra over there. Isn't that a Jewish thing?"

"Yes."

"Never knew a Jew before," she mused, taking a first sip from her beer, "'cept for the Minskys, I guess."

"We're kind of like everyone else," Henry said. "Just different traditions."

"Hmm," she responded blankly before moving on to another topic. "What made you decide to become an artist?"

Henry answered her question, and the ones that followed, to her apparent satisfaction. It was clear they had little in common, but he found her more intriguing than he'd anticipated. Rather than the guarded reserve she'd adopted during their lunch at the automat, Alice had been unusually open and engaging. She sounded, he thought, less like the jaded chorus girl and more like the young woman he might have hoped she would be. After their break, Henry pursued an entirely different line of inquiry.

"When did you meet Jake Powell?"

"About a year ago, just before Minsky's closed. Came to the show one night with Bump Hadley and Lefty Gomez." Henry was familiar with both of the Yankee pitchers. "They offered to take a few of us girls to a nightclub after the show. There were five or six of us . . . you know, strength in numbers . . . so we figured, what the heck." Alice took another swallow of beer. "Lefty and Jake were having marital troubles. And, ya know . . . well . . . one thing led to another, I guess."

"You knew Jake was married?"

"Yeah. Didn't hide it . . . but he swore it was over. She was in Dayton and wouldn't come to New York." Alice broke from her pose and turned toward the young artist. "Look, Henry . . . I'm not sure why I'm telling you all this. I probably should have just walked away after that night with Jake . . . but I didn't."

"Are you in love with him?" Henry asked brazenly.

"Jesus, why should I tell you?"

"Sorry, you're right . . . I shouldn't have asked."

And yet Alice seemed somehow driven to respond. "Some days I am," she said. "And some days he's a goddamn drunken bastard!"

Startled by her outburst, Henry turned silent. But he couldn't help but notice the tear descending from her left eye. Alice wiped it away and resumed her pose.

Henry had made good progress to this point, sketching his subject directly onto the canvas, first with charcoal and then in oil. He captured the contour of her delicate chin; the soft flesh of her nose; the pleasing curvature of her moist, cherry red lips; the striking blue of her eyes; the gentle swell of her breasts. The more she revealed in her words, the more he revealed in her portrait. He knew now that he had enough to work with—that he could finish the painting without her. It was just as Yas had preached: first, paint from the model; then let the picture dictate its progress.

"I think that's all I need for today," he told her. Alice sighed and lifted herself wearily from the chair. She circled to the other side of the easel to examine her image on the canvas.

"You're not done, are you?" she asked, troubled by the picture's decidedly unfinished look.

"Not yet. But the rest will develop from what I've got here."

"But—"

"If you want, come by in a couple of days. I think you'll be pleased at how different it'll look."

His words reassured her, at least for the moment. Henry paid her the agreed-upon fee and she donned her coat to leave. "Come by in a couple of days, okay?" he repeated. She nodded and left.

For much of the next forty-eight hours, the portrait of Alice consumed him. He realized that what he'd started to paint from life, he was now painting from deep within himself. What she'd told him, and how she'd spoken and acted, were as much a part of what he was now creating as the *actuality* of her physical being. He remembered the fist Kuniyoshi had placed on the table in the classroom, and the shadow it cast. He'd captured the *actuality* of his model in their session two days earlier, but it took the succeeding couple days of laborious effort for the *truth* to emerge. He studied the painting closely. What had begun as a likeness of an extraordinarily beautiful young woman had evolved into a portrait of both beauty and vulnerability. This was not the hardened, streetwise woman that had surprised and disappointed him at the automat, although that was certainly a part of what she'd become. There was much more—and it thrilled him to discover it peering out from the canvas.

Waiting was the title he chose for the painting. It made sense to him. He perceived a young woman waiting to make sense of her life, to comprehend and reconcile the choices she'd made, to find a path forward.

Three days after the modeling session, Alice knocked on Henry's door. "Is it finished?" she asked.

Henry nodded and led her to his easel. Alice stared at the painting—and wept.

CHAPTER TWENTY-THREE

There's a Naked Girl on my Couch

H enry found a note under his door when he returned with the week's groceries on a hot, muggy Friday in late May.

Henry—

Dropped off some new paintings with my dealer, Frank Rehn. Said he's looking for new talent, so mentioned your name. Said he noticed your work at Nat. Acad. exhibit. Suggested you call him, arrange studio visit soon. Good luck!

Reggie

If he'd had a phone, Henry would have dialed the gallery instantly. Instead, he dumped his groceries, bolted out the door, and hopped the subway to Midtown.

Henry took the little elevator to the fifth floor. The whir of electric fans filled the gallery, providing slight relief from the sweltering heat. Rehn sat at his desk in the rear, poring through papers. As the young artist approached the gaunt, mustachioed dealer, his assistant, John Clancy, accosted Henry like a lineman protecting his quarterback.

"Can I *help* you?" Clancy inquired.

"I'm here to see Mr. Rehn."

"Mr. Rehn's busy. Can I help you?" he repeated. Noticing the commotion, Rehn interceded, rising from his desk to address Henry. He looked comfortable in his wool suit and tie in spite of the heat.

"I remember you," Rehn said. "You were here when we had the Marsh show. You and your lady friend wanted to see some Hoppers, right?"

Henry nodded. His intervention no longer required, Clancy retreated to his desk.

"I'm Henry Kapler. I'm a painter. Mr. Marsh said you might be interested in seeing my work?"

"Ah, yes, of course. Reg spoke highly of you." Rehn offered Henry the chair opposite his desk. "I saw for myself what you can do at the Academy show. Especially impressed with your Savoy Ballroom painting. Beautifully done."

"I appreciate the compliment," Henry said, taking his seat. He was hard pressed to temper his excitement.

"Where did you train?" Rehn asked him. Henry cited Yale, Kuniyoshi, and his practical apprenticeship with Marsh at the Custom House. Satisfied with Henry's credentials, the dealer asked if he might arrange a studio visit. An appointment was scheduled for the second week in June. It was as simple as that.

To show at Rehn Galleries would be like cracking the Yankees' lineup. He'd be in stellar company. In addition to Hopper and Marsh, Rehn had represented such stalwarts as George Inness, Theodore Robinson, Childe Hassam, George Bellows, Charles Burchfield, and Kenneth Hayes Miller. More importantly, it would be a chance for Henry to sell his work, an opportunity that could have hardly come at a more critical juncture.

The impending studio visit prodded Henry to ramp up his production. He had but five significant pieces to show: *Gastonia*

Renaissance, Night at the Savoy, 7th Avenue Express, Tenements,
and now *Waiting.* He wanted one more. The subject matter was
hardly in doubt—he longed to paint Alice again.

Pleased with her modeling debut, Alice agreed to an encore.
She agreed to come by on the afternoon of May 31st, the day
after Decoration Day.

While awaiting his muse, Henry thumbed through the
sports pages of *The New York Times.* The Yankees had played
a holiday doubleheader at home. The headline was strangely
familiar: FISTS FLY AS YANKS TRIUMPH. And right below the
headline was a photo of Jake Powell in the middle of the scrum.

This time, Powell had taken offense to a high, hard one from
southpaw "Happy" McKain. McKain's next offering was
evidently more objectionable, grazing Powell in the abdomen.
According to the *Times*:

> On picking himself up, Jake marched belligerently to the
> pitching mound. McKain seemed willing enough to
> meet him halfway.

> But before the two had a chance to mix, Cronin dashed
> over from his shortstop position and decided to take an
> active hand. In fact, he opened fire on Jake at once, and
> with the latter retaliating, there was a spirited struggle
> until umpires and the other players pried the combatants
> apart.

It didn't end there. After their ejection by the umpires,
Powell and Cronin exited the field through the only means of
egress available, the Yankee dugout. Several Yankees
shadowed Cronin, at which point the umpires rushed down to
head off the posse. Within moments, the remaining players
had emptied their respective benches to witness round two of

the brawl beneath the grandstand. An all-time record crowd of 83,533 was left "to view in bewilderment nothing but the grass while Cronin and Powell resumed hostilities under the stands." Based on its tally of scratches and bruises, the *Times* declared Powell the victor.

"I gather yesterday set a world record for largest attendance at a light heavyweight fight," Henry clucked at Alice shortly after her arrival.

"Yeah," she responded. "I was there. Jake won the fight," she said, "but lost the battle. League fined him . . . the others got off scot-free."

"Doesn't it bother you?" he asked, referring to Powell's penchant for fisticuffs. Her close-lipped silence answered his question.

Henry had draped his couch with a fragment of fabric scavenged from a local furnishings store. "I'd like you to recline on this," he said. "What do you prefer, elegant or provocative?"

"It's hot today," she said. "How about naked?"

Henry was taken aback. "Are you *sure* that's what you'd like to do?"

"Yeah . . . why not?" There was a decided edge to her voice.

Alice removed her clothing and spread herself across the couch. It was clear she'd chosen provocative. Henry was accustomed to painting from a nude in the classroom—he'd done it for years. But he was thoroughly flummoxed by Alice's choice. He perceived it as an act of defiance. She was peeved. He assumed it related to Jake.

Henry positioned Alice on her right side, her left leg bent over strategically to cover her pubis. Her breasts were fully exposed and, he couldn't help but notice, exquisite. She rested her head upon a pillow wedged up against the arm of the couch. Her body language and facial expression shot well beyond provocative, bordering on reckless.

Henry grasped her left wrist loosely—and *very* carefully— as he placed it over her breasts to partially hide them, beguiling the viewer as much with what was visible as with what was not. When he moved her arm into position, he noticed a deep purple bruise above her elbow. "It's nothing!" she said indignantly. Her reaction foreclosed further inquiry.

Henry went to work, sketching quickly for fear she'd change her mind. No model he'd ever sketched was as physically perfect. As diligently as he'd worked, it took him three hours to get it right. Through it all, she'd been a trouper, interrupting the session only twice for breaks.

In stark contrast to her previous sitting, Alice had little to say. Henry tried to engage her, but she was in no mood for chatter. When they were done, Henry paid her and she quietly departed.

"Where on earth did you find her?" Frank Rehn asked seconds after he'd entered Henry's studio. He'd made a beeline to the paintings of Alice—*Waiting*, and the latest one, which Henry called *The Goddess.* "She's absolutely breathtaking," Rehn gushed, "and yet these paintings convey so much more." He bent down to inspect *Waiting*. "She looks exposed and susceptible in this one—emotionally naked though fully clothed. And in the other," he said as he shifted his attention to *The Goddess*, "it's the other way around. She looks fierce, angry, dangerous." Rehn sighed. "I hope you'll expand your series with this gal. She's remarkable . . . and marketable."

Rehn moved on to *Gastonia Renaissance* and *Night at the Savoy.* "Both wonderful paintings," he said. Rehn extracted a magnifying glass and examined *Gastonia Renaissance*, assessing the Corcoran's handiwork in repairing the damage incurred in the knife attack. "They did a good job," he said. "And the notoriety should enhance its salability."

The dealer believed that the prospects for *7th Avenue Express* and *Tenements* were also favorable. "My city clients love city scenes," he said. He turned from the paintings and addressed Henry. "Let's start with *Night at the Savoy, 7th Avenue Express* and *Waiting . . .* and see how it goes. I'll send someone by to pick them up next week. In the meantime, I'll draw up a proposed price list and the terms of our representation. I'm pleased to have you join us."

Henry was ecstatic. Gallery representation for an artist during the Depression was a rare circumstance, and while it offered no guarantee of sales, it was an enviable accomplishment and an endorsement of worth. It was impossible to sell what no one could see, and the exposure his work would receive at Rehn's was something that money couldn't buy.

But Henry needed money for what money *could* buy. And with his mother's gift nearly gone, he needed it desperately.

"Uh . . ." Henry stammered as Rehn turned to leave.

"What is it, Henry?" Rehn said.

"I'm not sure how to say this, Mr. Rehn, but . . . is there any chance—"

"You'd like an advance," Rehn interrupted. He was well aware of the financial straits in which the vast majority of artists now found themselves.

Henry nodded. Rehn extracted his wallet, peeled off ten twenties, and handed them to Henry without hesitation or judgment. It was an astonishing show of both confidence and compassion.

Henry was overwhelmed. "Th-thank you . . . *so* much," he said, thrusting the bills into his pocket.

Henry was surprised to find Fiona at his door again later that week. She'd been upstairs to see Edward, but had a dubious message to pass along to her former lover.

"Something screwy is going on between my cousin Jake and your pretty little muse," Fiona said.

"What do you mean?"

"Jake telephoned me . . . he was looking for your name and address."

"Why?"

"I could hazard a guess, and it wouldn't be pleasant."

"Did you give it to him?"

"Of course not," Fiona assured him. "He sounded drunk on the phone and kept mumbling something about Alice's posing naked and some other innuendo I won't repeat . . . Oh, and for some reason he seemed to know that you're Jewish." Fiona paused before asking him whether what Jake had said was true.

"Of course I'm Jewish," he said.

"Not that, Henry. The part about posing naked."

"She did pose naked," Henry conceded. "I didn't ask her to. She insisted. Come here, I'll show you." Henry led Fiona to the back of his studio where *The Goddess* was propped against a wall.

Fiona gasped. "My God, Henry, she looks . . . *ferocious*!" She stepped back and reconsidered the painting. "I've got to admit . . . it's an interesting painting. Raw . . . and so different from this other one here, which I *really* like." She nodded in the direction of *Waiting.*

"Okay, Fiona, let's take a breather," Henry said. "Why don't we start with a whiskey?"

"Fine," she replied edgily.

Henry strolled over to his three-bottle liquor collection, corralled a couple of glasses, and poured them each an inch or two of the golden liquid. "So, Jake is *your* cousin. Is this anything more than a harmless drunken rant?"

"I really couldn't say. Jake's been increasingly out-of-control these last couple of years." Fiona took a sip of her whiskey. "The fights on the field are just the tip of the iceberg. He's drinking a lot and is more impetuous than ever. I definitely think he's jealous, but I don't know what Alice might have said to taunt or incite him."

Henry told Fiona about the bruise he'd noticed on Alice's arm when she posed for *The Goddess*, as well as her refusal to address it.

"Maybe posing that way was her way of acting out," she said, "a way of getting back at him for something." She paused for another sip, grimacing as the liquor went down. Her eyes narrowed. "Or maybe she was trying to seduce you . . . to make him jealous." She suddenly put her glass down hard against the tabletop. "*Did* she seduce you, Henry?"

"Come on, Fiona. Don't you think that question is a bit out-of-bounds? You're my *ex*-girlfriend, dammit." Henry emphasized the point with a long swig of his own drink. "But no, she didn't seduce me. I don't think she was trying. But I can't in good conscience tell you that having *that* lying there in front of me for three hours wasn't tempting." He gestured with his glass toward *The Goddess*.

"Maybe you should ask her what's going on," Fiona suggested, her voice calmer. "Are you going to continue to work with her?"

"She's supposed to come by next week for another sitting. I have no idea what she'll want to do . . . or whether she'll even choose to wear clothes. At this point, whatever she wants to do seems to work, so I'll give her whatever leeway she desires."

"Seems like you should get to the bottom of this," Fiona said, "for your own good . . . and that of your precious muse."

CHAPTER TWENTY-FOUR

The Face of Fear

Henry wasted little time in interrogating Alice when she returned for her third session the following week.

"Why is your boyfriend calling Fiona looking for my name and address?"

She looked at him blankly, as if genuinely perplexed by the question.

"What did you tell him, Alice?"

She hesitated, unsure how to respond, loath to open the emotional floodgates.

"Come on, Alice. *What did you say*?" He reached out to grab her wrist but stopped himself. "Please, Alice, talk to me!"

She sat down heavily on the couch. Resignation gripped her face and tears welled up in her eyes. Her lips were trembling. She held back as long as she could, and then it all burst forth. "Jake thinks I'm cheating on him!" she blurted out. "But *I'm not!*" She exhaled deeply. "He refused to believe me. He lifted me up . . . slammed me into a wall!" She stroked the back of her head with her left hand. "He swore he'd break my arm if I didn't come clean!" The tears were pouring down her cheeks. "He was stupidly drunk. I had to tell him *something* . . . or he'd have killed me!"

Henry sat beside her. He placed his arm around her

shoulder in an awkward attempt to comfort her. At first she recoiled, then she relented. "It's okay, Alice ... calm down. Tell me what happened."

"I told him the God's honest truth," she insisted. "I said all I was doing was posing for an artist ... nothing more." She paused to catch her breath. "He asked if I was posing nude. I told him 'yes, but nothing happened.' He called me a liar, asked who you were. I didn't tell him ... *I swear it, Henry* ... so he smacked me," she recalled through a veil of tears. "I ... I ran out ... before he could ..." She was gasping for air, unable to finish her sentence.

"When did this happen?"

"Last week."

"You're living with him?"

"Not anymore. I haven't been back since." Alice wiped the tears from her cheeks with the handkerchief Henry handed her.

"How did he know to call Fiona?"

"Jake went to my girlfriend's apartment the next day. She said he was plastered again. Threatened to punch her if she didn't tell him who you were. But she didn't know ... all I'd told her was that you were an artist friend of his cousin's. Might have mentioned you were Jewish ... don't know why, really. Maybe it made you different somehow. So that's what she told him ... and I guess that's why he called Fiona."

Alice's explanation made sense. Henry had no cause to doubt her. But the revelation of the monster on their trail was disconcerting. "Where are you staying now? Not with your girlfriend, I hope."

"No. Back in my old boardinghouse in Brooklyn ... with a girlfriend Jake doesn't know."

"Are you safe there?"

"I think so . . . yes."

Henry rubbed his forehead. He remembered Peyton's mocking suggestion that Powell would attack Henry with a baseball bat one day. What seemed like a joke then was a real possibility now.

Henry studied the expression on Alice's face, the tears still streaming from weary, bloodshot eyes. Suddenly, he sprung from the couch to his easel as if launched by a slingshot. "Stay right where you are. Don't move! You're here, so let's make the best of it."

"But—"

"Just hold that pose." Henry slid his easel toward the couch. Whatever force had compelled Henry at that moment also froze Alice in place.

Henry painted Alice exactly as she was that afternoon. Broken, riddled with fear. Embarrassed. Hurting. And yet, despite it all, still hauntingly beautiful. He painted the damp trail left by the tears that descended her cheeks. He captured the terror that engulfed her as she'd related her story. And somehow, he also registered the strength that allowed her to maintain the same position, in spite of her inner turmoil, for more than an hour, breaking only to stem the recurrent flow of tears. He worked furiously, afraid of losing his tenuous grip on the intense emotion that had overtaken them both in his studio that afternoon.

When he'd reached the point where he could finish the painting without her, he thanked his muse for her stamina and courage. He poured her a whiskey, then made them dinner—a reasonable facsimile, he contended, of Horn & Hardart's macaroni-and-cheese. When they had finished, he accompanied her on the subway to her boardinghouse in Brooklyn. Then, returning to his studio, he worked into the wee hours of the morning on the painting he called *Fear*.

CHAPTER TWENTY-FIVE

Monster of the Night

He appeared on Fiona's doorstep, haggard, reeking of alcohol. She foolishly let him in.

"Jake, you're drunk. Let me make you some coffee," Fiona said. "You need to sober up."

"Fuck that, Fiona. Who is he?" Jake Powell demanded. "Who . . . *the fuck . . . is he!*" He lurched over to the coffee table, picked up an ashtray, and hurled it across the room where it shattered into a thousand pieces.

Fiona was no shrinking violet, but Jake was no shrinking drunk. She'd seen him plastered before, but never this violent. It was Sunday, July 24th, about nine in the evening.

Her cousin was anything but lucid. He ranted about a batting slump, a reduction in playing time. His wife had threatened to divorce him, he wailed, and his girlfriend had abandoned him. He was angry and blamed the world for his troubles. But he had "a special hell in store" for this "asshole artist" who'd compelled his girlfriend to pose in the nude before ravishing her mercilessly.

"Take it easy, Jake," she pleaded. "You need to calm down."

He staggered toward her, his speech slurred but unambiguous. "I don't wanna hurt you, Fiona . . . but I fuckin' will if I have to. Now who's that kike who's been fucking Alice? Where . . . *the fuck* . . . does he live?"

Fiona retreated as Jake drew perilously closer. When she'd backed herself into a corner, she knew it was too late.

"Tell me, goddammit!" he hollered as he stumbled forward, grabbing her by the throat and slamming her head into the wall. Fiona panicked. Her head throbbed like a drum. She knew she couldn't hold out for more than a few seconds. She knew that the fury of Jake's drunken delusion was infinitely more powerful than the ties of kinship.

"*Stop, Jake, please!*" she begged him as she gasped for air.

"Last chance, bitch!" he screamed, releasing his grip only enough to allow her to speak.

"Henry Kapler! 12 East Seventeenth Street!"

With that he peeled his hands from her neck. She plummeted to the floor, struggling for breath. Moments later, she lost consciousness.

Jake upended the coffee table and a lamp as he bulled his way from the apartment and into the night.

Henry met Peyton at the corner of Seventh and West 54th at six o'clock. They planned to see the hit movie *Algiers* with Charles Boyer and Hedy Lamarr at Radio City Music Hall. Only one issue remained to be resolved: where to eat.

"The Stage," Peyton insisted.

"The Carnegie," Henry shot back.

"Come on, Henry, the Stage has a nicer dining room, and the best pastrami."

"It's more expensive," Henry countered. "And anyway, what would a gentile like you know about good pastrami?"

"The Carnegie's noisy, cluttered, and crowded all the time."

"Exactly!" Henry said. "No one would put up with that crap unless the food was spectacular, right?"

Henry eventually prevailed, playing the Jew-card to the hilt.

And while the service was rude and the kitchen slow, the pastrami was as good as advertised.

Henry couldn't have known at the time, but the notorious sluggishness of the Carnegie kitchen made all of the difference that night. Dinner took forever. As a result, they missed the seven o'clock showing at Radio City. So they stopped for drinks and caught the nine o'clock movie instead. It lengthened their evening—and, quite possibly—Henry's life.

It was ten o'clock when Jake arrived at Henry's building. His bloodshot eyes were barely able to register Henry's apartment number from the directory posted inside the front door.

"Gonna thrash that motherfucker," he mumbled repeatedly as he climbed the stairs. Second floor. Third floor. Finally, he reached the fourth floor landing. He was winded and drenched with sweat. His head felt the way he imagined a ball would after colliding with Gehrig's mighty left-handed stroke.

He knew he'd done something unthinkable. He'd gone to Fiona's apartment—he remembered that much. She'd given him the name and address of the fucking Jew artist. But he couldn't recall leaving her place, or how he managed to find himself where he stood now, at the threshold of Henry's apartment. But he knew why he was here. *Gonna thrash that motherfucker!*

Jake pounded on the door. No answer. He pounded again, harder, louder. "Open up, motherfucker!" he bellowed. Still no answer. He slumped to the floor. A paper bag hung from his right hand. A bottle inside. Whiskey. *Where'd this come from?* He screwed off the cap, raised it to his lips, and poured. He grimaced as the liquid seared his throat. He caught a second wind.

Jake lifted himself from the floor and staggered down the

hallway, away from Henry's apartment. Then, summoning all of his energy, he turned, lowered his right shoulder, and plunged forward, crashing into Henry's door with devastating force. The sound of splintering wood reminded him of the night he'd driven his father's car through the garage door of his family home as a drunken fifteen-year-old. That, in turn, conjured in his mind the sting of his father's leather belt as it cracked across his back and buttocks until he bled.

Jake kicked at the shattered carcass of the door until it gave way completely, forcing his way into Henry's dark studio. He pawed at the wall for the light switch and flipped it on. There was little inside: a couch, a few chairs, a table, a bed in the far corner. And paintings. *Where's the one of that whore, Alice?*

The first painting he encountered was a dark scene of tenement buildings. He grabbed it and flung it against a wall. Nearby, a larger painting. Two baseball players. One white as snow, the other black as coal. *Fucking kike paints fucking niggers!* Three bottles of liquor sat on a nearby table. "Don't mind if I do," he said as he helped himself to the remaining contents of a bottle of Gordon's. Then, grasping the fully drained bottle by its neck, he smashed it against the edge of the table, scattering shards across the room. He carried the jagged neck in his fist, lifted it up to the baseball painting, and plunged its serrated edge through the canvas.

Teetering in front of the torn canvas, he saw a sight that confounded him: blood dripping from the wound in the chest of the Negro ballplayer, *the wound he'd inflicted moments ago.* How was this possible? He shuddered in fear and disbelief. Only then did he realize it was he who was bleeding. The alcohol had dulled the pain from the laceration on his right wrist.

He searched for a towel to wrap the wound. Before he

found one, he found *her*. She was naked, splayed across a couch, her face the face of a temptress. Her likeness stared at him from the large canvas, mocking him unmercifully. *Mocking him!* Enraged, he thrust her into the air and slammed her down across the top of Henry's easel, ripping her to shreds in his mania. "Why, Alice?" he cried out. "Why?"

Jake was losing steam. But he was gaining clarity. He found a towel in the kitchenette and wrapped it around his bleeding wrist. It was then that he spied the last painting. Alice again. Clothed this time, a trail of tears on her cheeks, a look of utter fear in her eyes. He remembered that look. It was the way she'd looked at him the last time he'd seen her. It crushed him to see her like that. He adored her. He couldn't bear to look at her, yet he couldn't pry his eyes away from her. Like a mortally wounded beast, he dropped to the floor in agony. "I'm sorry, Alice," he whimpered, "I'm . . . so . . . sorry, babe." No sooner had he stanched the flow of blood from his wrist that the tears began streaming from his eyes. He cried like a baby.

He must have passed out. The clock on the worktable read 11:30. His head spun as he lifted himself from the floor, trudged over the scattered debris, and walked out the door, down the stairs, and back into the darkness.

CHAPTER TWENTY-SIX

Down for the Count

Henry had slept sporadically during the early morning hours, his lanky frame contorted into the armchair he'd drawn up beside her hospital bed. Staring at her for hours at a stretch, he'd seized on each tiny movement in the hope she'd regain consciousness. The dawn light that penetrated the window bore harsh witness to the damage done: gruesome bruises on her face and neck, a cut on her forehead, a blackened right eye. He longed to hold her, to will her back into the world, but all he could do was wait . . . and worry.

It had been a long and tortuous night. Henry had returned to his apartment from Radio City at midnight to find his door a jagged mass of splinters hanging from a single hinge like a loose tooth. His heart pounded as he tiptoed tentatively past the shredded door and into his ravaged studio. The only sound he heard was the crunching of glass beneath his feet. His apartment was in shambles, furniture upturned, his easel toppled, broken liquor bottles scattered across the floor. The stench of alcohol was nauseating.

Henry exhaled deeply, surveying the ruin. His paintings looked as if they'd been gnawed and regurgitated by some comic book monster. He shivered when he noticed the fresh blood splattered randomly across the studio, then gasped when he saw it dribbling implausibly from the lacerations carved into Bunny's image in *Gastonia Renaissance. The Goddess*, the picture he'd painted of Alice in the nude, had been mutilated beyond repair, while *Fear*, which exposed her dread and anxiety in the aftermath of Jake's attack, remained curiously untouched.

Henry harbored no doubts over the identity of the intruder. It had been only a matter of time before Jake Powell, in an alcohol-induced rage, would pay him a visit. He shuddered to think of what might have happened if he'd deferred to Peyton earlier that night, dined more quickly and efficiently at the Stage, and attended the earlier movie. The blood on the floor could have been his . . . instead of . . . whose? He hoped it was Jake's . . . or was there another victim?

Only then did it dawn on Henry: only Fiona or Alice could have revealed his identity and address. Alice had assured him that Jake was unaware of her temporary lodging in Brooklyn. But Jake knew where Fiona lived—and Henry knew that she wouldn't have led her violent cousin to his apartment voluntarily. *Could Jake be vicious enough to attack his own cousin?*

Henry didn't wait to find out. He hurtled down the stairway and out to the street. He hailed a taxi to Fiona's apartment. He arrived well after midnight. Persistent ringing of the buzzer yielded no response. Frantic, he rang every buzzer in the building until some poor soul let him in, then bounded up the stairway to Fiona's apartment.

Her door was ajar. He entered warily. The floor was littered with broken glass. A lamp lay on its side across an overturned coffee table in the center of the room. And then his heart stopped. There she was, slumped against a wall, unconscious.

Her breathing was labored, but—thank God—she was alive.

Henry had frequently teased Fiona for indulging in the luxury of a telephone on a WPA salary, but at this moment he was grateful for its presence. The ambulance arrived within ten minutes. Henry climbed into the back to accompany Fiona to St. Vincent's Hospital where she was rushed into the emergency room. He waited. And waited.

"Your friend has sustained a nasty blow to the head," a doctor explained when he emerged from the emergency room a half hour later, "and probably a concussion." Henry blanched. "We won't know the extent of the damage until she regains consciousness," he said, fumbling at the stethoscope draped around his neck. "We'll move her to a room upstairs . . . you can sit with her there if you like."

And so Henry had begun his vigil, leaving the room only once to find a phone booth. He called the Lanings to explain, in briefest terms, what had happened. He'd feared that they'd pass his ruined apartment, wander in, and panic when they saw the blood.

"She's in a room at St. Vincent's," Henry told a distraught Mary. "I'm staying here until she awakens. They won't know much 'til then."

Henry awoke from a catnap in the early afternoon. Fiona had begun to stir. She moaned softly. He reached out and grasped her left hand. Her eyelids fluttered. Suddenly she gasped, her eyes wide open. "Where . . . am I?" Her voice was weak and hoarse. She spoke with obvious discomfort.

"Welcome back, Fiona," Henry said, smiling broadly. As he explained where she was, she began to recall why.

"Oh my God, Henry! You're okay!" she cried out, her eyes

tearing. Henry bent down and gathered her into his arms. They embraced like lovers.

After an afternoon of examination, reexamination, testing, pricking, and prodding, a legion of doctors announced their verdict: Fiona had suffered a concussion, but was otherwise remarkably sound. If all went well, she could expect to be released on the following day.

Henry's relief was matched only by his impatience in addressing the looming elephant in the room. He'd already described for Fiona the wave of destruction unleashed upon his studio. The cause was yet to be discussed. Now that they were alone, Henry was eager to talk.

"Don't you think it's time we addressed the obvious?" Henry asked her. Fiona grunted, then tried to change the subject.

"Jake almost *killed* you, Fiona! And he'd have killed me had I been there when he arrived. He ravaged three of my finished paintings. Haven't you anything to say?"

"What do you want me to say, Henry?"

"What are you going to do . . . just let it pass?" Henry was incredulous.

"He was drunk. He needs help."

"He committed attempted murder, breaking and entering, destruction of personal property. He should be put away!"

"Would that make you feel better?"

"Yes," Henry said, "and a whole lot safer, too."

"Look, Henry," she began, her voice raspy and halting. "If I press charges against my own cousin, it'll probably end his baseball career. It will tear apart my family. I haven't called my parents about what happened because I don't know what to tell them. Whatever I say will explode into full-scale familial warfare. I don't see how that would help matters."

"What kind of family condones homicidal behavior?"

"My family's not like your family, Henry. We don't sit around at Thanksgiving smiling at each other, sharing our hopes and our deep inner thoughts. My family is completely dysfunctional. We've got drunks, abusers ... name a social defect and we've got it. But as crazy as they are, they coexist. This would rip apart the fragile peace and incite a war."

"Let me get this straight, Fiona." Henry was becoming angry. "He nearly strangles you, he undoubtedly still wants to kill me ... and you just want to let sleeping dogs lie?"

"No. Not exactly. He needs to be confronted ... when sober ... to acknowledge what happened and to convince us it won't happen again."

"What, he's gonna quit drinking and become a boy scout?" Henry abruptly stood up, trying to tame his emotions. "What if I press charges even if you don't?"

"How are you going to prove it was him without my testimony?"

"Fiona, this is ludicrous!" She watched as he stalked about the room.

"I can't testify against him, Henry. I won't."

"He knows where I live, Fiona," he said, waving his hand for emphasis. "And what about the destruction of my paintings?"

"When you first approached me about your damn muse, I told you I couldn't be responsible for Jake's reaction if he found out. You wouldn't listen to me ... and I was foolish enough to let you talk me into contacting her. Now that the genie is out of the bottle, you're looking for me to put it back in?"

"Jake's always into the bottle, according to Alice."

"Can't you get some other goddamn muse? If you finish with her, you'll be finished with Jake."

"Did you see the paintings she posed for?"

"I did. They were very good. But it wasn't because of her, Henry, it was because of you! *You* painted them, she didn't."

"Okay, Fiona . . . I can't debate this anymore. I need to get home, clean up, sleep. I'll see you tomorrow."

"Wait . . . Henry. Please don't go home angry." She grimaced as she sat up straight against her pillow. "You were there for me last night when I really needed you . . . and you haven't left my side since. I'm grateful for that . . . no, Henry, I'm more than grateful." She looked at him earnestly. "Come here." She motioned him over with her hand, drawing him to the side of the bed. He sat down beside her. She took his hand and pulled him closer, then kissed him softly on the lips. "I guess I've missed you a lot more than I thought," she said.

Henry was touched. The last eighteen hours had been an emotional roller coaster. He wasn't sure he could trust his feelings, but he knew he felt something for Fiona at that moment that transcended mere friendship. "Stay with me for a few days," he suggested, "until you're back on your feet. You've got a concussion . . . you can't be alone in your apartment right now."

"Henry, I—"

"Fiona . . . *please.*"

Though she was reluctant to admit it, she knew he was right. And besides, where else would she go? "Okay . . . that's very sweet of you." She smiled. "Thanks."

"Good. Now I've got to do a bit of housekeeping," he quipped, "and I've got to see a man about a door."

CHAPTER TWENTY-SEVEN

An Uncomplimentary Reference

Mary cringed when she saw the bruises on Fiona's face and neck. "I hope you feel better than you look," she said. Henry and Fiona had just arrived at Henry's hastily reassembled apartment after her release from the hospital. Mary and Edward were there to greet them.

"That wouldn't be saying much," Fiona said, "but I do. A little dizziness and some tenderness, but otherwise I feel pretty good . . . under the circumstances."

Edward surveyed the studio. "Like what you've done with the place, Henry. Quite a transformation."

"Wish I'd been able to do as much with the paintings," Henry lamented.

"I know a good restorer," Edward said, glancing at the jagged hole in the heart of *Gastonia Renaissance.* "Can make absolute wrecks look as good as new."

"Sign me up!" Fiona quipped, drawing laughter.

Henry had already briefed the Lanings on the events that occurred two nights earlier. They'd found it hard to digest. But he'd asked them not to mention Jake Powell in Fiona's presence. It was awkward, but they complied.

Jake Powell woke up in a cold sweat the morning after his rampage. His sheets were stained with blood. His head throbbed and his right shoulder ached. A grisly wound screamed out from the top of his right wrist. *What the...?* He had no recollection of the injury, though he vaguely recalled a tussle with someone. He'd dodged a bullet last night—he knew that much. Had the wound been on the underside of his wrist, he'd have probably bled out. He arose with some difficulty, disinfected the wound with whiskey, then bandaged it up... rather neatly, he thought.

The Yankees were scheduled to depart that morning on a two-week road trip. He packed his suitcase, gobbled up a few aspirin, and washed them down with what remained of the whiskey. On the cab ride to Penn Station, he concocted the excuse he'd need to explain the bandage.

Yankee manager Joe McCarthy noticed it the second Jake filed onto the train. "What the fuck is that, Powell?" he asked.

"Nuthin', Mac. Cut it whiles fixing a broken window pane."

"You live in a fuckin' hotel, Powell. That's the best you can do?"

"Well... uh, I—"

"I know you're full o' shit, Jake," McCarthy said, "and so do you. Better cut down on the boozing... *and soon*... or you'll find yourself back in Dayton playing in a beer league."

"Aye, aye, Skip," he said glibly.

The long train ride to St. Louis gave Jake plenty of opportunity to reflect on the events of the previous evening— or at least what he recalled of them. Most of the night was a blur. He'd amped up the drinking in recent weeks, what with his lengthening batting slump and his troubles with Alice, and the blackouts were occurring more frequently.

His recollections from last night were like a random

collection of hazy snapshots scattered across a tabletop. Several involved his cousin, Fiona. *Sweet girl, that Fiona . . . and smart.* There was a look of disapproval on her face in one snapshot . . . a look of terror in another. Had something to do with her artist friend. Right . . . the Jew! Needed to find the Jew who was diddling Alice. *Damn him!*

Jake glanced out the window at the lush green landscape as the train clattered westward. Across the aisle, Joe "Flash" Gordon, the Yankees' sharp young rookie second baseman, was snoring like a buzz saw. Jake continued to plumb the cobwebs of his mind for bits and pieces of the previous night. Had he gone to the kike's apartment? He wasn't sure.

More random snapshots. A nigger in a baseball uniform. Uppity. Shaking a white guy's hand. Did he fight him? Blood . . . he remembered blood, but whose? His tortured brain also coughed up an image of Alice. Yes, it was Alice, all right. She looked at him in horror. He closed his eyes and grimaced, shaking his head, as if the back-and-forth motion would erase that particularly unwelcome fragment of his splintered memory.

More than anything, Jake harbored a profound sense of guilt—like he'd done something he'd regret if he could only recall what it was. But he couldn't—and maybe that was just as well.

The Yankees were in Chicago on July 29th, the fourth day of their road trip. White Sox radio announcer Bob Elson scoured the field after batting practice in search of a pre-game interviewee. Jake, who was slated to play left field that day, agreed to talk with him.

"Hello, fans," Elson began. "We have with us today Jake Powell, left fielder for the New York Yankees. Hello, Jake. Welcome to the airwaves."

"Uh, thanks."

"Tell us something about your background, Jake . . . where you grew up, how you broke into professional baseball."

And Jake blathered on. He'd been born and raised in Silver Spring, Maryland, was scouted and signed by Clark Griffith, owner of the Washington Senators, and been traded to the Yankees in 1936 in exchange for Yankee outfielder Ben Chapman.

"How do you keep in trim during the winter months in order to keep up your batting average?" Elson later asked him. The question was as soft as a lazy fly ball.

"Oh, that's easy," Jake said. "I'm a policeman in Dayton, and I beat niggers over the head with my blackjack."

While Elson gasped in disbelief, the radio engineers at WGN quickly pulled the plug. The interview was over, and so, for all intents and purposes, was Jake Powell.

The next day, a delegation of prominent black Chicagoans turned up at the ballpark with a petition demanding that Powell be "barred from professional baseball." Later that day, Powell and his manager were summoned to the Chicago office of the Commissioner of Baseball, Kenesaw Mountain Landis.

Landis kept the pair waiting in his outer office while he talked on the telephone. Jake had never met the Commissioner, though he'd incited his wrath on more than one occasion with his on-field fisticuffs. Thirty minutes passed; then an hour. Finally, Landis' personal secretary ushered them into his office.

Kenesaw Mountain Landis was a legend. A onetime Federal judge, he became Commissioner in 1920. His harsh condemnation and ultimate expulsion of the alleged participants in baseball's infamous Black Sox World Series betting scandal of 1919 was generally credited with restoring the integrity of professional baseball. A gaunt, stern-faced, white-haired Midwesterner, Landis ruled the sport with an iron fist.

Landis's office was as imperial as he was: mahogany desk, matching bookcases, big leather chairs. It seemed to Jake even larger than the Yankee Stadium clubhouse. He was nervous as he took a seat across from the Commissioner.

"The coloreds in this city are in an uproar," Landis said. He stared at Powell. "How'd you manage to make such a stupid statement? You were on the radio, for God's sake!"

Though thousands had heard otherwise, Jake denied any wrongdoing. "They got it wrong, Mr. Landis. I didn't say anything like what they say I said. In fact," he allowed, "I've got some very good friends among the Negroes of Dayton."

Landis scoffed. "Your testimony is very much the minority view, Jake. I've got very little choice here. The Negroes in this town . . . and every other . . . are part of baseball's constituency. You can't utter that nonsense and not expect repercussions."

"I didn't mean no disrespect, Your Honor, sir."

"I'm going to have to suspend you, Jake . . . at least for the rest of the road trip. Maybe next time you'll think first and talk later."

"But—"

"That'll be all, gentlemen." Landis waved his hand dismissively, ending the discussion.

While McCarthy was livid with Powell, he'd never disparage a player in public, no matter the transgression. So it was not surprising when he assigned primary blame for the blowup to the radio station. "The ball players don't want to engage in these broadcasts," he told the press. "But they're pestered and pestered until finally one of them gives in. Then in an unguarded moment something's said, maybe only in a joke, but it's taken the wrong way and then there's trouble." McCarthy was more annoyed than outraged. "I don't know what Powell said, but whatever it was, I'm pretty sure he meant no harm. Probably just meant to get off a wisecrack." Yankees General Manager Ed Barrow seemed equally impervious to the gravity of the matter, assuring beat writers that even his two "colored servants" considered it no more than an unfortunate mistake.

"Jake Powell of the New York Yankees made an uncomplimentary reference to a portion of the population," Commissioner Landis proclaimed in his official statement later that day. "Although the commissioner believes the remark was due more to carelessness than intent, player Powell is suspended for 10 days."

CHAPTER TWENTY-EIGHT

The Harlem Apology Tour

"Jesus Christ!" Henry blurted out as he read the article on Powell's *faux pas* in *The New York Times*. "Your cousin's not only an incorrigible bigot but a certifiable idiot! And instead of condemning him for being a racist pig, the Yankees simply excuse his conduct as innocuous and unfortunate," Henry fumed, pounding his fist on the table. "And that hypocrite of a commissioner slaps Jake's wrist while he doggedly preserves the color line."

"I don't know what to say," Fiona conceded after Henry had passed her the newspaper. "But I can tell you that he invented the part about being a policeman."

Henry shook his head in disgust. "Still wanna protect him?"

"I don't want to, Henry, but I have to," Fiona said for the hundredth time.

It had been a week since Jake's attack on Fiona and his demolition of Henry's studio. Fiona had made steady progress in her recovery. The headaches were now less frequent and the dizziness was gone. The bruises on her face and neck were rapidly fading.

When he'd brought Fiona home with him, Henry had set her up in the bed in his alcove while he slept on the couch. Fiona felt guilty depriving him of his own bed, but Henry insisted.

He'd gone to great lengths to accommodate her, buying their groceries, preparing meals (a few too many servings of macaroni-and-cheese, she'd noted), and straightening up.

Their temporary living arrangement felt different to Henry from their days as lovers. They'd eased into a comfortable rapport, enjoying each other's company as Fiona recuperated. They didn't discuss it, and there was no physical intimacy between them, but it was obvious to both that a spark was reigniting.

On their fifth night together, as Henry headed to sleep on the couch, Fiona intercepted him. Wordlessly, she took his hand and led him to her bed in the alcove. For the first time in a year, they were lovers again.

Afterwards, they smiled at each other knowingly.

"Are you thinking what I'm thinking?" Henry asked her.

Fiona grinned broadly. "Mary will be ecstatic," she said.

The Yankees returned to New York on August 9th. The fallout from Jake's bigoted wisecrack had still not dissipated. Newspapers—particularly the influential Afro-American press—were relentless in their condemnation of the Yankee outfielder. Ownership finally took notice. On orders from the Yankees' brass, McCarthy corralled Powell shortly after the club's train pulled into Penn Station in New York.

"You're going up to Harlem tonight," Mac said.

"No fucking way," Jake replied.

"Bosses' orders."

"They'll fuckin' lynch me!" McCarthy shook his head at the irony.

"You'll be accompanied by some colored guy," Mac told him. "He's your ticket through Harlem. You'll visit newspaper offices, shops, bars. You'll say you're sorry for being such a fucking asshole. You'll buy a round of drinks and then you'll move on to the next place on the list and do the same fucking thing."

"Nigger payin' for the drinks?"

McCarthy gave Jake a cold Irish stare. "No, asshole, you are. And watch your mouth or they *will* fucking lynch you."

"Shit," Jake said, reluctantly acknowledging the terms of his penance.

Powell was too radioactive to insert into the lineup that first day back, and by now it appeared that George "Twinkletoes" Selkirk had supplanted him in left field. So his only public appearances that day would be in Harlem.

Hubert Julian, a Trinidad-born aviator who'd been the first African-American pilot to fly the nation coast-to-coast, accompanied Powell on his Harlem Apology Tour. Jake figured the guy was being paid to babysit him, but was grateful for the protection he afforded. First stop was the office of the *Amsterdam News*, Harlem's most respected newspaper. After Julian's introduction, Powell sat down with a reporter.

"So what brings you here today, Mr. Powell?" The reporter was amused by Jake's unease and curious about his agenda.

"Came to say I'm sorry."

"Sorry for what, Mr. Powell?"

"Uh ... for dis— ... dispar'gin' Negroes."

"*Disparaging?*"

"Yeah, you know, saying *nigger*," Powell said, shifting uncomfortably in his chair. "Ya know, it was that radio fella that said it first." Hubert Julian winced.

"The radio announcer used the word *nigger*, Mr. Powell?" The reporter seemed surprised by that revelation.

"Yeah ... I think so. Probably wouldn't have used it myself ... but—"

"So that constitutes your apology, Mr. Powell?"

"*Constitutes?*"

"Sorry. So that's your apology, then. You're sorry you 'dispar'ged' the Negro race by bragging about hitting niggers over the head with a blackjack, but only used *nigger* because the radio announcer had used it first?"

"Uh . . . right, I guess so."

"So if you'd said 'hitting *Negroes* over the head with a blackjack' it would have been okay?"

"Aw, come on. Look, I'm sorry. I'll be more careful next time, I promise."

"With your language or with the blackjack?"

"Both."

"Well, thank you for coming in, Mr. Powell. It's been a special privilege to talk with you. I can hardly imagine how you got yourself into this fix," the reporter chuckled, "you've got such a way with words."

"Uh . . . thanks." Julian shook his head as Powell got up. "Where to next, fly boy?" he asked the befuddled aviator.

The Harlem Apology Tour lasted two nights. Powell was more at home in the bars than the newspaper offices, but his awkward expressions of contrition were consistently underwhelming. When the ordeal was finally over, he asked McCarthy to restore him to the lineup. The Yankee skipper demurred. "You're toxic, Jake. Brass wants you on the bench for the rest of the homestand. We'll see what we can do when we get to Washington next week." *Shit*, Jake thought. Washington's Griffith Stadium was no bed of roses: the Senators despised him to a man for his brazen attacks on first baseman Joe Kuhel back in July. And the fans were prone to expressing their displeasure by peppering him with bottles.

But he wanted to play in the worst way. If returning to the lineup meant submitting to the hostile environment of Griffith Stadium, he'd just have to take his chances.

McCarthy paroled Jake from the doghouse on August 16th, starting him in the second game of a doubleheader at Griffith Stadium. A 16-1 drubbing in the first game left the Washington crowd in a decidedly uncharitable mood.

Jake swaggered to the plate in the first inning, his bat perched on his shoulder like a warclub. Twenty-three thousand angry fans showered him with a chorus of boos. The boos turned swiftly to cheers when he slapped into an easy double play. *Fuck!*

When the Yanks took the lead in the sixth, the crowd became restless. Jake jogged to left field in the bottom of the inning. Suddenly, as if commanded by a guerilla general, the bleacherites let loose with a barrage of pop bottles and other assorted projectiles. "You shitheads couldn't hit me if I was fuckin' standing right in front of you!" he taunted them as the missiles plopped harmlessly at his feet. When a defiant Powell reached on an infield error in the seventh, a bottle whizzed by his head. "That was intended for you," Powell said to Zeke Bonura, the Senators' first baseman.

Even his manager seemed oblivious to the plight of the most hated ballplayer in America, leaving Jake exposed to ever-larger projectiles (a tin pail was hurled at him later while he chased down a triple). The umpires did little more than periodically dispatch the grounds crew (all Negroes, *The New York Times* noted ironically the following morning) to rid the field of errant bottles and other paraphernalia. Jake's sole consolation that afternoon was the fact that the fans were no more capable of hitting him with their projectiles than their players were of hitting Yankee pitching with their bats.

CHAPTER TWENTY-NINE

Fettuccine Alfredo

Jake became the forgotten man on the Yankee bench, playing in only seven more games over the last third of the season and making only a cameo appearance in the 1938 World Series, which the Yankees swept from the Cubs. By the second week of October, he was back in Dayton chasing Negroes with blackjacks. Even though neither Henry nor Fiona had encountered him since that awful night in July, they were relieved to know he'd be out of the city for the next six months.

After two weeks of pampering from Henry, Fiona had been well enough to return to her apartment and resume work on Edward's mural. She'd received no pay during her absence and badly needed the money.

Although Henry's inventory of salable paintings had been decimated in Jake's studio assault, he did receive some encouraging news from his dealer. *Waiting*, the first painting for which Alice had modeled, had sold. Henry received a note from Frank Rehn, along with a check for $400 (after deduction of his $200 advance), enough to pay his rent for another year. "I'll send someone by for your other Alice painting," Rehn wrote. He was referring to *The Goddess*, which Jake had destroyed. "And Henry," he'd noted in closing, "I'd urge you to continue your series with that delectable creature. She's irresistible!"

Flush from the proceeds of his sale, Henry invited Fiona to dinner. He met her at an old warehouse in Hell's Kitchen, where Edward had moved his mural project after the WPA lost its lease on the Tenth Avenue church.

Perched on a scaffold, Fiona wore a paint-splattered smock much like the one she was painting onto the figure of Johannes Gutenberg on a panel for the New York Public Library's McGraw Rotunda. In a scene imagined from the 1450s, the inventor of moveable type proudly displayed a leaf from his seminal Bible to an official of the City of Mainz. It was the third of four thematic panels that Edward had designed to illustrate *The Story of the Recorded Word.*

"Looks like a waiter with the sandwich list from the Carnegie Deli," Henry joked, pointing to the figure of Gutenberg.

"Your way of telling me we're going to the Carnegie again?"

"Its shitty service saved my life. I feel I owe it my business," Henry said.

"I'd kill for a plate of lasagna at Carlito's."

"That's way down in the Village!"

"Right . . . three blocks from my apartment," Fiona said. "We can do a nightcap at my place afterwards."

"Jeez, guys," Edward said, emerging from behind the canvas he'd been painting in another corner of the room. "Am I also gonna have to listen to you negotiating where you'll spend the night *after* the nightcap?"

"I'm sure Mary would be pleased if you'd convey all the details, so pay attention!" Fiona said.

"Okay, Fiona, you win. Carlito's it is." Henry said, graciously conceding defeat.

Fiona climbed down from the scaffold, put away her paints and brushes, and peeled off her smock. Henry laughed.

"What's so funny?"

"You've got a blue streak running east to west across your forehead. Nice touch . . . it matches your outfit."

Fiona flashed a faux pout and strolled to the worktable to erase the wayward brushstroke. After she'd retrieved her coat, they said their goodbyes to Edward and scurried to the Ninth Avenue El for the journey downtown.

For reasons Henry couldn't explain, Manhattan's elevated railway lines had always fascinated him. It was a guilty pleasure, particularly at night, passing by second and third story flats, catching the briefest glimpses of life inside the unshuttered windows. He made a mental note to consider it as subject matter for a future painting.

It was Henry's first visit to Carlito's, the little Italian restaurant on Bleecker Street. A small, rotund maître d' with an exuberant moustache and slicked-back hair led them through a low-ceilinged room to a small table set against an old brick wall. Adorned with a red-and-white checkered tablecloth, the table was lit by a candle protruding like an exclamation point from an empty, wax-caked wine bottle. The little Italian smiled obsequiously and handed each of them tattered menus splattered with remnants of tomato sauce.

"It isn't elegant, but the food's great," Fiona assured Henry as they took their seats.

"I could save us a few bits by ordering a bowl of plain pasta and just scraping the sauce off the menu," Henry mused. Fiona strained to suppress a smile.

"I'm having the lasagna," she said after perusing the menu perfunctorily.

"What, tired of mac-and-cheese?" Henry grinned. "Don't even see it on the menu," he said in mock despair.

"It's called fettuccine alfredo."

"Oh." So that's what he ordered, along with a bottle of Chianti.

Later, as they dug into heaping plates of pasta, Henry contemplated how to approach a subject that he knew would displease her.

"Got a check today from Rehn's. Sold one of my paintings."

"That's terrific, Henry," Fiona said. "Which one?"

"*Waiting*, my first painting of Alice."

"Oh," Fiona replied.

"Unfortunately, Rehn wanted *The Goddess* next."

"I could sew it together" was her tight-lipped reply.

"I'll give him *Fear*, the painting I did after his studio visit. It's the only one I have left of her... the only one Jake *didn't* destroy."

"Fine," she said, barely looking up as she raised a forkful of lasagna to her mouth. A look of annoyance spread slowly across her face.

"He urged me to continue my series with Alice." Henry delivered that line warily, twirling pasta around his fork as he braced for Fiona's reaction.

"Really, Henry? We haven't endured enough because of that girl?"

"Well, I knew you wouldn't be thrilled ... and in fairness, I think it was because of Jake, not Alice." Henry took a sip of his Chianti. "But as far as we know, Jake's out of our hair for the next several months ... and as frightened as she was, I don't think Alice would have seen him again anyway."

"Look," Fiona said, putting down her fork, "you do what you've gotta do, Henry. You'll do it no matter what I say."

Fiona's resistance to Alice unnerved him. Was it fear, jealousy, or both? He could understand fear. For months now, they'd adopted the 'let sleeping dogs lie' approach she'd advocated, against his better judgment. It left them exposed. But was there reason for jealousy? Was Henry motivated by purely rational considerations—the salability of paintings—or by an irrational compulsion to see Alice again? Was Alice Woodley a muse or a siren?

"I don't plan on putting either one of us at risk," Henry said.

"You didn't plan on it the last time, either."

You could have put him in jail and solved the problem, he wanted to say, but wisely restrained himself.

"I felt bad about bringing this up . . . knowing how you feel about Alice," Henry said. "But I didn't want to deceive you." He would've been hard pressed to paint Alice covertly; Fiona would have seen the paintings in his studio whenever she came by. "Are you okay with this?"

"No, Henry, I'm not. But I'll live with it."

Henry's announcement that evening accomplished two things. First, he got his plans to paint Alice off his chest, which made him feel at least marginally better than he would if he'd chosen to conceal it. Second, it dissuaded Fiona from sharing her bed that night, a regrettable but somewhat foreseeable consequence of his honesty. It had been, he realized in retrospect, a classic no-win proposition.

Looking at the bright side, he'd refined his palate, graduating from macaroni-and-cheese to fettuccine alfredo.

Henry purchased the full-length mirror-on-stand from a second-hand furniture store, hauling it across Union Square and up three flights of stairs to his studio. He positioned it so that he was visible from the knees up. He then nudged it slightly so the back edges of his canvas and easel appeared along the left edge of the mirror. Until he secured Alice again, or devised an alternative plan, he'd serve as his own model.

It was November 11, 1938, another day of bad news in an increasingly perilous world. Three days earlier, New Deal Democrats had been crushed in mid-term Congressional elections, threatening the future of the New Deal programs that had been crucial to the subsistence of so many artists. Even more distressing was the news from Germany and Austria, where government forces and civilian mobs terrorized Jews by torching synagogues, trashing Jewish-owned businesses, and taking thousands into custody. NAZIS SMASH, LOOT AND BURN JEWISH SHOPS AND TEMPLES read the headline in *The New York Times*. Later referred to as *Kristallnacht*—the night of broken glass—it seemed to herald the point of no return for the countless Jews already suffering the indignities rained upon them by the Third Reich.

After braving the harrowing account in the *Times*, Henry employed his first true indulgence, a brand new telephone, to call his parents. The sale of *Waiting* convinced him that he could finally afford the luxury of instant communication. Lifting the heavy black receiver and twisting the rotary dial gave him the same thrill as mastering the wonders of the Horn & Hardart automat.

Ruth was concerned when she heard Henry's voice. "Are you okay, dear?"

"Just fine, Mom," Henry assured her before mentioning his new telephone.

"Morris! Henry's got a telephone!"

"Will wonders never cease?" Henry heard his father utter in the background.

As the call stretched to a half-hour, Henry began to question the wisdom of his new toy. Thirty minutes of long distance charges would cripple him. Next time, he hoped, his parents would place the call, sparing him the financial repercussions.

Henry talked with his father about the news from Germany. "It'll get much worse," Morris prophesied, as was his wont. "Wrote cousin Yuri in Amsterdam just this morning," he said. "They've got to get out. Hitler won't be satisfied with the annexation of Austria. Just a matter of time before he moves south and west."

His conversation with Ben was even more troubling. "I'm thinking about enlisting," Ben said. "Dad says I can enter an officer's training program and be prepared when the mobilization comes."

"Really, Ben? Is that what you want . . . or what Dad wants?"

"Well, it's sure not what *Mom* wants."

"Finish college first," Henry implored his brother. "Then, if it's something you still want to do, fine. Just don't let Dad manipulate you."

"Just *thinking* about it," Ben insisted in an effort to placate his pacifist sibling.

"Okay, okay," Henry said. "Oh . . . and by the way . . . I'm seeing Fiona again." Henry neglected, however, to disclose the frightening circumstances that had reunited them. "But do me a favor: don't tell Mom or Dad. Now that I've got a phone, they'll drive me nuts if they know."

"Your *shiksa* secret is safe with me," Ben said.

After two self-portraits, Henry was chomping at the bit for something—or someone—more inspiring to paint. Not that he was unsatisfied with the work he'd done; the full-length self-portrait that pictured him in the act of painting himself was, he thought, among his better efforts. But it was time to move on.

He'd deferred any reunion with Alice, electing first to mend any damage he'd inflicted on his relationship with Fiona by merely raising the specter of Alice's return. With their romance now back on a solid footing, Henry decided the time had come to reconnect with his muse.

But where *was* Alice? He had no phone number, nor the address of the apartment she'd occupied before her blowup with Jake. And if Fiona had any of that information, he wasn't foolish enough to ask her for it. All he had was his memory of the Brooklyn boardinghouse to which she'd escaped, having escorted Alice there the last time he'd seen her—the day he painted *Fear*. It was a place to start.

An elderly woman answered the door when he arrived at the boardinghouse on a chilly afternoon in early December. It was an old Victorian, and so was she.

"How can I help you, young man?" she croaked. She was ninety if she was a day.

"I'm looking for Alice Woodley."

"Alice . . . Woodley . . ." She turned her wrinkled face toward the sky as if the clouds might supply a glimmer of recognition. "Alice . . . Woodley."

"Beautiful blond girl . . . curls . . . worked as a burlesque dancer?"

"Ah . . . yes . . . I'm afraid I do remember her now," the old lady sniffed. "Don't condone that sort of thing, you know . . . no loose morals in my house." She puckered her lips in disapproval. "Sent her packing . . . ages ago." Henry was getting nowhere.

"She might have had a friend here," Henry said.

"Yes . . . Miss Winters, if I recall. Funny," she muttered, "I seem to remember seeing them together not long ago." Good news, at last.

"Does Miss Winters still live here?"

"She does," the relic responded, her tone suggesting that the conversation was rapidly approaching its limits.

"Might I talk with her?"

"I'm rather certain she's not here now . . . don't know when she'll be back."

"Could I leave her a message?" That, apparently, was neither impermissible nor immoral. The old woman grudgingly allowed Henry into the house where he scribbled a note for Miss Winters, urging her to have Alice contact him at her earliest convenience. All he could do now was wait.

CHAPTER THIRTY

Hot Pretzels

Henry had heard nothing from Alice in the month since his visit to the boardinghouse. But he hadn't been idly waiting. Like a surfer riding a serendipitous wave, he'd harnessed a surge of creativity, swelling his inventory by the addition of two new works. While New Yorkers indulged in holiday revelry, Henry anchored himself to his easel, painting fiendishly.

Ninth Avenue El was his paean to the elevated railway lines, rusting relics of the late Victorian epoch whose days were numbered. His subject was the crumbling old station at Christopher and Greenwich Streets near Fiona's West Village apartment. It was an architect's nightmare—a gingerbread cake floating precariously atop an Erector Set base—but its very incongruity was irresistible to the young artist. After working in his studio until mid-afternoon, he'd traipse to the station, sketchpad in hand. He'd draw until chilled to the bone, then repair to Fiona's apartment to thaw. If sufficiently motivated, he'd putter around Fiona's kitchen, treating her, upon her return from work at the warehouse, to a selection from his tiresome repertoire of largely indigestible cuisine; otherwise, they'd hoof it over to Carlito's for a more palatable meal. Later, they'd burn off the excess calories in bed. After breakfast, he'd return to his studio and enthusiastically repeat the cycle.

Henry took his time on *Ninth Avenue El*—prolonging his agreeable routine—while he worked simultaneously on a larger picture he called *The Pretzel Vendor.* The pretzel vendor was a Union Square institution. A Jewish immigrant from Russia, of indeterminate age and ample girth, she could be found every day at numerous locations in and around the square, serving up hot pretzels from a rickety wooden pushcart. Her cart was fitted with wooden rods through each of which she threaded at least a dozen pretzels, each neatly separated from the ones above and below by a sheet of waxed paper. She was bundled in a heavy black overcoat, worn at the elbows and cuffs, a vestige of the old country. Her feet were clad in heavy, fur-lined boots, even in the summertime. A long white apron was invariably tied to her waist while a red knit cap covered her graying hair like the cherry atop an ice cream sundae. Except for her familiar, throaty chant of "Hot Pretzels," she rarely spoke or smiled. But her pretzels were worth a thousand words, baked fresh every morning before dawn, with a slightly crusty exterior that surrendered to a silky softness within.

Henry painted the pretzel vendor in her favorite rush hour spot at the mouth of the Union Square subway station. He painted her from behind and slightly to the right, an angle from which her face was hidden but her stock in full display. It was how she wanted it. He hadn't planned to hide her face, but each time Henry had tried to sketch her frontally, she'd furiously waved him away. His final composition featured the subway station prominently in the background, as if rising to embrace her. And in a respectful nod to Yas, he placed a discarded newspaper on the ground near her feet. The headline mimicked the one from the *Times* that had so upset him several weeks earlier: NAZIS SMASH, LOOT AND BURN JEWISH SHOPS AND TEMPLES.

As for Kuniyoshi, Henry was both surprised and delighted to find him at his door on a snowy Saturday in January of 1939. The two of them had stayed in touch, meeting occasionally for lunch, but this was Kuniyoshi's first foray to his former student's studio.

"I was in the neighborhood," Yas said.

"Your studio's three blocks away... you're *always* in the neighborhood!"

"Yes, yes... of course. But I didn't want to come by too soon." He removed his wide-brimmed hat and scarf. "I wanted to allow you time to evolve."

Henry took Yas's overcoat, shaking out the snow that clung to the shoulders like powdered sugar. Yas accepted his offer to make tea. While waiting for the water to boil, the older artist gravitated toward Henry's easel where *The Pretzel Vendor* sat in anticipation of a few final brushstrokes.

"You *have* evolved, Henry," Yas said with evident satisfaction. "This is much softer... more ethereal... than your earlier work." He smiled broadly. "I know this lady... buy pretzels from her now and then." He bent over the canvas, carefully scrutinizing the background, the handling of paint. "I can actually *see* the atmosphere... *smell* the pretzels... *feel* the old woman's presence. And the newspaper in the foreground... is a clever touch." Yas smiled, acknowledging the young artist's tribute to his mentor.

The teakettle whistled. Henry grabbed a pair of cups off a shelf, poured the hot water over a couple of tea bags, and joined Yas at the easel. "Careful, it's hot."

"You know, I saw your painting of the dancers at the

National Academy last spring. I thought it was wonderful," Yas said as he took his first sip. "But in some ways I like this better." As he delivered the compliment, his eyes wandered to a larger work propped against a wall in a back corner of the studio. It was Henry's *Self Portrait at the Easel.* Yas put down his cup to take a closer look. On the canvas before him stood a self-confident young artist clad in a white shirt, collar unbuttoned, his red tie hanging loosely beneath a light brown V-neck sweater. His eyes were fixed upon an unseen mirror in the vicinity of the viewer, whose vantage point was behind and to the left of the canvas as it rested on the easel. The artist clenched a paint-spattered palette in what appeared to be his right hand while applying paint with his left (because this was a mirror image, it reversed reality). Kuniyoshi expressed his admiration at Henry's reconciliation of the four broad planes in the work: the floor, the rear wall, the palette, and the canvas itself. "Very nicely done," he said. Henry was buoyed by his mentor's kind words.

Yas withdrew a handkerchief from his pocket, removed his round, dark-rimmed glasses, and rubbed them absent-mindedly as if massaging the scruff of a cat. "Listen, Henry . . . I'm bringing a work down to Philly next week for the Pennsylvania Academy annual in February. If you'll permit me, I'd like to bring your self-portrait with me as well. It's an open competition . . . and I think this piece would please the jury." Yas was too humble to admit it, but he'd won the Temple Gold Medal for best painting at that very exhibition four years earlier.

"Absolutely!" Henry replied, jumping at his offer.

"And it wouldn't hurt to have one less self-portrait staring you in the face all day."

"To the contrary," Henry said, "I use it to scare off the mice."

CHAPTER THIRTY-ONE

Picasso and the Paddy Wagons

"**N**o More Pink Slips! . . . Artists Gotta Eat!" The chant and refrain went on all morning as they paraded up and down the sidewalk outside WPA headquarters on Columbus Avenue. Fiona waved a "Down With Somervell!" placard as she chanted along with the dozens of other artists, craftsmen, and even artist's models who had gathered to protest a recent spate of layoffs announced by city WPA chief Colonel Brehon Somervell. Fiona had shamed Henry into joining her on the picket line, while Henry had bribed Peyton to come along, promising to spring for lunch at The Stage after the protest.

By early 1939, attacks on the WPA had intensified. Republican leaders, buoyed by recent election gains, spearheaded efforts to curtail funding and prosecute alleged waste and graft. Funding cuts, often sudden and unexpected, were devastating to artists, like Fiona, reliant upon the program for their survival.

By noon, the picket line had grown to almost fifty. The administrators in the building grew restless. Audrey McMahon, director of the city's WPA art programs, engaged the picketers, offering to speak in her office with a small delegation of representatives. No sooner had she tendered the olive branch than Colonel Somervell emerged from the building and angrily overruled her. "Out of here, you Reds!" he screeched. "You're wasting your time . . . and mine!"

On several occasions in the past, Edward had regaled Henry and Fiona with tales of run-ins with McMahon and Somervell. Despite saddling the former with the nickname "Arsenic and Old Face," Laning respected her judgment and grace under increasingly challenging circumstances. She'd been whipsawed between the (mostly) legitimate grievances of the artists she supervised and the iron will of Somervell, her superior, whom she despised. Like the fox guarding the henhouse, Somervell—an Army colonel whose WPA charges ran the gamut from ditch diggers to easel painters—never acknowledged the creation of art as "work" and considered the WPA a hotbed of Communism. During the earlier years of his reign, he was an obstructionist; now, he was openly committed to dismantling the program.

Somervell's outburst angered the protestors. "Restore Our Jobs! . . . No More Cuts!" they screamed, only louder. Fiona was particularly agitated and vocal. Henry wasn't sure whether to be impressed or embarrassed when she started the entire group chanting "Somervell, Go to Hell!"

The stone-faced Colonel refused to back down. "Disperse now, or I'll have the police drag you out!" he bellowed. Audrey McMahon was livid, pleading with Somervell to back off and allow her to talk with the protesters. "Someone will get hurt," Henry heard her say. But it was to no avail. Within minutes, three paddy wagons pulled up to the curb. Policemen with billy clubs streamed forth like ants from an anthill.

"Let's get the hell out of here!" Henry cried.

"No way!" Fiona shouted. "Bring 'em on!"

"This isn't worth the pastrami," Peyton said. "I'm skedaddlin'!" He discarded his picket sign and, like a giraffe evading a stalking lion, beat a hasty retreat down Columbus Avenue. Henry, of course, had little choice but to stand by his woman.

"Get your damn hands off me!" Fiona shrieked as a burly officer grabbed her by the arm and dragged her toward one of the paddy wagons. Seconds later, an officer shoved Henry in the same direction. He didn't resist. Dozens of other protestors suffered the same fate. When the wagons were full, they pulled away to the local precinct house.

Miraculously, no one was injured in the confrontation. When they reached the police station, the picketers were paraded in, single file, past a uniformed desk clerk armed with pad and paper. "Name?" he barked to the first poor soul as he passed through the gauntlet.

"Pablo Picasso!" croaked the artist-picketer-arrestee.

"How do you spell that?" the clerk inquired.

"P . . . I . . . C . . . A . . . S . . . S . . . O," recited the artist.

"Okay, next!" hollered the clerk.

"Homer," the next man said. "Winslow . . . fucking . . . Homer!"

Vinnie van Gogh, Leon da Vinci, Johnny Vermeer, and Michael Angelo followed in swift succession. Despite the sniggering and occasional guffaws, the desk clerk was none the wiser. Fiona was booked as Mary Cassatt while Henry claimed the moniker Remy van Rijn (which, of course, he was compelled to spell).

The three dozen arrestees were divided into four holding cells, three for males and one for the half-dozen women, including Mary Cassatt and Carrie Vaggio, who had incurred the wrath of the powerful Colonel Somervell. The cellmates passed the time singing songs. At one point, all four cells were engaged in a four-part rendition of *Row, Row, Row Your Boat* to the delight of both the participants and their increasingly sympathetic jailers.

After several hours, an officer called out "da Vinci, Vermeer, Angelo . . . van Rijn," which he pronounced as *van ridge-in,* along with eight more names, assembling the group in front of the cells and then escorting them out of the building and back into a paddy wagon.

"Where are we going?" Henry asked.

"Riker's Island . . . max security," the policeman said, straight-faced, as he reveled in the shudders his pronouncement elicited. "Nah," he chuckled, "you're just going down to city court." Henry, as well as each of his wagon-mates, was visibly relieved.

At the courthouse, the dirty dozen were taken in handcuffs into a courtroom, where they appeared before a judge. A clerk began to read off the names of the picketers. "John Vermeer, Michael Angelo, Remy van Rijn . . ."

"Stop right there," the judge said, laughing. "You've got to be kidding me." He addressed an assistant district attorney who was not yet in on the joke. "Please tell me why these people are here in my courtroom, Mr. Daniels."

"Your Honor, they participated in a demonstration this morning outside WPA headquarters at 70 Columbus Avenue."

"And why were they arrested?" the judge asked pointedly.

"Colonel Somervell made a complaint. Claimed they were disturbing the peace."

"Do you care to comment, Mr. Popper?" Martin Popper, lawyer for the United American Artists union, was present to represent the prisoners.

"Your Honor, these are nothing more than starving artists who expressed their First Amendment rights by assembling on a city sidewalk to protest WPA funding cuts. There was no violence and no one was injured. They'd like to go home now," Popper said.

"Case dismissed!" the judge proclaimed. As the newly freed contingent congratulated each other, the judge interjected. "One second," he said. "Which one of you is Michael Angelo?"

"I am, your Honor," one of the artists alleged.

"Nice work on the Sistine Chapel," the judge said.

CHAPTER THIRTY-TWO

The Deputy's Grandson

Just days after his deliverance from the slammer, Henry received word that *Self Portrait at the Easel* had made the cut and would be shown at the Pennsylvania Academy in early February.

"It'll be a tad more personal when some thug carves a hole in this one, don't you think?" Fiona said.

"Very funny," Henry replied.

Henry had every reason to be pleased. The exhibition was one of the country's most prestigious. He had even more reason to celebrate when the critic for the *Philadelphia Evening Bulletin* praised the work in his exhibition review.

Unwilling to rest on his laurels, Henry began work on a picture inspired by a glance out Fiona's rear window. From the adjacent apartment, a young woman leaned out her window to hang laundry. A clothesline stretched across the void separating the building from its neighbor. A snippet of streetscape appeared in the distance under a patch of blue sky. Garments in a rainbow of colors hung limply from wooden clothespins. It was a fleeting moment of ordinary life, unremarkable but for Henry's attraction to it. He'd sketched the scene quickly, stressing mood over detail.

Commencing work on the painting, Henry was reminded of

his debt to Kuniyoshi. In the past, his work had required extensive periods of direct observation. He recalled the many hours Bunny and Ben had posed for him as he meticulously appropriated their images for *Gastonia Renaissance*. Now, he needed only the spark of an idea and a few sketches for guidance; the rest came from his imagination, just as his mentor had preached.

As he plugged away one afternoon at the painting he'd call *Wash Day*, a letter arrived. It was from Homer Saint-Gaudens, director of the Carnegie Institute, the Pittsburgh art museum renowned for its annual exhibitions of international art. "It gave me great pleasure to see your *Self-Portrait* at the Pennsylvania Academy," Saint-Gaudens wrote. "I'd like, if I may, to see more of your work." The director would be in town on March 8th and proposed to visit Henry's studio that day "at precisely a quarter to three."

Henry was bowled over. The visit could have wide-ranging implications for his career. Recent exhibitors at the Carnegie International included Matisse, Braque, and his recent cellmate, Pablo Picasso.

Henry's mind raced. He scanned his studio. *Gastonia Renaissance* was relegated to a corner, too damaged to display (and too hard to explain if he did); *Night at the Savoy*, *7th Avenue Express*, and *Fear* were at Rehn's; and *Waiting* had been sold. Except for *Self-Portrait at the Easel*, which Saint-Gaudens had already seen (and would still be at the Pennsylvania Academy at the time of his visit), only four paintings remained in his studio: *Tenements, Ninth Avenue El, The Pretzel Vendor*, and *Wash Day*. He'd prevail upon his dealer to temporarily return the works in his inventory, but even so, a mere seven paintings was hardly enough.

Henry climbed upstairs to share his news with the Lanings. Edward was at the warehouse, but Mary expressed sufficient excitement for the both of them.

"I'm not assured of anything yet," Henry reminded her.

Mary had a visitor in the loft that day. "Henry, I want you to meet my nephew, Curtis Overton." A handsome young man, perhaps fifteen, stepped forward and politely shook Henry's hand. "Curtis is my sister's son from back home. He's visiting during his school vacation." 'Back home' was Canton, Ohio, where Mary had grown up. "Curtis, this is Henry, our downstairs neighbor . . . and a very talented artist."

Even as he uttered a reflexive "pleased to meet you," Henry's wheels were spinning.

"What is it, Henry?" Mary asked, detecting his momentary self-absorption.

Henry looked at Curtis, then back to Mary. "At the risk of being presumptuous—" He cut himself off mid-sentence and turned to the teenager. "Curtis, would you permit me to paint your picture?"

Mary and Curtis looked at each other, neither knowing quite what to say.

"I'd just need you for a few hours . . . and there's a little spending money in it for you if you're interested. You can dress as you like, and if you decide after starting that you'd rather not continue, that'd be perfectly okay."

Curtis perked up with the talk of remuneration. "Aunt Mary?"

"Okay by me." Mary put her hand on her nephew's shoulder. "You might just find yourself hanging in a museum one day!"

Curtis came downstairs the next morning dressed in a white cotton sweater, rolled at the cuffs, over a white collared shirt, all of which he'd tucked neatly into a loose-fitting pair of brown corduroy trousers supported by a plain leather belt. He'd pinned a star-shaped, brass badge, like a sheriff might have worn in the Old West, on his left pants pocket.

"Why the badge, Curtis?"

"My granddad gave it to me. He was a sheriff's deputy out in Iowa in the old days," he explained. "Aunt Mary thought it might tear my sweater, so I wore it on my pants. You said I could wear whatever—"

"Sure. No problem," Henry said. "I'm glad you wore it."

Henry had already prepared his palette and set up his easel. He'd decided to sketch directly onto a canvas. He could work faster that way, unsure how much patience Curtis would bring to his modeling gig.

"Relax, Curtis . . . just stand naturally," Henry said, leaving it to the young man to find a comfortable position. "Look out toward that baseball painting against the wall over there . . . the big one with the hole in it." Henry had turned *Gastonia Renaissance* face-forward so as to reveal both its subject matter and its damaged state. He thought it would interest the boy, and that a discreetly edited description of what it had endured might engage him.

"What happened to it?" Curtis inquired almost immediately. The ensuing explanation succeeded in distracting him, easing his self-consciousness. As he listened, Curtis placed his left hand casually into his pocket, his right hand clutching at his belt. The pose was perfect, so Henry began to draw.

Curtis was a clean-cut young man with warm brown eyes, a chiseled nose, and a small but well-defined mouth. He had a full complement of thick, slightly tousled black hair. He projected the image of a bright but sensitive youth on the precipice of manhood.

The layered narratives underlying *Gastonia Renaissance* captivated Curtis for close to an hour, even though Henry had adroitly skirted the issue of the intruder's identity. They'd taken several breaks, during which they talked mostly about baseball—the relative strengths and weaknesses of Henry's Yankees and Curtis's Cincinnati Reds. Curtis's favorite player was southpaw Johnny Vander Meer, a fifteen-game winner in 1938 who'd shocked the baseball world by pitching consecutive no-hitters within a span of just four days in the middle of June. "No one will do that again," the young man confidently predicted. Henry concurred.

Curtis returned the next day, posing for another hour as Henry honed his picture. Mary wandered down with a plate of warm brownies, teasing her nephew about what she called his "Gary Cooper movie star good looks." When they'd all had enough—posing, painting, and brownies—Henry thanked them and urged Curtis to drop by before the end of his visit to check on the painting's progress.

Henry was pleased with the completed portrait. He felt it captured the boy's intelligence, confidence, and maturity, none of which eclipsed the vigor of his youth. He'd been so enchanted by Curtis's decision to display his grandfather's badge that he titled it *The Deputy's Grandson*. A few hours before escorting him to the train station, Mary and Edward stopped by with their nephew to view the painting.

"Remarkable," Edward said.

"I love it!" Mary chimed in.

Curtis said nothing, but the smile on his face said it all.

CHAPTER THIRTY-THREE

Breasts and Corn Flakes

H e knocked on Henry's door at *exactly* 2:45 P.M. on March 8, 1939. At almost sixty, Homer Saint-Gaudens was still a handsome man, his gray hair combed straight back, with a well-trimmed moustache and wire-rimmed glasses. A gold watch fob dangled from the vest pocket of his tailored three-piece suit. The son of the distinguished sculptor Augustus Saint-Gaudens, he'd spent his entire life steeped in the world of art and artists.

Henry's suit looked shabby by comparison. He hoped to make a better impression with his artwork.

Saint-Gaudens came well informed. He knew of Henry's training at Yale and his studies with Kuniyoshi. "I've just come from Yas's studio," he said. "When I told him where my next appointment was, he perked right up. He gushes about you, Henry ... and I greatly respect his judgment ... especially when it comes to young artists."

Saint-Gaudens focused immediately on *The Deputy's Grandson.* "I can see Kuniyoshi's influence," he said. Henry followed him as he advanced toward the large vertical canvas. "Tell me about this."

Henry described the inspiration behind the painting, the technical details, and the choices he'd made in organizing and executing the composition.

"Hmm ... Edward Laning's nephew! Small world," Saint-Gaudens said. "I remember sitting for a portrait myself ... back in 1890. The artist was none other than John Singer Sargent," he recalled, inserting his right thumb absentmindedly into his vest pocket. "I was sitting on a straight-backed chair in front of my mother, dressed in a black velvet Fauntleroy suit." He winced at the memory. "I was ten years old and the very last thing I wanted to do was to sit still. My constant squirming annoyed Sargent ... and Sargent annoyed me! I cringe each time I see that painting," he said, "and that's more often than I'd like—the blasted thing's in the Carnegie's collection!"

Henry worried that Saint-Gaudens' unhappy experience with his own portrait might have doomed *The Deputy's Grandson.* But, to the contrary, the director praised it. "This is so much more appealing to me than Sargent's portrait. The young man here has a presence ... a certain depth and maturity." Saint-Gaudens pivoted away from the easel. "Show me more."

Henry walked him through his studio. Saint-Gaudens took particular note of *The Pretzel Vendor* and *Wash Day,* then lingered for an extra few moments before *Night at the Savoy.* "I love the energy of this one, but I'm guessing it preceded the last several you've shown me. More Yale and less Yas, perhaps?"

"It *is* earlier," Henry confirmed, "before Yas."

Pressed for time, Saint-Gaudens quickly reviewed the rest of Henry's work, pausing in particular to scrutinize Alice's portrait, *Fear.* "Haunting, I'd say ... very emotional."

Then, as if a silent alarm had gone off, Saint-Gaudens snapped to attention. "I must be going," he said, thanking Henry and turning to leave. There were many more visits to make before works could be chosen for the International, he explained. "But make no mistake, Henry, I'm very taken by your work." He promised to be in touch soon.

In fact, it would be three months before Henry would hear back from Homer Saint-Gaudens. Much would transpire in the interim.

Fiona's sharp eye caught the article buried on page 25 of *The New York Times* on April 12, 1939.

"Look at this, Henry," she said as she sat at the breakfast table, clad in a diaphanous negligee, her breasts peeking playfully through the partially unbuttoned front. "WORLD'S FAIR PROVIDES BUILDING FOR CONTEMPORARY AMERICAN ART."

"So they finally came to their senses," Henry said, strolling in from Fiona's bedroom wearing nothing more than a smile. "How can you put on a World's Fair and stiff the American artists?"

"Interesting choice of words," Fiona said, smiling, as she lowered her gaze. "Uh . . . you should submit something, Henry."

"Don't move . . . I'll get my sketchpad. I'll do a portrait of you just as I see you right now . . . luscious breasts poking out over a tasty bowl of Corn Flakes," Henry teased. "No way *that* fails to make the cut." He walked to the table and gave her a mischievous peck on the cheek.

"Thanks, but no thanks . . . and will you *please* put something on?" Fiona returned to her cereal, lifting a spoonful to her mouth as she continued to peruse the newspaper. "Why don't you submit *Wash Day*?" she said, a trickle of milk dribbling down her chin. "I can picture it hanging at the Fair . . . it'd be like looking out my apartment window."

Henry did indeed submit *Wash Day*, though it took some effort to navigate the chaotic selection process. To mount a "democratically selected" national exhibition in just seven weeks, the organizers divided the country into six regions, each of which was subdivided into smaller geographic districts. In New York City, a jury of nine was appointed to review the avalanche of submissions. Its mandate was to select the best available works in categories designated as "modern," "conservative," or "middle-of-the road." Henry really didn't care how they made the sausages, so long as he got a fair shake. He hadn't a clue which category he represented . . . and he didn't care.

Once he'd made his submission, all he could do was wait. As he waited for word from Saint-Gaudens about the Carnegie International. And as he waited, his hopes rapidly fading, to hear from Alice again.

CHAPTER THIRTY-FOUR

Alice—Back from the Rabbit Hole

He'd barely heard the faint knocking on his door. Henry put aside his palette and brushes. He slid the heavy bolts on the pair of latches he'd mounted on the replacement door that his landlord had grudgingly installed after Jake's break-in nine months earlier. He turned the knob.

Alice.

Henry stood there with his mouth open.

"Can I . . . come in?"

"Yes . . . yes, of course!"

Alice smiled demurely as she entered. She looked different. No less beautiful . . . but different. Her hair was shorter, for starters. Her eyes were free of mascara, her lips unadorned.

"Didn't think I'd ever see you again," Henry said. "I looked for you in Brooklyn, at your boarding—"

"I know. I was away. I've *been* away . . . for a while."

"Where?"

"Home . . . Iowa."

"Can I get you something? A cup of tea?"

"Sure, Henry, that'd be nice."

As Henry filled the kettle and fished out a couple of tea bags, Alice sat on the couch. The last time Henry remembered Alice on that couch she was naked, posing for the ill-fated painting called *The Goddess.* As the kettle heated, Henry pulled up a chair.

"How are you?" He asked the question with a hint of trepidation. She seemed subdued, but not sad.

"I'm good," she said somewhat tentatively. "I'm *better.*" When he'd last seen her she was terrified, falsely accused of infidelity by her physically abusive boyfriend. He'd captured her fear on canvas that day. In fact, he couldn't help but notice Alice wince when she spotted *Fear* across the studio, propped against a wall awaiting its return to Rehn's.

"The incident with Jake . . ." she began, her voice trailing off, "really scared me. It made me think . . ."

"About?"

"About what I'd done with my life since I came to New York. It wasn't what I'd hoped for . . . I didn't like what I'd become."

Henry excused himself as the kettle whistled and returned with two cups of steaming hot tea. "I didn't mean to interrupt. Please continue."

"I decided to go back home for the holidays . . . to the farm in Iowa." She turned suddenly wistful. "It was the same place I'd so desperately wanted to escape seven years ago." Her tea was too hot to drink. She put it down to cool. "But when January came along, I didn't want to leave." She twirled a strand of her hair. "Oh, not so much that I didn't want to leave the ice-cold, snow-covered prairie," she said, "I just didn't want to come back to New York."

Henry blew the steam off his tea as he lifted the cup to his lips. "So when *did* you get back?"

"Last week. My girlfriend in Brooklyn told me you'd come to find me, so here I am."

"But if you didn't want to come back, why—"

"Because all I was doing in Iowa was hiding." She sighed. "I needed to come back . . . face my failings . . . start over. I'm not a quitter, Henry. That's why I came back." She took her first sip of tea, then gently replaced the cup in her saucer. "Also, my lease runs out at the end of April and I needed to move my things."

"What'll you do now that you're back?"

"Got a job as a waitress at a diner on First Avenue at 12th Street. I start next week . . . not too far from here, actually."

"Where will you live?"

"Found a little place in the East Village . . . 6th between B and C," she said. "I move in at the end of April." Alice swirled her tea bag in her cup while she glanced through the studio. "I see you've been busy."

"Gotta make ends meet." Henry hesitated before shifting to a more troublesome topic. "What about Jake?"

"There is no Jake," she said firmly. "Jake was a huge mistake . . . it just took me a little too long to realize it," she said. "I was taken by the glamour of it . . . you know . . . running around with a ballplayer and all that. But it wasn't worth it."

Henry wondered whether he should tell her about Jake's July rampage. She seemed to have moved past him, so he decided not to mention it—at least for now. But he still had one more question.

"Will you pose for me again?"

"Of course! That's why I'm here, isn't it?"

Henry was elated. They made arrangements for the following Monday, May 1st, in the late afternoon, after she got off from work.

Henry blurted it out over dinner at Carlito's.

"Alice Woodley came by a couple of days ago," he told Fiona. She dropped her fork. It clanged off the edge of her bowl and tumbled to the floor along with the forkful of *spaghetti carbonara* that had been otherwise destined for her open mouth.

Henry gave her a sheepish look. *Hey, it's not my fault*, he wanted to say, but that wouldn't be entirely accurate. Now, having let the cat out of the bag—*he had to tell her, didn't he?*— he quickly piled on. "She's been in Iowa since the holidays . . . just came back to New York. Says she's done with Jake . . . and agreed to resume posing for me." Henry braced for Fiona's reaction.

"Okay," Fiona said, making no effort to retrieve her errant fork. She looked him in the eye while gathering her thoughts. "I'm obviously not thrilled," she conceded, "but it's something I'll have to deal with. You're an artist . . . she's *salable*, as you keep telling me . . . so I just need to be a big girl about it."

"Thanks, Fiona," Henry said, hugely relieved. It could have been worse. But not having to defend himself made him feel even guiltier. "Now let's get you another fork."

CHAPTER THIRTY-FIVE

The Last Days of an Heirloom Vase

The grogginess lifted haltingly, like a slowly evaporating fog. It was nighttime—that much he could see—but he recalled little of the daytime preceding it. He remembered going 0 for 5 against the Senators that late April afternoon, his batting average plunging accordingly. Then there was the post-game rendezvous with his three best friends, Jack Daniels, Jim Beam, and Johnny Walker . . . after which the trail went cold.

Jake lifted himself off the floor, scrutinizing his surroundings as he shook away the cobwebs. The room was familiar, but something was awry. The sofa and chairs were gone; so was the dining room set. Boxes were everywhere, some neatly piled in stacks, others upended, their contents strewn across the bare floor. *Alice's place* . . . but no Alice.

He struggled to maintain his balance as he forced himself upright. His dizziness gave way to an infernal pounding at the rear of his skull. His hand rose to the source: a throbbing bulge the size of a golf ball on the back of his head. Sticky, partly coagulated blood coated his fingertips. Jagged ceramic shards covered the floor—the remnants, he surmised, of that stupid Kraut vase that Alice so foolishly cherished.

Jake had longed to see her from the moment he'd returned

to New York ten days earlier for the start of the '39 baseball season. He'd obsessed about her day and night. He was haunted by the memory of the last time he'd seen her . . . in that painting in the artist's studio. She'd glared at him . . . with that searing look of fright in her eyes. That terrified countenance was etched indelibly into his alcohol-addled brain.

He'd hoped to win her back . . . persuade her to give him one last chance. But if not, then *shit,* at least he would touch her soft, warm skin and make her smile—just one last time.

Jake's blackouts had become like jigsaw puzzles: the evidence was in pieces before him, but the task of putting them together was daunting. But judging from the chaos before him and the bump on his head, the inference this time was as plain as a 6-4-3 double play. Jake had failed in his quest to reclaim his fair Alice. Failed miserably.

Alice looked at Henry self-consciously as she stood at his door. The reason was evident: a shiner the size of a baseball encircling her eye like a hungry vulture. "Don't even ask," she said as she strode past him and into the studio. She was still in her waitressing uniform, a short-sleeved, blue-and-white-checkered dress with oversized starched white lapels, white cuffs, and a crisp, white apron. "I wasn't gonna come," she said, "but that wouldn't've been fair to you. You can still paint me anyway, right?"

Henry felt a sense of déjà vu. His emotions ran the gamut: sympathy, frustration, anger, annoyance, pity, disgust. "Uh . . . sure," he said in response to her question.

Alice began to unbutton her dress. "What'll it be?" she snapped. "Clothed? Naked? What?"

"Whoa, Alice . . . wait a minute!" Henry gently grasped her arm. "First tell me what happened."

"What do you *think* happened?"

"Jake?"

"No, the Pope."

"How?"

Alice sat down on the sofa. "Came to my old apartment Saturday night as I was finishing packing. Drunk ... as usual. Said he loved me ... couldn't live without me ... *bullshit, bullshit, bullshit!*"

"Easy," Henry said. "Let me get you a drink. Bourbon okay?"

"Uh ... yeah, okay. Sure."

Henry poured a shot of the amber liquid into each of two glasses and gave her one. She took a healthy swig.

"I said I was through and asked him to leave. Dope started to cry! Can you believe that shit? He actually started to bawl like a two-year-old." She took another gulp and put down the glass on the coffee table. "Told him again to get out. So he says to me 'I wanna hold you ... just one last time.'" Her eyes telegraphed her anger. "So he lunges at me ... and I slap him on the cheek with all my might! Reacts like an animal ... throws a right cross ... *smacks me right in the eye!* Like I was that first baseman on the Senators that he hates so damn much!"

Alice finished the bourbon and motioned for more. Henry refilled her glass.

"So he staggers forward. I pick up the vase I'd been wrapping ... family heirloom ... from Germany, I think ... and I *whack* him on the back of the head with it." She exhaled deeply. "Hits the deck like he'd been beaned by a Dizzy Dean fastball."

Henry no longer felt pity. Instead, he found Alice's gumption intoxicating. "Then what?"

"Then I just ran the heck out of there to my girlfriend's

place, leaving Jake on the floor, bleeding . . . didn't care if he was dead or alive." She finished her second bourbon before Henry had taken a sip of his first. "That's it!" she said triumphantly.

Henry smiled. "Jesus, Alice. I didn't know you had it in you. I'm impressed!"

"At least I know he got the worst of it," she said. A broad smile filtered across her face.

"Okay," Henry said. "So now I know exactly how I'd like you to pose for me today." He put down his drink, got up, and walked to the closet near the front door. He fished out the baseball bat he'd bought to defend himself in the event Jake Powell reappeared one day on his doorstep. He slid a low-backed chair to a spot near his easel, the chair back facing him. "I want you to sit—dressed as you are—straddling the back of the chair, leaning forward, looking straight at me." Alice did as he asked. "Hold the bat vertically on your right, with your right hand clutching the knob, pressing the barrel to the floor." Again, she complied. "And then I want you to think about what you'll do with that bat if that bastard Jake Powell ever drags his sorry ass into your life again! . . . I want you *defiant as hell!* Can you do that?"

"Hell, yeah!" she shrieked with a murderous grin.

CHAPTER THIRTY-SIX

Amazon Warrior Women and Reindeer Steak: A Day at the Fair

It was late May when Henry got word of *Wash Day's* inclusion in the hastily assembled World's Fair exhibition *American Art Today.* The letter of acceptance included an invitation to the opening, at four o'clock on Thursday afternoon, June first.

"Come with me to the opening," Henry said. Fiona was busy arranging a dinner of lamb chops and baked potatoes in Henry's ill-equipped kitchenette. By volunteering to make dinner, she was preempting another lame attempt by Henry to prepare them an edible meal. "Maybe you can persuade Edward to give you the whole day off to spend at the Fair."

"Sounds swell to me," she said as she drew the potatoes from the oven.

While they waited for the chops to roast, Henry offered to unveil his latest painting. Fiona knew that the subject was Alice, and he'd already told her of Alice's brawl with Jake. She'd been disappointed, but hardly surprised. She'd not heard a single word from her cousin since he'd nearly strangled her almost a year ago. Fiona seemed content with that and appeared to have put the episode largely behind her. And while she remained no fan of Alice, she was nevertheless curious to see Henry's most recent work.

Henry had laid the canvas against the back wall of the studio. Fiona followed him as he retrieved it, flipped it over, and placed it on his easel. "I call it *Jake's Ex (Defiance)*."

"Holy moly!" Her reaction was involuntary. She studied Alice's mutinous expression, the "don't tread on me" look in her sizzling blue eyes. Her body language bespoke confidence, courage, and determination. "Jake did *that?*" she asked, pointing to the prominent black eye that Alice displayed like a war medal.

"Afraid so," Henry said, "but I can assure you that Jake got the worst of it." Fiona allowed herself a half-smile as she scrutinized the canvas.

"I know I've been uncompromising about Alice," she said. Henry wondered where this was heading. "But she certainly brings out something in your art that's . . . well . . . *remarkable*." She looked at him sympathetically. "It's as if she's a conduit for whatever emotion you want her to convey. It's raw . . . it's powerful . . . and yes, Henry, it's very good."

Henry's eyes lit up. He'd given up hope that Fiona would ever modulate her resistance to Alice. "I can't tell you how pleased I am to hear you say that," he said.

At Mary's insistence, Edward granted Fiona the day off she'd requested. It was, of course, without pay—strictly in accordance with WPA regulations. So on the morning of the appointed day, Henry and Fiona caught the special express train from Times Square to the World's Fair. An overpass led them from the spanking new subway station to the ticket kiosks where lines formed in advance of the Fair's opening. Henry plopped down a buck-fifty for two admissions.

"My treat," Henry said, segueing into his best Jimmy Cagney

impersonation. "Whole day's on me, dollface."

"That's sweet, Henry," Fiona replied before channeling Bette Davis. "I'd love to kiss ya, but I just washed my hair."

"What?"

"Never mind, Henry. Let's just go in."

The entrance led into the Amusement Zone. To their left loomed the world's largest cash register, a bright red, Gulliver-sized replica that sat atop the pavilion of the National Cash Register Company. The day's attendance figures flashed across its outsized screen. Turning left, they strolled along the Great White Way, past the Living Magazine Covers, where half-naked models posed for "art-conscious visitors" for a twenty-five cent fee.

"Gee, Henry, that's less than you pay Alice! Should've brought your sketchpad and set up shop for the day."

"And miss *that*?" he said, pointing to the Savoy Ballroom exhibit just ahead, where couples jitterbugged to a live jazz band on a balcony beneath a banner that billed them as "the World's Greatest Colored Dancers." In the bright sunshine, Henry squinted at the latest couple to take to the narrow dance floor. "I'll be damned if that isn't Frankie Manning and Frieda Washington!"

"It'll cost fifty cents to find out for sure," Fiona advised, studying the comprehensive Fair guide she'd extracted from *The New York Times*, "money that could be as easily spent at the Amazon Warriors booth right over there." Fiona read the description aloud: "Girl athletes stage gladiatorial combat in helmets and shields—"

"*Only* helmets and shields?"

"For those hussies, the helmets would seem superfluous, don't ya think?"

Passing the gruesome display of Nature's Mistakes (a two-headed cow?) and the Sun Valley ski slope ("real skiing, real skating, on real ice"), they reached the Parachute Jump. "To the top of a twenty-five story tower . . . and then down to earth in a foolproof parachute equipped with shock-absorbers," Fiona recited.

"Fifty feet up on a scaffold in the Custom House scared the bejesus out of me," Henry reminded her. "There's no damn way I'm gonna strap myself into that."

"Oh, *puh. . . leeze*, Henry!" Fiona teased. "It's *foolproof* . . . it says so right here!" Henry grabbed Fiona's hand and dragged her past the parachute jump as quickly as possible. But no sooner had they cleared one death trap than they came to another.

"Come on, Henry. We've *gotta* do the roller coaster!" Fiona squealed, obtaining more pleasure from teasing Henry than she could have possibly garnered from the ride. "It's the Giant *Safety* Rollercoaster, Henry," she laughed. "Safety is its middle name!"

"Jesus, Fiona, really?" Henry trembled at the prospect of mounting the wooden, three-thousand-foot express train to oblivion.

"Bigger, faster, steeper, more thrilling—"

"Okay, already!" Henry relented, regretting it immediately. He studied Fiona as they waited in line. The anticipatory smile on Fiona's face was genuine. Perhaps it was his sense of impending doom that, at that strangely uncomfortable moment, served only to intensify his admiration for her. He loved her spunk, her intelligence and wit, her grace. No, she wasn't the goddess that men saw in Alice, but there was plenty to like about her engaging smile, soft brown eyes, and her long, lean looks which were stunningly enhanced by the blue-and-white flowered mid-length dress she wore to great effect on that pleasant June morning.

Henry laid down fifty cents for the privilege of enduring several harrowing minutes of utter torture. "Geez, Fiona, the sign says it reaches speeds of seventy miles-an-hour!"

"No, Henry, that's wrong," she said with a smirk. "According to *The Times* . . . it's eighty."

When their car settled before them, they climbed aboard, Fiona enthusiastically, Henry as if confronting an execution squad. They strapped themselves in and waited. In a few moments, they felt a jerk, then a gradual build-up of speed. The car began to rise . . . faster and faster. Then, dramatically and without warning, it plunged, along with Henry's innards. They shrieked involuntarily as the process repeated itself, only now with the addition of terrifying twists and hairpin turns. While Henry sweated bullets, Fiona savored the ride. When they reached the summit, Fiona marveled at her bird's-eye view of the Fair—and the city beyond—while Henry looked only at his knees, as if to will away the reality of his precarious perch. The car paused a moment, then began a death-defying descent that elicited yelps of exhilaration from Fiona and expletives from Henry.

When the ordeal was over, Fiona looked to her seatmate. "Are you okay?" Henry didn't respond. His face was ashen, his lips purple and gnarled in panic. As she stepped from the car, she leaned over to help him to his feet. Henry stepped forward gingerly, like a drunk after an all-night bender, weaving as he tried to negotiate the platform and short stairway that would return him to *terra firma.* Fiona grabbed his arm, guiding him like a blind man. Suddenly, Henry bolted to the side of the path, leaned over a railing, and deposited his breakfast on a patch of grass that would forever bear the scars of his moment of ignominy.

He turned back a few moments later. Fiona had all she could

do to keep a straight face. Henry looked at her soberly. "Let's do it again," he muttered wearily as Fiona convulsed with laughter.

When they'd had their fill of the Fair's frolics, Fiona and Henry left the Amusement Zone, strolling down the Avenue of Pioneers toward the thematic and symbolic center of the Fair, the Perisphere and Trylon. "Looks like a massive golf ball lying beside the swollen shaft of a broken putter," Henry said.

"Or a javelin thrown by one of those Amazon Warrior women alongside an egg laid by one of Nature's Freaks," Fiona countered.

A slender, three-sided spire the height of two football fields, the Trylon was a symbol of man's aspirations. From its base, they mounted the world's longest escalator to the world's largest sphere. Inside the Perisphere, a moving sidewalk transported them over a dioramic representation of a city of the future. They finally exited the massive freak egg via the Helicline, a 950-foot spiral ramp that wrapped around the Perisphere's shell like a cobra.

It was two o'clock when they'd finished their march down the Helicline, marveled at Paul Manship's massive sculptural sundial just beyond, and grabbed a bite to eat. Fiona consumed her customary salad, while Henry inhaled two corndogs and a Coke.

"You're crazy, Henry," Fiona said, unimpressed by his flagging nutritional IQ.

"No, I'm hungry," Henry insisted, reminding her that he'd already surrendered his breakfast.

They ambled down Constitution Mall with its monumental statue of George Washington by James Earle Fraser (the Fair also marked the 150th anniversary of Washington's inauguration) and the modernistic rendering of The Four Freedoms by sculptor Leo Friedlander.

"So what are the four freedoms again?" Fiona asked.

"Speech, press, religion, and the right to eat corndogs without criticism from your girlfriend," Henry said.

They followed Constitution Mall until they reached the Lagoon of Nations in the heart of the Government Zone, where sixty countries had mounted exhibits. Pools, lakes, and fountains were ubiquitous, and well-manicured flowerbeds lined every walkway.

Returning to the Theme Center, they evaded a swarm of buzzing schoolchildren on a field trip with a flock of chaperones rounding up stragglers like cowpokes. They ducked briefly into the RCA pavilion, mesmerized by its display of live television. "This will change the world," Henry predicted. "Can you imagine watching a baseball game from your living room?" In fact, the first such broadcast was only months away.

A striking mural by Philip Guston adorned the exterior of the WPA pavilion. Entitled *Maintaining America's Skills*, it featured four stylized figures—an engineer, a scientist, a surveyor, and a laborer—boldly rendered in primary colors. "The scientist—the most intelligent one—is a woman," Fiona observed. Inside, a Seymour Fogel mural depicted a family's transition from unemployment and starvation to work and self-sufficiency, a transformation presumably achieved through participation in the programs of the WPA. "You won't find a Republican within a block of this pavilion," Henry said.

It was almost four o'clock, time for the opening of the contemporary arts exhibition. The couple hustled toward Bowling Green, past the Gas Industries building. "Let's skip it," Henry said, "got enough gas from the corndogs."

The dedication ceremonies took place in the Main Hall of the Contemporary Arts Building. A. Conger Goodyear, president of the decade-old Museum of Modern Art, served as emcee, introducing speakers including Holger Cahill, National Director of the Federal Art Project and principal organizer of the exhibition; Gertrude Vanderbilt Whitney, founder of the Whitney Museum; and New York City Mayor Fiorello LaGuardia.

Henry and Fiona grew antsy as the speakers droned on. Fair Corporation President Grover A. Whalen hailed the show as "a demonstration of what a great democratic institution art is becoming."

"Blah, blah, blah," Henry whispered.

"Jabber, jabber, jabber," Fiona replied.

But then came the speech that delivered them from boredom. Moments after Mayor LaGuardia waddled up to the microphone—which had to be lowered at least six inches to accommodate all five-feet-two of the stocky ball of energy—he launched into a colorful tirade against modern art, condemning the twisted and abstracted human forms that appeared with increasing frequency in contemporary compositions. "I don't know where those fellows get their models," he moaned. "No one I know looks even *remotely* like that!" He blathered on. "I don't see why it's necessary to make those faces all contorted and out of proportion." The Mayor likened the chasm between traditional and modern art to the contrast between music and noise. "I don't like noise," he declared. "If I want noise I can go under the Third Avenue El." Most of the artists in the audience snickered—even those like Henry whose work remained rooted in more traditional realism. Everyone found the Mayor's diatribe amusing, although it was hardly conceived as a comedy act.

"Thank you, Mayor LaGuardia," Goodyear said, grabbing the microphone before the man they called "the Little Flower" could dig himself a deeper hole. "Next time, Mr. Mayor, perhaps you'll let us know how you *really* feel about modern art."

At the conclusion of the LaGuardia jeremiad, much of the crowd (the Mayor excepted) filtered into the twenty-three galleries that displayed over twelve hundred works of art. Henry and Fiona perused works by Thomas Hart Benton, Isabel Bishop, Stuart Davis, Philip Evergood, Edward Hopper, Yasuo Kuniyoshi, and Reginald Marsh, as well as hundreds of others entirely unknown to them.

"There it is!" Fiona said excitedly when she spotted *Wash Day* in Gallery No. 14.

"A masterpiece!" Henry declared.

"The cat's meow!" Fiona confirmed.

Henry was pleased to see his painting prominently displayed in the center of the room. It was hard for any painting—however meritorious—to stand out in a sea of artwork spread among 40,000 dizzying square feet of gallery space.

After trudging through all twenty-three galleries, Fiona and Henry were spent. A journalist had likened the experience to a journey through a Tunnel of Love "with no escape until the bitter end." To Henry, it was like passing through the gastrointestinal tract of King Kong.

At Fiona's suggestion, they stopped for dinner at a restaurant in the Finnish pavilion. It was a random choice, possibly Fiona's way to keep Henry from sabotaging their evening with yet another nutritional indiscretion. Henry hemmed-and-hawed his way to a plate of reindeer steak, the only thing on the menu he could pronounce. Fiona was more adventurous, electing to try the *harillihakaariloita* (rolled beef with vegetables).

"It's unpronounceable . . . how can you eat it?" Henry asked her.

"I'll not only eat it," Fiona said, "but I'll *Finnish* it."

"It's time to go home," Henry said, laughing.

It was nine o'clock when they headed for the exit, a dozen hours after they'd arrived. The Fair at night was yet another revelation. Dancing lights frolicked with dancing waters in the fountains and lakes while fireworks lit the sky.

Henry and Fiona fell asleep on the train to Times Square, jolted to consciousness by the good graces of another Fair attendee who could well relate to their exhaustion. They emerged like zombies from the underground at the Union Square subway station, staggered to Henry's apartment, and fell asleep beside each other, fully clothed, on Henry's bed.

CHAPTER THIRTY-SEVEN

Sauerbraten and Lederhosen

For weeks, Henry had scoured his mailbox for word from the Carnegie. In late June, the letter arrived.

"I was greatly impressed with your work when I visited your studio earlier this spring," it began. "Accordingly," Homer Saint-Gaudens wrote, "I'm hoping that you'll grant us the privilege of including *The Deputy's Grandson* in this year's Carnegie International beginning on October 19th." Henry reread that second sentence over and over, savoring it like a delicate crème brûlée, before telephoning his parents, Fiona, and Peyton, with the news.

"You've arrived, Henry," Peyton said. And he had. Few, if any, exhibition venues were more selective than the Carnegie International, particularly for American artists. His co-exhibitors would rank among the finest artists in the world. "And," Peyton added, "we're gonna celebrate, old pal . . . big time!" Peyton went on to announce *first*, that he'd fallen "head over goddamn heels" in love with Lucille, a "perty young thang" whom he'd met at the Art Students League; *second*, that he was "rollin' in the dough," having just cashed a "fat fuckin' check" from his trust fund; and *finally*, that he, Peyton Jackson Small, IV, was taking Henry, Fiona, and Lucille to dinner Saturday night at Lüchow's to celebrate Henry's achievement, "all goddam expenses paid by my motherfuckin' trust fund."

Fiona met Henry at his apartment on Saturday evening. "You're a knockout!" he said when she appeared at his door in a long, form-fitting, burgundy red dress in ribbed crepe with an embroidered white collar and gray pumps.

"And you look like the Good Humor man," Fiona said, laughing. Henry wore a blue and white pinstriped seersucker suit with matching vest and a regimental stripe tie. "But you know how much I adore ice cream, don't you Henry?"

The night was warm and pleasant, with a refreshing breeze that tousled Henry's hair. Crossing Union Square, they passed the pretzel vendor whom Henry had immortalized; dog walkers yielding to periodic yanks and jerks from the leashes of their prancing four-legged companions; and a young busker strumming his guitar above an open guitar case primed with his own dollar bill. Grinning young couples strolled arm-in-arm in contemplation of the evening to come, she anticipating a luscious meal or the pleasure of watching the debonair Cary Grant romancing Katharine Hepburn in *Bringing Up Baby*, he plotting more amorous nocturnal activities. Their destination was Lüchow's, the world-famous German restaurant at East Fourteenth Street and Irving Place, a New York institution for half a century.

Fiona and Henry were the first to arrive. The maître d', dressed like a Tyrolean peasant, escorted them through the dark, wood-paneled dining room to a four-seater covered with a starched, white tablecloth. Beer steins lined the walls like targets in a shooting gallery. Music from a string quartet wafted languorously through the huge room, mingling harmoniously with the sweet-and-sour aroma of traditional

German cooking. A waiter, clad implausibly in knee-length lederhosen supported by leather suspenders over an embroidered white shirt, flashed an obsequious smile while filling their glasses with water.

Within minutes, Henry noticed Peyton entering the room. Like a skyscraper, he towered over everyone and everything. Trailing behind him was a tiny waif-like creature, a veritable Tinker Bell beside her elongated escort.

"How y'all doin'?" Peyton crowed as he approached the table. Dressed in a tuxedo, he'd be mistaken for the maître d' in any other restaurant. "Hey ... I want you to meet my girl," he said, motioning toward his pixie partner. "This is Lucille Baker." Henry and Fiona rose to greet her. Lucille was barely five feet tall, at least a foot and a half shorter than Peyton. Her hair was as red as a sugar maple in autumn.

"Pleased to meet you both," she said in a confident, unaccented voice. "I know how we must look together," she added, laughing.

"So ... how'd you guys meet?" Fiona asked after they'd all settled into their seats.

"In William Zorach's class at the League," Lucille said. She described herself as a recent transplant from Michigan, an art major who'd recently graduated from the university in Ann Arbor.

"We're both knee-deep into abstraction now," Peyton said, "so it'll be a decade before we're as famous as you, Henry."

"By the way," Lucille said, "congrats on getting into the Carnegie. That's pretty heady stuff ..."

"Thanks," Henry acknowledged, "though I'd probably make a better living selling caricatures in Union Square."

"Patience," Fiona counseled. "It'll come."

"So ... why the tux?" Henry asked his taller counterpart.

"Shit, Henry, we're here to celebrate your ascension into the pantheon of American artists," he said. "Besides, my lederhosen were at the cleaners."

Henry scanned the large, modestly populated room. "This place is legendary," Henry said. "Thought it'd be jammed on a Saturday night."

"Hitler's fault," Peyton said. "Nazi barbarianism isn't so much in vogue among the New York intelligentsia."

Henry leaned forward, whispering across the table. "They do serve Jews, don't they?" He was only half joking.

"Shit, yeah," Peyton said. "It's still America." He then leaned in conspiratorially. "Not Commies, though." Everyone laughed.

Instead of cocktails, they began the evening with a round of Würzburgers, the imported Bavarian beer for which Lüchow's was famous.

"I'm gonna have the Koenigsberger klops with caper sauce," Peyton said to the hovering waiter.

"What the—" Henry muttered.

"Meatballs," Peyton said, "nothing more . . . nothing less."

The ladies both ordered sauerbraten with potato dumplings. Henry, the most unadventurous gastronome among them, was paralyzed by the range of unfamiliar offerings.

"Try the pig's knuckles," Peyton teased.

Fiona came to his rescue. "Try the venison, Henry. . . it's like the reindeer steak you ate at the Fair."

"Except that it's actually roadkill from New Jersey," Peyton said.

Lucille poked him hard in the ribs. "Give him a break, honey."

Despite the ribbing, the couples enjoyed a pleasant evening peppered by good-natured banter as well as serious conversation. Henry and Fiona shared their misadventures at the World's Fair while Peyton and Lucille revealed the latest gossip from the Art Students League. Prompted by their Teutonic surroundings, they engaged also in more somber discussions about the excesses of Nazism, the plight of European Jews, the paradoxes of Communism, and the future of art.

On a lark, they chose to share an unpronounceable dessert. It was a pancake the size of a manhole cover, filled with jam, rolled up, drizzled with rum and liqueurs, and set ablaze at the table. "Looks like a Nazi book burning," Henry said as the waiter ignited the delicacy.

As they were finishing, Fiona reached into her purse for an envelope. She withdrew two tickets, handing one to each of the gentlemen at the table. "This is my celebratory gift to you, Henry . . . and our thanks to you, Peyton, for such a pleasant and generous evening." The tickets were third row box seats at Yankee Stadium for the July 4th doubleheader against the Washington Senators. More importantly, it was Lou Gehrig Day, the farewell tribute to the star athlete who'd been cruelly felled by a mysterious, debilitating disease.

"This is amazing, Fiona. I'm speechless," Henry said as he reached over and kissed her.

Peyton was equally floored. "These are incredible seats," he said. "But how—"

"Connections," she said . . . and left it at that.

Henry avoided the question until they'd already made love later that evening. It was a question that she'd certainly known was coming.

"You didn't . . . I mean, you couldn't have . . ."

"Of course I did . . . sooner or later I had to."

"But . . . how?"

"I wrote him a note the day you called me about the Carnegie," she said, brushing a lock of hair from her eyes. "I took it to his hotel . . . and left it with the front desk to deliver."

"What did you say in the note?"

"Told him I wanted two tickets to the games that day . . . and that he owed me that much."

"That's all you said?"

"Yup, pretty much."

"And?"

"And a couple days later a clubhouse boy comes to my apartment with an envelope. Inside are the two tickets and a little note." Fiona arose from Henry's bed. Henry never tired of observing her lithe body, especially unclothed. She switched on a reading lamp, dug into her purse, and returned to bed with a folded scrap of paper.

"I knew you'd ask," she said before unfolding it and beginning to read.

> Dear Fiona
> Here's the ducats you asked for. Least I can do. Glad to hear from you. Afraid I hurt you, but can't remember that night. Really hope you're okay, cuz. I'm REALLY, REALLY sorry.
> Your cousin, Jake

"Well, it's hardly eloquent," Henry said, "but it's pretty much what we suspected. Drunk out of his gourd that night." Henry stroked her cheek. "But why? Wasn't it tempting the fates . . . contacting him at all?"

"If I thought so, I wouldn't have done it." She rolled from her side onto her back. "He's still family . . . and sober, he's not as bad as you think."

"You didn't need to do that for me," he said.

"I didn't do it for you, Henry . . . I did it for *me*."

CHAPTER THIRTY-EIGHT

The Luckiest Man on the Face of the Earth

A heady buzz of anticipation permeated the cavernous ballpark on that historic July afternoon. It was Independence Day—and the day New York would bid farewell to its beloved hometown hero, Lou Gehrig, the man they revered as "The Iron Horse." The crowd of nearly 62,000 was caught up in the waning moments of the first game of the holiday doubleheader against the Senators, a game the home team threatened to salvage with a rousing ninth inning rally. With two away and the leaden-legged Bill Dickey on first base representing the tying run, manager Joe McCarthy inserted a pinch runner—the nefarious Jake Powell.

"Will Powell slug the first baseman, spike the second baseman, or call the umpire a nigger?" Peyton asked. Henry failed to respond. His stomach churned as he imagined a crazed Jake Powell peering into the seats, picking him out of the crowd, leaping into the stands, and pummeling him to a bloody pulp before a horde of horrified witnesses.

"Henry?"

"Uh... sorry, I was... um... distracted," Henry said, snapping back to reality.

In the end, McCarthy's maneuver made no difference, as knuckleballer Dutch Leonard retired Charlie "King Kong" Keller on a weak tapper to third, sealing the rare Senator victory.

"Lucille's a real doll," Henry said during the lull as the groundskeepers readied the field for the between-games ceremony. "Smart, cute . . . and remarkably tolerant of your countless quirks and inadequacies."

"She's a peach, Henry. Just wish she were a half-foot taller," he said with a grin. "Walkin' around, I tend to lose track of her." Peyton took a gulp of the beer he'd been nursing since the seventh inning. "And in bed . . . well . . . I'm afraid someday I'll crush her."

"Yeah . . . that'd be a tough one to explain to the authorities."

"You and Fiona . . . you seem to be goin' strong," Peyton said, flipping kernels of popcorn into his mouth with abandon.

"So it would seem," Henry said. "I think we're in love . . . but neither of us seems willing to admit it."

"I see," Peyton said, though it's doubtful he understood it any more than Henry did. So he changed the subject. "Powell's moll still posin' for you?" he asked.

"Haven't seen her since May," Henry said. He'd already told Peyton about Jake's assault on his muse and the powerful painting he'd done in the aftermath.

"Why not?"

"To avoid irritating Fiona," Henry said. He hijacked a fistful of popcorn from Peyton's stash. "But I'm dying to paint her again."

"Shit, Henry," Peyton said, washing down the last of his popcorn with the rest of his beer, "who wouldn't be?" Peyton scratched at the stubble on his chin. "I honestly don't see how you keep yourself in check with a dame like that spread-eagled across your studio couch." Although he hadn't actually met her, Peyton had ogled Henry's paintings of Alice in his studio. "That one you did of her in the nude?" he said, shaking his head. "Thought I'd cream my pants."

Henry shot his friend a dismissive look. "Strictly platonic," he insisted. "And just to be clear," he added, "she doesn't pose spread-eagled on my couch."

"Hmm," Peyton sniffed. "So Powell got *that* worked up about somethin' he merely *imagined* between you and Alice?"

"Is that so hard to believe? He's a lunatic . . . a jealous drunk with a wild imagination and a habit of acting before thinking."

"So how do you know this . . . uh . . . *lunatic* won't come back again to bash your brains out?"

"He's the one who got us these tickets, Peyton. Fiona's convinced he's repentant," Henry said, "and Alice insists she's done with him. Crowned him with a ceramic vase to prove it."

Peyton rolled his eyes. "Still think she's potential trouble . . . one way or another."

"You sound just like Fiona!" Henry chirped, his eyebrows rising.

A murmur arose from the crowd. From a gate near the corner of the Yankee dugout, a parade of former athletes filed onto the field. They were a motley crew—balding, graying, dressed awkwardly in ill-fitting suits and ties, all proud members of the greatest Yankee team of all time, the 1927 juggernaut better known as "Murderers Row." Among them were "Deacon" Everett Scott (whose then record 1,307 consecutive games-played streak was eviscerated by Gehrig), Wally Pipp (who'd be forever remembered as the poor sap whom Gehrig replaced at first base, a position he steadfastly retained for the next 2,130 consecutive games), the great Tony Lazzeri, and the legend himself, Babe Ruth. The old ballplayers ambled to the centerfield flagpole, raising the coveted 1927 World Series banner, before reassembling on the infield grass with the current Yankees and Senators.

At last, to the deafening cheers of the crowd, the guest of honor emerged, his bowed head and halting gait betraying his unease. Friends, teammates, and former diamond adversaries showered him with a cavalcade of gifts. Famously shy, Gehrig stared at the ground through the tributes, pawing at the earth with his spikes.

Then The Little Flower, the indefatigable Mayor LaGuardia, shuffled forward to speak.

"Probably another savage attack on modern art," Henry predicted.

But the Mayor had come to praise Lou Gehrig, not to bury modern art. He heralded the weary slugger as the paragon of sportsmanship and citizenship. "Lou," he said, speaking as one native New Yorker to another, "we're proud of you."

As the tributes wound down, the emcee addressed the crowd. "Mr. Gehrig," he said, "has asked not to speak. Thank you very much for coming." But the throng would not have it. "We want Lou! We want Lou!" they chanted. Joe McCarthy offered his friend words of encouragement—and a gentle prod toward the microphone.

Gehrig stepped forward tentatively. "Fans," he said, his voice cracking, "for the past two weeks . . . you have been reading . . . about the bad break I got." His accent revealed his humble Manhattan roots. He raised his right hand to his eyes, his head bowed. "*Yet today . . . I consider myself . . . the luckiest man . . . on the face of the earth.*" Henry and Peyton looked at each other, tears trickling down their cheeks as Gehrig's simple, warmhearted pronouncement echoed through the cathedral of baseball.

Gehrig paused to gather himself. "I have been in ballparks for seventeen years and have never received anything but kindness and encouragement from you fans," he said. He then cast his eyes upon the weeping ballplayers surrounding him. "Look at these grand men," he said. "Which of you wouldn't consider it . . . the highlight of his career . . . just to associate with them . . . for even one day? *Sure, I'm lucky.*" He praised former Yankee owner Jacob Ruppert, who had passed away just six months earlier, and longtime Yankee general manager and team president Ed Barrow, whom he hailed as "the builder of baseball's greatest empire." He heaped accolades upon the managers under whom he'd served, "that wonderful little fellow, Miller Huggins . . . and that outstanding leader, that smart student of psychology, the best manager in baseball today, Joe McCarthy. *Sure, I'm lucky,*" he repeated.

Gehrig exhaled deeply. He surveyed the throng of admirers, brushing away his tears. In measured, heartfelt words, he praised and thanked his parents, wife, and mother-in-law; his former teammates and opponents; even the ushers and groundskeepers, for their unrelenting support and admiration. He paused again, waiting for the cheering to subside, preparing to launch one final sentence.

"So I close in saying . . . that I might have been given a bad break . . . but I've got an awful lot to live for."

Someone nudged the Babe toward the microphone. Never bashful and ever brash, the Bambino addressed his old friend, the old-timers, and the assembled multitudes in his familiar, gravelly voice. "It's good to see all my old friends here . . . the stalwarts of the '27 Yankees . . . the best damn team in history," he said, "better even than McCarthy's current crop . . . swell as they are," he declared to general applause and laughter. "And while Lazzeri here pointed out to me that there are only about thirteen or fourteen of us here, my answer is ... shucks, we only need nine to beat 'em!" The Babe then wrapped his arm playfully around the shoulder of the guest of honor, bringing a smile to Lou's face for the first time all afternoon.

There was, indeed, a second game to be played that day, albeit a mere formality. The fans had seen what they'd come for, and they'd share it with their children and grandchildren in the decades to come. As they filed out of the Stadium, Henry turned to his friend. "It's hard to imagine," he said, his voice still tinged with emotion, "a man more courageously facing a bleak destiny ... finding so much to live for ... despite the hand he's been dealt. I hope I'll remember that," he said, "when my own time comes."

CHAPTER THIRTY-NINE

The Burgundy Dress

On September 1, 1939, Germany invaded Poland. Within forty-eight hours, Britain and France, honoring their commitment to the defense of Poland, declared war on the Third Reich. The nightmare had finally begun.

In the preceding weeks, Henry had been enjoying his most sustained stretch of artistic and financial success. His participation in the World's Fair exhibit and his upcoming appearance at the Carnegie International validated his status as a notable "emerging" artist. More importantly, Frank Rehn had managed to sell both *7th Avenue Express* and *Night at the Savoy* while a "hold" had been placed on *Fear*, the third of his portraits of Alice. While parting with one's creations was bittersweet, Henry found solace in solvency.

Henry's curiosity about the buyers would remain unsatisfied. "Look at your contract," Rehn sniffed. "I'm not obliged to reveal the identity of my clients. I'm bound to respect their privacy." Henry suspected that the constraint was designed instead to prevent him from circumventing his dealer on future sales. Rehn did allow that *Night at the Savoy* had gone to "an important collector," and that the prospective purchaser of *Fear* was the person who'd acquired *Waiting*, the first painting of Alice. "Keep the Alice paintings coming," he implored the young artist while adding *Jake's Ex (Defiance)* to inventory.

With his dealer's advice as cover, Henry decided to reconnect with his muse. The lunch crowd had begun to disperse when he slid into a booth at Johnny D's, the East Village eatery where Alice waited tables. A yellowing newspaper clipping touting the diner's debut decades earlier hung crookedly from a nail on the wall.

Henry watched Alice swap friendly banter with her regulars. By the time he caught her eye, he'd studied the menu. "Club sandwich, pickles, side of fries," he said as she approached.

"Sissie's lunch," she said, grinning broadly. "What you *really* want is Johnny D's mac-and-cheese—a stick-to-your-ribs kind of lunch!" Her hair, tied in a loose ponytail, bobbed playfully as she spoke.

"Sounds swell. And while you're at it, there's an artist itching to do a portrait of Gotham's prettiest waitress ... whaddya say?"

"Sure, Picasso. Tomorrow afternoon ... around four?"

Henry's smile signified his approval.

Alice chuckled as she turned toward the kitchen. For all of her trials and tribulations, she seemed happy now, as if a weight had been lifted from her shoulders. As he watched her walk away, Henry couldn't deny the tinge of attraction he felt. But he caught himself quickly, banishing the thought from his mind.

It was four-thirty when Alice arrived at his studio. "Sorry, Henry. Took a little longer to straighten up today." She discarded her coat and hat, revealing the blue-and-white-checkered uniform she'd worn in *Jake's Ex (Defiance)*. It hadn't occurred to him to ask her to bring a change of clothes. "What's wrong?" she asked, sensing his disappointment.

"It's the uniform. I should have asked you to bring along something else." It dawned on him that Fiona kept clothes in the apartment—for those occasional mornings after. Henry hesitated. It made rational sense, but there was something not quite kosher about it.

"I can pose for you nude if you'd like," she said.

Henry was torn. To clothe Alice in something of Fiona's felt sacrilegious; at the same time, he was suddenly uneasy about painting her nude. His growing attraction to Alice was straining his self-control. In the past, his defenses had been formidable. But his perception of Alice had changed. She'd returned from her Midwestern pilgrimage softer, more open, more self-aware. He wavered for what seemed like an eternity, then blurted it out: "Fiona has some dresses in the closet."

"I'll take a look." Henry stole brief but longing glances as she shed her tacky waitress garb and slipped into the long, shimmering, body-hugging burgundy red dress that Fiona had worn on their night at Lüchow's. "Will this do?" she asked as she stepped toward the easel.

Henry was tongue-tied. "Uh . . . you look . . ."

"Thanks," she said, reading his expression if not his words. "Fits nicely, don't you think?"

Regaining his composure, Henry engaged her in small talk, seeking the bolt of inspiration he'd need to drive his next portrait. He asked if she'd found a new boyfriend. He meant it only as innocuous banter, he swore to himself.

"No," she said, untroubled by the inquiry. "I've had opportunities," she conceded, "but after Jake, I want to be more . . ." She paused as she sought the right word: "*discriminating.*" Alice lifted herself onto the stool beside Henry's easel. Henry could plainly see that Fiona's dress was a trifle tight, particularly in the bust. "I hope you won't mind my saying this," she said, "but when a guy asks me out, I find myself measuring him up against you." She fixed her eyes on his. "So far, no one's passed the test."

The ingenuousness of her remarks floored him, and the admiration that she professed for him was more than he could endure. As he stood there, mesmerized by her beauty, guilt-ridden for allowing himself to clothe her in Fiona's dress, he found himself drawn to Alice as never before. He thought about Peyton's admonitions—his near certainty, despite Henry's confident denials, that Alice would prove his undoing.

"I'm flattered," he said, summoning all the professionalism he could bring to bear. "We've channeled your emotions in our last pictures," he told her, urgently struggling to control his own. "We've done fear . . . we've done defiance. We've captured you looking off into space . . . waiting." He was finding his way back. "What do you *feel* today, Alice?"

"Gratitude, admiration." She said it without thinking . . . and with a reverence that was disarming. "You've been a rock for me, Henry." He felt himself blushing, ever so slightly; but her expression—the way she looked at him—revealed those emotions more passionately than her words.

"Don't move," he said. "Don't change your expression . . . it's perfect!"

And so he began to paint, fueled by the adoration in her eyes.

CHAPTER FORTY

International Incidents

KAPLER DEBUTS AT CARNEGIE INTERNATIONAL
Prodigious Year for Ex-Springfield Painting Prodigy

Special to the Springfield Union
by W. D. Danforth, Art Critic for the Springfield Union

PITTSBURGH, Penn., October 21, 1939. When last we checked in on him some nineteen months ago, Henry J. Kapler, Springfield's crackerjack contribution to the New York art scene, was collecting kudos for his impressive showing at the annual exhibition of the National Academy of Design. *Night at the Savoy*, his energetic depiction of a Negro couple jitterbugging in Harlem's legendary Savoy Ballroom, even garnered special praise from my esteemed colleague at *The New York Times*.

Well it seems that Mr. Kapler is not quite done making waves. On a lark, he put himself on display—quite literally—in the City of Brotherly Love this January, submitting his *Self Portrait at the Easel* to the annual exhibition of the Pennsylvania Academy of the Fine Arts, where it caught the discerning eye of Homer Saint-Gaudens, director of the Carnegie Institute, host of this country's premier international art exhibition. Saint-Gaudens was sufficiently impressed with the work of our hero to arrange a visit to his New York studio, which led to a coveted invitation to exhibit at this year's International, now on view here in Pittsburgh.

The International is a truly important event, one that draws art critics to the Steel City like bears to beehives. The guest list for the preview alone numbers five thousand. And this year's International is doubly significant, as the outbreak of war in Europe virtually guarantees a suspension of the annual until peace is restored.

Consider the numbers: of the 348 paintings accepted for display at this year's International, 243 are by European artists. Of the 105 American entries, only seventeen (including Mr. Kapler's) are from artists invited for the very first time. To display your work with the likes of Picasso, Matisse, Dix, Léger, Miró, Soutine, Chagall, Vuillard, Braque, Rouault, Kokoschka, Ernst, Klee, Kandinsky, and Nolde, along with Americans such as Hopper, Marsh, Soyer, Wood, Miller, Biddle, and Kuniyoshi, is a prodigious honor.

And it didn't take long to discover Mr. Kapler's brilliance, for there he was in the midst of the first American gallery, beside a canvas by John Marin, on a wall that also featured major works by Kenneth Hayes Miller and George Biddle. Springfield's favorite son of palette and brush acquitted himself admirably. His entry, *The Deputy's Grandson*, is a warm, sensitive portrait of a teenager, a poised, intelligent, and thoughtful young man rendered in yellows, browns, and blues—with a panel of purple polishing off the painting along its left margin. In the estimation of this reviewer, Kapler's place in such heady company is well deserved. The influence of Yasuo Kuniyoshi, the noted Japanese-American artist who taught Henry at the Art Students League and who has mentored him ever since (and who, incidentally, earned overall second prize honors at the exhibition), is apparent in those feathery passages that impart such depth of feeling to this work.

And while we sing Mr. Kapler's praises, let us not overlook yet another in his cascading catalogue of accomplishments, the inclusion of his painting *Wash Day* in *American Art Today*, the show of contemporary American work currently on display at the World's Fair in New York. While a seemingly pedestrian scene, it is portrayed in anything but a pedestrian manner. The artist has spread his verticals in such a way as to make the picture seem to open up, rising to provide a stage for the young woman in the foreground who leans out her window to hang out her wash.

Now represented in New York by Rehn Galleries, Henry Kapler is on his way. We look forward to his continuing success.

CHAPTER FORTY-ONE

Shiksa in Disguise

H enry's phone rang late Sunday morning, just as he and Fiona were finishing breakfast.

"You're a celebrity!" his mother declared, moments before reciting every word of W. D. Danforth's weekend art column in the *Springfield Union*.

"Breathe, Mom," Henry advised.

"Your father and I are both so proud of you," she added. Though often partisan, the praise of mothers was always welcome. Praise from Henry's father, on the other hand, was a revelation.

"Father?"

"Yes, Henry, Father too," she said.

"Thanks," he said, smiling at Fiona, who hadn't a clue as to the subject of the conversation.

After the praise came the inevitable question: "Will you be joining us for Thanksgiving, dear?"

"Can I call you back, Mom? Someone's at the door," he lied, merely deferring the moment of reckoning.

Henry returned to the breakfast table, describing the column and his mother's inquiry. He looked adoringly at Fiona and popped the question. "Will you come to Springfield with me for Thanksgiving?"

"Hell, no," she said.

"Come on, Fiona. I'd go with you to your parents' if you asked me."

"But I didn't. And you know damn well I wouldn't. That's a scene not even a daughter can stomach." Henry frowned like a toddler denied ice cream. "Geez, Henry," she said, rather less harshly, as she grasped his hand across the table, "does your family even know I *exist*?"

"Well, my brother and sister do . . . and I've at least dropped some hints with my parents." He stood up and strolled toward the window. "And what were you planning on doing for the holiday anyway? Carving a turkey with cousin Jake?"

"I'm gonna really regret this . . . I just *know* it," she said through gritted teeth.

They sat together, huddled in scarves and overcoats in the ice-cold railcar. The trip to Springfield should have taken four hours, but the engine had broken down three times, the heat functioned only intermittently, and they were already four hours into the journey and yet to reach New Haven. The train was crowded, noisy, and reeked of diesel fuel. A young mother and her two bratty children occupied the seats across from them. A six-year-old bruiser kicked Henry repeatedly in the shins while yanking the pigtails of his younger sister as if he were ringing church bells.

"This is fun," Fiona growled.

After consultation with Henry, Fiona had bought his parents a *babka*, a doughy, Jewish dessert with streusel topping and chocolate and cinnamon-sugar filling. Henry had brought them a watercolor, *Off Allen Street*, a winter scene he'd painted from memory depicting a small farm on the outskirts of Springfield.

Despite their tardy arrival, Ben was waiting at Union Station to meet them. Henry introduced Fiona to his brother. "Henry's told me all about you," he said, smiling. He turned to Henry. "What've you told Mom and Dad?"

"That I was bringing my girlfriend home for the holiday," Henry said. Fiona glanced at him apprehensively. "What have you and Edith told them?" he asked his brother.

"Not a thing," Ben insisted.

"Not even that she's a *shiksa*?"

"What's a *shiksa*?" Fiona asked.

"It's Yiddish for a non-Jewish female," Henry said.

"Henry?" The challenge of Thanksgiving was coming swiftly into focus for Fiona. "Do you mean to tell me . . . they think I'm *Jewish*?" Ben broke out laughing. "Henry!" Fiona protested. "How *could* you?"

"I didn't do anything, Fiona."

"My point *exactly*!" she fired back.

"Seems to me you've got a couple of options," Ben said. "You can go in there as Fiona . . . I'm sorry, what was your last name again?"

"Harlsweger."

"Right, Harlsweger." Ben steered the truck onto his parents' street. "So . . . as I was saying . . . you can be Fiona Harlsweger, of German *Aryan* descent, perhaps, in which case they'll probably hate you . . . or you can be Fiona Rosenberg, Henry's Jewish girlfriend."

"Jesus Christ!" Fiona muttered, snickering as she grasped the irony of her rejoinder.

"Mom, Dad, this is my girlfriend, Fiona Rosenberg," Henry said as they entered the white frame house his parents had called home for over a decade. Fiona clenched her teeth. Ruth gave her a warm hug; Morris deemed a handshake sufficient. Ben left the room to giggle.

It was nine o'clock on Wednesday night; they'd planned to stay until Friday morning. That left only about thirty-six hours of deception. In lieu of dinner, they gobbled up some cold cuts in the kitchen, retiring early to strategically separate bedrooms. In the morning, Ben took them on a tour of Springfield that lasted until the early afternoon. But the holiday dinner loomed like a pulsing thunderhead.

Thanksgiving dinner at the Kaplers was a mostly secular affair. It was just the seven of them: Henry and Fiona; Morris and Ruth; Edith and her husband, Bill; and Ben. The turkey was kosher, but looked and tasted like any other turkey. It wore no yarmulke.

Ruth's inquisition began modestly, with Fiona fielding innocuous questions about her artistic endeavors. She described her work with Edward Laning on the New York Public Library murals. And the Lanings connection explained, in turn, how Henry and Fiona had met.

Henry did his best to deflect attention from his girlfriend, discussing not only the paintings his parents had read about in W. D. Danforth's column but also mentioning his series with Alice. That, too, annoyed Fiona. But it was only when they delved into her family roots that the going got sticky.

"What kind of synagogue does your family attend back in Maryland?" Ruth asked. Fiona looked blankly at Henry.

"I think Mom's asking whether it's Reform, Conservative, or Orthodox," Henry said. "It's Reform, Mom. Right, Fiona?"

"Uh . . . yes. Reform." Fiona flashed an anemic smile.

"Does your family observe Shabbat?" Morris asked, referring to the Jewish sabbath. Henry shook his head almost imperceptibly.

"Uh, no, Mr. Kapler, I'm afraid we don't."

"I see." Ben and Edith tried desperately to suppress their laughter.

Fiona's growing irritation was etched on her face. Henry surmised that the ruse was about to unravel. He needed to say something, but Fiona preempted him. "This is ridiculous," she snapped. "Mr. and Mrs. Kapler, I owe you both a huge apology," she said. "I'm about as Jewish as Eleanor Roosevelt." Henry's jaw slackened.

Morris cleared his throat, preparing to speak. But instead of speaking, he burst into laughter. Such mirth was unprecedented in the Kapler household. "We knew from the moment we met Fiona that she wasn't Jewish, Henry," he said. "Mother and I just wanted to see how long you could drag out the subterfuge."

"Ben won the bet," Edith said with a broad smile. "He said they wouldn't make it through the *babka*." Ben patted his napkin to his eyes, he was laughing so hard.

"It's okay, Henry," Ruth said. "Fiona's a charming young lady and you should be proud of her as she is."

Henry was as embarrassed as Fiona was relieved. "I'm sorry . . . I didn't want to upset you. I know how important it is to you that Ben and I marry into the faith."

"Unless you're announcing your engagement," Morris said, "there's nothing more to discuss."

"*Are* you announcing your engagement?" Ruth asked.

"No!!!" Henry and Fiona shouted in unison.

"Now that that's settled, please pass the turkey," Morris demanded.

"Well, *I* have an announcement," Ben said.

"You're converting to Catholicism?" Edith quipped.

"No, I'm enlisting in the Navy."

"You're *what*?" Henry was dismayed by his brother's revelation.

"I've been considering it for a while . . . you know that, Henry. And with the war and all, it's only a matter of time. I'd like to get a head start, the proper training, maybe even be commissioned as an officer."

Morris broke into a proud smile. Ruth registered a look of concern followed quickly by tears. Edith and Bill offered expressions of support. Fiona was only glad that the focus had shifted from her.

"I'm proud of you, Ben," Morris said. "And Mother will get used to the idea . . . just give her some time."

Later that evening, when they were alone, Henry apologized to Fiona for the ordeal he'd put her through in his misguided attempt to appease his parents.

"You can be a pretty stubborn jerk sometimes," she said. "But I love you anyway." It was the first time she'd said the magic word.

"I love you too," he said, hoping that his verbal acknowledgment would obliterate any lingering doubts. But what most concerned him was the vision of Alice that slithered into his mind as he said it.

"And that comment about marrying into the faith. Is that your plan, too?"

The question was pregnant with ramifications, none of which Henry cared to address. "I'll cross that bridge when I come to it," he said with an indecipherable smile.

Fiona elected not to linger, moving quickly on to another topic. "I couldn't help but notice your lack of enthusiasm over your brother's enlistment."

Henry exhaled deeply. "I'm not a fan of war," he said.

"None of us are, Henry."

"No, Fiona. I mean . . . I'm a pacifist. I always have been. It's been a sore spot, in particular, with my father, who's as enthusiastically pro-war as I am against it."

Fiona looked puzzled. "I don't understand," she said. "Do you mean that you wouldn't fight if war were declared?"

"That's what it means to be a pacifist . . . but it gets a bit tricky when you factor in an enemy that persecutes and massacres Jews."

"Why haven't you told me about this before?"

"Because I thought you'd think less of me . . . or perceive it as cowardice."

Fiona stared at him. "I respect your judgment about everything," she said, "well . . . everything but Alice, I guess." She tempered her qualifier with a half-smile. "But we should talk more about it . . . when you're ready . . . if we edge toward war."

"We'll discuss it," Henry conceded, "if and when the time comes."

CHAPTER FORTY-TWO

Conversation Piece

"We come here almost once a week," Fiona said to him as they consumed, almost orgiastically, another midweek dinner at Carlito's. "So how can you order the same damn dish every single time?"

Henry twisted another few strands of his fettuccine alfredo around his fork. "I love it, Fiona. Isn't that sufficient reason?"

"That doesn't mean you shouldn't try something new and different."

"I love *you*, Fiona," he replied after withdrawing the emptied fork from his mouth. "Should I try someone new and different?"

Fiona shook her head wearily and smiled in graceful defeat.

As they continued eating, they found themselves drawn to the drama unfolding at a nearby table. A young couple faced each other uncomfortably, he nursing a stein of beer, she idly fingering the stem of her wine glass. Their body language telegraphed the rift between them. Fiona leaned across the table. "I've got a feeling," she whispered, "that the guy at the next table did just that."

"Did just what?"

"Tried someone new and different."

"So, what's their story ... do you think?" Henry asked conspiratorially.

"Well, they're engaged ... living together. She walks into their apartment one afternoon unexpectedly—she's been shopping during lunch hour and drops off her purchases before returning to the office—and she finds him in their bed, his face buried in his secretary's crotch." Fiona paused, searching for additional inspiration while Henry snickered. "She freaks. He looks up at her, but his face is covered in ... *whipped cream!*" While Fiona giggled, Henry began to laugh out loud. "She says ... 'that was tonight's dessert! How could you do *that* with tonight's dessert?' and she runs from the bedroom in tears. So here they are. He takes her out to dinner to apologize, but she's still furious. 'I'd never have used the whipped cream if I'd known you'd been saving it for dessert' he says, digging a deeper hole for himself." They both convulsed with laughter.

"No," Henry said when he'd caught his breath. "I think it's the other way around. She's trying to break up with him ... says she's met someone new ... 'He pleases me in ways you never could,' she tells him. 'What, is his dick bigger than mine?' he asks her angrily. 'It is, but that's beside the point,' she says. 'You're slovenly, you snore, and you fart in bed,' she tells him. 'Is that any reason to dump me?' he asks. 'Yes, yes, and yes,' she replies."

"Wait," Fiona said. "I've got one more." Her expression turned suddenly somber. "He's an artist ... and she's his girlfriend," she said, taking the last sip from her nearly empty glass of wine. "He's got this model ... *insanely* gorgeous ... it gnaws at her ... but she trusts him ... so she keeps her emotions in check." Henry's smile evaporated. "He paints this picture of his model practically bursting out of this blue dress." Fiona exhaled, her eyes averting Henry's gaze. "His girlfriend says to him, 'That dress looks a lot like mine.' 'Isn't yours red?'

he responds, feigning innocence. 'Burgundy,' she answers, 'but you changed the color, hoping I wouldn't notice.'" Fiona cut the scenario short, waiting to see how it would play out in real life.

Henry felt as if he'd been bludgeoned between the eyes. "The dress . . ." he said haltingly, "I shouldn't have allowed—"

"It's not about the dress . . ." she interrupted, her voice trailing off. In the process of exposing him, Fiona had exposed herself, articulating her feelings as she never had before.

"Fiona," he said apologetically, reaching across the table to grasp her hand. The hint of a tear emerged from a corner of her eye.

"I'm sorry, Henry," she said softly, squeezing his hand. "I couldn't help myself . . . it just came out." Fiona looked at him tenderly. "It's been there . . . festering . . . for a while."

Henry had a sinking feeling that he and Fiona were about to plunge into the same murky depths of anxiety that they'd witnessed at the adjoining table. He pondered what he might say to her next. That he'd abandon Alice—for the sake of their relationship? Or should he defend himself, reminding her of his dealer's advice—that Alice's remarkable beauty sells paintings? But the one thing he couldn't possibly tell her— because he couldn't admit it to himself—was that Fiona's jealousy was not entirely misplaced.

Fiona wiped the nascent tear from her eye, quickly recovering from her uncharacteristic display of vulnerability. "Look, Henry. I'm not asking you to banish Alice. I understand. I dropped my guard a little. Let's just forget about it," she said stiffly.

"Sure," he said, though he knew he couldn't.

It was mid-December, three weeks before the deadline for the Pennsylvania Academy's 1940 annual. Henry regarded it as a critical opportunity; after all, his participation in the 1939 event had catapulted him into consideration for the Carnegie. He debated submitting his latest work, the portrait of Alice he'd titled *Adoration with Blue Eyes*. But with matters involving Alice so sensitive to Fiona, he decided to send it to Rehn's instead. Meanwhile, the Herron Art Museum in Indianapolis had requested a loan of *The Deputy's Grandson* for a show opening on New Year's Day. Henry had readily agreed, rendering that work unavailable as well.

With the Carlito's episode still weighing heavily on his mind—and devoid of other options—Henry boldly decided to draw on the harrowing experience as inspiration for a new work to submit to the Academy. It would serve, in a way, as his penance.

"No way," Fiona said when he revealed his concept and asked her to model for him. It wasn't clear what troubled her more—the idea of recreating a painfully emotional moment or the prospect of serving as Henry's model, a role she dreaded and had thus far eluded.

Henry was persistent. He bent down and kissed the nape of her neck. "Pretty please," he begged, "with whipped cream on top?" His daring reference to a suddenly scandalous dessert topping instantly defused the tension. Fiona's grudging smile sealed her capitulation. But she made him promise that he'd never ask her to pose again.

At Henry's request, Fiona wore a simple but flattering blue dress with black pumps. He positioned her on a wooden chair, legs crossed, her left arm in her lap. He placed her right elbow on his kitchen table, arm bent upward, right hand resting loosely under her chin in a contemplative gesture. "Just stare into space," he said, "as if slightly peeved with me."

"Piece of cake," she said.

Henry persuaded the equally reluctant Peyton to pose as Fiona's male counterpart. By drawing him separately—he conducted the session in Peyton's Midtown apartment—it would be easier for Henry to reduce the six-foot-eight colossus to more conventional scale in his final composition. He drew him seated on his sofa (a stand-in for the restaurant's banquette), his left arm resting atop the sofa back. "I need a downcast expression... a mixture of disappointment and heartache," Henry directed. "Imagine how you'd feel if your trust fund ran dry."

Angelo Carlito, the ruddy, mustachioed proprietor of his eponymous eatery, allowed Henry to drop by the restaurant between lunch and dinner to execute the sketches he needed for the painting's background and details. "Whatever you want, Fettuccine Alfredo," he declared.

Henry put the pieces together in his studio. And if he'd harbored any doubts about the wisdom of his plan, the finished product would put them to rest. Fiona's figure dominated the painting, her blue dress contrasting nicely with the orange hue of the leather banquette on which he'd placed the shrunken Peyton. But most importantly, Henry captured the emotional stalemate between the figures, their discord heightened by comparison to a couple in the distant background, a pair so engrossed in conversation that they're oblivious to the waiter standing before them. He gave the completed painting the ironic title of *Conversation Piece* and, as was his wont, shipped it to the Academy just ahead of the deadline.

CHAPTER FORTY-THREE

The Anonymous Donor

For the next four months, Henry enjoyed an unprecedented series of artistic successes. It was an encouraging way to begin the new decade.

Conversation Piece not only made the cut at the Pennsylvania Academy, but pleased the critics in attendance for the unveiling of the exhibition on January 28th. "The painting marks a departure for Kapler," wrote W. D. Danforth, "exploring human interrelationships in a manner not previously seen in his figural works." The *Philadelphia Inquirer* hailed it "a perceptive work, speaking volumes about the awkward silences that come between us."

Fiona's reaction was more direct. "We should quarrel more often," she said. "My displeasure's your best inspiration." Henry rolled his eyes without comment.

In February, Henry triumphed without even trying. Unbeknownst to him, his parents had submitted *Off Allen Street*, the little picture he'd given them as a Thanksgiving gift, to the Springfield Art League annual. "Mr. Kapler's simple winter scene is eloquent of the versatility and craftsmanship of this rapidly developing young artist," wrote Richard Brooks in the *Springfield Republican.* Eloquent enough, in the jury's judgment, to earn him first prize honors in the watercolor division.

"An impressive achievement," Fiona joked after Henry had shared the news. "First place without lifting a finger."

"Good thing they didn't enter your chocolate *babka* instead," Henry replied.

With March came a milestone: Henry's first one-man exhibition, a selection of his earlier oils, temperas, and watercolors mounted by the Women's Club of Springfield. His parents did much of the work, combing through the pieces Henry had left behind when he'd moved to New York. But the Club's chairwoman wanted one more picture, the one Springfield knew best, the one that cowered in a corner of Henry's New York studio like an injured beast, a gaping hole torn through its heart.

"*Gastonia Renaissance* is in no condition to display," Henry explained in a telephone conversation during the show's planning stages. Though he'd long since wiped away the bloodstains, he was loath to admit that he'd patched the rips with Band-Aids.

The chairwoman was tenacious. "It's a Springfield icon!" she insisted. "The damage is part of its allure!"

The damage she referred to was that inflicted by the pen knife-wielding moron in Washington and not the manic leftfielder in New York. In the face of the chairwoman's persistence, Henry reconsidered the facts. Only a handful of people (and no one in Springfield) knew of Jake Powell's satanic rampage. Many, however, had read the account of the harm wrought at the Corcoran, where the painting was famously displayed even after its disfigurement. As far as anyone knew, *Gastonia Renaissance* still bore the battle wounds incurred in Washington, wounds that could now be proudly exhibited—even if misattributed—to an audience none the wiser. So Henry relented, packed the mangled masterpiece, and shipped it to Springfield.

While delighted with the prospect of Henry's show, Fiona declined to join him for the opening. "Thanksgiving in Springfield was more than enough for me," she said with a scowl.

The provincialism of his hometown was never more apparent. Instead of sipping champagne at the opening, Henry was obliged to endure a lecture by a superannuated speaker on the "Romance and History of Silver" before joining the Women's Club matrons for a "spot of tea." Nevertheless, he was deeply honored by the recognition and gratified by the community's enthusiastic response. W. D. Danforth hailed the exhibit as "a tantalizing taste of what this talented artist can do." As to *Gastonia Renaissance*, he wrote: "It was a pleasure to revisit Kapler's best known work, though it appeared a trifle more under the weather than I had remembered."

April brought the most exciting news of all. With funds provided by an anonymous donor, the Springfield Museum acquired *Gastonia Renaissance* for its permanent collection. "The Museum is proud to acquire this important work by our own Henry J. Kapler," announced museum director Conrad Gilmore in a press release, "a superbly talented young artist whose early accomplishments portend a very bright future." The gift even included an additional sum sufficient to replace Henry's Band-Aid patchwork with a full and proper restoration.

Henry was ecstatic. *Gastonia Renaissance* had been his landmark achievement. Along with controversy and notoriety, it had brought him national recognition. While conveying a powerful social message, it paid tribute to a young Springfield athlete whom Henry respected and admired. Its permanent presence in Springfield would honor Bunny Taliaferro as well as the artist who painted him.

Henry would often ponder the identity of the donor who had financed the museum's acquisition. Anonymity, he'd been informed, was an absolute condition of the donor's largesse. As a result, he would never learn that his most generous benefactor was the person he'd least have expected: his father.

CHAPTER FORTY-FOUR

The Invitation

He hadn't seen Alice in nine months—not since the infamous modeling session in Fiona's dress that had spawned *Adoration with Blue Eyes*, precipitated the awkward discussion at Carlito's, and inspired the creation of *Conversation Piece.* Henry had taken to heart Fiona's misgivings about Alice, and his recent triumphs had diverted his attention from what his dealer had come to refer to as his *Alice Series.* But events would soon conspire to change all that.

The first occurred in mid-June, when Rehn reported the sale of the last three paintings of the *Alice Series.* Thrilled as he was with the sales, Henry was unnerved by the fact that they'd all been made to the same collector. Was the buyer legitimately enamored with Henry's uncanny ability to divine emotion through the medium of his muse, or some creep with a sordid obsession with Alice? Even worse—almost unthinkable—was the possibility that the unidentified buyer could be the dastardly Jake Powell.

The plot thickened several weeks later when Rehn called Henry on behalf of the collector with two unusual requests. The first was for yet another painting of Alice—with the stipulation that she be portrayed in the nude. The second was an invitation—to Henry, Alice, and Rehn—to "an intimate dinner party" hosted by the collector in early August. "This is more than an invitation," Rehn advised, "it's a summons. We can't possibly refuse."

Henry was equivocal. His curiosity was piqued, but he was ambivalent about the commission for the nude. "I'll need to talk to Alice on both counts," he told his dealer.

"This client's vital to us both," Rehn insisted. He minced no words. "I need you to make this happen."

"I'll talk to Alice," Henry reiterated.

"One more thing," Rehn added. "He'd like you to deliver the new painting on the night of the dinner party."

Though Rehn still doggedly withheld the collector's identity ("you'll find out soon enough," he said), the odds it was Powell were diminishing. Even had he been inclined to construe this entire scenario as an odious trap set by a diabolical mastermind, Henry knew two things. First, that Powell was anything but a mastermind. And second, that the ballplayer's alcohol-addled brain had been further compromised by a grave concussion incurred when he'd rammed his head into the right field fence at Cleveland's League Park in June. Although the papers indicated he "was somewhat improved," his doctors declared him "a very sick man," a diagnosis Henry would most certainly endorse.

Still heedful of her sensitivity about Alice, Henry consulted Fiona, hoping she'd endorse, at least tacitly, the course of action that Rehn had laid out.

"I don't see that you have much choice," she said, much to Henry's relief. "I doubt the collector's the Frankenstein you imagine him to be. And as to Alice unclothed," she sighed while arching an eyebrow, "it insures she won't burst the seams of any more of my dresses." Henry thought he detected the hint of a smile.

"So you're okay with it?"

"Yes, Henry," she said. "I trust you implicitly."

Henry caught Alice's eye as he slipped into the booth at Johnny D's. She emerged balancing a trio of luncheon platters. A scene worth painting one day, he thought, but *not* in the nude. After distributing the plates, she hurried to his table.

"Where've you been?" she asked, slithering onto the facing bench. "I've missed you!" She gave him an endearing smile; he returned it in spades.

"Been busy," he said. "How've you been?"

"Oh . . . life goes on," she said, her tone decidedly upbeat.

Henry told her about the sales of the *Alice Series* paintings, the single purchaser conundrum, the unusual dinner invitation, and lastly, the request that she pose in the nude. Her reaction was surprisingly measured.

"It's all very interesting, Henry," she said, "but I'm not sure what to make of it." She tucked an errant lock of her hair behind her ear. "What do you think?"

"I think it's a little strange . . . and a little disturbing. But I'm mostly concerned about you," he said, his eyes narrowing. "Do you want to pose nude for some guy who's obsessed with you?" He nearly shuddered when he recognized the ambiguity lurking in his words.

"Not particularly," she said, interpreting his question the way he had meant it, "but I'm willing to do it for *you* . . . for your career."

The pang of guilt cracked him like a whip. To put Alice at risk to promote his career and preserve his relationship with Frank Rehn was unseemly and selfish. But Alice wasn't overly troubled by the collector's request.

"Look, Henry. I'm a big girl. I can take care of myself. I've posed for you naked before and I can do it again ... and frankly," she said, "I miss our sessions together."

"And the dinner invitation?"

"Dinner at some swell's place with you and your dealer? How bad could that be?"

"Thanks, Alice."

She got up, reached over, and kissed him on the forehead. "Shall I come by tomorrow after work?"

"Sure," he said. "See you then."

His breathing quickened as he watched her walk off. He felt fear—for Alice, not knowing what he was getting her into; and for himself, afraid he could no longer resist her. He felt gratitude—for her willingness to do whatever he asked, simply because it was *he* who was asking. But more than anything, he felt guilt and trepidation, knowing that Fiona trusted him more than he trusted himself.

CHAPTER FORTY-FIVE

Olympia Redux

It was as inevitable as America's advance toward war, with the potential for equally calamitous consequences.

Alice arrived at Henry's studio at precisely four o'clock. She carried only a small pocketbook. "No need for a change of clothes," she said. "Right?" He nodded, smiling weakly.

Henry had prepared for the session by scouring art books for a reproduction of one of the most famous nudes in the history of art. *Olympia*, painted by Édouard Manet in 1863, reveals the artist's luscious model in her *boudoir*, reclining provocatively, her head and back nestling luxuriously against a soft pillow. She wears a bracelet, slippers, a flower in her hair, a ribbon about her neck, and nothing more. Her head tilts to her right as she looks toward the viewer, her left hand covering her pubis. She's accompanied by a black cat and attended by a Negro maid who presents her with a bouquet of flowers, the gift of an admirer.

The moral outrage that greeted the exhibition of Manet's masterpiece at the Paris Salon two years later was attributable less to its frank display of nudity than to the confrontational nature of the naked figure. Henry proposed to position Alice in a similar fashion, without the maid, cat, or flowers, but with the same unabashed expression, a pride in her beauty that required no apology or display of false modesty. She'd be seductive without being coy. He shared the reproduction with Alice, as well as its history. "I can do that," she said as she began to undress.

Henry chose a huge canvas, over five feet in width, nearly the size of Manet's original. But while Manet's painting was set in a plush bedchamber, Henry was obliged to pose Alice on the sagging mattress of his humble bed. At least he'd applied a fresh set of sheets. He'd improvise a suitable background later.

A brief shopping spree that morning had produced the requisite accessories—a black ribbon for her neck; a mauve flower for her hair; a second-hand copper bracelet for her wrist. The red leather shoes with narrow ankle straps that she'd worn that day were adequate substitutes, he thought, for Olympia's slippers. Fully adorned as Olympia, Alice was equally beguiling.

Henry rolled the bed to his workspace, setting up his easel about six feet away. He watched as Alice approached the bed, gracefully swiveling her hips as she sat on its edge. She then leaned back, shifting her shapely legs onto the mattress, her back supported by a stack of pillows. "Is this okay?" she asked. Henry nodded tentatively, swallowing hard.

He studied the reproduction that he'd set on the worktable beside his easel. "We need to prop you up just a little bit more," Henry said, scurrying to the couch to collect his last available pillows and adding them to the growing mountain beneath her. "Better," he said.

Finally ready to begin his preliminary sketch, he selected a piece of charcoal and gazed once again at his model. Alice's body was flawless, her skin supple, her breasts magnificent. He made a final check of her posture, comparing it with Manet's *Olympia*, noticing this time a disparity in the positioning of

Alice's shoulders. Henry put down the charcoal, wiped his hands on a rag, and approached his model. He placed his fingers tentatively upon her bare shoulders, delicately adjusting her posture. He inhaled her fragrance. She moved with the subtle pressure of his fingertips, her eyes fixed on his. He trembled when his arm inadvertently brushed against her left breast. By now, his heart was pumping feverishly. He was powerless to extricate himself from her gravitational pull, hurtling toward the point of surrender like a meteor crashing to Earth. He froze as he lost himself in the tenderness of her eyes.

"I want you," she whispered, reaching her hands to his face and drawing him down gently until their lips met.

CHAPTER FORTY-SIX

The Paint-Splattered Canvas

For three nights, Henry couldn't sleep. He barely ate. He avoided everyone, especially Fiona. He hid his homage to *Olympia* in a corner of his apartment, its half-finished surface pressed to the wall. He couldn't so much as lift a paintbrush.

But on the fourth day, he did something he'd never done before—not at Yale, not at the Art Students League, not during some idle moment in his studio. It was something he never even imagined he *could* do. It was lazy, undisciplined, an affront to his rigorous training, an insult to traditions dating from the Renaissance and beyond.

He grabbed a square canvas, about three feet wide, and placed it on his easel. He went through his litany of preparations unconsciously. He reached into the old, repurposed Maxwell House coffee tin that held his brushes and selected the broadest one he owned. He unscrewed the cap of a tube of Bocour's "Midnight Black" paint, squeezing a generous dollop onto his palette. Finally, he swirled his brush into the paint and stared at the empty canvas.

Henry exhaled, positioned his overloaded brush near the upper right corner of the canvas, and yanked it diagonally downward, slashing like a madman with a butcher's knife. He replaced his brush and repeated the process, lacerating the canvas with successive strokes of cadmium red, zinc white, and cadmium yellow, each diluted with a liberal dose of paint thinner.

Henry's colors had been applied so thinly and with so much force that they began to meld with each other, dripping like a toddler's runny nose. As he watched the streams of color trickling slowly down the surface, he had a sudden impulse to rotate the canvas ninety degrees, thereby shifting the direction of the oozing lines of color. And then he rotated it another ninety degrees . . . and then another.

Finally, in a fit of unrestrained pique, he dashed his brush across his muddled palette and flung it at the canvas, inflicting a blemish on its surface like the bloom on a rotting peach.

Henry recognized that he was painting with raw emotion. His anger and self-loathing expressed itself with bloody reds, the intensity of his sexual energy in yellow, his depressive state through black. The white, he imagined, represented something he'd suddenly lost, an innocence, perhaps . . . or the sense of order that had previously regulated his life. It was the white, he realized, that had been virtually eviscerated by the onslaught of red, yellow, and black.

Henry knew he was lost, that he'd crossed a line and could never go back. He loved Fiona, but he'd betrayed her. And yet his submission to Alice was no mere sexual escapade: he adored her as much as she adored him. Fiona and Alice were opposites, each attracting and nurturing a different part of him, each with her own attributes and flaws. And yet no one, it seemed to Henry, was more flawed than he.

Henry needed desperately to talk to someone—someone other than Fiona or Alice. He telephoned Peyton.

"You sound down in the dumps, my friend," Peyton observed. "Listen," he said, "I'll pick up a couple of pastrami sandwiches and meet you at your place in an hour." He paused. "But I'm going to The Stage," he said adamantly, "not the goddamn Carnegie."

"You look like shit," Peyton said when he arrived at Henry's apartment. About six steps in, he stopped in his tracks, his eyes drawn to the abstract canvas on Henry's easel. "What the . . .?" He made a beeline toward the painting.

"I don't know what it is, Peyton. I haven't slept for days . . . I'm a wreck . . . so I wasn't myself when I painted that . . . *whatever* it is."

Henry was well aware of Peyton's preference for abstraction.

"Jesus, Henry. It's fantastic! The way you manipulated the dripping paint is ingenious!"

"You're full of crap, Peyton," Henry said.

"No, Henry. This is really good." Peyton studied the canvas closely. "You really piss me off sometimes, you know that? You don't give a good goddamn about abstract art and then you produce . . . *this!*" He shook his head. "Everything comes so easily for you," he complained. "I'm so fucking jealous!"

"Well, I *still* think it's a piece of shit, Peyton," Henry said. He inhaled deeply. "Forget the damn painting . . . I can smell the pastrami."

Peyton retrieved the brown paper bag that he'd deposited on the coffee table. The heady, intermingling aromas of pastrami, onions, and pickles were as seductive to Henry, at that particular moment, as the fragrance of Alice Woodley.

Henry grabbed a couple of plates, two glasses, and a pair of beers and set them on his kitchen table. Peyton lumbered over, commandeered a chair, and pulled himself uneasily beneath the table, his oversized legs jammed against its apron. "So

what's eating you?" Peyton asked as he devoured his
sandwich, his words muffled by the sheer volume of food he'd
stuffed into his cavernous mouth.

Henry swallowed his first bite of pastrami on rye, washed
it down with a swig of beer, and turned silent.

"Come on, out with it!" Peyton demanded.

"I slept with Alice."

Peyton nearly choked on his sandwich. "You didn't!"

"Yeah . . . I did."

"Well, I warn—"

"I don't want to fucking hear it, Peyton! I know what you
said . . . and I know what I said. And I did what I did!" Henry
was clearly amped. He'd already drained his first Rheingold
and walked over to the icebox to grab another. He gestured
toward his friend with the bottle, offering him another as well.
Peyton nodded.

"How'd it happen?" Peyton asked during a momentary lull
in his pastrami intake.

Henry told him what little he knew about the collector
who'd purchased his *Alice Series* and about the nude he'd
commissioned. "Look, I'll show you." He rose from the table
and led Peyton to the corner of his studio. His friend gasped
when Henry revealed the painting he called *Homage to
Olympia*. It was still missing a background and the foreground
details. But the figure of Alice as Olympia was breathtaking.

"Jesus Christ!" Peyton exclaimed, unable to wrest his eyes
from the picture. "You should draw hazard pay just being in
the same room with her!"

"This was *not* a conquest," Henry insisted. "Yes, she's the
most beautiful creature on earth, but it wasn't just sex,
Peyton. . . . I *adore* this girl. And, for reasons I can't adequately
explain, the feeling seems to be mutual."

"Well that certainly complicates matters," Peyton snickered.

"What am I going to tell Fiona?" Henry asked, articulating for the first time the question he'd wrestled with for the last several days and nights.

"Are you crazy? You tell Fiona *absolutely nothing!*"

"I can't be that much of a cad, Peyton."

"You're already a cad for sleeping with Alice. How's it going to help matters to inflict pain on Fiona?" Henry shook his head in bewilderment.

"Listen, buddy. You've got to figure out who you want to be with—Alice or Fiona." He massaged his chin with the fingers of his left hand. "But my guess is that you don't really know." Henry's expression confirmed Peyton's assumption. "So you give it some time . . . and the answer will emerge."

Much as Henry hated to admit it, Peyton's logic was persuasive. If he told Fiona now, he'd almost certainly lose her. And, at least for now, Alice already understood that Henry had a girlfriend. Yet the burden of his continuing duplicity would be overwhelming. "Okay," he said wearily. "But promise me, Peyton . . . *promise* me that you won't say anything to Lucille or to anyone else. *Please.*"

"You've got my word, buddy," he said. "And Henry . . . I just figured out the perfect title for your abstraction."

"This better be good," Henry said.

"You came up with half of it yourself already," Peyton said. "I'd call it *Dripshit.*"

CHAPTER FORTY-SEVEN

The Trophy Room

Frank Rehn was comfortably ensconced in the back seat of the black limousine as it pulled up to Henry's building. The artist and his model waited outside, accompanied by an enormous canvas, swaddled in blankets and secured by leather straps. Henry and Alice were suitably dressed for the dubious occasion, he in a conservative gray suit with white shirt, blue tie, and a snappy gray fedora; she in an elegant, mid-length, black silk, button-front dress with a cherry red hat, matching high-heels, and stylish evening gloves.

Alice had arrived by cab just a few minutes earlier. She'd greeted Henry with a warm smile and a passionate kiss. It was the first time he'd seen her since that fateful afternoon when so much had changed between them. A second modeling session hadn't been necessary for *Homage to Olympia*, and Henry had needed every available moment to complete the painting before their rendezvous with its mysterious purchaser. But the hours spent on his spellbinding image of Alice had sorely tested Henry's equanimity.

The chauffeur, clad in a gray uniform with shiny gold buttons and matching cap, leapt from the front seat to open the rear door. "My name is Guido," he said with a jack-o-lantern smile and an accent that left little doubt as to his heritage.

Rehn helped Alice into the limo while Henry climbed in behind her. "You're even more lovely in person," Rehn cooed as she settled into the middle seat between them.

Before returning to the wheel, Guido tapped on Henry's window. "I'm sorry, sir," he said as Henry rolled down the window, "your package won't fit in the trunk." Before Henry could respond, Guido hoisted the painting onto the roof of the limousine and began strapping it down. Henry vaulted from the car with alarm.

"Careful with that!" Henry barked.

"Not to worry, sir," the chauffeur replied. "Your parcel's secure." As Guido lashed the painting to the roof of the limo, Henry imagined it shorn from its moorings by a strong gust of wind, clattering onto the roadside. A curious trucker would retrieve it and haul it home. As he patiently unwrapped his treasure, Alice would be revealed in all her glory. Delirious over his good fortune, he'd place the risqué painting proudly above his threadbare sofa. The trucker's wife would vehemently object to the salacious nude in his living room. She'd angrily confront his Alice-infatuated husband, a nasty argument would ensue, and she'd leave him, their three uncomprehending children in tow.

His horror-fantasy having run its course, Henry returned to the back seat, a bit less confident than Guido that the nude Alice would arrive at its intended destination concurrently with the clothed one. "Guido," he begged, "drive slowly . . . *please!*"

When they reached the highway, Henry leaned over to Rehn. "Isn't it about time you tell us who we're meeting for dinner?"

"Colonel Horatio Melrose and his wife, Zelda," Rehn said with a slightly patronizing smile. "He's a retired Army

Colonel . . . a World War I hero, I'm told . . . now in the firearms business." Hardly a fan of firearms, Henry was less than enthusiastic; but he was relieved to confirm that his biggest collector was a legitimate businessman instead of a Yankee outfielder.

"And where exactly is this dinner?" Alice inquired.

"At the Colonel's residence in Greenwich, Connecticut," said Rehn.

Henry stewed as they motored north, still fearing the imminent flight of his painting from the limousine roof and peeved at the graceless efforts of his dealer to endear himself to his muse-turned-lover. But he said nothing, wary of suggesting that anything more than a professional relationship existed between artist and model.

Guido finally steered the limo onto a narrow path that led to an elaborate iron gate. He pressed a button. The gate clanked and rumbled open. A line of tall oaks beckoned them toward the house, a palatial stone residence the likes of which Henry had never seen.

The limo stopped in a large circular driveway. Guido scurried to the passenger door on the opposite side, opening it with a flourish. Benedict, the butler, emerged from the stately front door to greet, in his own dour fashion, the guests of his employer.

"Don't imagine you experience *this* too often in Iowa," Henry whispered to Alice.

"Or anywhere else," she murmured, her eyes wide as saucers.

Opulence buffeted them as they ascended the brick stairs and stepped onto the marble floor of the stone foyer. A cut-glass chandelier burned brightly above them while a grizzly old English portrait glowered at them from within its jewel-encrusted frame. The walls were crammed with antique firearms sufficient to equip a battalion. While they stood in the foyer, Guido trudged in behind them bearing *Homage to Olympia*, still bundled and apparently none the worse for the wear. He placed it discreetly against the wall of the foyer.

Benedict led them down a short passageway into a massive, high-ceilinged room he referred to as The Trophy Room. "Your host and hostess will join you presently," he announced.

Neither Henry nor Alice was prepared for what they encountered in the Trophy Room. Even Frank Rehn, more accustomed to the idiosyncrasies of wealth, was nonplussed. Mounted just below the ceiling, and continuing in an unbroken procession along the perimeter of the room, was an endless array of big game trophy heads: wild boar, caribou, bear, elk, all manner of deer, bighorn sheep, wildebeest, bison, antelope, cougar, puma, even tiger. To the right, before a broad window, loomed a huge, alarmingly lifelike stuffed lion, his powerful jaw opened to reveal ravenous teeth, his reddish-brown mane and golden coat as fresh as the day he was killed. Across the room, a leopardess roamed the stone mantel above the imposing fireplace, her glistening eyes trained on the viewer as if preparing to pounce, her sleek body frozen in time by the morbid art of the taxidermist.

But it was the display below the parade of slaughtered game that left Henry and Alice reeling: a collection of paintings, mostly contemporary, of women. Beautiful women. Seductive women. Women amassed and showcased like the severed heads that hovered above them. At least two dozen elegantly framed sirens jockeyed for position on the crowded walls. Alice's mouth was agape as she spotted her likenesses scattered about the room: *Waiting, Fear, Jake's Ex (Defiance),* and *Adoration with Blue Eyes.* She turned to Henry, her eyes bursting with indignation. "Is *that* how men see me... a trophy... to gawk at?" she whimpered. "Is that how *you* see me?"

Henry was no less offended by the crass display of human and bestial mementos. He felt, at that moment, more like a pimp than an artist. He gathered Alice into his arms and held her, trembling, until she recovered from her initial shock. Henry looked harshly toward his dealer. "Did you know about this, Frank?"

"God, no!" Rehn said. He, too, seemed repulsed by the brutish and provocative spectacle.

Henry and Alice wanted to leave immediately, but Rehn resisted. "Not yet," he pleaded. "We haven't even met our hosts."

Moments later, Colonel Melrose appeared, entering the room through a side door. He was a man of considerable girth, sixtyish, with thinning, salt-and-pepper hair and dark, heavy-lidded eyes. He brandished a half-smoked cigar between the index and middle fingers of his meaty right hand. Following closely behind him was a voluptuous woman barely half his age, tall, blond, and buxom, with green eyes and full lips. She wore a white lace gown, cut low enough to expose her enviable cleavage, and enough jewelry to sink a ship. She struck Henry as the living, breathing manifestation of the trophies populating the Colonel's walls, a domesticated playmate who'd bartered her beauty and self-respect for the trappings of money—and plenty of it.

"Welcome to all of you," the Colonel bellowed. "Zelda and I are honored to have you join us this evening. Please sit down while Benedict collects your drink orders."

Henry requested a scotch. "Make it a double," he said, bracing for whatever further surprises might be in store.

"Me, too," Alice said with a despairing look. Henry understood her reluctance to face the evening unfortified.

"Let me show you around," Melrose said, leading them toward the lion by the window as he drew on his cigar. He proceeded to relate the circumstances of the once-regal being's slaughter, noting the weapon he'd used and describing, in excruciating detail, each shot required to fell the beast. Alice and Henry were appalled. They drained their drinks to dull their anguish as the Colonel heralded his murderous accomplishments. Zelda Melrose shadowed her husband attentively, saying nothing at all.

When he'd finished relating his bloody exploits, the Colonel summoned his guests to his bedchamber, a room six times the size of Henry's apartment. Alice turned deathly pale when she saw, prominently displayed above the marital bed, a larger-than-life portrait of Zelda, unabashedly nude, curled seductively on a white bearskin rug. "Half-ton polar bear," the Colonel boasted. "Bagged him on an ice floe in Newfoundland back in '34." He took as much pleasure in describing his conquest of the polar bear-turned-rug as in flaunting the extravagant physical attributes of his wife. Once again, Zelda remained mute.

"And there," he said, pointing to a blank wall directly across from the monumental bed, "is the spot that I've chosen to display Mr. Kapler's latest rendering of our exquisite guest, Alice." Alice nearly gagged on what little remained of her scotch. Henry was aghast. "Well, I think it's time we retire to the dining room for dinner," the Colonel said, pointing the way with the smoldering stump of his cigar.

"I can't handle any more of this," Alice whispered to Henry as they followed at a respectable distance behind the others. She was livid. "To be naked, exposed to that murderous creep . . . titillating him every night as he ravishes her . . . I can't live with that, Henry!"

"I know, Alice," he said, his voice resolute. "I won't allow our painting to hang on that wall—or any other wall in this dungeon. I'll think of something, I promise." Rehn, for his part, appeared determined to endure virtually anything to ingratiate himself to one of his most profitable clients.

The dining room was vast, with oak-paneled walls. A matching pair of Venetian chandeliers hung from the coffered ceiling. Instead of carcasses, the room was plastered with old Dutch still lifes, most depicting bloody cuts of meat.

Colonel Melrose, prompted by an endless procession of flattering questions from Rehn, monopolized the dinner conversation. Zelda seemed resigned to a purely ornamental role. The Colonel offered opinions on everything, his confident, booming pronouncements discouraging debate. "Roosevelt's mucked up this country far too long," he said. "Too many handouts . . . timid on the war in Europe." He pounded his fist on the table, startling Alice. "Wendell Willkie is the antidote," he declared. "A Wall Streeter . . . friend of business . . . not afraid of taking on those blasted Nazis!" It seemed to Henry a logical stance for a man intent upon selling munitions.

Henry and Alice responded to a few innocuous questions but were otherwise largely uninvolved in the conversation, such as it was. Henry wondered why the Colonel had even bothered to request their presence, though he formulated a credible hypothesis as the night wore on. Horatio Melrose, it occurred to Henry, needed to confirm that Alice was real—and as alluring as advertised—in order to feel that he'd bought and tamed her, adding a verifiable victim to his growing collection of conquests.

Not surprisingly, dinner consisted of meats—venison, elk, and bison. Rare and bloody steaks and chops were heaped like plunder upon their plates. Henry and Alice were served enough meat to feed even the most ardent carnivore for a week.

As he gathered the courage to eat, Henry glanced at the serrated steak knife to the right of his dinner plate. He leaned over and whispered to Alice. "Say you're not feeling well . . . ask for the bathroom. I'll meet you there."

Alice looked up from her plate. "I'm afraid I'm feeling a bit ill," she said, interrupting the Colonel's soliloquy on the evils of the WPA. "Too much scotch, perhaps . . . where can I find a bathroom?"

The Colonel motioned to Benedict, who directed Alice to a washroom off the drawing room near the foyer.

"I'd better go check on Alice," Henry said a few moments later. As he rose from his chair, he slipped his steak knife into his suit jacket pocket and proceeded toward the washroom, knocking softly on the door. Alice opened it and let him in.

"Listen. I need you to stand guard outside the foyer," he said. "Don't let anyone come in."

"What are you—"

"Trust me," he said, revealing the knife. She understood immediately.

Henry entered the foyer. The painting was still there, leaning against the wall exactly where Guido had left it. He quickly loosened the straps and peeled away the blankets. For what he was about to do, he was grateful that he'd exposed the back of the canvas instead of the front. As he reached into his pocket for the steak knife, he heard footsteps and voices. "I just came out to make sure you're okay," he heard Zelda say to Alice.

"I'm fine, thanks, Mrs. Melrose," Alice said. "Henry'll be back in a few moments." Alice had little choice but to accompany Zelda back to the dining room.

The intrusion averted, Henry reached back and plunged the knife into the back of his painting, slashing it like a serial killer on a midnight spree. The sound of ripping canvas was jarring. Within a matter of seconds, *Homage to Olympia* had been reduced to ribbons of canvas dangling like streamers from a gold leaf frame.

Henry replaced the blankets around the mangled carcass of his painting and secured it with the straps. He leaned it against the wall, in the same position in which he'd found it. He returned the knife to his pocket and walked calmly back to the dining room.

"This has been a lovely evening, Colonel Melrose ... Mrs. Melrose," Alice said after they'd finished the dessert course. "But I'm due at work at six in the morning," she fibbed. "Can we call it a night?"

"Of course," the Colonel said. "I'll summon Guido and we'll have you on your way." As he rose from the table, he remembered the painting. "Wait! We've yet to unveil the painting!"

"Uh ... Colonel Melrose," Henry said, "I think Alice would much prefer if you do that after we've gone. I'm afraid she's a bit more timid about revealing herself than you might have assumed." Alice nodded demurely, on cue.

"Uh ... well ... of course ... I understand, my dear Alice. We won't embarrass you tonight," the Colonel said with a decidedly wicked grin.

Frank Rehn raised no objection, as he too had grown weary of groveling to the Colonel. "You can send me your check tomorrow, after you've inspected the painting," Rehn told the

Colonel. "I'm sure you'll be more than satisfied."

Not likely, Henry surmised as he and Alice exchanged conspiratorial glances.

The limousine was well south of Greenwich when Henry leaned forward, closing off the partition that separated the front seat from the passenger compartment.

"I owe you some money, Frank," Henry said. Alice squeezed his hand. "You can deduct it from my future share of sales."

"What're you talking about, Henry?"

Henry described how he'd butchered *Homage to Olympia*, and he and Alice took turns explaining why.

"I'm not a piece of meat," Alice said bitterly, "or some trophy to be displayed like an animal head by some demented arms dealer."

"And I'm not a purveyor of naked flesh for the edification of that bastard," Henry said with comparable fervor.

At first, Rehn was speechless. Henry had braced for a reaction commensurate with the violence of his action. When the dealer finally spoke, he measured his words carefully. "You committed a sacrilege tonight," Rehn said, shaking his head, "but I've got to applaud you for your audacity." He exhaled deeply. "I learned this evening that there are limits to what I'm willing to do for a hefty commission. I can't control what that man does with his money, but I don't have to facilitate it." He removed his spectacles and rubbed the bridge of his nose with his left thumb and index finger. "If I knew then what I know now, I would never have allowed you to accept the commission. And Alice, I wholeheartedly agree ... you don't deserve to be treated in that manner."

Henry and Alice let out a mutual sigh of relief. Rehn smiled. "You know," he said, "I wish I could see his face when he unwraps that bundle of shreds."

"Guess you won't be receiving his check anytime soon," Henry said.

"Not likely," Rehn laughed, "and don't worry about the lost commission . . . it'll cost you more than it did me as it is."

"Thank you both," Alice said.

"And tomorrow I start my life as a vegetarian," Henry said with a broad smile. "I've seen enough raw meat for a lifetime."

CHAPTER FORTY-EIGHT

Behind the Eight-Ball

His studio was pitch black but for the sliver of red neon light that slipped beneath the drawn shade. Alice lay beside him, still asleep, her golden hair and delicate features dimly outlined in the dull neon glow.

It was midnight when the limo had dropped them off in front of Henry's apartment. She'd followed him willingly into his studio, and onto the same bed on which he'd transformed her into a latter-day Olympia. She made love to him fiercely, as if her passion could somehow obliterate the sting of being dehumanized, hung in a Trophy Room, and marked for ultimate humiliation in the bedchamber of a depraved arms dealer.

As he lay awake hours later in the gathering dawn, Henry pondered the price that Alice had paid for her beauty. She'd been exploited at every turn—paraded half-naked on a chorus line, abused by an obsessive lover, cheapened by a barbarous trophy hunter. But she was not Zelda Melrose. Whereas the Colonel's wife had fully resigned herself to a life of shameless exploitation, Alice had vigorously recoiled from it.

"I'll never forget what you did tonight," she'd said before their lovemaking. "You sacrificed your art . . . and a great deal of money . . . for my self-respect. No one's ever done anything like that for me."

Henry felt it strange that for all of her incandescent beauty, it was Alice's vulnerability that aroused the greatest devotion in him. Curiously, the same had been true with Fiona. Their initial infatuation had waned, but the brutal attack she'd endured from Jake Powell had exposed a vulnerability in her that he'd never perceived—a vulnerability that drew them together again.

Yet just as Henry approached an epiphany, he fell back to sleep.

Henry had accepted Fiona's invitation to dinner at her apartment for the day after the debacle in Greenwich. He'd called her that morning, requesting that she not serve meat. "Why not?" she'd asked.

"I'll tell you when I see you," he said.

And so, as he devoured a plateful of her cauliflower and broccoli casserole ("not half bad!" was his backhanded compliment), he related the tale of his bizarre evening in the Colonel's hall of horrors.

"I can't believe you'd sabotage a major painting like that," she said, "especially one of your naked muse."

"I really had no choice," he replied. "It was the only honorable thing to do."

"You realize, of course, that this brings to three the number of your paintings carved up by cutlery. Probably a world record."

"That had occurred to me." He smiled wanly.

"So," Fiona said tentatively, "since this butcher cornered the market in Alice paintings, will you paint her again?" It was a loaded question.

"Don't know," he said, and left it hanging.

She took another tack. "Did Alice show proper appreciation

for your heroic act in defense of her honor?"

"She made delirious love to me." Henry smirked. Although he'd said it in jest, he felt a small sense of relief to have actually told her the truth. "Kind of like we're going to do ourselves later tonight, right?" A clever follow-up, he thought.

"We'll see," she said, and left it hanging.

It had been Peyton who'd discovered Diamond Mike's Bar and Pool Hall on Sixth Avenue. It was, by any measure, a dump. The upstairs was a sleazy dive bar, the kind of place where a handful of regulars spent their entire afternoons and half their paychecks getting plastered on watered-down drinks until the heartless barkeep hauled them off their barstools and tossed them onto the street. But in the basement, down a rickety flight of stairs, were three regulation-sized pool tables where you could play for hours for the cost of a drink or two. Henry had taken up pool at college, but Peyton had grown up with a fancy table in his parents' parlor. He'd managed to supplement his trust fund income by suckering opponents into betting against him in the fraternity houses at the University of South Carolina and the pool halls of Charleston. So when Peyton had a break in his schedule at the Art Students League and Henry needed a breather from the easel, they'd meet in the basement at Diamond Mike's for some straight pool or a game of eight-ball. Henry rarely won.

On this particular June afternoon, Henry was behind the eight-ball . . . literally. He'd sunk his last remaining striped ball and had only to sink the eight to record a rare victory over his elongated friend. "Eight in the right corner pocket," Henry announced. He drew back his cue, took aim . . . and missed.

"You slept with Alice on Saturday night . . . and with Fiona on Sunday?" Peyton asked, shaking his head in wonderment, after Henry had filled him in on his trip to Greenwich and the events of the days—and nights—that followed. While Henry retired to a nearby chair, Peyton gamboled about the table, evaluating the options for his next shot. He'd need to sink the four solid-colored balls remaining on the table to earn a chance at pocketing the eight for a come-from-behind victory.

"Uh . . . yeah," Henry said sheepishly.

"I hope you changed the sheets."

"Different venues."

"I see." Peyton buried the four-ball in the side pocket. "But destroyin' that painting, Henry . . . that took balls." Peyton marched around the pool table evaluating his options. "Such a waste, though," he said as he pocketed the six-ball. "So how long you think you can manage to juggle two girlfriends before you get burned?"

Peyton kissed the seven-ball off the three-ball, sinking the former and setting himself up for an easy tap-in of the latter. "Let's make a chart—consider their respective pros and cons . . . then ditch the loser." He tapped in the three.

"Articulated with the eloquence I've come to expect from you," Henry said.

"I call 'em how I see 'em," Peyton said, "like any good umpire." He idly chalked the tip of his cue. "So let's get to it," he said, abandoning the table to finish the scotch-and-soda he'd transported from the bar upstairs. He placed the empty glass on a tray table beside Henry's chair. "Whaddya see in Alice . . . other than the fact that she's drop-dead gorgeous?"

"C'mon, Peyton, are we really doing this?"

"Can't hurt, can it?"

Henry relented. "Okay," he said. "Alice is sweet . . . and she's . . ."

"She's what?"

"Vulnerable."

"Hmm. Gorgeous, sweet . . . and *vulnerable?* Is that a pro or a con?"

"A pro . . . I think."

"And Fiona?"

"Smart, strong, self-reliant, attractive, cooks well." The attributes poured off the tip of his tongue.

"Didn't hear *vulnerable.*"

"She was—once," Henry said.

"Cons?"

"Jealousy?"

"Not exactly misplaced, I'd say. So no demerits for that." Peyton rested his cue stick against the wall. "Okay. So I've got Fiona up five to three on the pros. Double-shutout on the cons. So here's what I think," he said, peering at Henry. "You're blinded by beauty . . . and inexplicably attracted to women who *need* you . . . which, if you hadn't noticed, is inconsistent with your admiration for Fiona's self-reliance. And don't forget, Henry: ridiculously beautiful girls are magnets for trouble . . . like your paintings are magnets for sharp objects." Peyton reclaimed his pool cue and returned to the table to line up his potentially game-winning shot at the eight-ball. "So, basically, Henry, I've got Fiona up by a nose."

Peyton bent his towering frame over the edge of the table. "And now I'm gonna put the eight-ball back up here in this corner," he said, pointing at the pocket to his right. He retracted his cue stick and propelled the cue ball forcefully into the eight, banking the latter hard off the far cushion, and smiling smugly as he watched it roll all the way back across the expanse of green felt and drop cleanly into the designated pocket. "Guess you lose," he said.

CHAPTER FORTY-NINE

Bobo's Butt

There was good news and bad news. The good news arrived in early August: a letter from Juliana Force, the dynamic director of the decade-old Whitney Museum of American Art and the doyenne of the New York City art scene, inviting Henry to exhibit at the Whitney's 1940-41 annual beginning in late November. For Henry, it was like winning the grand slam of tennis. He'd already conquered the Corcoran, the Pennsylvania Academy, and the Carnegie. The Whitney was the fourth major, the icing on the cake.

In Europe there was only bad news. Hitler's malevolent war machine had invaded and quickly vanquished France, Belgium, Norway, and the Netherlands. Henry thought of the Davidovs, his father's relatives in occupied Amsterdam. The campaign in Holland had lasted but five days before the vastly outgunned Dutch surrendered. With rumors of the harsh treatment of Jews multiplying, the family's outlook was increasingly bleak.

And there was bad news closer to home. Much closer. Henry, it seemed, had become the consummate fraud. He'd succumbed to late afternoon trysts with Alice, covering his tracks with increasingly convoluted lies to Fiona. His infatuation was matched only by his self-loathing.

Convinced that he loved two women, he was constitutionally incapable of choosing between them. The pressure of maintaining the untenable was tearing him apart. He turned morose. His paintings turned gloomy. Beggars and winos crept into his canvases. He'd become an addict—Alice had gone from his muse to his craving.

His friends had surely noticed. He was no longer himself with Fiona. When she'd inquire if something were wrong, he'd deny it . . . or become irritable. Alice sensed it, too—the tension in his manner, the deepening furrows in his brow.

If it weren't for Peyton, Henry would have imploded. With Peyton he could be himself—a diminished version, to be sure, of what he once was—but there were no lies to manufacture or truths to avoid. But not even Peyton could free him from his torment.

Henry's art, though compromised by his mood, had become his refuge. But it came less and less easily until, for the first time in his career, he contracted a crippling case of artist's block. It came at an inopportune time. He needed something to show at the Whitney, and it had to rise to his customary standards.

It was during an evening in Fiona's apartment—evenings that had become alarmingly less frequent—when he stumbled upon his next subject. Fiona was cooking him dinner—a vegetarian meal—when she caught him staring at a bowl of fruit on her kitchen table.

"Why don't you just do a still life?" Fiona suggested in her continuing effort to rouse him from his studio stupor.

"I've already done a still life or twelve," he grumbled.

"Why not submit the one you did a couple of months ago," she said. "You know . . . the one I said I liked?"

"You hated the other eleven?"

"That's not what I said, Henry." Fiona pulled the bean casserole from the oven and placed it on the stovetop to cool. "I'm talking about the one with the apples and lemons on the green felt cloth ... you know, *Two Lemons and an Apple* ... or maybe it was *Two Apples and a Lemon.* Jesus, Henry, I don't remember ... it was something like that!"

"I don't know, Fiona," he said, "it's too dull. Three pieces of fruit on a green felt cloth ... it looks more like three billiard balls awaiting a cue shot."

"Well, there's your answer," she said.

"*Where's* my answer?"

"That pool hall on Sixth where you and Peyton hang out."

Henry ordered himself a gin-and-tonic at the bar at Diamond Mike's, transporting it, along with his sketchpad, to the pool room below. Only one table was occupied—by three middle-aged men he'd seen there before. He nodded to them, grabbed a chair, placed it a respectable distance from the trio, and sat down to sketch.

"Hey, buddy, whatcha doin'?" one of them inevitably inquired. Tall and gaunt, he wore a blue sweater vest and a gray fedora.

Henry explained he was doing studies for a painting. "You don't mind, do you?" he asked.

"He's okay, Stretch," another said. "I seen him here before."

A husky player in a wrinkled white shirt with rolled up sleeves leaned over the table to line up a shot. A cigarette dangled from his lips. "Six in the corner," he said.

"Shit, Bobo, Rembrandt here's gonna paint your ass bendin' over the table," Stretch said. "And then your ass is gonna be hanging on some fuckin' museum wall some day." He laughed. "Everybody's gonna stare at your big fat ass!"

"Fuckin' ass'll be immortal!" laughed the third player, whom they referred to as Woody.

"More like *immoral*," Stretch shot back with a maniacal chuckle.

Bobo ignored the ridicule, barely raising his eyes from the barrel of his cue stick. The distinctive *crack* of colliding billiard balls rang out followed by the *thump* of the six-ball as it plopped into the leather netting of the corner pocket.

As the banter continued, Henry sketched in pencil, scribbling color notes as he outlined his composition. The lush green color of the felt that covered the pool table reminded him of the manicured lawn of Yankee Stadium. He recorded the harsh, yellowish tinge thrown off by the massive lighting fixture that hung over the pool table like an inverted feed trough. He would count on those broad passages of green and yellow to anchor and unify his painting. Henry also made quick studies of the ball racks and triangles arrayed against the back wall.

But he spent most of his time on the pool players. He captured Bobo from behind (just as Stretch had teasingly predicted), draped over the table, the bottom of his drawn cue stick hanging limply in his right hand, his left arm stretched across the table to guide his shot. He drew Stretch standing off to the right, his eyes fixed on Bobo's impending shot while clutching his own cue like a farmer grasping a pitchfork. Henry balanced the composition by placing Woody on the left, behind the table and facing forward, cuddling his cue stick in the crook of his neck like a toddler caressing a teddy bear.

Stretch wandered over to Henry's chair and glanced over his shoulder. "Damn, you're good!" he said. "C'mon over here, guys ... get a load a' this!" Bobo and Woody rested their cue sticks against the pool table and strolled over to see what had so impressed Stretch.

"Well, I'll be goddamned," Bobo said. "You really did paint my ass!"

"More like a pit-cher of the ass *of* an ass!" Woody said.

"'Stead of a half-ass, it's a double-ass!" Stretch said, cracking himself up again. "Or," he continued, "the whole ass of an asshole!" By now Stretch was convulsing with self-induced laughter.

Woody prolonged the agony. "When we tell the guys back at the Lodge . . . Bobo'll be . . . the *butt* of every joke!" And so it continued until Henry gathered his drawings, bought his subjects a round of thank-you drinks, and repaired to his studio to paint Bobo's butt.

The line stretched around an entire city block, threatening to lap itself like a dog chasing its tail. It was October 16, 1940, the day on which every American man between the ages of twenty-one and thirty-five was obliged to register for the first peacetime draft in American history.

Bundled in topcoats and hats, Henry and Peyton were among the early arrivals at P.S. 17 on West Forty-Eighth Street, one of 712 public school buildings pressed into service to register close to one million men from the five boroughs of New York. They'd claimed their places in the swelling line before the seven o'clock opening, hoping to minimize the wait.

"Is it always this cold at this hour?" Peyton asked Henry as they shivered in the unexpectedly brisk chill of the early fall morning.

"How the hell would I know?" Henry said. "Artists are bohemians. We go to bed with the first light and wake up for lunch . . . right?"

"I obviously didn't get that memo," Peyton said. He reached into his coat pocket for a cigarette and lit it, cupping his matchbook against the force of the crisp breeze.

"Can you see any movement up ahead?" At six-foot-eight, Peyton had a bird's-eye view of the proceedings.

"Not on the line," he reported, puffing intently on his Chesterfield, "but check *this* out!" Peyton motioned toward a group of at least a dozen men heading across the street in their direction. What was remarkable was that none appeared over four feet tall. The shortest in the group marched right up to the tallest man in the line.

"From the sublime to the ridiculous!" he said in a high-pitched voice, craning his neck to gaze at Peyton. He wore a newsboy cap and spoke with an Irish lilt.

"I trust I'm the sublime," Peyton said from his vantage point almost three feet above him.

"That's ridiculous!" the small man said, laughing hysterically. Henry was stupefied by the spectacle of this random conversation between the abbreviated and the elongated. The former explained that he and his colleagues were members of a circus troupe in the midst of a two-week engagement at nearby Madison Square Garden. "Gotta register, they say, even though there ain't a snowball's chance in hell they'll induct a wee guy like me . . . or a giraffe like you, for that matter," he said with a smirk.

"What's *that* mean?" Peyton asked, removing the cigarette from his lips. By now, the snickering was universal among those in the vicinity of this bizarre exchange between radically disparate physical specimens.

"They's got limits, ya know. Uncle Sam ain't gonna be bothered making uniforms and helmets for the odd dwarf or giraffe." The diminutive fellow smiled meekly. "Well, good luck, pal," he said, scampering back to join his compatriots at the end of the line.

Peyton was taken aback by the encounter. "Are there *really* height restrictions?" he asked Henry with alarm.

"Beats the hell out of me."

"Jesus Christ!" Peyton groused. "I'll be damned if I have to sit out the war tightening lug nuts in some factory with a platoon of broken-down geezers and dames with thighs like tree trunks! *You're* the one who wants out . . . not me."

"Think about it, Peyton. The boys'll be gone and you'll have your pick of the Amazon women!"

Peyton wasn't smiling. "Look, Henry. Y'all know war's coming . . . and *most* of us . . ." Peyton raised an eyebrow at Henry as he articulated the word *most*, "wanna do our part." He took another drag on his Chesterfield. "Jesus . . . I'd be devastated if I couldn't—"

"I *get* it, Peyton," Henry said, a pained look on his face. As the inevitability of American involvement in the war had become increasingly apparent, the two friends had often debated Henry's pacifist convictions. "I'm still mulling it over. But I know that if I go with my conscience, my father'll probably disown me."

"Thought he pretty much had," Peyton said. "Not to mention that your girlfriends—and note that I use the plural— will think you're a coward, even if they don't say so to your face."

"I'm not ashamed of my pacifism," Henry said. "But I'd have to convince the draft board my that belief is religion-based to qualify as a conscientious objector." Henry blew on his ungloved hands. "I'm a Jew, not a Quaker," he said as the long line finally lurched ahead several feet.

"Just tell them in Yiddish," Peyton said.

"It's no laughing matter."

"Neither is what Hitler's doin' to your fellow Jews . . . as you keep remindin' me."

"I couldn't agree more."

"Want my advice?" Peyton asked.

"No."

"Well here it is . . . it's the same advice I gave you about your other so-called *conundrum.*" He took one final puff on his cigarette before flicking it into the gutter.

"I said I didn't—"

"My advice is to give it a rest. Today's only registration . . . we're not at war. You've still got time to figure it out. I'm willin' to wager that when the day comes that you've gotta choose between sittin' it out on principle or defendin' your country and religion, you'll know *exactly* what to do."

It was a twenty-minute cab ride from P.S. 17 to the East Village, but Henry had insisted—and paid—so Peyton acceded. They were famished when they piled into a corner booth at Johnny D's.

"This place better be special," Peyton said. "It's a long way to come for break—" When a smiling blond waitress with a model's body and the face of an angel approached them, he suddenly understood. "Oh my God . . . that's *got* to be Alice!" Henry smiled like a Cheshire cat.

"Alice . . . I'd like you to meet Peyton Small, who's . . ."

"Ridiculously tall!" Henry and Alice roared in unison.

Peyton grinned. "You two rehearsed that, didn't you."

"Maybe," Alice allowed, sliding into the open seat beside Henry.

"I've seen you in Henry's paintings . . . but you're even prettier in the flesh."

"And I suspect you've seen a lot of that flesh in those paintings," Alice said with a playful grin.

Since the breakfast rush was over, Alice relayed their

orders to the kitchen and returned to chat with the duly registered duo. Henry told her about the unusual encounter between Peyton and the pint-sized circus performer. "Even the munchkin called him *ridiculous,*" Henry recalled.

"Then scared the shit out of me by suggestin' I'm too tall to qualify for the military," Peyton said. "So I asked the draft guys . . . but they didn't know crap . . . said I'd find out when I took my physical."

"They must have top shelves on military bases . . . figures they'd need someone to reach 'em, right?" Alice quipped before slipping out of the booth. "Let me go check on your breakfasts," she said, heading back to the kitchen.

Peyton wrenched his eyes from Alice and turned to his friend. "Okay, Henry, you've made your point."

"So what would you do?"

"Screw 'em both 'til my head exploded . . . and then I'd join the Navy."

CHAPTER FIFTY

Upside Down

"Never before," President Roosevelt had declared in his year-end 'fireside chat,' "has our American civilization been in such danger as now." Only the most quixotic of observers could envision a scenario without war. As Henry's father was wont to say, it was merely a matter of time.

The pre-Christmas madness had given way to the relative calm of the final week of 1940. Fiona had returned to Maryland to endure the holidays with her dysfunctional family. Alice had embarked for Iowa on a similar mission. Peyton had decamped to Dixie to appease his parents and shoot some pool. Henry had politely declined invitations to join each of them, preferring the peace and quiet of his studio and the time to think.

While his head hadn't yet exploded, the complexity of his love life had taken its toll. To love two women was more exhausting and emotionally draining than he'd ever imagined. At the same time, the struggle continued between his pacifism and his abhorrence of fascism. He'd deferred decisions on both fronts for as long as he could, but had little appetite for prolonging the agony.

Alone in his tiny apartment on New Year's Eve, Henry made himself a solemn resolution. He would make the two most important decisions of his life and would endure the inevitable repercussions, as painful as they might be. And he'd do it quickly, before the return of his friend and his lovers. The year 1941 would be a year of destiny, whichever path he chose.

But before he applied himself to the formidable task at hand, Henry allowed himself one final indulgence, like a last cigarette before the firing squad. Preoccupied with his personal problems, he'd failed to visit the Whitney Annual, now nearing the end of its six-week run. He'd make that visit, and then he'd tackle his future.

Light snow had begun to fall in the early afternoon as Henry stepped through the elaborate doorway of The Whitney Museum on West 8th Street. An Art Deco eagle glared at him like a sentinel from the lintel above.

Founded by heiress and sculptor Gertrude Vanderbilt Whitney, the museum was housed in an interconnected trio of century-old, red brick townhouses. Graciously furnished, the galleries gave the impression of a series of intimate drawing rooms.

On that particular day, the museum was nearly empty, a serendipitous circumstance that pleased the young artist. His mood was wistful, his circuit through the silent galleries assuming the aspect of a pilgrimage. Emotions bubbled to the surface. He felt a sense of accomplishment—to be represented among the artists acknowledged as the best in America. There was gratitude as well, for among this pantheon of artists were several who had played major roles in his own evolution, beginning with his arrival in New York City just over four years earlier, a fresh-faced artist with lofty dreams.

A large painting by Edward Hopper dominated the first gallery Henry entered. Its spare title, *Gas*, was emblematic of its haunting simplicity. A filling station sprouts up on a quiet country road on the forest's edge. Artificial light from the sterile white building intermingles with the fading light of dusk. Three red gasoline pumps dwarf a solitary figure at the center of the canvas while a *Mobilgas* sign shoots skyward like an unchecked weed. Here were Hopper's trademarks in art as in life: loneliness and isolation. Henry thought about the phlegmatic Hopper, a man he hardly knew, but whose favorable assessment of his talent bolstered his confidence and launched his career.

Henry broke into a smile as he strolled into the next gallery. He adored Reginald Marsh's teeming paintings of frolicking New Yorkers. *Swimming Off West Washington Market*, a watercolor as large as Hopper's *Gas*, fit the bill. Muscled men and bathing beauties cavort at one of the few remaining swimming venues along the lower Hudson, near the West Washington Market in Lower Manhattan.

Henry reflected on what he'd gleaned from his apprenticeship with Reginald Marsh. The Custom House murals exposed him to Marsh's vibrant technique, his loose brushwork, and his unique ability to synthesize great quantities of artistic material into a single composition. But more importantly, Reggie had taught Henry how to look at the world around him, how to see artistic possibilities in the most banal aspects of everyday life. It was Marsh, too, who had connected Henry with his dealer, Frank Rehn. As he sat on a sofa in the middle of the gallery admiring Marsh's latest handiwork, Henry recalled the eureka moment in Marsh's studio when he'd stumbled upon that first painting of Alice.

Weaving through the rooms, Henry was charmed by Paul Sample's *Noon at the Fair*, a marvelous depiction of a classic New England country fair, complete with carousel, Ferris wheel, and assorted amusements; and Clyde Singer's hilarious *Shotgun Wedding*, in which a country preacher unites a pregnant bride and her dazed groom in holy matrimony beneath the barrel of a shotgun brandished by her sullen father. He was even drawn by the largely abstract *Report from Rockport*, a riot of colors, signs, symbols, and shapes through which Stuart Davis effectively captured the bustling activity of the town square in the seaside community of Rockport, Massachusetts.

In Gallery VII, Henry found the work of his upstairs neighbors and friends, Edward and Mary Laning. Edward's *Camp Meeting* was the energetic portrayal of a rural revival meeting that he'd seen, in its earliest stages, the first time he'd ventured into Edward's studio. Henry was glad to see the finished product, which impressed him greatly. Alongside Edward's painting hung a delightful work by Mary entitled *Outlet Store*, a lyrical parody featuring a bevy of half-dressed women in contorted poses as they feverishly slip in and out of bargain-priced garments in a crowded dressing room. It was a wonderful work, a hint of the heights to which Mary could ascend if she could only find the time to paint.

It was fitting that Henry's own *Pool Room* hung in that same gallery, directly opposite the Lanings' works. It was their friendship and generosity that sustained him when he first arrived in New York. They had introduced him to the denizens of the art world . . . and to Fiona. He thought of the heartache Mary would endure if he chose Alice over Fiona.

Henry owed a tremendous debt of gratitude to Reggie, Edward, and Mary. But artistically, his greatest obligation was to the man whose work he encountered as he swept into the final room of the exhibition. Yasuo Kuniyoshi had transformed him from a technically competent painter into an artist who could imbue his work with spirit and emotion.

Henry sat on a sofa in the center of the room to contemplate Kuniyoshi's enigmatic still life, *Upside Down Table and Mask*. At first glance, the painting appeared as an incoherent aggregation of objects—an inverted tripod table with a missing leg; a blue vase lying precariously on the upturned underside of the table top; a folding wooden ruler twisted haphazardly around the table's base and shaft; a traditional Japanese kabuki mask hanging from the broken stump of the missing table leg; a crumpled copy of the *Daily News*, its bold headline no longer legible. That was, perhaps, the *actuality* portrayed, but not the *truth* that Kuniyoshi sought to convey. The more Henry pondered it, the more he understood. He read the composition as commentary on a world turned upside town. Traditions (symbolized by the blue vase and the Japanese mask) stood on the verge of shattering. Henry recalled Yas's explanation of the symbolism of the newspaper, a motif that appeared so often in his paintings. "It's my way to tie the inner soul of the painting to the world beyond," Yas had said. For Henry, this confirmed his suspicion that *Upside Down* was Kuniyoshi's reflection on the irrationality of a world at war.

But there was another more personal level on which the painting spoke to Henry alone. His own life was also in shambles, its logic upended. World events required that he measure his moral convictions against the exigencies of war. The precarious balance of the blue vase was as untenable as his duplicitous love life.

Henry sat in that room, staring at the painting for what must have been hours. He contemplated his circumstances, evaluated his options, considered how his choices would impact the lives of those he loved. There were bursts of anger and frustration, moments of sadness and tears, and flashes of clarity and enlightenment. These were the hardest decisions he would ever have to make.

Henry was engrossed in his thoughts when a uniformed guard tapped him on the shoulder. "I'm sorry, sir, but the museum's about to close," he said. Henry wiped a tear from his cheek, donned his overcoat, and stepped into the biting January cold. As he walked back to his apartment in the darkness, past the office workers scurrying home to their families, the shoppers hauling their bagfuls of bargains, and the newsboys hawking their evening papers, he felt a sense of relief. After months of agony, he'd formulated a plan. All that remained was to implement it.

CHAPTER FIFTY-ONE

The Plan

Peyton was the first to return from his holiday sojourn. He met Henry at Diamond Mike's for the post-mortem.

"Daddy gave me the third-degree at the dinner table on Christmas Day, so he'd have plenty of witnesses to my feeble defense of my dissipated life as an artist," Peyton said as he and Henry lingered at the bar with their watered-down drinks. "Didn't help that I'd wrapped up an abstract as a Christmas gift to my parents." Peyton laughed out loud. "Should'a seen my Daddy's face when he confronted *Untitled No. 12.*"

"I can imagine," Henry said, sipping his scotch through a smile.

"But I turned the tide right then and there," Peyton said. "Told 'em about Lucille—to dispel their fears of my homosexuality—and then blasted them between the peepers with the announcement that I'd decided to enlist."

This was news to Henry. "Since when?"

"Since summer, I guess... when war began to feel inevitable."

"Uh ... what about your ... stature?"

"Yalie word for height?" Henry nodded while Peyton took another gulp of his gin-and-tonic. "Well, I'll list myself a couple inches shorter and stoop a lot when I go for my physical."

Peyton watched the bartender emerge from behind the bar to usher a dissipated regular out the door. "Can't figure out why these guys come back here when he treats them like that," Peyton said.

"Cheapest drinks around," Henry replied.

"So, Henry, how about you? Settled on anything yet?"

Henry smiled. "In fact, I have."

"Well, then, by all means, spill the beans."

Henry hopped off his bar stool. "Let's take it over there." He pointed to an empty table in the back corner, retrieved his drink, and sat down as Peyton followed.

"So?"

"The Nazis won," Henry said.

"Meaning?"

"That my disgust for the excesses of fascism has trumped my distaste for the obliteration of my fellow man."

"Thought you'd come to your senses," Peyton said, "eventually."

"My chances of making a case for conscientious objector status were slim to none," Henry said, "and I'd have shamed my father and my friends if I'd tried."

"Hope you don't think that I'd—"

"No. I know you'd have been supportive." Henry drained his scotch. "Anyway, it doesn't matter . . . I couldn't even convince myself anymore."

"So will you enlist?"

"Yeah . . . in a month or two, I think. Better off to get in before we're in the thick of it." Henry put both hands around his scotch glass, staring at the melting ice. "But I need to accomplish a few things first."

"Like?"

"Like telling Fiona about Alice . . . and breaking it off with Alice."

"Are you crazy?" Peyton bellowed. "You'll lose both of them!"

"Since I can't commit to either of them, neither of them should commit to me. It wouldn't be fair."

"I thought you said you loved them both."

"It's *because* I love them," he said solemnly, "that I need to set them free. Who knows when ... or if ... I'll ever come back?"

"So this is the cockamamie plan that you dreamt up while I was gone?"

"Yup."

Peyton shook his head. "This is gonna tear you apart, Henry ... you know that," he said. "And it will crush both Fiona and Alice."

"I can't have them both waiting for me ... and I can't choose between them," Henry said. "So it's really the only way."

"There's gonna be a world of hurt around here when you put this crackpot plan into action." Peyton shook his head again, but this time with a sense of resignation. "So when do you swing the axe?"

"Wish you wouldn't put it that way ... it's hard enough just to think about it. But to answer your question ... I need some time to paint something first ... something important. And I want to include both Fiona and Alice in it."

"You're nuts," Peyton declared.

"I've got an idea, but it needs refinement. I'll tell you about it when I've got it figured out."

"This is all too bizarre for me," Peyton said. "Let's go downstairs and shoot some pool ... that's somethin' I can understand."

Peyton signed his enlistment papers at the end of January. He lied about his height. Two weeks later he reported for his physical. He stooped. Again he lied about his height. But the height rod didn't lie back. Six feet eight-*and-a-half* inches. A half-inch over the limit. *He'd grown!* Peyton pleaded, stooped some more, requested a recount, but to no avail. Peyton Small was indeed ridiculously tall—and ridiculously tall was a tad too tall for Uncle Sam.

Peyton was devastated. "Relegated to the home front," he grumbled as he leaned over the bar at Diamond Mike's, furiously puffing on his cigarette. His eyes were sunken, his cheeks flushed. Though he couldn't show it, Henry was envious of his friend. Had Henry been five inches taller, he, too, would be relieved of the obligation to kill . . . and without the need to prove or justify his pacifism. Peyton, however, could never see it that way.

"It's not your fault," Henry said in a feeble effort to comfort him.

Peyton finished his second bourbon, rubbed out his cigarette, queued up another. "Maybe I can get a job in the circus . . . juggling dwarfs," he moaned. He was inconsolable. He even lost to Henry in pool.

CHAPTER FIFTY-TWO

Home Front

It was Peyton's disparaging remark about the home front that crystallized Henry's thinking about his farewell painting. The war, or at least some aspect of it, would provide his subject matter. He'd already done a powerful anti-war picture, a battlefield scene called *Soldiers*, while at Yale. But to glorify war, or expose its horrors, was not his objective this time. Instead, he wanted this next painting to resonate with the people who would be stateside to see it, while others were off to war. Henry would paint a heroic portrayal of the contributions he anticipated from those on the home front, on the farms, in the factories, in the hospitals and rehabilitation facilities—from the people who would keep the industries humming while ministering to the needs of the wounded.

Henry toyed with a variety of approaches before settling on the one he thought would best convey his message. *Home Front* would be a monumental, full-length triple portrait, painted in a muralist style. A tall, muscular farmer in faded blue denim overalls would rise like a tree trunk from the center of the canvas, his sleeves rolled up, a wide-brimmed straw cap on his head, an iron rake held vertically in his left hand, a burlap seed sack draped over his right shoulder. He'd be silhouetted against a field of wheat below a cloudless sky. A simple farmhouse would appear in the distance, a large American flag waving from the flagpole beside it. In the foreground on the right third of the composition, Henry envisioned an attractive young woman, clad in a gray work shirt with sleeves rolled up to her elbows, her blonde locks creeping out from beneath a bandana adorned with stars and stripes. The woman's head would be turned slightly to the viewer's right. Her left hand would support the barrel of a rivet gun, while her right would be poised at its trigger. Behind and to the viewer's right he'd paint a vignette of the inside of an aircraft factory. The figure of a second young woman would fill the foreground on the left third of the picture. He'd outfit her in a crisp, white nurse's uniform with a matching cap bearing a bold red cross, a stethoscope around her neck. With her left hand and forearm, she'd press a clipboard gently to her chest, her right arm hanging at her side. A glimpse of a hospital ward would fill in the space behind her, to the viewer's left. The expressions of the figures would radiate their solemn determination.

Henry knew exactly whom he wanted to model for each of the figures in *Home Front.* Fiona would pose as the nurse, Alice the riveter, and Peyton the farmer. These were the people he'd be leaving behind; it was his way of paying them tribute. Alice would certainly be game; Fiona and Peyton would be harder to coax.

Henry spent the middle two weeks of February refining his composition, preparing ever larger and more detailed sketches as he distilled his ideas. He wouldn't dare to assemble his intended models together. He'd arrange for separate sessions with each, incorporating the drawings into his final composition much as Reginald Marsh would have done for one of his Coney Island scenes.

Henry approached Fiona first. Without yet revealing his plans to enlist (or, for that matter, his relationship with Alice), he showed her the final charcoal study he'd developed for the composition. She was impressed with the drawing, but loath to pose.

"You *promised* me I'd never have to pose for you again!" she protested, reminding him of the commitment he made when she'd modeled for *Conversation Piece*.

"I know," Henry said. "But this might be my most important piece yet—my contribution to the upcoming war effort." His eyes implored her. "I can see it hanging in a museum one day . . . you'll bring your children to see it . . . and you'll point proudly to your image and say, 'kids, that's your mother up there.'"

"What a crock," she said, struggling to suppress an incipient smile.

"*Please*, Fiona!" he begged, "with whipped cr—"

"Okay! Jesus, Henry, I'll do it already."

Henry rented a nurse's outfit from a local uniform supplier, scraped up a stethoscope from a Yale classmate studying medicine at Columbia, and supplied his own clipboard. While she groused during much of her sitting, Fiona admired the sketch he produced. "I look rather good as a nurse," she said. "When Edward's library murals are finished, maybe I'll go back to Georgetown, get myself a degree in nursing . . . or better yet, medicine. What do you think, Henry?"

"I think you'll be terrific at whatever you do, Fiona," he said, gently squeezing her hand while his heart slowly smothered with guilt and remorse.

Peyton was another hard sell. Still uncomfortable with his prospects on the home front, he was reluctant to embrace the role on canvas.

"Look, Peyton," Henry said, "I'll make you shorter and more muscular. Lucille will go nuts over it!" Henry punched him playfully in the arm. "And if you want, I'll reciprocate and model for you."

"I paint non-objectively," Peyton reminded him.

"All the better," Henry said.

Henry pored through the racks of countless second-hand clothing stores to find a suitable pair of overalls. Even the 'extra large' he settled on was a tad too small. It took a generous application of Lucille's tailoring skills—she let out the seat and extended the straps—before her outsized boyfriend could even hope to climb into them. A hardware store supplied the rake as well as an empty burlap sack to serve as a seed bag.

Alice was thrilled to model, especially in the role of the lady riveter. "This painting of yours would make more of a splash if I was naked, don't you think?"

"Hmm," Henry grinned, momentarily savoring the thought.

From Edward, Henry borrowed an electric drill to stand in as a rivet gun. He'd find one later in a local factory, whip up a working drawing, and incorporate it into the painting before its completion.

Henry absolutely loved painting Alice. He'd have loved for his *Alice Series* to go on forever, but the creepy repercussions associated with those paintings had effectively halted the cycle. So he treasured these modeling sessions with his muse, realizing they could well be their last. And what was better . . . or worse, depending upon his mood . . . was the fact that each session ended with a spirited session of another kind, under the covers of Henry's bed.

CHAPTER FIFTY-THREE

You'd Have Preferred Groucho Marx?

Henry took his time on *Home Front*, recognizing that its completion was the only thing delaying implementation of the rest of his plan. But except for postponing the heartbreak of abandoning lovers and friends, there was little to be gained by procrastination. The war news in Europe had become increasingly dire. By early April, the Germans had invaded Yugoslavia and Greece. If Henry stalled much longer, the benefits of early enlistment would evaporate.

Home Front was a departure for Henry, a return to the heroic Regionalist style he'd perfected at Yale. The softer edges, scumbled backgrounds, and emotional overtones that had crept into his work under the tutelage of Yasuo Kuniyoshi were absent. Henry envisioned *Home Front* as a tribute to those he loved and would soon be leaving, and as a balm for Peyton's despair. It was his parting gift, even if it might have been a step backward in his artistic evolution.

Peyton was the first to view *Home Front* when Henry unveiled the newly finished work in his studio during the first week of May, 1941.

"Jesus, Henry ... I look like Henry Fonda in *The Grapes of Wrath*!"

"You'd have preferred Groucho Marx?"

"Absolutely not . . . but Fonda's not as good looking as I am." Henry grinned while Peyton lit a cigarette. "It's a damn good picture," Peyton added, "but a bit premature, don't you think?" He casually launched smoke rings into the air. "It'll resonate more when we're in this bloody war."

Peyton was right. Henry's best strategy was to withhold the painting from exhibition until America joined the fight. Besides, there was no significant exhibition venue appropriate for such a work until the late fall or winter. And by then, war might well have become a grim reality. Henry contemplated the logistics of arranging for the painting's exhibition *in absentia.* He could leave it with Peyton, but a better approach would be to entrust it to someone with impeccable art world connections, someone who might champion the work and expose it to the right people. He decided to call Yas.

Kuniyoshi stopped by Henry's studio on the following afternoon. Henry welcomed him, plied him with a glass of scotch, and fixed one for himself. He sat on the dilapidated wing chair, reserving the couch for his mentor.

"Saw your *Upside Down Table and Mask* at the Whitney in January," Henry said. "You probably won't believe this . . . but I sat in front of it for hours."

"I've been accused of all kinds of things with regard to my paintings," Yas said, "but putting fellow artists to sleep is a first."

Henry laughed. "Actually, the emotion you unleashed in that painting struck a chord with me that day . . . helped me to make some difficult decisions."

"What decisions . . . if I might ask?"

"I've decided to enlist . . . get a jump on the war." Henry took a sip of scotch and set his glass down on the coffee table.

"Big decision," Yas acknowledged, "especially for a pacifist."

"Caught between a rock and a hard place," Henry said. "But pacifism seemed an indulgence given Hitler's imperialism and anti-Semitic agenda."

"Sara's been in contact with relatives in France," Yas said, referring to his Jewish wife. "Jews are being stripped of rights and assets. And the Non-French Jews are being rounded up and banished to camps." He shook his head. "We live in a frightening world."

"How is Sara?" Henry asked.

Yas grimaced. "We've separated," he confessed.

"Sorry to hear that." Henry had heard rumors of an affair between Yas and Lily Harmon, a young artist in Kuniyoshi's building. But as one deeply troubled by his own infidelity, Henry was disinclined to pursue the matter further.

Yas reached into his coat pocket for his pipe. "Mind if I smoke?" As Henry shook his head, Yas began the ritual of filling and lighting it. "So let's see this new painting of yours!"

Henry led him to his easel by the window. Yas gazed at *Home Front* for a few moments before reacting. "Rather ambitious," he declared. "But a reversal of course, Henry, wouldn't you say?"

"Filled an emotional need," Henry said. He knew that Yas would be disappointed, but, on this particular day, it wasn't his opinion that he sought. "This work has a special purpose," he told him, "one for which my earlier style seemed more suitable."

"This has the potential to be a very popular painting," Yas said. "It's beautifully composed and powerful. I *do* like it, Henry . . . it's just a bit of a surprise."

"I'm leaving friends and lovers behind," Henry said. "They need encouragement . . . I guess it's my way of providing it."

Kuniyoshi sat on the stool, reconsidering Henry's creation. "Well, then," he said, "when you explain it that way, I can see it differently." He took a couple of hearty puffs from his pipe.

Henry then explained his reason for summoning Yas to his studio. He asked if he might entrust the painting to his mentor and rely on him to determine the best time and place for its exhibition. "I owe you a great deal, Yas," Henry said, "and I know I have no right to ask for more . . . but it would mean a lot to me if I could leave *Home Front* in your capable hands."

"It's as good as done," Yas said, placing his hand on Henry's shoulder in a gesture of friendship and support. "I'm honored that you'd ask me."

Henry exhaled deeply. "Thanks, my friend," he said, shaking his hand, wondering when—or if—he'd do so again.

CHAPTER FIFTY-FOUR

Dino's

The easy part was done. The rest would be agony.

He called his parents to let them know of his decision to enlist. He sensed the pride in his father's voice as he applauded Henry's decision. It felt strange to be at peace with him after so many years of turmoil. Though his mother said nothing, Henry could hear her muffled sobs in the background. With both of her sons joining the service, her angst was palpable.

"We'll be fine, Mom," Henry said in a feeble effort to reassure her. "We'll be home before you know it."

"Your mother will be okay," his father said. It was more a command than a prediction.

Henry signed his U.S. Army enlistment papers on June 2, 1941. He passed his physical a few days later. He'd have two weeks to put his life in order. Except for *Home Front* and a handful of paintings he'd leave with his dealer or Peyton, most of the contents of his studio, including all his remaining works, would be packed and shipped to his parents in Springfield.

Henry stopped by Johnny D's long enough to buttonhole Alice. She flashed him a luminous smile as she balanced a platter of pancakes in one hand and an order of scrambled eggs in the other. The smile he returned was more ominous than luminous. "Be with you in a sec," she said as he slid into his customary booth in the back of the diner.

"Is everything okay?" she asked him a few moments later.

"Sure, everything's fine," he said. "Listen, if you're free tonight, I'd like to take you to Dino's for dinner."

Henry knew that an invitation to the classy Midtown restaurant would arouse her suspicion: it was the first time he'd offered to take her out publicly since they'd been lovers. They both knew they were stealing time from Fiona, and you don't flaunt one lover in public if you're intent on maintaining another.

"So what's the occasion?"

"I'll tell you at dinner," he said. He slid from the booth, kissing her on the forehead. "Pick you up at six?" He was out the door before she could nod her assent.

The cabbie waited as Henry climbed the stairs to Alice's apartment. She greeted him in the same black silk, button-front dress she'd worn to Greenwich. Her phenomenal beauty taxed his already precarious resolve.

"You look amazing," Henry gushed. He smiled when he noticed the modest copper bracelet he'd bought her for *Homage to Olympia* adorning her left wrist.

Dino's was a culinary playpen for the prosperous. Its walls were clad in streamlined panels of glass and aluminum, its tables groomed with starched white tablecloths. Alice drew stares from countless pairs of male eyes as the maître d' ushered the couple to a small table in the rear of the smoky restaurant.

Henry ordered a round of drinks, as fortification for him and anesthetic for her.

"It's mostly steak," Alice said as she glanced at the menu. "I thought you'd sworn off meat since our night at the Colonel's."

"It couldn't last forever," Henry said, his words eerily portentous.

"Henry, why are we here tonight?"

Henry felt a roiling in the pit of his stomach. Until now, he'd never seen Alice happier. Released, at last, from the abusive clutches of Jake Powell, she'd slipped eagerly into Henry's warm embrace. Her gradual transformation from hard-shelled chorus girl and ballplayer's mistress to artist's muse and lover had been attended by a corresponding escalation of contentment and self-respect.

Their love affair had been improbable. Attracted by her breathtaking beauty, he found in her an unexpected warmth, vulnerability, and capacity for love. For Alice, romance with a talented artist with Ivy League credentials and a Jewish heritage seemed unimaginable. He'd peeled away her defenses, reset her emotional compass, and reawakened her passion and confidence. He respected her for who she was, not how she looked (not that he hadn't noticed). She'd reveled in his love, and he in hers. And now he would shatter it all.

"I've enlisted in the Army," he said. "I report in two weeks."

Alice's face flushed. She took a gulp of her martini to steady herself, then uttered a single word: "Why?"

Henry offered his well-rehearsed explanation: the likelihood of war, the benefits of proper training, the Nazi menace.

"When," she asked, brushing an errant curl from her newly furrowed brow, "did you decide on this?"

"Early January," he said.

"January?" The gleam disappeared from her eyes. "And you wait until now to tell me?"

"I couldn't summon the courage to tell you sooner." A wave of guilt enveloped him.

Alice looked at Henry uncomprehendingly. She finished off her martini in a single gulp. But when she registered the anguished expression on Henry's face, she cringed. "There's more, isn't there."

"Yes."

"It's over, isn't it," she said, tears seeping into the corners of her eyes.

"Yes."

Alice was crushed by the prospect of Henry's abandonment. She sighed deeply. "You were my rock, Henry," she said haltingly. "You were the only man in my life I could count on ... the only one I could trust. You never disappointed me ... until now." Her words pierced him. As she fumbled through her pocketbook for a tissue, Henry reached across the table with his handkerchief.

"I love you, Alice," he said. "But I never stopped loving Fiona. I can't do this anymore, to either of you ... or to myself."

"I never asked you to choose, Henry," she reminded him. While half of Henry's love had been enough for Alice, she was still the 'other woman'—just as she'd been with Jake.

"I know," Henry said, "but you deserve so much more than a part-time lover."

As much as he'd wounded her, he'd leave Alice stronger than he'd found her. Henry was sure of it. From the depths of her grief, she'd cling to her rediscovered self-esteem. He believed in her and she'd thrived on his confidence. He'd leave her a better version of herself, capable of loving and worthy of the love of someone more deserving than he.

Alice paused, pressing his handkerchief to her eyes. Her resistance was pointless. His departure was a *fait accompli*. "I'll write to you," she said, trembling.

"No," he said, his heart fracturing with each new obstacle he imposed. "You have to get on with your life," he said. "All I can offer is heartache." Henry wanted to take her into his arms and hold her. It took all of his willpower to resist. He had to let her go. He owed her that.

Mutually despondent, neither could face the charade of dinner. When they'd finished their drinks, Henry paid the bill and hailed a cab.

The cabbie weaved through the evening traffic like a halfback evading tacklers. The blare of car horns, screeching of brakes, and angry epithets of the taxi driver were the sounds that filled the void between them as they returned to Alice's apartment. When they exited the cab, Henry escorted her to the entrance of her building.

Alice folded her hands into his. "Stay with me tonight?" she pleaded.

Henry was sorely tempted. "It would only prolong the pain," he said as tears poured down her cheeks. She lunged forward, throwing her arms around him. They embraced fiercely. After a few heartrending moments, Henry released his grip, his eyes filled with tears. "Goodbye, Alice," he said tenderly, before dissolving like a phantom into the warm city night.

CHAPTER FIFTY-FIVE

The Parting Gift

Still reeling from his break-up with Alice, Henry spent the better part of the next week holed up in his studio, surrounded by boxes, half-packed trunks, and general clutter. A mélange of drawings of Fiona and Alice were scattered across his worktable and tacked to the wall. He'd collected the studies he'd made of each of them for *Home Front*, of Fiona for *Conversation Piece*, and of Alice for the paintings from his *Alice Series*. Now, after a week's work, he put the final touches on half-length portraits of each of his lovers.

As Henry approached his reporting date, he became increasingly mindful of his mortality. Through his initial twenty-six years, the subject had barely registered on his consciousness. But now, faced with the uncertainty of a two-year Army stint and a widening war, it became an obsession. His artistic legacy was hardly assured—a five-year career is far too brief to make a lasting impact. His personal legacy was another matter entirely. How would he be remembered by the people he'd loved or befriended, especially now, in the case of Fiona and Alice, when his parting actions would inflict such pain? If he never returned, he'd want them to know that it was *because* he loved them that he'd set them free.

Henry painted the portraits to underscore his love and to

assuage his guilt. Before he left, he would also write them a letter, to be delivered, along with the portraits, in the event he didn't come home.

Henry had called a cab to transport the portraits to Peyton's apartment. He'd wrapped them securely, along with a third painting, a gift to Peyton. He carried them individually down three flights of stairs while awaiting the taxi's arrival.

Peyton was waiting on the front stoop of his building when the cab pulled up. The two friends extricated the paintings from the back seat and hauled them to Peyton's apartment.

Owing to the miracle of trust fund money, Peyton's place was twice the size of Henry's. His walls were hung with his own works, blotchy abstracts in red, green, and black—like the aftermath of a bloody massacre on a mobster's front lawn.

Peyton placed the two wrapped portraits, each carefully inscribed with the subject's name on the wrapping paper, into a storage closet. Henry's instructions were precise: Peyton would retain the portraits until Henry returned to reclaim them. If, God forbid, Henry were to "bite the dust," as he termed it, Peyton would deliver the paintings personally, if at all possible, to each of Fiona and Alice, together with a letter addressed to both of them that Henry would compose and mail to him before leaving New York.

"I've got it, Henry," Peyton said, "morbid as it is." He lit up a Chesterfield. "So, what's the third one?" he asked, referring to the third wrapped object.

"My parting gift to you," Henry said, smiling.

"Gee . . . you shouldn't have." Peyton flashed a wry grin.

"Open it up, you elongated fool."

Peyton tore away the paper, revealing the one and only abstraction in the oeuvre of Henry J. Kapler, the slashing, dripping monstrosity in black, white, yellow, and red that

Henry had created at the height of his turmoil over the complications of his love life.

"*Dripshit!*" Peyton shouted. "I absolutely *love* this thing! It'll have a place of honor over my dining table," he proclaimed.

"Then don't invite me for dinner," Henry said.

"I'll expect you here for dinner in two short years."

"Only if you seat me with my back to that abomination," Henry laughed. His mission accomplished, he stood up to leave. "Goodbye, my friend," he said as he embraced his vertically enhanced companion.

"Take care, old pal," Peyton commanded, his eyes betraying the melancholy of their parting.

CHAPTER FIFTY-SIX

The Longing Goodbye

There was something unusual in the tone of his voice when he'd called to invite her to dinner at Carlito's. An urgency, a sense of determination, a hint of nervousness. For months he'd seemed preoccupied, as if burdened by some weight he was loath to reveal. She'd pressed, but he'd denied there was anything wrong. She understood that the looming war had imposed uncertainty upon the plans of young men everywhere. She knew he'd wrestled with his options, torn by the inevitable conflicts arising from his pacifism, his father's outsized patriotism, and his disgust for the atrocities committed by the Nazis against the Jews.

And while she'd never have admitted it to him, Fiona had also considered their prospects for the future. Except for a brief hiatus, they'd been a couple for four and a half years. They were comfortable and compatible, yet respected each other's independence. Was he planning to propose? Would she accept? And how would that calculus be affected by the likelihood of war?

It was a quiet night at Carlito's, so Henry was able to wrangle a secluded table in a far corner of the restaurant. They'd both grown accustomed to the less-than-fussy ambience, the faint red sauce stains on the tablecloths, the stray breadcrumbs lingering from the luncheon service. They'd always been comfortable here—it was *their* place.

"What'll it be tonight, Miss H?" Lorenzo asked Fiona. The grandfatherly Italian immigrant was their regular waiter. He was quick with a smile and unbiased advice regarding the quality of the evening's specials or the wine that would best complement the spaghetti bolognese.

Fiona considered the menu, though she knew it by heart. "Think I'll try the spaghetti carbonara," she said.

"Excellent choice," Lorenzo said. "Fettuccine alfredo for you, Mr. K?"

"No, thanks, Lorenzo . . . how's the veal scaloppini?"

"Superb, as always, Mr. K." Lorenzo was amused by Henry's unexpected deviation from the norm, but refrained from comment, making his way toward the kitchen with their order.

"We've been here . . . what . . . twenty, thirty times?" Fiona said. "You've never, *ever* ordered anything other than fettuccine alfredo." She gazed at him earnestly. "What's up, Henry?"

"Sometimes," Henry said with a disarming resolve, "things have to change."

Fiona responded with a steely glare. "I know you better than that." The tension was killing her. "Tell me what's on your mind," she insisted, a bit more firmly than she'd intended.

He broke the news of his enlistment dispassionately, enumerating the same reasons he'd cited to Peyton and Alice. She took it in stride. She knew how much his uncertainty had weighed upon him and she respected his decision. "I thought something was afoot when you chose to paint *Home Front*," she said. "You put Peyton, Alice, and me in your picture . . . but there was no you."

Henry seemed disappointed by her equanimity. "I thought you'd be upset."

"I *am* upset, Henry. I'm upset that we didn't discuss this *together*," she said, her tone mildly scolding, "because it affects us both." She paused. "But I knew this was coming—if not now, then soon."

Lorenzo delivered their entrées and a carafe of wine. "A new house red," he explained. "Try it . . . with our compliments." Fiona thanked him, less for the wine than the distraction.

"There's something else I haven't told you." He articulated the words gingerly, like a man traversing a half-frozen pond. The sound of his voice was unsettling. This was no prelude to a proposal, Fiona deduced, but something infinitely more ominous. She reinforced herself with a sip of wine, gazing at him suspiciously as she swallowed.

"I've been seeing Alice . . . romantically."

Fiona laid down her fork. Her shoulders tensed, her lips tightened. She felt slightly nauseous. "You bastard!" she screamed. Diners at the adjoining tables took notice.

"Fiona, I—"

"How long?" she hissed, too loudly, squeezing her wine glass nearly to the breaking point.

"It began last summer," he said with a calmness that infuriated her, "and ended two nights ago."

Fiona bit her lower lip, struggling to maintain her composure. "You've slept with her?" she asked, a bit more discreetly.

"Yes," he said, studiously averting her accusatory gaze.

Fiona stared blankly into her bowl of pasta. Moments passed in awkward silence. It occurred to her that they'd taken on the aspect of the star-crossed lovers in *Conversation Piece*, the tension between them as tangible in life as Henry had rendered it on canvas.

"Please," he begged, "say something . . . *do* something."

Fiona clenched her teeth. Her face turned crimson. "*Do* something?" she said, her nostrils flaring. "How's *this!*" She sprang from her chair, clutching her bowl of spaghetti carbonara with both hands. With remarkable precision, she flipped the contents squarely onto Henry's head, twisting it savagely into his scalp before letting it drop to the table with a thud. Henry looked at her plaintively, groaning as the warm Italian concoction slithered down his temples and forehead. Not yet satisfied, Fiona snatched the half-full carafe of house red and emptied it over his lap.

"Dio mio!" cried Carlito, his hands rising to his temples in astonishment, while a roomful of diners gasped at the spectacle. Lorenzo watched in open-mouthed horror as Fiona stormed from the restaurant into the warm, misty night.

A half-block from her apartment building, Fiona heard Henry pursuing her on the dead run. She quickened her pace, hoping to avoid a confrontation. When he reached her, he clutched her left arm from behind.

"Let go of me!" she demanded.

"Fiona, please!"

Tears streamed from her eyes as she turned to him, trying in vain to wriggle from his grasp. Henry refused to let go. A light rain had begun to fall.

"What do you want from me?" she cried, confronting him now. Her eyes were like daggers. "I feel like a fool!" Henry released his grip, tears welling in his own eyes. "I'd always feared this would happen," she whimpered, almost breathlessly, "but I trusted you. You knew how I felt about her. And still . . ." She exhaled a mournful sigh of exasperation, then turned to walk away. After a few steps, she stopped and pivoted. "Why in the world would you tell me this now?" she barked at Henry. "You could have gone ... to wherever the hell they're sending you ... and said nothing!" She shook her head. "Why humiliate me like this?"

Henry reached for her hands, anguish etched in his eyes. This time Fiona didn't resist. "I've been in love with you for a long time," he said, his voice unsteady. "Then I fell foolishly in love with Alice, too." He gripped her hands tightly. "But I never loved you any less ... you have to believe that!"

His words were little consolation on a night on which Fiona had been anticipating a completely different discussion. She turned her back to him and resumed walking home.

"I just couldn't bring myself to choose between you and Alice," Henry said, nipping at her heels. "You complemented me more than she did ... but she needed me more than you did." These details were of no interest to Fiona.

"You haven't answered my question!" she stammered as she reached the front stoop of her walk-up. "Why tell me this at all," she snapped, "when you're about to leave anyway?" She sat down on the steps, emotionally drained.

Henry stood above her, placing his hands upon her heaving shoulders. "Because I love you," he said. "Because I owed you the truth and ..."

"And *what?*" she sneered as he sat down beside her.

"And because I knew that if I told you the truth, you'd be angry enough to go on with your life ... without waiting for someone paralyzed by indecision." Henry exhaled. He removed a handkerchief from his pocket, raising it tentatively toward her sodden eyes. She recoiled for a moment, then plucked the handkerchief from his grasp and dabbed at her tears.

A grudging half-smile emerged as she studied him in the porch light. A lone strand of *al dente* spaghetti peeked out from his mane of thick, brown hair. His white shirt and trousers were saturated in house red, giving him the appearance of a Mafia hit victim. Bits of bacon adhered to his left eyebrow and the bridge of his nose. She wiped them away with his handkerchief. Her rage evolved into regret.

Fiona's mind wandered to the New Year's Eve party at the Lanings' almost four and a half years ago, the night he spotted her pouring herself a glass of wine at a makeshift bar—a night she punctuated with a delightfully spontaneous New Year's kiss. She remembered the evening she took him to the Onyx Club to celebrate the "slashing" debut of his painting, *Gastonia Renaissance*, at the Corcoran—the night they first slept together. And with a shudder, she recalled the harrowing night her life was nearly snuffed out by her crazed cousin—a night Henry sat vigil at her hospital bedside, willing her to emerge from unconsciousness.

Henry broke their awkward silence. "I don't want it to end like this, Fiona."

A profound sadness engulfed them. *Was* it over? It was Henry who'd decided that she shouldn't wait for him. Wasn't that her decision to make? Should she protest her liberation or accept his decision to set her free? She'd always been sure of herself, in control of her emotions. But her heart was now riddled with confusion. She felt helpless. "Neither do I," she said, her voice dripping with melancholy.

"I'll miss you, Fiona," Henry said, rising from the stoop. Though barely able to contain his distress, he remained resolute, committed to releasing her.

"Me, too," she replied, thoroughly heartbroken. Tentatively, he bent down to kiss her. Without thinking, she stood up and returned the gesture with a passion that surprised them both. Their long, deep kiss opened the floodgates to a mutual torrent of tears.

"Take care of yourself, Henry," she said when she broke from their embrace. She knew now that she had capitulated to her release. "Come home safely," she murmured.

Fiona turned and climbed the porch steps through a veil of tears and raindrops, disappearing slowly behind the frosted glass door of her red brick building. "Goodbye, my love," she heard him say, his voice cracking, as their lives changed forever.

CHAPTER FIFTY-SEVEN

The Boogie Woogie Bagel Boy of Company B

Henry collapsed on his cot, thoroughly spent. His uniform was caked with mud and steeped in sweat. His face was raw with sunburn. Every joint and muscle in his body ached.

Fort Leonard Wood was a hellhole, but at least it was an American hellhole. Henry had survived Day One of basic training. Not all of his platoon-mates were as fortunate. Jimmie Landry, a skinny eighteen-year-old from the backwoods of West Virginia, tumbled halfway through their six-mile jog through the Missouri Ozarks. The drill sergeant, a foul-mouthed, mean-spirited Georgia redneck, challenged the kid to get up, prodding him as he writhed on the ground in agony.

"Get up, Landry, you piece of shit!" he bellowed. The panicked recruit curled into the fetal position, howling with pain as he cradled his injured knee. "What're you gonna do, lie down and wait for the Krauts to rescue you? You're a dead man, Landry!" And to the rest of the platoon, he barked: "What're y'all lookin' at? Keep on running, you motherfuckers! Forget that bastard!"

Henry had all he could do to restrain himself from stopping to aid his platoon-mate. But he, like the others, ran on, until they could no longer hear the teenager's shrieks.

Fifteen cots, no more than three feet apart, lined each side of the barracks of Company B, First Platoon. Twenty-nine were occupied as the weary trainees unwound that night from their brutal introduction to boot camp. Jimmie Landry's cot was empty. His fate remained a mystery.

Henry and most of the others had arrived the previous day. They'd come by train and bus from cities, towns, and hamlets throughout the country. Their arrival was met with a deluge of paperwork. Dog tags were issued, barracks and cots assigned. They stood naked for an hour in the supply hut awaiting uniforms before waiting again to have their locks shorn. All day long it was 'hurry up and wait,' the stop-and-go cadence of life in the Army.

Intimidation was the norm. Commands were laced with expletives. Racial and ethnic slurs were *de rigueur*. As the only Jew in the platoon, Henry was addressed with variations of *hymie* and *kike*, as in "get that hymie ass down and give me twenty!" A drill instructor with more imagination took to calling him "The Boogie Woogie *Bagel* Boy of Company B," or "Boog," for short, a clever riff on the pop hit debuted by the Andrews Sisters' earlier that year. The name would stick.

Ben, who'd already endured his own basic training, had coached his brother on boot camp survival skills. "Lay low and keep your mouth shut, unless and until spoken to. Act dumb," Ben said, "but not too dumb. And for God's sake don't tell them you're a Yalie! Drill instructors will crucify anyone with a brain."

Day One had begun at five that morning. Henry was awakened by an ear-splitting clamor. The crashing of a baseball bat against a metal trashcan had served as the substitute for reveille. Thirty recruits sprang to their feet, washed, dressed, made their beds, and lined up for roll call. "Here, Drill Sergeant!" cried out thirty young men in rapid succession as the sergeant butchered their surnames. Then came breakfast at the mess hall, where servers slopped unidentifiable mush onto metal trays.

Henry had barely time to swallow the gruel before calisthenics. Then came the obstacle course, followed by marching drills. "Forward, march!" the sergeants hollered. "Column right! To the rear, march!"

Breaks, tailored for smoking, punctuated the tedium. Cigarettes were ubiquitous. "Smoke 'em if you've got 'em," was the common catchphrase.

Henry made it to lunch. Despite his hunger, he cringed as a mess hall drudge deposited a slab of bread on his tray and drowned it in a milky, lumpy muck.

"What kind of shit *is* this?" Henry muttered to a platoon-mate as he sat down beside him.

"*Shit-on-a-shingle*," he said, "the Army's answer to creamed chipped beef."

"If the jog doesn't kill me, the food will," Henry lamented.

A half-hour later, at the height of the afternoon's heat, came the dreaded six-mile jog. Henry had never run half that far. But fear of humiliation was a powerful motivator. Unlike Jimmie Landry, Henry completed the ordeal, much the worse for the wear.

As he lay on his cot that evening, Henry took stock. His reasons for enlisting no longer mattered. There was no turning back. He'd left behind the life he knew and embarked upon another. Henry Kapler was now Private First Class "Boog" Kapler. No longer would his life revolve around "painting pretty pictures," as his father once alleged. From now on, it was all about survival. He was in the Army now.

CHAPTER FIFTY-EIGHT

You're in the Army Now!

KAPLER TRADES PALETTE KNIFE FOR ARMY LIFE
Ex-Springfield Artist Serving at Westover

Special to the Springfield Union
by W. D. Danforth, Art Critic for the Springfield Union

SPRINGFIELD, September 1, 1941. He's got the Corcoran, Carnegie, Whitney, Herron, and the Pennsylvania and National Academies on his resume. And now he's added one more stop: Westover Field in nearby Chicopee. Henry J. Kapler, the Springfield native and Yale grad who stirred up the art world with such masterful works as *Gastonia Renaissance* and *Night at the Savoy*, has exchanged his New York City studio and white painter's smock for a bottom bunk in the Westover barracks and a footlocker brimming with olive green.

Kapler, the son of Springfield physician Morris Kapler and his wife, Ruth, volunteered for service in the U.S. Army on June 2nd. Shipped initially to Ft. Leonard Wood in Missouri, he was transferred three weeks ago, joining the 803rd Engineer Battalion currently training just a dozen miles from here.

We caught up with PFC Kapler during a weekend leave at his parents' home. He reports that he's added a good ten pounds of muscle since his enlistment, and it shows. Tall and lanky, he has exchanged his studio prison pallor for a deep Indian brown. "Haven't lifted a brush since June," he informed this reporter, but added that he hoped to "crack out the watercolors" at least once during his brief respite in Springfield.

The Army, it would seem, is missing out on his prodigious talents. At the very least, it could get some museum quality camouflaging out of him cheap—at the rather stingy $20-30 per month the Army pays its lowly privates. An artist good enough to do a painting for Homer Saint-Gaudens' Carnegie International is certainly good enough to do some Westover Field concealment work for Saint-Gaudens, who now serves as chief of camouflage for the U.S. Engineers.

Private Kapler professes a lack of knowledge as to his next posting, but wherever he may be destined, we wish him Godspeed.

CHAPTER FIFTY-NINE

The Telegram

Sixteen days following the publication of the article in the *Springfield Union*, Henry sent word to his parents that his battalion would be deployed to the Philippines. He wrote them again on November 14th, three weeks after his arrival on the South Pacific archipelago. "It's ironic," he noted as he prepared to defend against the Japanese menace instead of the Nazi plague, "that the devil I'll face isn't the devil I chased." He revealed he'd been promoted to Staff Sergeant and professed to be in "high spirits," busily engaged in defense activities he was not at liberty to divulge. Nor was he permitted to disclose his exact location. By the time Henry's letter reached his parents, the Japanese had attacked Pearl Harbor and America was at war.

The three weeks following Pearl Harbor had seemed an eternity to the Kaplers. The Japanese invaded the Philippines on December 8, 1941. While early communiqués from General Douglas MacArthur assured the country that the American forces had matters "well at hand," each succeeding day brought bleaker news. By the end of December, reports of the "stubborn resistance" of the "vastly outnumbered" American defenders against relentless air and ground attacks by Japanese invasion forces were steadily eroding the Kaplers' shrinking reservoir of hope.

The doorbell rang at precisely 10:30 P.M. on Monday, December 29, 1941. Ruth's heart began to race. She and her husband had just gone to bed. No one would be expected to call at such an hour.

Morris rose quickly, nervously donning a robe and a pair of slippers, while his wife began to panic. "I'm sure it's not what you fear, Ruth. Be calm," he said. The bell rang again as Morris flipped on the stairway light and plodded down the steps toward the front door. Ruth followed, breathing heavily. Morris opened the door.

"I have a telegram for Mr. and Mrs. Morris Kapler," the visitor announced, waving a slim envelope. "Sign here, please."

Morris's hand trembled as he signed for the telegram. Ruth said nothing, the look of terror on her face sufficient to convey her fears. She clutched his arm as he tore the envelope open.

YOUR SON STAFF SERGEANT HENRY J. KAPLER CORPS OF ENGINEERS REPORTED A PRISONER OF WAR OF THE JAPANESE GOVERNMENT IN THE PHILIPPINE ISLANDS. STOP. LETTER TO FOLLOW.
THE ADJUTANT GENERAL

"He's alive, Ruth," Morris said with a sigh, "he's alive." It was more good news than bad, but little cause for celebration. His continuing safety, Morris well knew, was hardly assured.

The follow-up letter from the Adjutant General revealed only that Henry was interned at Cabanatuan Camp #1, north of Manila. His parents received reassurance of his continuing survival in April, when a bare-bones, multiple-choice postcard bearing his signature and a date of February 14, 1942 revealed that he was well (indications of hospitalization or injury having been crossed out). With little more to sustain them, Morris and Ruth could only hope and pray for the best.

CHAPTER SIXTY

On the Home Front

April 10, 1942

Dear Henry,

Word of your capture has filtered through your circle of friends and acquaintances in the New York art world. While deeply saddened, we are all grateful that you are alive and pray urgently for your health and safety.

When news broke of the American setbacks in the Philippines, your friend (and my former student) Peyton Small contacted your parents in an effort to ascertain your well-being; he was kind enough to encourage me to do the same. Your parents, of course, are immensely concerned, but draw strength from their religious convictions and their confidence in your resourcefulness. It was they who graciously furnished the mailing address c/o the Red Cross that I hope will secure this letter's path to you.

Before your departure, you entrusted me with your latest masterpiece, *Home Front*, a painting that has, indeed, become most topical. I had intended to submit it to the Whitney, but, like a number of venues, it elected to suspend its annual exhibitions due to the war. The National Academy of Design, however, chose to proceed with its annual, and I submitted your painting to its jury on your behalf. It was enthusiastically accepted. At the opening two days ago, I was (as you will be) thrilled that *Home Front* was accorded pride of place at the very entry of the exhibition, a result I attribute as much to its fine workmanship as to its timely theme. Although it was not accorded a prize, there is no doubt that *Home Front* was the public's favorite—and by a wide margin. Crowds amassed before it all evening long and photos appeared in each of the *New York Times*, *Daily News* and *New York Post*. It is, in a word, a sensation!

On a matter less sanguine, it behooves me to disclose that your parents have appealed to me to use any connections I may have in the Japanese hierarchy to obtain such concessions as might be possible in terms of your incarceration and treatment. While I understand their motives are honorable in that regard, I fully suspect that you would disavow any such preferential treatment in respect for your mates. Be that as it may, I must tell you that, at present, I am considered, on the basis of my heritage alone, an "enemy alien," and am effectively a prisoner in my home and studio. I've been obliged to surrender my camera and my binoculars, am denied access to my bank accounts, and am subject to daily curfew (it took a special dispensation for me to attend the Academy show). I am not permitted to conduct classes at the League, but have arranged at least to have my students join me with their artworks at my studio. I should, perhaps, be grateful, as the plight of those in the west who share my heritage is far less agreeable, as many of them have been relocated to government camps from which they are not permitted exit. I relate all this, Henry, not to complain, for in the face of your misfortune I suffer comparatively little, but to explain why, even if I had sufficiently influential contacts in Japan, any effort on my part to reach them would be surely construed as a conspiratorial offense.

I saw Edward and Mary Laning just the other day, and while Mary is deeply distraught over your predicament, she is holding her chin up and praying for your safe return. Reggie Marsh, whom I encountered at the Academy exhibition, also sends his best wishes. I join them all in wishing you a prompt and safe return.

Your friend,
Yas

CHAPTER SIXTY-ONE

National Icon

P.O.W.'S PAINTING MAKES SPLASH IN NATION'S CAPITAL
*Kapler's **Home Front** Becomes Rousing Symbol of Stateside War
Support*

*Special to the Springfield Union
by W. D. Danforth, Art Critic for the Springfield Union*

WASHINGTON, D.C., April 1, 1943. It was exactly six years ago,
on this very date, that this reporter covered the remarkable artistic
debut on the national stage of Springfield's own Henry J. Kapler,
whose magnificent painting *Gastonia Renaissance* attracted
unprecedented attention at the prestigious Fifteenth Biennial
Exhibition of Contemporary American Oil Paintings at
Washington's Corcoran Gallery of Art by enduring a knife attack
from a misguided museum-goer offended by its theme of racial
harmony. Now, six years later, at the Corcoran's Eighteenth
Biennial, another work by the same artist has elicited an equally
momentous response here in the nation's capital. The painting,
entitled *Home Front*, is a paean to the wartime contributions of the
men and women whose stateside endeavors are critical to the
support of our fighting men abroad. The picture is as noteworthy
for its subject matter and skillful execution as for the irony that its
creator now languishes in the Philippines as a Japanese prisoner of
war.

Home Front is a large and ambitious work, a reminder of the
epic Regionalist compositions with which the artist first gained
recognition. The painting depicts a young man (in farmer's garb)

and two attractive young women (a nurse and a factory worker) posing together, a steely determination etched on their faces as they clutch in their hands the tools of their respective wartime trades. It is said that the models for this work were the friends the painter left behind when he closed his New York City studio and enlisted in the Army two years ago.

Kapler, the son of Dr. and Mrs. Morris Kapler of Springfield, was reportedly captured while defending Bataan and Corregidor from the Japanese invaders who attacked the Philippines in the weeks immediately following the bombing of Pearl Harbor. Kapler's captors have permitted him to send only the briefest of messages to his parents, enforcing a strict fifty-word limit. The artist's most recent note stated that he was "getting along very well," while he urged his parents not to worry. "I am hoping to see all of you soon," he wrote.

This observer's visit to the Corcoran exhibit last week confirmed what has been generally reported in the Washington newspapers: that *Home Front* has effectively stolen the show. Great hordes congregate before it, reinforced in their commitment to the war effort on the home front. Rumor has it that the painting will grace the cover of an upcoming issue of *Time Magazine*, following which it is destined, in this writer's opinion, to achieve something of the status of a national icon. We only wish that the creator of this masterwork might have been able to share its success with those whom it has inspired. We offer our best wishes and prayers to the artist and his family for his swift and safe return.

CHAPTER SIXTY-TWO

The Last Voyage of the Arisan Maru

They'd been aroused at the crack of dawn. Soldiers with bayoneted rifles prodded them from their filthy, bug-infested cots, ordering them, in barely intelligible English, to collect their belongings and mass at once in front of their crumbling barracks. Henry dressed quickly, shoved his meager belongings into a fraying backpack, and took his place in the first of three rows of emaciated prisoners.

Henry had been among the lucky ones. He'd been seriously ill only once in the thirty-three months he'd spent at the hellhole in Cabanatuan. Many of his colleagues were less fortunate. Lack of food and proper sanitary facilities had contributed to the demise of hundreds, while scores had been beaten to death as punishment for some alleged misdeed or a perceived lack of respect for their ruthless captors.

If one can become accustomed to subhuman conditions such as this, Henry had nearly accomplished the impossible. Routine yielded a modicum of equanimity, enough, at least, to preserve the will to survive. But now a change was brewing, and change, like the hated Japanese, was his enemy.

It was the tenth of October of 1944. Rumor, though never reliable, had it that the American Far East forces had at last gained the upper hand in the South Pacific and would soon launch a massive military assault to repatriate the Philippines. But whatever the rationale, it was now clear that the prisoners at Cabanatuan would be relocated, and with haste.

Henry and his prison mates were herded into troop transport vehicles and driven south. It was a jarring, unforgiving ride over badly pockmarked roads. When the convoy reached Manila Bay four hours later, the haggard prisoners were funneled like bleating sheep into the cargo hold of a battered old freighter, the *Arisan Maru*. Henry was among the many who had noticed, upon boarding the rusting vessel, that it bore no identification of nationality—a precaution, they surmised, to minimize exposure to Allied attack. A staggering number of men, possibly as many as a thousand, climbed over each other like ants, desperate for a few square feet in which to settle for a journey they speculated would take them north to Japan.

If conditions at Cabanatuan were deplorable, those aboard the *Arisan Maru* defied description. Temperatures soared in the poorly ventilated hold, food and water supplies were woefully inadequate, and sanitary facilities were instantly overwhelmed.

For two unbearable weeks, the freighter drifted. The engines were employed sparingly, giving rise to a growing fear that they were little more than a floating target in the South China Sea.

Then, at five o'clock in the evening on October 24, 1944, their worst fears came to pass. The oppressive stillness that had characterized their journey to nowhere came to a sudden, calamitous halt. An American torpedo tore into the hull of the *Arisan Maru*, its explosion splitting the aging freighter in two. In that terrible split second after impact, Henry felt the warmth of fresh blood escaping from his left shoulder as a jagged piece of shrapnel sliced through his flesh. Bodies and body parts scattered until, just seconds later, a massive wall of water poured into the ruptured hull, plunging the mortally wounded freighter beneath the surface of the sea.

Inexplicably, Henry found himself bobbing on the water's surface, the *Arisan Maru* sinking into the ocean like a rock in his wake. He gasped for air. But when he tried to move his arms to tread water, he felt a staggering pain in his shoulder— or what remained of it.

Henry struggled for less than a minute before recognizing the futility of his effort. He thought, for a moment, of the farewell speech of the late Lou Gehrig five years earlier, recalling his courage and serenity in the face of inalterable destiny. Henry's mind grew suddenly calm, summoning images of family, friends, and lovers. He thought of his parents' grief . . . and of Fiona and Alice. A strange and unexpected peace enveloped him as he floated in the barely rippling sea, warm as bath water. Other men were caught in the same currents, some furiously flailing arms and legs, emitting muffled screams of terror; others, like him, had resigned themselves to their fate, mercifully released from the terrible burden of survival. Finally, Henry began to sink, descending slowly into a murkiness punctuated occasionally by prismatic shafts of light. He drifted gently into the gathering darkness like an autumn leaf liberated from its mooring, twisting slowly but inevitably toward the ground, borne by the soft evening breeze. His vision grew hazy as the salt stung his eyes and throat. Fish swam by, oblivious to the human drama unfolding before them. As his lungs filled with seawater, Henry felt, impossibly, as if he'd shed a tear, his miniscule contribution to the enormity of the sea, the earth, and time.

CHAPTER SIXTY-THREE

The Letter

June 12, 1941

Dearest Fiona and Alice,

If you are reading this now, you'll know that I'm gone. I'd entrusted to Peyton the solemn task of sharing this letter with each of you in the event of my passing. Dutiful friend that he is, I'm confident he will have executed my instructions faithfully.

Writing this letter, which I pen on my last night in New York, is an excruciatingly painful task, though it pales by comparison to the agony I've already endured in bidding you each goodbye. It's not for lack of time or energy that I address it to you jointly; I do so because you are forever intertwined in my heart.

It may seem premature to contemplate one's mortality at twenty-six. But with the world as it is and the choices I've made, it is unavoidable. I write this in the fervent hope that I'll return, laugh at the pretense of this letter, tear it to pieces, and resume my life in the city I love. I'll sit down at Carlito's, devouring a bowl of fettuccine alfredo in the company of a woman I cherish, catching up on the events that occurred in my absence. I'll drop by Johnny D's, where I'll order a burger and fries from the waitress and model I adore. Or maybe I'll simply content myself with the knowledge that somewhere you are happy, with someone by your side whom you'll love and cherish for the rest of your life.

But if, instead, circumstances dictate that you read this letter, I want each of you to know that I loved you with all of my heart and soul. Few men are accorded one true love in life, and two at once would seem to most an unforgiveable extravagance. I hadn't planned for that to happen; but the heart, it seems, makes plans of its own.

Had the world been a safer place, I'd be here still, obliged to finally choose between you, assuming you'd both still have me. It was for want of a decision that I made the most difficult choice of all—to leave you both. I made that choice because I loved you both. Only a fool would expect a lover to await his return without an unqualified commitment in exchange.

By now, I trust, you've each received from Peyton a portrait I painted of you during my final days in New York.

Fiona, you were never too keen on my painting you. It was all I could do to persuade you to pose for *Conversation Piece* and *Home Front.* But using the sketches I did of your fictional roles in those compositions, I was able, I think, to capture the Fiona I loved and knew best: a strong, independent, and lovely young woman destined for a life of accomplishment. You had spoken, as I painted you in *Home Front,* about returning to school, becoming a nurse, or even a doctor. You have it in you, Fiona, and I hope you'll pursue what you love the most, be it art, medicine, or some other calling.

Alice, you were always a pleasure to paint. You were a chameleon, an artist's dream, channeling the emotion *du jour,* being whatever I wanted you to be in the picture upon my easel. This time, I tried to paint the Alice I'd come to love, a beautiful, vulnerable young woman with a heart of gold. You told me once that you were wary of men, that you measured them against me and found them wanting. I was flattered, of course, but I know that with patience, and faith in yourself, you'll find a man who loves you unequivocally and treats you accordingly.

Suffering no embarrassment in death, I can readily admit to you now that painting these portraits reduced me to tears. As my brush pressed against the canvases, it was as if I were gently stroking your cheeks with my fingertips. These paintings mean more to me than all of my previous works combined. I hope they'll mean as much to you.

Please convey my gratitude to my good friend Peyton for carrying out these last indulgent wishes. And, if you're so inclined, check in on him from time to time. Make sure he's still the same smartass he's always been, that he has someone to beat in pool, and that he doesn't grow any taller.

As I sit here in contemplation of the possibility of death, though still stinging from the pain of your loss, I recognize how fortunate I've been to share my love with each of you. My life, as abbreviated as it has turned out to be, was richer for loving you both.

My love forever,
Henry

CHAPTER SIXTY-FOUR

Henry

D r. Conrad Gilmore, the youthful, nattily attired director of the Springfield Museum of Fine Arts, made his first visit to the Kapler household in April of 1945, a respectable six months after Henry's tragic loss at sea. He offered his belated condolences, then got right to the point: the museum wished to honor Henry with a full memorial retrospective. As the bulk of Henry's work remained in the hands of his parents and siblings, it should be relatively easy, the director believed, to mount a comprehensive exhibition, and the combination of pride and grief that the community felt for its favorite son would surely guarantee its success.

Morris Kapler looked at his wife, then mournfully shook his head. "It's too soon," he said, "too much for my wife to bear."

That was only half of the truth. Ruth's grief was eclipsed by Morris's guilt. He had never forgiven himself for insisting that his sons go to war. Ben was eager to go and came home safely; Henry wasn't . . . and didn't. And guilt, it seemed, lingered longer than grief.

For six years, Dr. Gilmore persisted while the Kaplers resisted. Finally, Gilmore's perseverance prevailed over Morris's remorse. At long last, family, friends, collectors, and institutions were poised to collaborate on a three-week memorial exhibition opening on Sunday, February 3, 1952, just two days after what would have been the artist's thirty-seventh birthday.

With equal parts anticipation and trepidation, Fiona Harlsweger Phillips climbed the stairs to the Springfield Museum on that chilly Sunday afternoon in early February. So much had happened in the seven and a half years since she'd learned of Henry's death. She'd returned to Georgetown University, acquiring both a degree and a husband. Dr. Bill Phillips, the handsome man who followed her up those steps that day, had interrupted his studies at Georgetown Medical School in the summer of 1942 to join the 4th Marine Medical Battalion in the South Pacific. He'd met Fiona four years later while completing his degree on the G.I. Bill. Their son, a rambunctious four-year-old, gripped Fiona's hand tightly as she coaxed him up the museum stairs while their three-year-old daughter rode like a princess on her father's broad shoulders.

"Mommy, that's you!" cried the little boy, pointing to the right as they entered the building.

"Yes, honey, that's your Mommy." Her voice, like the artwork, exuded melancholy. The painting was *Conversation Piece*, in which Fiona figures prominently in the foreground, fidgeting with her wine glass while engulfed in an awkward standoff with her paramour. Inspired by a lovers' spat that Henry and Fiona had witnessed one evening at Carlito's, it reminded her now of the heartache they endured on the night that they parted.

"Are you okay?" Bill asked.

"Fine," she said, turning away from the picture. But the view on the opposite wall staggered her like a hard right cross. Henry stared out at her, large as life, as he labored over a composition in *Self-Portrait at the Easel*. Fiona felt his presence as intensely as if he were painting her own portrait at that very moment. She wept.

"Why's Mommy crying?" the little girl asked her father.

"The man in the picture was Mommy's friend," Bill said. "He's not here today, so Mommy's sad."

"Where is he?"

Disinclined to explore the concept of death with a three-year-old, Bill diverted her attention down the hall where Fiona appeared yet again, this time in the role of a heroine in Henry's most iconic painting, *Home Front*. Fiona had been inundated with attention when the painting had graced the cover of *Time*. Even now, a decade later, people would stare at her on the street, convinced they'd seen her somewhere before.

"Fiona!" The cry came from just inside the gallery. A sturdy woman with graying hair approached her with a broad smile.

"Mary!" Fiona responded. "Edward!" Mary Laning greeted her with a hearty hug as Edward grinned, waiting his turn. It had been close to a decade since Fiona had completed her marathon assignment with Edward on the Public Library murals. "It's so wonderful to see you!"

"It's a stunning exhibit," Mary said, "and yet it breaks my heart. I lost it when we stood in front of our nephew's portrait, *The Deputy's Grandson*." She gently dabbed at the corner of her eye with a handkerchief. "How are you holding up, dear?"

"I broke down at his *Self-Portrait* ... barely in the front door," she said before turning to introduce her husband to Mary and Edward.

Mary bent down to greet Fiona's children. "And who are these delightful little ones?"

"I'm Caroline ... and I'm *three!*" the younger one volunteered.

"And I'm Billy," said the other, "and know what? I'm gonna make paintings when I grow up!"

"I bet you will," Edward said approvingly. Mary took Fiona's hand. "Don't let us keep you from the exhibition," she said. "We'll catch up again later."

Fiona hadn't progressed more than a dozen steps into the main gallery when she spotted Peyton Small, towering above the throng that had come to pay tribute to Henry's art and sacrifice. When Peyton spotted Fiona, his face lit up like a torch. He loped in her direction like some Paul Bunyan, his family in tow.

"What a wonderful surprise!" he said, gathering Fiona awkwardly into his endless arms.

"Lucille!" Fiona exclaimed when she recognized the tiny, redheaded woman at Peyton's side. "You two . . . are married?"

"Six years," Lucille said proudly. "These are our boys." She tapped her little ones on the shoulder in descending order of age. "Peyton . . . the *Fifth*," she laughed, "and Rembrandt."

Fiona chuckled. "Rembrandt?"

"Guess who's idea that was," Lucille said.

"Instead of a painter wannabe who ended up a lawyer, we'll have a painter *and* a lawyer," Peyton said. "Come on, let me show you around. It's a phenomenal exhibition!"

And indeed it was. The familiar paintings were all there. The show's seventy-four artworks (including fifty-two paintings) ranged from early masterpieces like *Eventide, Dust Bowl*, and *Gastonia Renaissance*, to the paintings with which Fiona had a more personal connection, works such as *Night at the Savoy,* the picture Henry had unveiled to her the night that they met; *Ninth Avenue El*, Henry's painting of the crumbling station on the old elevated line a few blocks from Fiona's apartment; *The Pretzel Vendor*, the old immigrant lady Fiona would pass each time she walked across Union Square; and *Wash Day*, the simple depiction of Fiona's neighbor hanging her wash from a clothesline suspended from her apartment window.

"And there's his tribute to that sleazy little pool room in the basement of Diamond Mike's," Peyton said, appraising *Pool Room*. "I beat the stuffing out of him down there every time," he said, chuckling. "He was too smart to play for money," he added, "or I'd've cleaned him out."

"What . . . in God's name . . . is *that*?" Fiona motioned toward the show's most incongruous work, an abstract painting characterized by broad slashes of red, yellow, black, and white, the colors dripping into one another at ninety-degree angles. "When . . . and *why* . . . did Henry paint that?"

"At the depth of his depression over his dual-lover dilemma," Peyton said. "He was a wreck . . . so in a fit of anguish he simply let his emotions run amok on canvas. He hated it, but he gave it to me as a parting gift when he delivered the portraits of you and Alice to me for safekeeping." A playful smile appeared on his lips. "I christened it *Dripshit* . . . the museum preferred *Untitled*."

From his superior vantage point, Peyton surveyed the swelling crowd. Hundreds milled about in the galleries, mesmerized by Henry's prodigious talent. But a bittersweet aura permeated the praise and chatter . . . and handkerchiefs were in evidence everywhere.

An Asian gentleman in his sixties lifted one of those handkerchiefs from his suit jacket pocket, removed his dark round glasses, and gently dabbed his eyes. Gaunt, with graying hair and a solemn countenance, he sat alone on a bench before the most audacious of Henry's *Alice Series* paintings, *Jake's Ex (Defiance)*, the portrait in which Alice sported a black eye like a badge of honor in defiance of her abuser. He was awed by how Henry had adapted his teachings in his own unique fashion, extracting hurricane-force emotion from the carefully crafted expressions of his remarkably beautiful model.

Yas Kuniyoshi was dying of cancer. He'd enjoyed a productive life as an artist and a stellar career as a teacher. Though he'd suffered the indignities of a Japanese man in America at an unpropitious time, he'd both endured and flourished. But he'd die with two regrets. The first was his failure to obtain the American citizenship he'd always longed for, a privilege his adopted nation had stubbornly denied him. And the second was the untimely death of his most promising student, even more painful for the fact that it flowed from the negligence and brutality of his country of birth. If there was, indeed, an afterlife, he would join Henry soon enough. It would be a happy reunion.

Yas arose from the bench gingerly. As he slowly exited the gallery, he passed behind an elegantly dressed woman standing alone in quiet contemplation of the portraits comprising the *Alice Series*. He glanced at her only briefly, failing to recognize her as the beautiful subject of the painting he'd just admired. Though a wrinkle or two had begun to invade the corners of her eyes, Alice, even in her late thirties, was still the belle of the ball.

Peyton had been engaged in animated discussion with Fiona when he saw a familiar figure in an adjacent gallery. "I think I see Alice," he said. Surrounded by the patter of little feet, Lucille and Bill forged their acquaintance while Peyton lumbered over in the direction of Alice. With mixed emotions, Fiona chose to join him.

Alice wiped the tears from her eyes as she revisited the paintings of the *Alice Series* for the first time since that bizarre night at the Greenwich mansion of Colonel and Mrs. Melrose. Her mood changed as Peyton delivered a robust greeting and a warm hug.

"You still look like the prom queen," Peyton told her.

"That's certainly gracious of you," she said, craning her neck to meet his eyes. But her smile quickly evaporated. "I wish Henry were here."

"That would make for a remarkable memorial exhibition now, wouldn't it?"

Alice's lips puckered in a feigned pout. "You know what I mean."

"Alice, you remember Fiona, don't you?"

Fiona offered a polite smile and a perfunctory hug. Though their fates had been indelibly intertwined, they'd spoken but once or twice since their meeting at the Yankee Stadium ballgame that featured the brawl instigated by Fiona's cousin, Jake.

"Still a painter?" Alice asked Peyton.

"Not by a longshot," he said. "My lack of talent finally caught up with me." He ran his long fingers through his thick hair. "Married . . . two kids . . . back in Charleston practicin' law . . . the one thing I swore I'd never do." He gave Alice an ironic little grin. "And how about you, Alice? Still at Johnny D's?"

"God, no," she laughed. "I married a lawyer, we've got a three-year-old son—and I'm sure you'll find this hilarious— we live in Greenwich, Connecticut."

"Is your family here?" Fiona asked.

"They're out there somewhere." She waved her hand in the direction of the larger gallery. "I told my husband that I wanted to mull over the *Alice Series* by myself for a few minutes . . . before he has a look. The only painting of me that he's ever seen is the one you gave me, Peyton, after Henry passed away." That painting was directly in front of them, and alongside

Henry's final portrait of Fiona. "That painting means the world to me," Alice said.

"As mine does to me," Fiona acknowledged.

Peyton glanced at the wall labels for *Waiting* and *Adoration with Blue Eyes*. "Lent by Mrs. Zelda Melrose," he recited. "What happened to the Colonel?"

"Killed himself back in '45," Alice said. "Used one of his own company's pistols... something about a war profiteering scandal."

"His wife should've had him stuffed and mounted," Peyton said. Alice flashed a guilty smile. Peyton noticed his son escaping from his mother's orbit. "Sorry," he said, "but I need to corral my wanderin' progeny. It was wonderful to see you again, Alice."

Fiona stood by as Peyton ambled off. "By the way," Alice said, "if you don't mind my asking... whatever happened to your cousin Jake?"

"He was arrested in Washington in '48 for passing bad checks. Shot himself to death right in the police station," Fiona said without a hint of emotion.

"Oh my God!... I'm so sorry!" An uncomfortable silence settled between them as they perused the wall of Henry's portraits. Finally, Alice turned to Fiona, a plaintive look in her eyes. "Fiona... I'm sorry..." she began, searching for the proper words to express her remorse, "for falling in love with Henry... for interfering with what the two of you had together." She paused, mustering her words as well as her courage. "I'd been hurt by Jake ... you probably know that ..." Her voice trailed off. "But Henry was there for me. He was the kindest, sweetest man I'd ever met." Alice's face was flushed. She reached into her purse for a tissue and wiped her eyes.

Fiona's steeliness began to melt. She had always blamed

Alice, in part, for becoming involved with her married cousin, yet she knew firsthand how manipulative Jake could be and how much pain he could inflict. They had both been his victims. "It's okay, Alice," she said. "It took me a while, but in time I understood Henry's dilemma. He deeply loved us both . . . and it took its toll on him."

Alice let out a long breath. "I often wonder," she said, "whether he'd be alive today if we'd never—"

Fiona reached out and touched Alice's arm. "You can't blame yourself," she said. "As Henry said in his letter: 'the heart makes plans of its own.'"

"He was right about another thing," Alice said. She shifted uncomfortably for a moment, fingering the simple copper bracelet she wore on her left wrist. "That with patience and faith in myself . . . I'd find someone as kind and loving as he was." Her lips tightened. "He gave me that faith and it *happened*, just as he said it would."

"He inspired me to finish school," Fiona said, "and to reach for more. I'm setting my sights on medical school . . . when the kids get a little bit older."

Alice smiled. "I was supposed to be his muse," she said, "but in the end, he was mine."

Henry's two lovers embraced, then returned arm-in-arm to the lobby of the museum where Dr. Gilmore had begun to address the large crowd that had gathered around him. He introduced Morris and Ruth Kapler; Henry's brother, Ben; and his sister, Edith.

While Henry's family members shared their recollections of Henry, a tall, well-built man in work clothes slipped quietly into the main gallery. His powerful right hand lovingly grasped the tender left hand of a little boy, four or five years of age. As they paused before *Night at the Savoy*, the father bent down to his son, whispering in his ear. A memory, perhaps, of a visit long ago to that very place with the man who had painted that picture. He gently squeezed the little boy's hand, leading him to a bench in front of *Gastonia Renaissance.* His son realized immediately that it was his father, Bunny Taliaferro, who looked out at them from the painting. Bunny told him of the hours he'd spent fifteen years earlier, posing patiently in the artist's studio while Henry miraculously brought him to life on the very canvas before them. But Bunny wasn't quite ready to tell him what it was like to be a black man in a white world— to endure abuse without objection, to struggle to maintain your pride while others belittle you because of the color of your skin. He couldn't tell him that it was racism that had brought his athletic career to a premature end. These, Bunny knew, were hard lessons for another day.

Gastonia Renaissance had meant as much to Bunny as Henry's portraits of Fiona and Alice had meant to them. Bunny was forever indebted to Henry Kapler, the warmhearted young man who befriended him and honored him for his athletic achievements as well as his courage. With that painting, he'd given Bunny an immortality he'd never expected or imagined. With this exhibition, perhaps Henry would achieve a similar destiny.

The activities in the lobby had drawn to a close. As the crowd slowly wandered back into the galleries for a last peek at the exhibition, Bunny arose. "Come on, Henry," he said, taking his son by the hand. "It's time to go home."

-The End-

AFTERWORD

A large wooden crate arrived on my doorstep on a winter morning in early 2006. Inside was the painting *Eventide*, by the artist Harold J. Rabinovitz (1915-44), the same painting described in the opening pages of **Artist, Soldier, Lover, Muse** and attributed to the fictional artist Henry J. Kapler. That so talented a painter could have gone unnoticed for much of the seven decades since *Eventide's* creation mystified me—and moved me to discover why. Eight years of on-and-off research culminated in a brief biography and catalogue raisonne, **At the Threshold of Brilliance: The Brief But Splendid Career of Harold J. Rabinovitz** (The Rabinovitz Project, 2017). I'd gathered the facts and located the artworks, but the soul of the man behind the powerful, evocative paintings would always elude me. Constrained by biography, I fled to fiction.

Henry J. Kapler is *not* Harold Rabinovitz, although their lives share a number of salient facts, a common timeline, and even some of the same artworks. Henry is a figment of my imagination, as are his thoughts, desires, motivations, quirks, and foibles. His sense of humor is also mine, for better or worse. Fiona, Alice, and Peyton, his inner circle, were fashioned from whole cloth—though Peyton required the lion's share of the fabric. While Henry's parents and siblings share superficial similarities with Harold's, their personalities and the nature of their relationships with Henry were dictated by fictional necessity. Beyond this, I've sought to portray the world in which Henry resides, the New York art world of the late Depression, including the artists, athletes, politicians, events, and institutions that contributed to the rich history of the period, with as much historical accuracy as possible.

In tackling historical fiction, one often uncovers little known characters and facts that prove the adage of Mark Twain that truth is stranger than fiction. In seeking a villain, an author could have done no better than Yankee outfielder Jake Powell, whose on-field belligerence was the perfect resume for his encounters with Alice and Fiona, and whose ill-fated radio interview and Harlem Apology Tour are little-known footnotes in the shameful history of segregation in professional sport. Similarly, the saga of Bunny Taliaferro, the gifted African-American athlete from Henry's hometown of Springfield, Massachusetts, seemed a natural inspiration for Henry's imaginary masterpiece, *Gastonia Renaissance*. Forgotten for generations, the 1934 incident in Gastonia, North Carolina was recently recounted in a delightful children's book by Richard Andersen, **A Home Run for Bunny** (Illumination Arts, 2013), which I highly recommend. The protest scene at New York's WPA headquarters and its curious courtroom aftermath are based on events that occurred several years earlier as described by one of the participants, artist Joseph Solman, in his essay "The Easel Division of the WPA Federal Art Project" appearing in Francis V. O'Connor's **The New Deal Art Projects: An Anthology of Memoirs** (Smithsonian Institution Press, 1972). Edward Laning's trials and tribulations with his Ellis Island mural, including the bubbling adhesives and the condom-filled harbor that dissuaded him from drowning his sorrows, are described in glorious detail in "The New Deal Mural Projects" in the same anthology. Laning's illuminating essay was the source for many of the other details relating to the federal arts programs.

One of New York City's best-kept secrets is the fabulous mural cycle by Reginald Marsh that graces the rotunda of the United States Custom House Building at the southern tip of Manhattan. I commend you to visit it. For details of its creation, I'm indebted to Margo Hensler, whose fascinating account of the project appears in "Art & Document: Reginald Marsh's Custom House Murals Are Great Paintings That Also Accurately Depict New York Harbor in its Glory Days" (*Seaport*, Winter 1997). While Mary Fife Laning did assist Marsh on the project, Marsh painted all of the murals himself, a remarkable accomplishment in light of the rapid timeframe during which he produced them.

Although the Japanese-American modernist artist and teacher Yasuo Kuniyoshi had a considerable influence upon the evolution of Harold Rabinovitz, his impact on and personal relationship with Henry Kapler is the product of the author's imagination. The character and teachings of Kuniyoshi were informed by Tom Wolf's enlightening exhibition catalogue, **The Artistic Journey of Yasuo Kuniyoshi** (Smithsonian American Art Museum, 2015) as well as a selection of the artist's own writings in the Archives of American Art. Background on Reginald Marsh was gleaned from a variety of sources, including **Swing Time: Reginald Marsh and Thirties New York** (New-York Historical Society, 2012), a collection of exhibition essays edited by art historian Barbara Haskell, and **The Sketchbooks of Reginald Marsh** (New York Graphic Society, 1973), written by his real life close friend, Edward Laning.

The Springfield Tech-Springfield Classical baseball game described in Chapter Three never actually took place, partly because the two best Springfield pitchers of their generation, Bunny Taliaferro and Vic "The Springfield Rifle" Raschi (who would later win 116 games with the Yankees from 1946-53), played for the same team (Tech). On the other hand, the descriptions of the events of Lou Gehrig Day at Yankee Stadium and the wonders of the New York World's Fair (including Mayor Fiorello La Guardia's no-holds-barred attack on modern art) adhere closely to contemporary accounts in *The New York Times*. Finally, the critical musings of the fictional W. D. Danforth were inspired by the columns of *Springfield Union* art critic W. G. Rogers.

Scores of artworks make at least a cameo appearance in **Artist, Soldier, Lover, Muse**. Paintings by artists other than Henry Kapler are works that might have been seen by a young artist in New York City at or about the times represented. In particular, the works described as part of the Reginald Marsh exhibition at Rehn Gallery were included in a similar show that took place at that venue at an earlier date. The paintings attributed to Henry are about evenly divided between purely fictional creations and works painted by Harold Rabinovitz, although the inspiration behind *all* of Henry's paintings, as well as the details of their creation, derive solely from the author's imagination. Any reader sufficiently intrigued to explore the oeuvre of Harold Rabinovitz, including over a dozen works described in the preceding novel, is invited to consult the author's biography and catalogue raisonne referred to above.

I am grateful for the assistance and encouragement of Richard Andersen and Margo Hensler, whose top-notch research made it possible for Henry to paint Bunny Taliaferro (as well as to watch him perform) and to paint with the incomparable Reginald Marsh. And my heartfelt thanks to Tim Neely, Gary Null, Ken Brooks, Richard Andersen, Tom Wolf, Lauren Rabb, Dea Illian, and Gerry Nielsten, each of whom plowed through one or more drafts of my opus, for their sage advice and useful suggestions, without which Henry's story would have been much the poorer. Finally, I thank my wife, Peggy, for putting up with Henry and me for all these years.

About the Author

ARTHUR D. HITTNER is the author of **Honus Wagner: The Life of Baseball's Flying Dutchman** (McFarland Publishing, 1996), recipient of the 1997 Seymour Medal awarded by the Society for American Baseball Research for the best work of baseball biography or history published during the prior year. He has also written or co-written several art catalogues, a biography and catalogue raisonne on the artist Harold J. Rabinovitz, and articles on American art and artists for national publications including *Fine Art Connoisseur*, *Antiques & Fine Art* and *Maine Antique Digest*.

A retired attorney, Hittner spent nearly thirty-four years with the national law firm now known as Nixon Peabody LLC, resident in the firm's Boston office. He served as a trustee of Danforth Art (formerly the Danforth Museum of Art) in Framingham, Massachusetts and the Tucson Museum of Art in Tucson, Arizona. He was also a co-owner of the Lowell Spinners, a minor league professional baseball team affiliated with the Boston Red Sox.

Married with two children and three grandchildren, Hittner currently divides his time between Oro Valley, Arizona and Natick, Massachusetts. He is a graduate of Dartmouth College and Harvard Law School.

CPSIA information can be obtained
at www.ICGtesting.com
Printed in the USA
BVHW04s2046010618
517940BV00003B/6/P